Black Crow Press LLC
P.O. Box 185626
2514 Whitney Avenue
Hamden, CT 06518

FIRST EDITION
Author's full text edition
10 9 8 7 6 5 4 3 2 1

Copyright ©2021 Kathy M. Umbricht Straka
ISBN   978-1-7321685-2-7
eISBN 978-1-7321685-3-4

Editor Judy Roth
Cover illustration Beth Janelle Stone

Published in the United States of America

PUBLISHER'S NOTE
This is a work of fiction. All characters, names, places, business
establishments, agencies, situations, dialogue and incidents are
the products of the author's creative imagination or are used in a
fictitious way. Any resemblance to persons living or dead is entirely
coincidental.

Cover Design and Interior Format

HABOR CHASE

SPRING HOUSE MYSTERIES · BOOK TWO

K. M. UMBRICHT

ALSO BY K. M. UMBRICHT

Spring House Mysteries

Mystery at the Spring House, Book One

Harbor Chase, Book Two

TABLE OF CONTENTS

CHARACTER LIST

Miranda Elise "Em" Huber, outsourced,
retired competitive intelligence consultant

Her family:
Ex-husband, Professor Harley Travis Huber, Geology,
returned to family Texas oil business
Deanna "Dee" Huber, rising college senior, youngest
daughter
Celina Huber, pharmacology graduate student, middle
child, specializes in natural medicines
Joshua Huber, acoustic engineer, the oldest child, wife
Miriam, psychologist
"Aunt Marlene" Albrecht, distinguished head of H.T.
Huber's family, owns the oil business
Robert Albrecht, "Uncle Bob," deceased WW II hero

Friends:
Allessandra "Sandy" Waitely, Deanna's best friend, their
resident guest
Professor James Stevenson, Geology, specialties geothermal energy, caves, DARPA alumni

The clients, inventors of game-changing solar technology:
Professor Ali "Al" Hussein, murdered in Book 1, *Mystery
at the Spring House*
Professor Francis Xavier "Frank" Kirbee, missing Books
1 and 2
The McGuffin, SunSpryte Version 5, Version 3 was stolen
previous to Book 1

The IIA Federal Agents:
Michael "Mike" Halloran, director of IIA, a post 9/11 armed federal agency
Senior Agent Pierre Anatole "Pete" Leonard, Halloran's former second in command, from Louisiana, murdered in human trafficking raid just prior to Book 1
Senior Agent Fernando "Andy" Vargas, veteran, earned his citizenship through Army service
Stefan Rankel, "ninja from NYU," grandson of a Hungarian freedom fighter
David "Dave" Anson, new recruit, younger disabled veteran, hired as Halloran's bodyguard and driver, "the man whose feet leave little scent"
Gladys Rodriquez, duty officer, IIA Control Center, pregnant Books 1 and 2
Bertha Wilkinson, the IIA group's armorer, collector of exotic weapons
Leroy, chief of the IIA motor pool, occasionally undercover, father is a judge
Dr. Roland Smithers "Smitty" Williams, III, the IIA's on call doctor and veterinarian

Local law enforcement officers:
Nancy Dombroski, "Nancy Drew," FBI field agent, Em's friend
Detective Nilsson, New Haven Police Department contact, his sergeant is Gianelli

Animals:
Sergeant Yaeger of Saybrook, "Jake," a coal black Shepherd semi-retired canine federal officer, wounded in the line of duty, lives with Em Huber at the Spring House
Ashurnasirpal, "Ash," Em's elegant half Siamese black cat, golden eyes, talks like a Siamese
Cleome, Professor Frank Kirbee's prized Siamese princess who talks back, left in Em's care

1

FIRE!

———————

"FIRE'S BLOODY WELL nearly, really almost
out here, Mom," Deanna Huber yelled over
her shoulder, twenty-something drama in her voice.
Awakened with a frightening start by the sound of a fire
bomb thrown in front of their country home and the
screeching of the smoke detectors, she barely recovered
to help fight the grass fire in the front yard. Although not
serious, it was no ordinary fire. It started in the middle
of the night with a container of gasoline lobbed from
a car to smash on the cobblestone paving before the
Spring House. She aimed the garden hose at the base of
the encroaching flames greedily heading for the stacked
cordwood at the edge of the lawn. Rubbing a wet hand
down the summer sleep shorts that clung to her slender
legs, she said, "*Sorta. Maybe.*" Rain boots were definitely
an asset, soon her feet would be the only dry spots on
her body.

Flames consumed the accelerant. Gas ran down through
the crevices in the paving seeking new tinder in the leaf
litter at pavement's end, the beginning of the woods.
Burning leaves, edges red with incipient fire floated
away unseen. Not totally a dark summer night, a quar-
ter-moon hung over her shoulder, but smoke clouded
their sight. Flood lights from the corners of the Spring

House reached across the wood pile but not behind it.

Towards the country road, in the way that fires do, flames leapt up from a tuft of long grass snapping and popping in defiance and sneaked off around a bush heading down the slope. A long way off in the quiet valley below the Spring House a heavy engine roared to life, chugged and thrummed, and then the siren sounded.

"Well, Dee, that worked. We can't let the Spring House go up in flames. I heard glass smash and a heavy car drove away. Fast. I was never so glad we have fieldstone halfway up the house, cold as it is in the winter." Her mother Miranda Huber, or Em, pointed a nearly spent kitchen fire extinguisher at the pile of glass shards and scorched stones then brushed a soot covered hand over one cheek, smearing it with black. Flying ash from burnt leaves and grass besmirched her slightly faded pink and blue striped pajamas. In haste, she had tucked them into stove pipe riding boots that were easiest to pick from the hall closet.

"This is about Professor Hussein's murder. Yeah, some clients. One's dead and the other's missing. It's got to be Professor Kirbee and his missing solar plans, doesn't it? They think you have them. What if they come back?" Deanna was anxious. "Like this afternoon. It's not everybody that gets mugged in their own backyard. You know I cracked that guy's ribs, right?" The summer before her senior college year was quickly turning perilous.

Em Huber gave a tight cough. The breeze shifted, giving her a warm shower of smoke and ash on her wavy dark grey hair. "Unlikely they will come back with the lights and all the noises from the security system. What was your brother thinking when he programmed it? All those crazy whoops and screeches. Josh's got to do something or the neighbors will never forgive us. They can probably hear them all the way to New Haven." She paused. "Sandy's inside, she should be on the phone with Joshua to get him to turn that noise off. What have I gotten my family into? I just needed to go back to work to pay for this place. In the company, competitive intelligence was … a whole lot of desk work, and just a seriously miffed vice president. Or two," she complained out loud.

"Wow, finally quiet. I hope the well holds out, we can't exactly pump the spring in the cellar. I thought we caught the guy this afternoon. He'd be in jail, right?" Deanna's voice quavered slightly, betraying misgivings. The water from the nozzle leaked, giving her spray.

"More likely in the hospital. Between the two of us, we saw to that. No, this is intimidation and has to be someone else." Em wiped a black smear across her forehead.

"You think, Mom? You've got smut on your hands. Now it's on your face." She gave a nervous laugh, her eyes watered from the smoke and the memory of the shock and fright she felt when held at gun point the afternoon before.

Her mother heaved a barely patient sigh as she tried hard to suppress both worry and anger. It was not a time to let anger overtake her. "It's just ash. Deanna, a good throwing arm could easily have pitched the bottle farther, right up to the house. The guy who taped you and Sandy to the Adirondack chairs demanded the solar plans. Then threatened you to get me to stop looking for the plans. A contradiction there. You were really brave, by the way."

"Yeah, well, I didn't have much of a choice…" Deanna grimaced, kicked a blackened tuff hard with the toe of her boot.

"Says you. Listen. The volunteers are on the way, hear them? We'll have help soon. I can't wait to explain this to the police. Again. I hope the feds get here first." The fire extinguisher now empty, slid from Em's sore, tired hand and landed with a clunk on the cobblestones at her feet.

"Any particular feds in mind?" Deanna could still pull out a joke.

"We will need the assistance. The fire, it gets away

from me along the road," came a man's softly accented voice from the other side of the wood pile. Their neighbor Philippe wielded a broom of thick bristles made to sweep grass fires. Turnout boots covered flannel sleep pants and his vee neck tee shirt showed growing sweat stains, broad black smears, and mud from the broom he dashed in the brook on his way up the hill to help fight his neighbor's fire. It was what you did in the country. The paid fire companies were too far away in the center of town. Fighting grass fires was smoky, dirty and tiring work. Embers lurked in the leaves smoldering, and the fire could go underground.

A newer emigrant from France, Philippe joined the volunteers and got trained. He knew they would need the approaching engine with its full tank to stanch this fire. It was clearly visible from his own farm house windows where his wife, Em's divorce lawyer, rocked a colicky baby boy with the lungs of a low land gorilla while he paced the floor. With her urging, like a shot he was in his boots and ran up to the Spring House fire broom in hand.

Siren howling, the lovingly polished red engine pulled over and came to a halt. Volunteer firemen and one firewoman in turnout coats, gloves and boots jumped off the back and out of the cab. One placed large wooden chocks behind the rear wheels to help hold the truck on the grade. Neatly folded canvas hoses were pulled from the back of the truck. At a signal, a fireman regulated the flow and the truck began to pump. The ground near it vibrated. It was a good sized pumper and carried ladders long enough to reach a third floor attic, about as high as any of the buildings within its fire district.

Behind the fire engine the much shorter brush truck, really a dusty red converted pick up with an enclosed metal back, came to a stop further down facing towards the approaching fire. To ferry air packs, portable water tanks carried on a fireman's back, stiff brooms to sweep a grass fire in against itself, rakes to turn over the ashes to find embers and shovels, the small truck could go up country where the large pumper could never reach. The two men on this truck and those who arrived in their own vehicles grabbed their equipment and started uphill to meet the fire as it advanced towards them. A single patrol car pulled in behind it with an officer dispatched to control traffic, especially onlookers.

"Watch out for the poison ivy. Stay the hell out of the smoke over there. Get respirators on." The fire chief had arrived, driving his pickup into the road side opposite the house. A farmer with a voice to call the cows home, the chief knew his business. This fire needed to be put out, his livestock was over the hill. The truck radio crackled, the dispatcher asked for a status update. Was the house engaged, should they call in a second alarm?

Inside the house, always shy of publicity Sandy Waitely, their resident guest and Deanna's best friend handled communications with the 911 operator. Practically leaning out the kitchen window over the sink, she called to Em and Deanna, "I'll be out soon!" Still glued to the phone, she kept up a running commentary describing the action to Joshua Huber and wife Miriam, who conferenced in his sister Celina.

With only Em Huber, her daughter Deanna, Sandy and Philippe to control it, the fire had taken the opportunity to head east up the ridge stealthily. A burning leaf had carried it away in the updraft created by the main blaze. Falling on matted weeds and leaves at the roadside, it was silent and dim until it gained ground. A thin trickle of smoke was spotted by a firefighter who stopped to assess. Sharp eyes with instinct developed over years and many blazes saw the new hot spot just as it shot into flame. Below the narrow column of smoke, flashes of yellow and red flames, the fire snapped in quick time. A shout sent three of the closest men running, brooms and rakes in hand, uphill to cut off the strategic advance towards the heavily wooded crest. Once into the fallen oak leaves, inches deep, slow to decompose, they might not have enough water to quickly stop the fire's spread to brush and up into the trees.

The fire company fielded so many able volunteers, it took less than an hour to extinguish the flames. Raking over all the ashes was another story. The fire passed by the feet of venerable sugar maple trees planted generations ago in a neat line along the road. Their thick crust like bark shielded the trunks. Their branches were carried high overhead, leaves safely away from the grass fire's reach. But not so the underbrush, brambles, fallen branches and weeds. The Spring House, like good properties in the wooded countryside, was surrounded by mown lawns that provided a pleasant yard and a firebreak. In the deciduous woods around the lawns, leaves piled up to disintegrate into rich forest soil, or to be burned. Last winter had been a stormy one, many dead branches had been pruned naturally by the wind gusts and lay where they fell on the forest floor, ripe for fire.

"You can turn that hose off now, miss, save your well water." A bearded young fireman approached Deanna carrying a sturdy rake. "I'm going over this area to make sure there's nothing going on around that pile of wood. Step over there onto the grass."

Another volunteer in full turnout gear came up behind him. She said to him, "You never call me 'miss.' Get a move on." They exchanged meaningful looks, laughed, and turned to their task.

"Like your boots," Deanna remarked to the young woman in the turnout coat. Standing in soaked sleepwear and half calf vinyl rain boots, Deanna proved a distraction for the bearded rake wielding fireman.

It took the fire chief to move Em Huber, who stood by

the corner of the house avidly watching the concerted efforts of the volunteers.

"Ma'am, you and your daughter can go back into the house now. We've got it under control. It's far enough away. We're wetting it all down now, probably won't even need to fill up at the pond." The engine carried a wide rigid hose with an oblong metal basket on one end to throw into the nearest pond to take in water if needed. The stream that flowed by the base of the hill was not deep enough and might require buckets. The firemen's first choice, draw clean water from a hydrant, but hydrants were often too far for a fast moving fire.

"We have to thank Philippe, and the rest of the volunteers. How about a year's supply of Blackmun's Wintergreen Spring Water?" With a sparkle in her eye, a tired sigh and a half smile Em thanked the chief. She gave one last resigned look at the shattered glass on the river washed cobblestones. Empty fire extinguisher in hand, she walked into the house and motioned Sandy to come too. Deanna declined to follow her mother, preferring to stay outside to watch the active fire scene.

Coming in fast, over the hill from the direction of the Interstate, a bland car could be described as tan, beige or maybe even putty, no insignia or badging and an odd license plate number, pulled smartly in front of the barn across the road. The lone police officer, night staff was minimal in quiet country towns, stood watching. The neighbors stayed a good distance away. There were no cars to direct. Prepared to approach the vehicle with due caution, the officer stopped short. The car doors popped open simultaneously. On the driver's side a pair of long legs in fatigues swung out together, and Army boots planted themselves firmly. They were followed by a man with powerful shoulders who used his arms to propel himself forward. The new agent, David Anson, lost both legs beneath the knees in service was still adjusting to a new job and new feet. A silver badge ill-concealed under a khaki short sleeved shirt was visible briefly as he unpacked himself from the car. More slowly, from the passenger side, right leg first in jeans followed by a stout cane, a tall lean older man emerged, cursing as his foot touched down. A dark knit shirt was pulled down over discrete bulges at his waist.

"Alright over there, sir?" Anson asked and received a barely audible growl in reply.

Into his radio the policeman announced, "Feds are back. Looks like the ones they told us showed up for that backyard invasion this afternoon. Anything they want. Got it." He was reluctant. "Huh, somebody got dragged out for this."

"How's it going?" the younger veteran asked the officer with an open, engaging manner.

"Fire's almost out. Never real close to the house. They'll be raking over, looking for hot spots to put out soon," was the reply.

Searching light grey eyes grazed over the house and the blackened yard. Taking the situation in quickly, the older man spoke. "We're from the IIA, don't worry if you never heard of it. This is Agent Anson." On command the new recruit flashed his ID a bit awkwardly. "I'm Michael Halloran…." His voice dropped, probably with intention, and was lost in the shouts of firemen as active embers burst into flames unexpectedly. His ID disappeared before the officer could do more than recognize the seal.

"Have you taken photos? Bagged evidence yet?" Halloran asked.

"No, sir." The officer addressed the man with the keen eyes. "They told me to wait, handle traffic, preserve the scene."

"Good. I need to speak to the chief."

On the lawn pointing to a small wisp of smoke at the base of a tree, Deanna stood with her back to the road. A glance over her shoulder at the new arrivals caused her to smile and give a surreptitious finger wave to David Anson. A grin rewarded her, and he was clearly distracted by the sight of her in wet and clinging tank top and sleep shorts, *sans* undies. This interaction did not pass unnoticed.

"Anson, get her into the house. Take photos, get enough detail to plot the scene. Sample trace evidence, scrape it off the stones for analysis. Leave the rest for the evidence crew. I'll be with the chief." This was said as Halloran walked with a measured step, favoring his right shin towards the man in the chief's helmet who stood on the road giving direction.

A brief discussion ensued between Agent Anson and Deanna who enjoyed the attention but ended up marching into the house as requested. Her offer to help gather evidence was firmly declined. Although Deanna's unrelenting encouragement helped him to get up and stay out of his wheelchair, Anson was determined to do his new job without assistance. It wasn't that girls from his home state of Maine weren't pretty. Smart, sassy sometimes with an active temperament, Deanna reminded him of another Connecticut girl, a young Katherine Hepburn. Only with a little more choice meat on the bone than Spencer Tracy once said about his Kate.

Using the soft sided evidence kit from Halloran's car, Anson's first crime scene work began. As he took the requisite photographs, he mused, *Could she still be interested me? With the feet and all. Can't screw up now. Got to finished six months' probation as an agent.* That was contingent on surviving serving as the boss's driver and bodyguard. Halloran was exacting, and Anson was never sure if he measured up. Close enough for government work, Anson measured the distance from road to point of impact and from there to the house's front door, plotting the original extent of the blaze. Finished with the easy part he contemplated how to get down on his knee or knees, gather evidence and get back up again, without compromising the scene.

Returning the camera to the kit, he dug around for the gloves and evidence bags and found a folded extendible wand with a pistol grip hand control. This might be used by people with mobility limitations. It was bagged with changeable heads, one a pick to stab litter, another with three fingers to grip an item, and a selection of different blades all carefully sheathed. He blessed the staff member who put together the kit. Only later did Anson realize that Halloran packed his own kit. Relieved, Anson set to work on the paving stones gathering samples for analysis under the canny eyes of the local officer.

Now moving a little more freely, walking exercise being generally beneficial, Michael Halloran leaned on his cane less and less. He greeted the fire chief with his name, an outstretched hand and identified himself by pulling his shirt away from a gold badge. Showing his ID long enough for the chief to actually read it, he asked if they might talk and stepped away from the working firemen.

"Tell me what you know, Chief." The men stood side by side observing the volunteers' progress. Halloran eased his weight onto one leg.

"Josephs, get that stump over there, around the back. I own the dairy farm over the hill. Around two o'clock the dogs started barking their heads off. Damned beagle starts baying. I let them out and they barked off in this direction. Couldn't see anything, got the call, we thought it might be the house. Go easy on the water Chuck, or you'll end up carrying it in a bucket."

He paused to speak to the radio operator. "Confirm. No second alarm needed. We got this.

"Once here, fire was just out front. We directed the fire away from the house, sometimes you have to do that if you can't get it all out at once."

"What do you think?" Halloran said.

"It's real quiet here. Very little traffic. No problems. People usually drive around this stretch of road. Wicked in the winter. Up past my house it winds around an S curve between stone walls, never been widened. Road still has the humps where the horse teams would rest pulling their loads uphill. Downhill this side is straighter, but people get fond of the easier ways around the hill, not over it."

"The residents here, any problems?" Halloran asked.

"Nice people, Mom and the older kids. They've lived here 'most two years and no trouble. Buy milk and my wife's eggs. Good customers. This place used to be part of our farm, long before we bought it. I still rent the maple trees for sugaring, like always. Music's kind of loud, sometimes."

"So what's really going on here? You able to tell me anything? All of a sudden twice in one day. Not the ex-husband, is it? Heard he took off to Texas. Didn't sound like the type. Horse's ass folks said. 'Course with these university folks, you never really know what they're into." Getting no response other than an interested look from Halloran, the chief paused.

"She bought this place from a physics professor. Nuclear physics, I heard. And you know what that means."

Halloran nodded this time, he knew very well what that meant.

After a quiet word with the chief to assure him they would be watching, Halloran received a pledge. In a neighborly way, the chief would keep an eye out and call them if concerned. Passing Anson at work on the paving, Halloran found his way into the house looking for Em, Deanna and Sandy.

Tired, shocked, arms aching with fatigue and stress Em Huber, propped against the kitchen counter, stared unfocused at Halloran. An inhaler was cupped in her red-

dened and lightly blistered hand. His steady gaze drew
her. Facing into the early shade of dawn, his eyes were
a clear ice grey under dark brows, one nicked by an old
scar.

At their first meeting, he'd requested an interview
concerning the disappearance of her client, Professor
Frank Kirbee. In his secure office building, she expected,
even dreaded, an interrogation. What she experienced
felt more like a professional meet and greet, a kind of
amity. Halloran seemed to know much about her already,
proving the value of good intel. Unexpected as it was,
they shared attraction right from the start. Go figure. Em
observed that his face, a warm coppery tan from summer sun on the water, showed emotion only in subtle
changes. She suspected he controlled it.

Never seeing senior federal agent Michael Halloran
quite this still and very close, she was absorbed. Wearing boat shoes, no socks, wire rimmed glasses, ripped
jeans spattered with paint and spar varnish and a tired
blue Henley, he was not the well-tailored man he had
been when they first met. Short dark hair peppered with
grey spiked straight up, uncombed. An overnight beard
was growing. Masculine jawline. It took her a moment
to notice he was looking straight into her eyes. His lids
slid down a fraction, the corners drew into creases. She
perceived he was smiling at her ever so slightly, even intimately.

"Alright?"

Em nodded and said in a low raspy voice, "Just about."

"Can you talk? Need your inhaler?" A gentle hand was
placed on her arm. "Miranda?"

Still recovering from mobilizing her daughter and
Sandy, and grabbing the extinguisher to put out the gasoline fire, she took a deep breath. "Yes, I can talk." Her
eyes fell closed. Tears ran from her left eye, and she began
to bat her lashes.

"Your soot is running." His voice resonated low and kind.

"I must have something in my eye." This was partially true, but also she didn't want him to see her lose composure. It had been a terrible day, even before the fire. Her hand came up as if to rub her eye.

"Keep your hand away from it. Don't move, I'll get it out." To cross the kitchen unimpeded Halloran placed his cane against the counter edge, went to the sink, found and dampened a tissue. Returning to face her, he said, "Look at me. I can see it. Stay very still." Holding her bottom lid down a bit he deftly swept the fragment onto the tissue and out of her eye. "Better?"

"Much. Thank you. You've done this before." Her eye lids fluttered, and then scrunched tight.

"I raised three boys alone. Minor injuries a specialty. Stay there. I'll get something to wash the soot off your face."

A renewed interest and inherent curiosity led Em to follow Halloran with her gaze, which took in the briar cane. It leaned on the Mexican tile of the counter not two feet away from her. Before she could stir, Halloran was back with a clean dishtowel drenched in warm soapy water and wrung out hurriedly.

"Close your eyes."

With fingers under her chin to hold her at a tilt, he scrubbed the charcoal smut from her forehead, down into the hairline by the affected eye and carefully around it to her cheek. His touch was warm and sparing. She sighed and her shoulders came down, relaxing. Although she couldn't see it, eyes closed after all, he was enjoying it. Once finished with one cheek, he turned her face slightly with a gentle pressure and crossed the bridge of her nose to complete cheek and chin. The warm towel grazed her lips and set them tingling.

"Let me see your hands. They must hurt." He reached

out for her, and she let him take them up. Too tired to resist and too intrigued Em allowed him to hold her hands, turning them over to examine the abraded skin and the patches of small blisters.

"Where's your First Aid kit?"

Em sniffed back tears from stinging eyes.

"The house is safe. What were you doing out there? Some people freeze, some run away, you just rushed right out. Second degree burns." He shook his head without dropping her hands. "Useless to tell you not to, huh?"

Is he flirting with me? She cocked her head a fraction to the side, asking without speaking. The smile on his lips spread slowly, invitingly. *OMG, he is.* She returned his smile with a soft, intriguing one of her own. Her breathing slowed and deepened.

Coming around the corner from the living room to the kitchen, Deanna made a fast stop, taking in the view of Halloran and her mother, their hands linked. Stepping cautiously, she backed away.

"They're having a moment, Dave Anson's boss and my mother," she whispered to their resident guest Sandy Waitely. Alike in age and similar in looks, the two girls might be sisters. Impish, about to retrace her steps to the kitchen, Deanna's bestie caught her friend's arm to prevent her.

"Let's stay in here, Dee. Leave them alone."

"Yeah, okay, but he's some kind of super scary fed. I need a shower. I smell like smoke and I can taste it, too. Yuck. Don't let Dave leave before I see him," Deanna said and was off up the stairs to the bathroom. An unusual throne room, it was painted with a proficient amateur rendition of a Mediterranean seascape, one of the idiosyncratic wonders of the house.

Halloran turned Em's hands over once again. It afforded him an opportunity to give her attention, gently running his fingers around the sensitive under sides of her wrists, making them tingle, and forcing Em to hide a grin. Firm capable hands, slightly roughened, used to work, strong fingers, not those of a man who spent his life typing code. *He is flirting, men are all so different. He can't think I don't feel it, can he? Oh my, no.*

"The First Aid kit is under the sink." Intuitively, Em knew they'd drawn an audience from the living room.

With half closed eyes, she watched as he bent down slowly, favoring his right shin, to reach into the cabinet. Revived by the touch of his hands, interest piqued, her eyes were attracted to his cane. Placed well within her reach, in one smooth move she grabbed the stout briar cane. With two sore hands she held it out in front of her, admiring the carved head. It was not of hefty weight as she expected, and might be hollow. Fascinated, she raised it until the creature carved on the handle stared directly at her with beady onyx eyes.

"Miranda!"

"You know, the first time we met, I thought this was a sword stick. You had it with you at the concert. When I asked you if you were armed, you said, 'Always.' Did you mean this?"

"No. Careful with that." Halloran straightened up with effort, First Aid kit in one hand.

The Irish briar cane, a burled wood, had an embossed silver band below the head of the cane. The shaft was smoothly polished but rather thicker than usual for a walking cane.

"It looks like a dragon or a head you see around the unknown parts on old maps. *Hic dracones?* Is it a sea serpent?" Looking closely, she could see a tiny line encircled a bump on the creature's forehead. "What's the bump do?"

"Don't touch that." He removed the cane from her grasp gingerly as if taking a dangerous toy away from an overly inquisitive child.

"What's it do?" This was met with silence. "If you can't tell me what it does, can you fly with it without special dispensation from TSA?"

"I can see you're feeling better. I prefer the train. Your hands need washing, then I'm going to wrap them. Leave the cane alone, please." The cane was now leaning against the counter well out of reach.

"Oh, I forgot, you would have automatic dispensation." Em's laughter rippled, not quite a chuckle, and she held out her hands.

"Can I come in and make coffee for the firemen?" Sandy asked, discretion in an undertone.

"Yes, fire people, there's a young woman out there, too. When we were younger, I was told I couldn't be a volunteer because I was a girl. Of course, I was *slighter* then. The equipment can be heavy depending what's needed for the fire."

"That's what Deanna said. Can I give them some of the cinnamon buns, too? The recipe made a lot."

"Of course," Em replied and patiently watched as he washed, dried and placed squares of gauze over blisters, then wrapped clean gauze strips around her hands securing them at the wrists.

"Feels better. Thank you, Mr. Halloran."

"It's five o'clock in the morning. Don't call me Mister."

"Director, sir?" she teased.

"You got that far, didn't you? Not in front of the locals. Michael is good."

The damp haired daughter of the house joined them in the kitchen. Sandy and Deanna exchanged looks over the percolator as Deanna reached for the grounds and Sandy filled the pot.

"Do you think firemen like French Vanilla?" Deanna asked innocently, without looking in her mother's direction.

"Use the Jamaican Blue Mountain," her mother replied.

Halloran smirked and eyed the buns in anticipation. Looking out the kitchen window into the distance, he listened to the chatter in his earbud.

"Apparently you have a friend in the FBI. They found Nancy Dombroski on stake out at Bradley Airport. She'll be here when her shift is over. I could use 'coffee and,' too. You and I need a few minutes alone, Ms. Huber."

Oh, dread. The wind's changed. Here comes another lecture on letting the professionals handle this. It's my competitive intelligence business and they are my clients. Hopefully Frank Kirbee's still alive. Alright for him, Nancy will help if I put it to her right. With a be-my-guest gesture, she sat down at the kitchen table while Halloran snagged a coffee for himself and cinnamon buns for both of them. Sandy passed a mug of sweet milky tea for Em.

With a tray loaded precariously with paper cups, sugar packets, a glass carafe of high test coffee and the remaining buns, the girls made their way to deliver the goods to the volunteers. Sandy carried the tray. Deanna caught the napkins as they slid off. A vociferous welcome met them, the firemen were almost finished with a good morning's work.

"The local police will be wanting a statement, be careful how much you say." The bun, one of the best in the batch, was disappearing rapidly, leaving him with sticky fingers. "Good."

"Wonderful. Detectives for breakfast." The tea soothed Em's smoke parched throat. "I'm exhausted. I couldn't sleep, there's something I'm missing. When the Molotov cocktail smashed on the stones I was actually in the kitchen with a mug of very hot tea in my hands. It splattered all over my knees." She winced and looked down at bandage wrapped hands, now holding another mug.

"Did you see the car?" he asked over the rim of his coffee cup.

"Too dark. Only the light by the front door was on.

But it sounded heavy, like a larger sedan. It pealed out, tires squealed, when the fire truck moves you may find a trail of burnt rubber on the road. Deanna's worried they will come back."

"Understandable."

"If you don't mind my asking, how did you get here so soon?" Em cradled the hot mug in her hands carefully.

"Your son called me. We had a talk last evening. We're closer than he is in Cambridge." This was said as if it was the most sensible thing.

"And you two just happened to agree on this on first acquaintance, did you?"

"He works for an old shipmate of mine. Time to go. Anson needs to get evidence to the lab. Try to stay safe. Stay here. The local police will patrol. Your neighbor the fire chief will watch his end of the road. *We will handle this*." Halloran suddenly spry on his feet, stood cane in hand before completing this exit speech.

"So you've said but here we are. It's my case and my clients, *Michael*," she said to his departing back while appreciating a good set of shoulders and especially the torn patch pocket on the seat of his jeans.

"Huh, do as I ask. Please. For once, Miranda," he replied from the hallway in a raised voice with little hope just before the front door closed behind him.

2
THRIFT STORE SHOPPING

MID-MORNING MONDAY AFTER the arson fire on their front lawn, which came just after a startling backyard home invasion threatened the girls with harm, all was quiet. Deanna Huber and her friend Sandy Waitely were still recovering. They were doing it in the living room of the Spring House on social media.

After a weekend of rest and recuperation, boredom had set in. Summer sun beat down on the converted farm building tucked under the brow of a southern Connecticut hill. The sugar maple trees, distinguished by their full rich canopy of leaves and rugged bark lined the country road and afforded shade. They moved gently in the breeze as if standing guard over the barn house with a free flowing spring in the fieldstone lined room in the cellar. The front lawn and the sides of the approaching road were blackened. The smell of smoke persisted and worked its way into the house.

"Mom, we're done here. We're going to the mall. I'm taking the car. By-ee!" Deanna sang out as she and Sandy ducked out the front door. It slammed behind them. "Wew, made it out alive." She laughed. "After what happened this weekend, I didn't think she would let us out of the house without an armed guard."

"Who do you have in mind for armed guard, I wonder?" retorted Sandy with snicker.

———

Em Huber was financially strapped by a messy divorce and a corporate layoff. She came out of an early retirement to create a business intelligence consulting firm, never thinking her one woman enterprise would place her family in jeopardy. Their backyard assailant was the leading suspect in the murder of one of her first clients, Professor Ali Hussein. He'd threatened Deanna and Sandy and demanded they turn over the missing strategic solar plans invented by her clients, Professor Frank Kirbee, now missing, and Professor Ali Hussein, now deceased. Unable to reach her children by phone, Em raced home followed by Michael Halloran, who made her quite uncomfortable in some very pleasant ways.

Em was confused, undecided. *Am I ready to reach out to another man after my ex-husband's embarrassing betrayal? Could it be a serious conflict of interest for him? How would he respond if I did? And for the love of heaven, what would the children think?*

One thing certain, she needed to find the solar plans fast to pay the mortgage and save her fledgling business. Although she'd been warned not to try, she was not deterred from trying to find Professor Hussein's murderer. An unresolved murder case, that was not going to happen on her watch.

Alone in the Spring House kitchen, the bread machine prepped for honey whole wheat, Em laughed softly to herself. With the kids out of her hair, it was time to get back to work. She picked up the wall phone as it rang. The caller was a younger woman friend from the boxing gym.

Hearing the laughter in her friend's voice over the phone, FBI agent Nancy Dombroski remarked, "You seem better. There's been a development. *Your friend Hal-*

loran was in a sharing mood. Usually it's one way traffic only between the FBI and that agency. I don't even have a good sense of what they do. One of his minions made an interesting report. Are you free for a field trip?"

"Sure thing. The girls took my van. Can you pick me up?"

"I'm out front."

Mention of Halloran gave Em a rush, unexpected and strong. She took a quick breath and a deep exhale as she sought to cover it, feeling the warmth in her chest spread up towards her cheeks. *I've got to get this under control*, she thought. *Oh, that's not going to happen.* She suspected Halloran shared information because of her. Frank Kirbee was her client after all.

"We need to continue this in person." Agent Dombroski was not a fan of unsecured communications, she was on her cell phone.

With the house secured, Em climbed into the black fleet car beside Nancy, finding the seats pushed way back to accommodate Agent Dombroski's long legs.

"Buckle up. Now we can talk. Here's the deal. A Spanish speaking agent, Vargas, you've met him, went back to Bacon Avenue this morning when landscapers were at work. Vargas made it clear he only wanted information, and he was not from Immigration. The guy he talked to is part of the regular crew that maintains lawns and gardens of several houses on the street. It's meticulous, skilled work and takes time, so he's there for hours."

"The places are beautifully kept," Em agreed, looking at her own recently cut but roughly tufted lawn. No smooth carpet of emerald green, it supported deer, wild turkeys and ground burrowing moles.

"The compadre remembered seeing a kid, maybe early twenties, go into the garage and probably the basement across the street. That would be Kirbee's house. Most likely he planted the incendiary devices intended to take out your client Kirbee. Maybe even created the one flung at your front door."

"Could he give Agent Vargas a description?"

"Better. He remembers seeing the kid before," Nancy continued, "but dressed differently. When the landscaper saw him go down the driveway to Kirbee's house he was dressed in grey work clothes and carried a case of tools. The kid didn't go to the front door or back door but straight into the garage. It was odd. Here's the payoff, first time he saw the kid, he was loading donations into the Mission's truck."

"Can it be a coincidence? Is he sure?" said Em skeptically and shook her head. "There's our link."

"The kid is pretty unmistakable. Thin, stringy looking, not strong like a worker, round shouldered, is how he described him. Only 5'6" or 5'7". The key is, he has extremely long very light blond hair. The landscaper remarked, *We don't have too many people around here like that.*"

"No, our ethnic mix here isn't like the upper mid-West where they have a good number of fair natural blonds," Em considered. "So the kid wasn't afraid he would be recognized?"

"Apparently not, probably not, maybe he thought a grungy baseball cap on his head would do it and walked by the landscaping crew like he owned the place. The informant got a good close look at him. That's what Vargas said in his report."

"You know it was just good luck when we searched for the woman missing from Professor Hussein's murder scene. We were in the Alcorn Inn *at the right* time to meet Shelli and McVeety trying to claim the missing woman's belongings to sell at the Mission. It still irks me. How would anyone know to call the Mission and offer a donation to have the missing woman's effects picked up there? Good thing Shelli had the sense to go back to the Mission to get Mr. McVeety to back up her story. The way the poor thing was dressed, the hotel manager never would have believed her. I know she's still young, but really, a sense of what to wear and when can make all the difference. Clean and neat is good." Em stated this quietly in a decisive voice.

"So you say, Em. Sometimes you get a lucky break in a case. A little old lady sees something and you slog until you find her. Like Vargas did. Or not. That's why we have cold cases," Nancy said ruefully.

"Time to go to the Mission, I'm guessing." Em smiled as she tried to adjust her seat forward.

"I've already called. McVeety recognized the description right off. You are not going to like this. He sounds a dead ringer for Shelli's ex-boyfriend, the one she's trying to avoid by living at the Mission. Seems he's horned his way in there. McVeety thinks it best we speak to Shelli directly. He'll let her know to expect us after they serve lunch. Of course, I didn't tell the good man why we're looking for this guy." Nancy concentrated on passing several bicyclists training for a race.

"Did he give you a name?" Em asked.

"Oh, yes, Curt. The last name varies apparently, mostly Orlov or Orlieve. I'm having background run as we speak. There is a question of residency as well. He speaks with a trace of an accent. Mr. McVeety thinks it may be central European, but his hearing is not acute as we have been told already. Curt's refused to discuss his background with either of them."

"Can we stop for lunch along the way? I'm a free woman. Deanna and Sandy got bored and took off for the mall. They will be there for hours."

"How do you live with those kids?"

"They are going back to college soon." Em smiled, relieved. "You'd never know they were duct taped to Adirondack chairs in the backyard only a few days ago.

By a murderously ugly assailant, yet. Ah, youth. How about a pizza in Wooster Square for lunch?"

"Fine with me." Nancy aimed the fleet car for New Haven's Little Italy and its famous coal-fired brick oven thin crust pizzas at Pepe's. Try the white clam pizza there if you are ever in New Haven.

After a satisfying lunch, Em and Nancy timed their visit to the Mission to arrive after the clients' lunch and cleanup. Nancy parked the fleet car discreetly two blocks away and around the block from the Mission's thrift store entrance. A well-known charity on a back street close to the boutiques on Chapel Street, the thrift store served many residents and area students. Furnishing student apartments was a cycle of donation, purchase, and many times, re-donation.

Originally an A&P grocery store, the Mission building was local red brick. The shop front windows looked in need of a good washing. Acid rain had pitted the surface, it would never look clean or shiny. They filtered the light inside the store, giving it a pleasant muted feeling. Treasures on display were a collection of sturdy toys, glassware and china and occasional silver plated items made in plenty in Connecticut years ago.

Em hadn't been to the store recently. To her surprise, Nancy was a regular customer. The agent gravitated towards the racks of tall women's clothes, making a quick sweep by them. Several other women were browsing industriously. Em wandered around tables of freshly washed household wares and stopped to admire a set of crystal wine glasses. Off in a corner, framed posters leaned against a wall gathering dust. Books stood loosely organized on shelves opposite the cashier with CDs and tapes. An antiques dealer who regularly cruised the store haggled with the woman behind the register over her selections.

When a price for several china figurines was finally

reached, Nancy approached the cashier, gave her a familiar greeting and asked if they might go in to see their friend Shelli. The modestly dressed elder woman replied that they were most welcome to go into the Mission.

Once inside, the noise level increased exponentially. In summer the teens' day program was in full swing. They found Shelli in a room converted from a walk-in double row coat closet. She was speaking on the phone, answering an inquiry about shop hours. They waited patiently in front of her rather battered desk. The wooden guest chair looked very much like one culled from the university dining hall years ago. In her twenties, Shelli Saunders was still finding her way in life. But today her hair was brushed with care and her skin seemed clearer, her color warmer, healthier.

"Mr. McVeety said you wanted to ask me some questions. He wanted me to be prepared to tell you about my old boyfriend, Curt. I told him I'd rather not, but he said I shouldn't be afraid to help you. He said it had nothing to do with me." The young woman looked down at the scarred desk top as she spoke.

Em glanced at Nancy, who said smoothly, "That's right, Shelli. We need a detailed description of Curt. Any scars, any identifying marks like tattoos. Do you have pictures?"

"No, only two and I burned them. Curt never wanted his picture taken." Shelli looked up at the older women.

"What does he look like? Can you show us how tall he is? How much taller than you? Than me? How much heavier?" Em asked.

Standing up behind her desk Shelli raised her hand only two or three inches over her head. "Not much taller than me. And he's not heavier, he's thinner, too thin. His chest is kind of funny, caved in like. I think he said he was sick when he was born."

"When and where was that?" Nancy faced her informant, appreciating that Em had coaxed her into a position of status behind her own desk. Now she looked straight out towards Em and Nancy.

"I'm not sure, he never liked to talk about it. We went to high school together, but I don't remember him being in town before. After high school, I wasn't happy at home. My mother's husband said I was old enough to be on my own, so I left. Well, not really her husband. Two girls and I had an apartment in Derby, but it was too small when he started hanging out. My roommates said he made them uncomfortable. They left. Probably he did it on purpose, now that I think of it."

"Sounds likely. Please tell us about the Mission and Curt," Em prompted gently. Nancy scribbled notes in her small pocket notebook with a stubby little golf pencil she kept for that purpose.

SHELLI'S STORY

"My name's really Angelique Sheldine Saunders, Angie for short. But, I like wasn't proud of some of the things Angie'd done. When I came to the Mission, Mr. McVeety thought I could hide from Curt. Mr. McVeety said I could make a new life for myself, and he started to call me Shelli so I wouldn't feel so bad about what Angie did."

Attentive, Nancy stood close enough to Shelli without looming over her to hear and to shield her from view of anyone passing.

"Like, he would give me money to go to the store, but it was never enough to buy what we needed. He told me to steal the rest. I knew he had the money, why not give me enough?" Shelli asked them balefully.

"Bastard," Em said loud enough for the other two to hear her.

"If I didn't come home with all the stuff, he'd yell at me and tell me I was stupid to worry about what people would think. Fat cow is what he called me."

Nancy could see the storm gathering on Em's brow.

"He'd always have money. Sometimes plenty of it. But he never had a job. Not a real one anyway. He would just go off, sometimes even for a few days. I liked him away. Then he'd come back really tired out or in bad shape."

"What kind of bad shape?" Nancy asked, professional suspicion in her voice.

"Bruises and scrapes and stuff like he'd been in a fight. Once he said he'd fallen from a moving car," Shelli replied.

"Did you ask him what happened?" Em interrupted.

"When I asked him what he did and where he got the money, he told me, 'It's none of your damned business. I freelance, that's what I am, a *free lance*.'" Shelli stopped to catch her breath. It seemed hard for her to speak about her past, especially about her relationship with the old boyfriend. She had a sympathetic audience in Em and a representative of authority in Nancy. They encouraged her to continue, as much for her own sake as for their inquiry. "He would never, like, answer my questions. It was like running into a brick wall."

"Stone walling is never a good sign. I've been through this, too. It destroys your trust, doesn't it?" Em observed. She'd seen enough of it from her ex-husband Harley Travis Huber to know this.

Shelli sniffed and nodded in agreement. "It can't have been good, what he did, I guess I always knew. You know, somehow, don't you?" She looked at the older women.

Sympathetic, with an edge to her voice, Em said, "Oh, you've got that right, honey."

"Any idea, any indication of what he was doing?" Nancy said, still all business. Her love life had not encompassed a truly despicable male.

Shelli thought, looking backing over an unpleasant

time in her life that she'd worked to put behind her. "He had these really heavy suitcases he brought home and put in the closet. They were always locked, you know? Once when I went to move them, he hit me in the face and told me to never touch them. I said I was only trying to get the vacuum." Shelli's eyes filled. "That's when I knew whatever was in the bags was bad. It took me a couple of weeks to get away from him. And that's when I came to stay here." Shelli brushed away a tear with a knuckle.

Em put her hand on Shelli's shoulder. "You made the right decision. We can see that."

"When I came here, Curt didn't find me for a while. I started to feel better, they're good to me here. I think the new name helped. But when he did find me, and I wouldn't go back with him, he started to volunteer. I told Mr. McVeety who he was, and I didn't like it, and he shouldn't trust him either."

"What did Mr. McVeety say?" Em fished a clean tissue out of her bag and handed it to Shelli.

"Same thing he said to me. 'Everyone deserves a chance to change.' He said he would make it clear to Curt he shouldn't bother me or try to get me to leave. He said they could watch him for me, and I would never have to be alone with him."

"Exactly what did he do here?" Nancy was on the hunt.

"They told him he could be maintenance like, cleaning and sweeping floors, 'cause he started to train to be an electrician." Em shot a glance at Nancy who frowned. Shelli saw Nancy's expression as well and misread it. She said, "No, no, he was good at it, but he couldn't stand the instructor or whoever, and they had a fight and he quit."

"Or got fired," Em added helpfully. For her and Nancy, learning Curt had been "good" as an apprentice electrician was not a welcome thing at all.

"Yeah, probably. If you listen to him, he's never wrong. It's always everybody else who's wrong. Sweeping the floors wasn't his thing, so they have him doing pickups."

"Picking up people?" This seemed unlikely to Em.

"Stuff. The Mission has this old beat up truck. If people really can't bring their stuff here to the shop, two of the guys go out in the truck to get it. It's little old ladies mostly who are cleaning out. Sometimes it's rich people, too, who call every once in a while. They clean out oftener and they can't be bothered to drop it off themselves. I shouldn't say that 'cause they can be generous. The stuff is nice, too. He liked doing it, said he got to see the insides of the houses, even the really big ones. He talked like he'd be rich someday and have a mansion, then he'd come back for me. I mean, how dumb does he think I am? If he was rich and had a big house, why would he come back for me?" Shelli held her head up, and Em thought this a good sign. The girl needed a healthy shot of self-respect.

"I think it must be in the genes. We think differently, so, some men can think we're dumb when really it's a matter of…" Em spoke, wound up on one of her favorite subjects.

Nancy cut in. "Okay, enough, Dr. Ruth. Tell us where he is now, Shelli."

"He's out with the truck to a house in Westville. An elderly lady called to say she's selling her house and needs to clean out. It's a nice neighborhood, so we're looking forward to seeing her donation. We have to be careful when things come in like this, especially if the person is elderly. They hide things and then forget, sometimes valuable stuff gets donated that shouldn't. Even loaded clips and loose bullets. We really have to check inside the shoes and everything. The lady sounded real sweet on the phone." Shelli spoke with concern and confidence in her new job.

"Now, about Curt…" Em prompted.

"Mr. McVeety said I should forgive Curt for the things

he had me do and for the way he made me feel. If I could do that, it would make me feel free, and I could move on with my life, to be the person I want to be. It was kind of hard to understand and all, 'cause I was mad and hurt, but it seemed to be working."

"That's good, Shelli, I'm glad." Em's heart went out to her.

"But when he came back and found me, and started volunteering..." she faltered. "He was all slick with promises. But I didn't believe him. Mr. McVeety encouraged me to talk to Curt to tell him I had forgiven him, 'to confront him with forgiveness.' But he warned me some people can't accept it, 'cause it means they have to accept they were wrong."

"Well, that's certainly true. So what happened when you confronted him?" Em could read the conflicting emotions on Shelli's face. Nancy shifted her feet. Em raised her hand to ask for her friend's patience to let Shelli continue.

Shelli wrung her hands. "He got angry at me. It was like Mr. McVeety said, some people are just like... It's their choice, you just have to let them go. Curt said it didn't matter about what other people think, we have to be out for ourselves. Rich people in big houses can steal things, too, only more of it. This woman offered him a job, an important one, not mopping floors either." Anticipating the next question, Shelli continued. "And he wouldn't tell me what it was. The way he said it scared me." She looked on the verge of tears again but took a deep breath and a good loud sniffle instead.

Em's mind worked away on this one. "Did he tell you who this woman was? How he met her?" Em asked quietly as she checked around them to see no one else was in earshot.

"Oh no, he wouldn't, would he? But, he said she had money and was a real good tipper. People sometimes tip the guys who pick up the donations. They're not supposed to accept it, or if they have to, they are supposed to turn it in as a cash donation. Pickup is supposed to be a free service, and we don't want them asking for money on their own."

Em looked at Nancy, who now frowned intensely, and said, "It's a woman, I could feel that from the planning."

"Shelli, when you answered the call from the person who wanted Marla Eisenstein's things picked up from the Alcorn Inn, did you recognize the voice at all? Could it have been someone who called for a pick up before?" This was leading the witness, but Nancy stood by quietly and let Em do it.

"Maybe, I thought so at first. But her voice was real low, like she was trying not to be recognized or like there was someone else in the room with her that she didn't want to hear. I really couldn't tell." Shelli looked perplexed.

Her eyes darted around her. "That's what frightened me, I thought it might be *her*, the woman who offered Curt the job, asking me to do something wrong, too."

"Would you recognize her voice if you heard it again?" Nancy's voice was firm, she'd been told 'no' more than once already. She needed to be sure.

"I think it was low because she was trying to change it." Shelli shook her head emphatically.

"Very likely. Any idea when you might have heard the voice before?" Em followed up with her question.

"Not recently, like last week or last month. No, I'd remember. Mr. McVeety says I have sharp ears." She smiled.

"One last question, I'm curious." Em smiled back at Shelli. "Did Mr. McVeety give Curt a new name, too?"

"No way! Mr. McVeety said he was afraid Curt was just the same as he always was. He didn't want to change. You have to earn a new name by being a new person, a better one. Curt didn't do that."

"When is the truck due back?" Nancy asked, conscious the interview with Shelli had taken longer than anticipated.

"Any time now. We can never tell what they will find. Stairs and things. They took three guys 'cause the furniture is supposed to be heavy. One of the guys is this big old friend of Curt's."

"Shelli, you've been a great help. Whatever happens, stay in the Mission," Nancy warned her, careful not to upset her. With one hand Nancy raked back her dark auburn hair, cell phone in the other to call for backup. She was not anxious to tackle three furniture movers with only Em for company.

Words of encouragement came easily to Em who had daughters close in age to Shelli, but Nancy's professional detachment rarely cracked. She let it do so that afternoon. Good at heart, but a thorough professional, Nancy knew she might need this important witness to be courageous.

"You can have coffee in the Rec Room. Mr. McVeety likes to have visitors we know in there. It makes people feel good to have other people to talk to. Do you play table tennis? We're always looking for new people to play with us. I'm no good at it," Shelli confided.

"I enjoy a good game of ping pong," Em allowed. *Lots of good harmless aggression.*

To cover the front and side entrances Nancy decided to browse the shop. As a frequent thrift store shopper, Nancy found some of her best undercover work outfits on the racks. Clothes often took a beating in the field. She was pleased that Em chose to cover the back entrance through the Rec Room.

The Rec Room presented organized chaos, cheerful, noisy and crowded with teens and pre-teens who owned it during the day. Most had homes to go to, but often they stayed for dinner and turned up again for breakfast. A good week for donations might mean leftovers to take to school. In the winter, there was always hot soup for lunch.

Several baleful elderly women sat in a corner sipping coffee and eating donuts. Homeless women residents might or might not choose to stay the night. Rules were strict for overnight stays — no alcohol, no drugs, no cigarettes, mandatory showers and health checks. Sometimes, a safe place to sit down was enough. In stormy weather, they had to get there early to get through the intake, but a hot dinner and a dry cot were worth it. Meals were prepared by volunteers and resident staff like Shelli who worked for a small stipend, room and board, and for the good of others.

Coffee attracted her attention as she walked, watching both the ping pong game in progress and the back door to the driveway. Donated Newman's Own coffee smelled inviting. The elderly women appeared to be savoring it. Too often single elderly women of that generation found themselves with only minimal financial support. One illness, or the loss of an apartment, were all it took for their needs to become dire.

To Em it seemed likely the bastard Curt would head first for free coffee and donuts before helping unload the truck to avoid as much work as possible. She chatted amiably with the supervisor of the Rec Room. Teens danced to music from a second or third-hand boom box commandeered from donations. In a relatively quiet corner, several volunteers gave homework help one on one to children. Halfway through her cup of coffee she spotted Curt through a back window. The silver blond head approached the back door. Em tensed. Nancy was out front and out of view.

Quick on his feet, Curt was up the steps to the door before Em could put down her coffee cup. Always on the alert, a consciousness of duplicity will do that, Curt opened the door, stepped in and surveyed the room.

Unfortunately for Em, he was quite familiar with the faces and the activities of the facility. Em started to move slowly towards the shop door. The well-dressed woman stood out to him immediately, and she could see he recognized her as a threat. With the instinct of the guilty, without the presence of mind of an older head, he turned sharply and went right back out the door.

Em sprang towards the door to the shop and yelled to Nancy, "Curt's here!" With that, she ran through the Rec Room and out the back door chasing the much younger man. Heads turned, but only for a moment. Curt was not well liked, and the wisdom of the Rec Room believed it only a matter of time before someone came after him. To them, Em looked like Social Services and so not a serious threat.

3

TUNNEL

———✦———

BURSTING OUT OF the Mission's back door, Em spotted Shelli's once live in boyfriend, hair nearly white blond, shallow chested as described. As she raced down the back steps, the blond headed man looked hurriedly first right and then left at the end of the driveway. Walking fast, he headed away from the busy shopping area on the main street. Em wearing her running shoes picked up her pace to follow him, and turned the corner sharply onto the sidewalk. This set him off at a run. Em kicked it into high gear. But let's face it, high gear at her age was unlikely to chase him down, only made him run faster.

"Oh, man. Does she have to do this? We had this covered. It's our stakeout," Agent Rankel asked into the mic placed in his collar. "She's running after the guy. I'm right here, I'm fast. Why can't she let me take him?"

"Vargas, assist Rankel. Cut him off," Halloran said to his driver from the back seat of the command car.

"Sir?"

Vargas got out of the car reluctantly, not entirely happy Halloran decided to do a ride along. Helping Rankel corner the fleeing man would leave the boss on his own in the car. Vargas shook his head, if the boss got hurt again on his watch, there would be no end to it. Being taken to task by one of the Joint Chiefs was not high on Vargas's bucket list. Although, why anyone in the five-sided squirrel cage, the Pentagon, should care was beyond his pay grade. A logical conclusion could be someone owed Halloran a favor, and Professor Kirbee's solar project was more important than Vargas knew.

Andy Vargas's instincts were correct. As soon as he rounded the corner out of Halloran's field of vision, the car door opened. Halloran stepped out and stood waiting. Looking like a distinguished visitor to New Haven, tall, hair shot with grey in a tailored business suit, he carried his weapons carefully hidden.

In the Control Center back at Halloran's office, Gladys Rodriquez, the duty officer, listened to the comm channel and moaned, "Mercy, he's out of the car."

Bertha, tall and stately in khaki work clothes, who was checking on her very pregnant friend Gladys, said, "You know, they ought to take me with them when they go out like that. He's too much for Rankel and Vargas to handle. I'm betting the only two of us who can stop him are me and the lady out there," referring to Em Huber.

"Let's hope she can manage it because you got yourself written up for it the last time," Gladys told Bertha, a woman with a lovely café au lait complexion who served as the federal group's Armorer. "You went out too prepared. Too well armed by half."

"Ha, ha, very funny. It was worth it. If we let something happen to him, who'll we get next? My mother used to say, you know the devil you got, you don't know the devil you'll get. This one's damned decent, 'cept he can't stay out of trouble. Vargas must be having fits."

"You can say that again," Gladys agreed. "He's just not your tied to the desk bureaucrat the way *some people* expect. You know, I'm feeling kinda funky today...."

"Oh? How so? Looks to me like you dropped some." Bertha stood by her friend. "You want me to call somebody, like Dr. Smitty maybe?"

"No, absolutely not. Not yet anyway." Gladys brushed off the suggestion.

"Okay, but you gotta tell us if you're not comfortable. Anson's almost ready to fill in for you. You've done a good job training him up."

"That man's a handful, but he'll do fine now," Gladys acknowledged. "Let's see if the agents give Lieutenant Anson any back chat." She placed a hand on her belly. "She sure can kick, this one."

Bertha realized Garvey, their security officer, whose attention was usually glued to his monitors, was listening intently. "Garvey, you're going to watch her like a hawk, right? She's looking about ready to go. If anything happens, and you can't reach her husband on the road, call Andy Vargas. You know that, right? Good!

"Listen, I need to get back to the Armory. 'Sparks' has me working on a tiny little armored case for special deliveries. Girl has more ideas. She takes that evidence courier stuff seriously."

Gladys's husband, certainly an attractive man, was a traveling salesman for high tech surgical gear. Conventions and trade shows were highly productive for him. On the road, he lived as if he were single. Gladys's pregnancy, a joy to her, was not his idea and he threatened divorce.

Andy Vargas's thoughts on Gladys were quite different, and everyone in the office who cared, knew it.

Out in the field, Em chased the young blond man down a side street where he unexpectedly detoured into the entrance ramp to an underground parking structure. Em came to an abrupt halt to let cars pass before crossing to the garage entrance. The delay enabled Halloran to come within pitching distance of her. She looked over her shoulder at him, and without waiting, headed towards the ramp.

"Miranda, stop! Don't go any further alone!" Halloran started down the winding ramp.

With a wave, she kept on going to reach the first parking level. Facing orderly rows of parked cars, she scanned for her quarry, who was nowhere in sight. Two parking levels were below. She turned towards Halloran who advanced on her from the ramp, his eyes blazing.

"I've lost him!" she cried.

"What the bloody hell do you think you are doing? Rankel and Vargas will get him. They're covering the exits." Halloran came towards her, limping on his injured right leg. "Get back onto the walkway, go back up the ramp. Stay out of sight. Leave now!"

"No," she said simply.

They faced each other, he was fuming, she was eager to pursue the fleeing man. Suddenly, all the lights went out, and they stood in pitch dark. Only a deep shadow showed the entrance ramp.

"What the hell!" Em exclaimed and involuntarily moved closer to Halloran.

"Someone hit the main power. Get back into the corner over here. We need to be where we can't be seen when the lights come back on." A firm hand on her arm steered her back to one of the irregular corners between the wall and a pipe chase. "Keep going, Ms. Huber."

Em continued to back up sideways. Halloran was quite close, well into the space Americans claim as personal. Encroaching still further, she needed to keep moving back to avoid contact with him. Realizing his purpose, she stopped short. The tall man with the cane bumped into her, quite gently actually.

"Why did you stop?" he asked in a low voice.

"I don't know where the wall is," she fibbed.

"Reach out and see if you can touch it."

The cold cement wall loomed close enough with only

one step back to reach it, which she chose not to do. Instead she stood still and said, "It's right here behind me."

"Good, now find the corner."

"We are there. I can feel the corner wall, can't you? What do we do now?" Em was in a quandary. So near, his face a few inches from hers, a federal agent, presumably armed, between herself and trouble could have benefits. It certainly had its attractions. All her senses were aroused, heart working faster from the run, hearing and touch on high alert in the darkness.

"We wait until Rankel and Vargas corner him."

From the garage level below them, echoing against the walls a car alarm whistled, whooping and honking loudly. Startled, Em jumped involuntarily and pressed right up against the man's chest. As a reflex, his arm reached around to hold her, although he faced away listening.

"Sounds like he's picked the most expensive car in the lot to jack." A second car alarm joined the first. "Idiot! He should find a plain old soccer mom's van." Halloran chuckled.

"I beg your pardon, nobody steals one of those!" Em could feel his chest rise and his arm low on her back.

"Less likely to have a security system you can't get around in a hurry, when you need a quick ride out of town. Like he does now."

"Is he armed? I couldn't tell," Em asked, stirring against him, unable to keep quite still.

"We assume they are all armed until we can be sure they are not." He gave no details about disarming suspects. "Vargas and Rankel are searching for him. I'm losing their signal," he replied calmly.

Em had been holding her breath. As she relaxed with a long exhale she felt something soft brush her face. She turned. His breath crossed her cheek. Her pulse rate climbed, breath came short and shallow, and her skin prickled in anticipation, though she was conscious that she felt warm, and slightly sweaty from her pursuit.

Although he had agents working around them, when she didn't move away from him, Halloran moved in. Her hair carried a floral scent and her own personal essence. He drew it in and liked it. He kissed her first lightly, surprising her, and she stood without moving. Thinking on his feet, he figured if she hadn't kneed him in the crotch or flipped him off he was good to go. Since she made no attempt to dodge him, he kissed her in way that asked for a response.

This was a most pleasant development. Em let instinct guide and pressed her moistened lips into his to gain a taste of him. Two soft hands wrapped up and around his shoulders to his neck above his collar.

When he could feel she needed a pause, he drew his mouth away, perhaps to let her think about it. He was standing without moving, close to her in the darkness.

Em reached up, nibbled his chin along the jaw line to get him to kiss her again, and could feel, rather than see, the smile on his face.

His kiss this time had a warmth that was heartening and unexpected from the seemingly dignified man. It was not only warm, but playful. He teased her with short smooches and enticed her to open her lips so his tongue could explore and find hers. When they parted, Em tried to gasp discretely for air. Bringing his hands down her side under her arm to rest below her waist, he hoped it left no doubt about desire for closer acquaintance. Halloran felt a teenage boy's delight in first contact and only realized then Em's arms were holding him more firmly than he was holding her.

"Well, I'm...." Em began in an intimate voice women use when they wanted words heard only by a lover.

Halloran quickly covered her mouth with his fingers to quiet her, and then removed them to snatch a quick ardent kiss that left her feelings well aroused. "He's coming up our way on foot. Vargas and Rankel lost him."

Em let out a deep breath. Now he was back in contact with his agents, speaking into his collar. Obviously, the fun was over, but the sensations lingered, warm and vibrant, with the taste still on her lips.

"Into the corner and stay there. No matter what happens." Halloran drew a gun from the holster at his waist. "Do it, Ms. Huber," he said with a deeper resonant voice, giving her the shivers.

Hearing the tone of command in his voice, Em made a face he could not see in the dark. She caught herself before she said out loud, *So, now I'm Ms. Huber again, a minute ago you had your tongue wrapped around mine.* The agents could hear and that might eliminate any more chances to feel the rush when he kissed her.

"Alright, but what if…" her hand drew slowly down his neck to rest on his well-tailored lapels and the collar bones beneath.

"Stay behind me no matter what happens. If you distract me, you could get me killed." And with that he nuzzled her ear, enjoying her scent, and gave her an affectionate push towards the corner.

As her eyes adjusted to the dark, Em could follow Halloran's movements. Typically prepared for the field, he pulled a diminutive flashlight out of his pocket. Protecting errant cars from hitting the cement wall were several half height cement barrier columns. In normal light they appeared a bright fluorescent yellow. Listening intently, he timed his movements to be complete before the approaching footsteps came up the ramp from below. He placed the flashlight on the top of one of the columns closest to the ramp, balanced it so its beam would strike the middle of the darkened ramp. Placing his cane down, he came to a kneeling position behind another yellow column.

It seemed a long few minutes. Em pressed her back against the cement wall. When the blond man rounded the corner and came to the first level, the flashlight caught him. He shot at it twice, and dodged to the ramp wall for cover. When it didn't move or return fire, he began to edge forward.

"Drop the gun!" Halloran bounced his voice off the opposite wall.

Curt fired repeatedly towards the wall, aiming where he thought the sound originated. Three shots ricocheted.

Tricky bastard, Em thought admiringly.

Halloran took aim from his low angle. His shot hit the wall next to the Curt's shoulder. A chip of concrete hit his arm and he cried out. Angered by the pain, he ran back up the ramp to the street, past Halloran, firing his last shots wildly for cover until he emptied his clip. As Em watched, to her surprise, Halloran let him go. Curt took off up to the street at a run. Halloran spoke quietly into his collar, reached for his cane, and stood up slowly.

Em stepped out of the corner to meet Halloran just as the lights went back on.

"You let him go?" she asked, astonished.

He took a gentle hold of her arm and walked her towards the ramp up to the street. "Rankel will get him. Vargas stopped to turn on the lights, he thought it might help. We're going."

"But he's got a gun! He's running up to the street, there are people up there!" she argued.

"The gun is empty now. I doubt he'll have time to stop and reload, if he has any with him." Halloran was making for the street up the inclined ramp with a hesitant step as Rankel ran by at top speed on the sidewalk. "See?"

"You could have shot him." Em was puzzled, blinking her eyes, now unused to the sun.

"Bad light. I couldn't see well enough to aim. I didn't want to maim or kill him." They were approaching the street level and could see each other clearly. Em stopped.

Halloran could tell an explanation was necessary. "I want him alive and well and talking. He's no good to us dead and no good to himself or his family."

"No time to answer questions, or to repent and be saved, if he's dead?" she asked. "I thought you were all trained to shoot to kill. Double tap to the chest."

"How would it serve justice? We're not paid killers. It takes a lot out of an agent to kill another person. We don't know this man's involvement yet. Everyone's entitled to self-defense and things happen in the field. We all know and have to accept that. But it doesn't mean it's always necessary to kill someone. Unavoidable is one thing, taking an easy shot is another." Halloran was adamant. He also had the sense after kissing Em, dropping the bleeding body of a young suspect at her feet was not the best strategy for initiating a relationship.

"But he fired at you. Curt matches the description of the kid who planted the explosives at Kirbee's house," Em probed.

"We don't know that definitely. Don't mistake me, we're not a catch and release agency. When we turn them over to local law enforcement, it's a solid case. The courts administer justice, it's their job, not ours," he said firmly, spoken like a lawyer.

Seeing his attention focused on her, Em took her chance. She placed her hand on his chest, over the collar covering the bump she assumed must be his mic, and he placed his hand over hers.

"So what was all the fuss down there? Was it because I took my cup away with me from your office the first time you had me in to visit? Are you pioneering a new way to collect DNA? Are you going back to the office to spit?" His eyes flickered. "Oh my bad, you hadn't thought of it. Of course, you would have to explain how mine got so thoroughly comingled with your own." She grinned, and he realized she was teasing and gave a short rusty laugh. Her hand slipped off his lapel.

"Anything goes in undercover work, right?" she said archly.

"How is this undercover, you've been to my office," he retorted, well aware her hand was off his mic.

Em tugged at his jacket collar. "Come on. Let's go see if Rankel has caught him."

"Oh no, you and I are going to sit this one out in the car." His leg ached. "They will handle this better without your help, or mine." Positioned behind Em, Halloran guided her across the street to the silver car. "I have photos I'd like you to review. Now. In the car." A brief but friendly tussle ensued as Halloran coaxed her forward. Em enjoyed giving a little friendly resistance but finally let him get her into the command car.

In the back seat, Em scooched over to let Halloran sit down next to her. For some odd reason, she did not slide over much farther than the middle of the seat. Halloran seated himself carefully, pulling his aching right leg around. He hoped Em would understand this particular back seat was a business only space, as had been his office.

"Miranda, Ms. Huber, would you please move over. I need to retrieve photos for you to review. Make yourself comfortable on the other side of the console."

Needless to say, Em got the message and shrugged her shoulders. As she shifted to the other side of the car, she said, "Please don't call me Miranda. I prefer Em and always have."

Halloran gave her a wry grin, rubbed his chin and opened a plain brown envelope. "We have surveillance photos we'd like you to look at. Tell me if you know or can identify anyone in them." He added, "Please take your time."

"What's going on with Rankel and Vargas?" Em stared at the first large format photos in the batch Halloran handed to her.

"A chase is in progress. Look at the pictures," he directed kindly.

The eight by ten inch glossies were not sharp and clear, they had been taken from a distance producing grainy quality and limited depth of field. The first showed two men talking to a third in front of an old brick industrial building. The third man's face was unclear.

"Well, these are my clients Frank Kirbee and Ali Hussein. I don't recognize the third man. Where was it taken?"

"Outside their lab. Next," he prompted.

The second picture caused a frown to cross her face. Kirbee, hands in his pockets, walked towards the camera. He was talking to two other men with a crowd behind them, many dressed in long flowing black academic robes. The 1930's American College Gothic buildings were unmistakable, carved stone gargoyles and all.

"What is it?" Halloran asked.

"In front there, this is Kirbee. There's the Dean of the Graduate School, and the guy next to him is a Geology Professor, Jim Stevenson. I didn't think they knew each other well. It looks like after a graduation. When was this taken?" she asked. "Who is man in the background? I've seen him before."

"Are you sure?" Halloran asked, doubt clear in his voice. Eyewitness identification from photos always had limited reliability as they both knew.

"Yes, he is quite distinctive, short light brown wavy hair, spit and polish. I think I saw him holding a gun on another man in an alley. It was the night Hussein was killed."

"Go on."

Em gathered her thoughts. "It must have been a while after Hussein was shot in the park by the river. My friends and I, we'd gone to the Irish pub for drinks and dessert after the concert in Woolsey Hall. I was on the way back to my car. As I walked by one of the alleys between the university buildings, I heard two men arguing. You know they try to light everything now, so when I looked down the alley, I could see them. This man was standing in the light, holding a gun on a man standing within several feet of him. I thought he looked like a cop, maybe a detective, with a suspect, so I just kept right on going." She watched Halloran's reaction.

"He was a cop, of sorts." Halloran sighed deeply. "Are you sure? He was killed shortly after that evening, during a raid down in New London."

"Oh, I read about a federal agent being killed and a police dog shot and not expected to live, too." She looked at him sharply. "You were close?"

"His name was Pete Leonard. Actually Pierre Anatole Leonard, he was Cajun from Louisiana. He and his family lived up north here because it didn't seem to bother people as much that his eighth great grandmother came over in the hold of a slave ship. We served together in the Navy, and I recruited him for this job. Pete left a wife and three kids." Halloran looked down at the photo in Em's lap.

"I'm sorry for your loss." She slipped her hand over his and squeezed it gently. He returned the gentle pressure. They sat together in silence for a moment. "So many of us have multiple heritages of ethnicity or religion, and it's not like your left foot is one thing and your right foot is another and your left hand is something else. It's a whole body and you're a whole person. Maybe it gives someone a little more insight."

"Pete would have agreed with you. You're sure he pulled his gun? He rarely did."

Em nodded.

"What did the other man look like?" Halloran asked tersely.

Retrieving the memory of the two men standing in

the alley, she thought for a moment. "The other man was standing more in shadow. Shorter, dumpy, looked out of condition, kind of flabby, without being heavy, rougher looking. Maybe a square face, greasy straight black hair, maybe sallow skin. Kind of unhealthy yellow."

"Could you identify him?"

"I'm sorry, probably not, he was not standing directly under the light. You know how, when someone is standing half in shadow their eyes look like black holes? That's how it was. I can eliminate someone by height, weight and build, but that's about it. I am sorry."

"Don't be. Pete seldom drew his weapon. It's the first indication we've had of an incident. I believe Pete was targeted. Out of all the agents on site during the raid, they killed him. The dog went after the shooter, that's why he was hit."

"Why was he in the picture with Kirbee, the dean and Stevenson?"

"Security. At graduation they had a special guest or two."

"As usual," Em remarked. "Anything I can do to help?"

"We may take you up on your offer. The memorial service is in a few days. We may ask you to attend with us to see if you can spot the other man." Halloran's face darkened, he looked lost deep in thought and memory.

Em watched him and thought, *If I were guilty of a crime, I would surely hate to have this man after me.*

"Ah, Rankel reports he has two men in custody with the help of a civilian," Halloran listened to the report feeding into his earbud. "You may know her. Apparently an old girl friend of Rankel's goes to your gym. Seems his cover is right good and blown. She helped him bring down the man from the Mission and another accomplice. They are being transferred to Agent Dombroski's custody." Halloran's hand found hers and squeezed it, ever so gently. "Certainly a worthwhile operation this afternoon."

"Praise be, they are back in the car. Now if we can only get Andy to drive them back to the office," Gladys Rodriquez, at her desk in the Control Center remarked.

"What about Rankel? Are you going to make him walk back?" Garvey liked the idea.

"Oh, no, I'm going to cut him some slack. Let him repair things with that very helpful friend of his." She smiled as she said this.

Gladys stretched, wrinkled up her brow and rubbed her hand across her belly in a way that made Garvey uneasy. He picked up his phone to call the Armory.

Em saw Halloran still looked troubled. "Why does he have two suspects? There are too many people turning up for this to be a random act of violence. Hussein's death, I mean. We're not done with this case yet, are we?"

"No, it's looking like organized criminal activity. They have patterns and behave like this. You can never be sure you've located everyone. It's not like a simple homicide or a string of robberies where the crime is solved and the perps are jailed. But with an organization, some come out of nowhere, and some slip away. The question is now, what is this organization built for? If we can figure that out, we have a better chance of stopping it."

"Patterns. I'm good at finding patterns and detecting organizational misbehavior." Em looked into the grey eyes. "Do you have *organizational* behavioral analysts?" she asked half smiling.

"Damn!" Halloran said out loud and dropped her hand. Anson had taken over the comm channel at the Control Desk. "We've got to find Andy Vargas! It's Gladys."

"Is Andy Vargas the father? The brother?" Em inquired.

"Not exactly." Halloran was not going to touch that one.

Two men came running down the street to the silver car. Vargas and Rankel pulled open the car doors and threw themselves into the vehicle. Vargas was about ready to burn rubber when Halloran said, "Slow up guys. No rush. Bertha says Smitty thinks it's Braxton-Hicks contractions. Whatever those are."

"Take it from me, if it's Braxton-Hicks, it's just practice for the main event." Em felt sympathetic. Three sets of eyes in crisis mode focused on her. She had never seen three men go into labor before. It was quite instructive.

4

FUNERAL

In the Armory

AGENT GLADYS RODRIQUEZ took hold of Em's elbow. "Come on now, we'll get you all set for the funeral. My friend Bertha is our Armorer. She's like really into all that weapons and gear stuff."

Gladys swiped her key card in the reader by the sliding glass doors, planted the fingers of her right hand one by one onto the print reader below. She announced her name and her guest's and smiled archly at the camera. The thick clear bullet proof panel door slid open. Gladys commenced a very pregnant lady walk down the hall with her new friend. In the hallway, right in the center of the building, Gladys stopped in front of an unmarked door, faced off with the retinal scanner, stared up and around the door, and waved a greeting. The door buzzed, it slid open revealing vertical steel bars in a narrow metal lined entryway.

Standing inside the door was a tall generously proportioned, well-toned woman with a light brown complexion and bright black eyes. Bertha unlocked the internal barred door. She wore a broad welcoming grin on her face, and khaki work clothes. "So, this is the woman! Welcome to my shop!"

Em liked her right off, she judged her good humored,

spirited and warm.

"Bertha, this is…." Gladys began the introduction.

The Armorer cut her off. "I know who she is. We all heard about you, lady. Come on in, we got to get to work on you. No time to waste. Got a team to get equipped for the field. It's what I do here." She gestured around the surprisingly large room. Weapons of all sorts and sizes were organized in locked shelves behind clear panel doors and in metal cases. Drawers below the shelves were labeled. Em guessed they might hold ammo for the guns above. Free standing shelves held still more unfamiliar equipment, some of it electronic. Em took care to stand well away from these things. A workbench stood along the far wall. Extremely fine tools were meticulously organized in containers on the bench. Larger hand tools hung by shape and size on the wall above it.

"Sit yourself down Gladys, and the little one. You can escort Ms. Huber back out front when we're done. I've got no time."

Em laughed. "You must be Q!" she joked to Bertha.

"Oh, yeah right, but this is America so you don't have to be some funny ol' white guy to do this stuff. I do have one though, he makes up special orders for us. I got in a new cane for the boss, something very special. Designed it myself." She measured Em with her eyes, "We need to start with a vest. I think I have one that will fit. Take off your sweater and we'll see. What are you planning to wear? Something dark and discrete? Suit with a jacket would be good." Bertha opened a metal locker to reveal a rod full of vests arranged by size. She selected three and brought them over to Em.

Obediently, Em put on the first vest. It bulged out. Looking down she couldn't see her toes. "I can't wear this one, it makes me look like Mother McCree."

"Well, I don't know who she is. Wrong shape. Try this one, standard issue."

Em swapped out one vest for another.

"No good on that one either for going under anything, you come out with a shape like a gun boat." Bertha chuckled to herself.

"I need one with darts, Bertha, and narrower shoulders," Em suggested.

"Darts! Interesting personal weapons choice. We heard about the arrows. We have throwing knives, would they do? I'd have to order the darts. Short range, semi-lethal, could be a good option for certain situations." The Armorer thought it through.

"Darts, little tucks in the bodice. For shaping. It's got to look natural. I'm going to a funeral, not a gunfight." Em laughed. Gladys and Bertha looked at each other.

"Well, here's hoping. It does need some shaping, doesn't it? Do you mind previously used? I had this one cleaned." Bertha dug through the vests in the locker, pulling out a smaller tailored bullet proof garment. "I was saving the best for last. This was custom made for an agent who needed something to wear under an evening gown. You might want to lose the padded bra when you wear it, you'll fill it out all on your own."

Em took one look at the quilted garment and slipped off her shirt, put the dark gunmetal colored vest over her head and wriggled into it. The sides adjusted to fit with strong snap closures. Sleeveless, it extended from her collar bones past her waist, and featured a snap crotch.

"There you go! Basic black. Suck it in girl!" Gladys encouraged.

"Damn, it's an armored bustier!" Em exclaimed with a hearty laugh. Gladys and Bertha joined in.

"Yes, nice piece of custom work, if I do say so myself. It worked well, too. You won't need a push up bra in this one. Might want a camisole under it. Now what else are you carrying? Pepper spray definitely." Bertha handed Em a small can, easily concealed. "Brand new. Test it first.

But not on anyone."

"She's not authorized to carry weapons. We can't have her shooting anyone," Gladys interrupted hastily.

"Good luck with that one, honey. You don't need an authorization to carry a slingshot, I know." Em and Bertha shared a good laugh at Gladys's expense.

"Go on back now. We're done here. I've got a line at the door."

On the way out Em asked Bertha, "If you don't mind me asking, how did you get into this line of endeavor?"

"I grew up with a bunch of brothers and cousins in a neighborhood where you had to have a gun to feel like you could survive. Some didn't of course. They had me cleaning things for them, so I learned young. I didn't want to bring up a family there. I made another career choice, with benefits."

MORNING OF THE FUNERAL

Em dressed with care on the morning of the funeral. She'd stopped at a fashion discount store and splurged on a finely knit top that would just cover the bustier. From her closet, she resurrected a dark charcoal pinstripe business suit with a decorous below the knee flaring skirt. Despite the thin lacy camisole, she did have to do as Gladys suggested, suck it in, to get the bustier on. Once put together on top, she paraded herself in front of the mirror on her bedroom closet door. She had to admit the look was not bad at all, high and full in the chest, slim in the waist. Everything fit well under the skirt, the jacket refused to button and had to be left open. Em wore no distinctive jewelry, only simple gold ball earrings.

Out in front of the Spring House, a silver car came to a stop on the cobblestones. Em stepped out to be greeted by Halloran, who was formally dressed in an impeccably tailored off the rack suit over a crisp white shirt. A black tone on tone foulard silk tie was done up with a knot Em did not recognize. Halloran opened the car door for her himself and slipped onto the honey brown leather of the back seat beside her.

"You've met my driver. Anson, I have two words for you. Speed limit," Halloran repeated his often heard injunction to his new driver.

"Yessir. Good morning, ma'am. How's your daughter?"

Em acknowledged Deanna's injuries from the backyard assault were healing well, and she was recovering her feisty spirit. Deanna had pleased her mother with a renewed interest in archery and had taken to practicing on the target in the cellar. Both men looked askance at Em.

"Well, think about it this way. Everyone is entitled to some means of self-defense. It's the nature of the species. We teach children the physical skills they need through sports and games." She paused to look at them, and thought, *they don't see it.* Em wanted to pursue this interesting topic, which made Halloran give up reviewing his eulogy notes.

"Take T-Ball, baseball and softball. I played right field. Okay, so here's the connection. During WWII American GIs could throw a grenade accurately because it was the size of the baseballs they'd learned to throw as kids. German grenades were shaped and thrown differently.

"Archery's been a women's skill for time out of mind. The Amazons cut off one breast to get a better draw on the bow string. For short distances, target shooting with the new bows, I hardly think that's necessary. What?" Em asked as she saw the look of astonishment on the men's faces. "By the way, what's the plan for this morning?"

"You and I are going in together. Watch everyone, see if you spot the man from the alley. I will be speaking."

Halloran sighed deeply, looking down at his notes.

"You'll be fine. Pause if you need to," Em replied softly.

Anson looked in the mirror at the two people in the back seat. *Damn*, he thought, *the boss has found a friend.*

5

ARRIVAL

———◆———

THE SILVER COMMAND car arrived at the church
in record time. No one in the back seat cared to
check the speedometer, and it was a fast car. It was in
time to survey the congregation as it arrived. Anson
stayed with the car. Em, closely followed by Halloran,
emerged in front of a church with a broad sidewalk on a
quiet city street. Em paused to appreciate its traditional
medieval style — grey stone with a circular stained glass
rose window over the heavily carved wooden doors. A
single bell tower formed the right side. Paint peeled from
the louvers on the bell chamber windows. Several slats
on the front window were askew, suggesting the need
for repairs.

Inside the church, the nave was dimly lit. The sanctuary
was lined with tall nineteenth century stained glass windows that glowed in the summer sunlight. Bible stories,
shipwrecks and psalms were illuminated along the side
aisles. The windows resembled those from the L.C. Tif-
fany studio. The Water Brooks window with its hart in
the forest clearing looked familiar.

A petite woman with wavy blonde hair, wearing deep
mourning approached Halloran as soon as she spotted
him. Without speaking they exchanged a hug. Em hung
back to give them a moment of privacy. To her surprise,
he turned and beckoned her to come forward to stand

by him. "Shari, this is…" he began rather awkwardly, as if he wasn't quite sure how to introduce her.

"I'm Em," she said as she reached out to take the other woman's hand. "I am so sorry for your loss." The warmth in her voice, and the touch of her hand conveyed her sympathy and rescued Halloran.

Seats on the center aisle, immediately behind those for the family were reserved for Halloran. Joel Schwartz and his wife were already seated there. Although she hadn't met Lead Agent Joel Schwartz, he most certainly recognized her and greeted her with a knowing smile. Em continued to scan the church, but it filled so quickly she lost track of those she had seen, and who was newly arrived.

The order of the service was simple, prayers and favorite readings, interspersed with hymns. Halfway through the service, a soloist in a black choir robe entered from a concealed door to take her position by the microphone at the front of the church. Em stared in surprise as the soloist began to sing the traditional spiritual "Swing Low, Sweet Chariot." Em turned to Halloran, holding her hand to her cheek to hide her words. "Bertha's a good sized woman, but she's not that big. What she got under her robe?"

He inclined his head towards her as if in close conversation. "See much, say little. Keep looking around."

"Lovely contralto voice. She's had some training." Em made a mental note to tell Bertha how much she enjoyed hearing her sing.

Soon it was time for Halloran to deliver the eulogy for his friend and colleague. Without his cane, he walked slowly and carefully up the steps to the pulpit. He began by telling the assembled he had known Pete since their days in the Navy and mentioned a particularly telling incident on a flight deck. Halloran paused to survey the church. Then, he proceeded to tell them the churchman they regarded as an amiable insurance salesman and baseball coach was a federal officer who died in the line of duty, demonstrating the courage and dedication that always characterized him. There was a stunned hush inside the great stone hall.

Halloran reminded them of recent news coverage of the rescue of illegal immigrants trapped in a cargo container and the ensuing pursuit. He continued by reasserting the commitment to end the trafficking that endangered so many innocent lives. He offered the condolences of Leonard's colleagues, many of whom could not be present at the service.

Em thought, *That's not quite the whole truth, they were all around, scattered in the pews.*

There were few dry eyes as Halloran returned to his seat, negotiating the stairs carefully. Leonard's sons, and daughter, their family, friends and teammates were heard openly grieving.

After the benediction, the officiant dismissed the mourners to follow the hearse to the cemetery. The family filed out from the front pews, and as she did so, the widow paused to ask Halloran and Em to join her. Halloran offered Em his arm. They walked with measured steps following the family down the center aisle, through the nave of the church and down the broad stone steps towards the sidewalk. Em searched the crowded back pews for the assailant's face.

The silver command car was parked behind the black family limousines, close to the church door. Halloran guided Em towards the car, his head up, eyes alert and searching. When they reached the sidewalk, Em noticed Halloran was checking the higher buildings around them. The warm wind ruffled their jackets. Em watched several people forming a wide perimeter around them and across the street towards a four story building.

"Your people are moving." Em felt the hairs on the

back of her neck rising.

"Get in the car," Halloran ordered in a low voice. He was standing straight, apart from her, highly visible. Andy Vargas, of shorter stature, stood behind him. As instructed, Em sat down on the back seat, ready to slide over to give him room to join her.

Em looked up at the tall man. *He's making the perfect target.* Her eyes were drawn up to the top of the crenellated bell tower. A small circular glint of light flashed in the sun. Several slats of the bell tower window were down at one end. Em reacted, she struck Halloran's sore shin with her leg, doubling him up in surprise. She reached up, grabbed his lapels and yanked him down. Using her weight as leverage, she pulled him in across the back seat. Halloran sprawled on top of her in a tangle of arms and legs. A rifle shot rang out, a bullet screamed across the roof of the command car.

To keep him down she pulled him into a Half Guard on the car seat by grabbing the back of his neck, cradling his head into her right shoulder, one leg clenched over his leg.

"Close the door!" Em yelled. Halloran and Em scrambled to get their legs into the vehicle. Anson hit the button to close the back door. Screams and shouted orders came from the church steps as mourners were forced back into the church for cover. Andy Vargas and the field agents changed direction, heading around the church.

Halloran raised his head to get a view out the back of the car. As soon as his profile appeared in the window, a shot hit the bullet proof glass. Em dragged his head back down towards her. "Get down!"

"Jaysus, woman, you're choking me!" He ended up face to face with her on the back seat. "Let go. It's my best tie." He struggled to get his arms under him, to get his tie loose.

"Italian silk? Nice." She had no intention of letting him

go. He was wrestling to get free without hurting her. Em wrapped her legs around his legs clenching her thighs together to keep him in the car. It was highly undignified and quite effective.

"What the hell did you think you were doing? That hurt! Bloody hell!" After thrashing around on the back seat, Halloran had landed between Em's knees, her skirt rode up to her thighs.

"Better embarrassed than dead. You were standing out there making yourself a big target. If anything happened to you, your team would be devastated. They've had one funeral today. I have no ambition to play Jackie to your John." The reference to the assassination of JFK, the only Irish Catholic President, gave him pause. Em and Halloran were of an age to remember the exhilaration of those early years of the Kennedy Presidency, followed by the fear and sense of profound loss caused by his death in Dallas.

"Let your team find the shooter. They're the field agents, you're supposed to be the general."

"Don't give me orders." Halloran took a deep breath. Her assessment was accurate, and he was conscious he had waited too long for safety. Lying on top of her, he could feel the rigid under structure of the bullet proof vest she wore.

"What on earth are you wearing, it feels like armor plate," Halloran said to Em.

"Bertha's best bullet proof bustier. It's a body suit, and it's pushing some parts way up, and it's too tight down in the crotch."

"Too many details." He laughed softly. "Any weapons I should know about?"

"None that I would care to disclose," she replied with mock dignity. The two steel crochet hooks were a less than comfortable addition to the bustier.

Like a gentleman, he held his weight on his arms.

Looking into her eyes, he came closer. A smile parted her lips. His eyes narrowed in anticipation. Pulse quickened with pleasure, she could feel his breath on her cheeks. And then he remembered his driver.

"Anson, report!"

"Andy says stay in the car, sir." Anson swung around, trying to listen to the open channel, ready to make a grab for Halloran to deter him from leaving.

Facing front, Halloran gave Em a close-up of his ear. She closed her eyes and tried to think about the attack and not about feeling the man's body pressing down on her. Two bullet proof vests sandwiched together was not exactly an intimate sensation. Between the back of the seat and his side, she searched cautiously. Conscious of her hand's progress, he gave her a sideways glance, and a corner of his mouth tugged towards a smile.

"No one hit, sir. They're trying to find how to get up to the roof of the church. McLaren's going to search the building across the street."

Em's eyes popped open. "It's not the church roof. It's the top of the bell tower. I saw a reflection and movement up there," she said urgently.

"There's no access to the bell tower, they checked. The door is bolted shut and the stairs are unsafe." Halloran was clear, it was a matter of fact.

"Then he rappelled up the outside wall to get in," she replied.

"You rappel down," corrected Halloran.

"Climbed up then," Em corrected.

"Anson, tell them to proceed with caution, search the bell tower. Witness saw movement on top."

While the exchange was going on in the back seat, Anson had been in communication with the Control Center on the open channel. Chatter went something like this:

"Command car under fire." Anson's voice was calm

and clear.

Gladys voice came through. "Anyone hit?"

"No one hit. Car is in lock down mode."

"We're reading that. What's going on in the background?" At the office, Gladys Rodriquez was surrounded by support staff, analyzing incoming data and coordinating communications. Seated at a console lined with monitors, headset in place, she had her feet up on a stool.

Anson snickered. "Someone is taking exception to being kicked on his sore shin and dragged into the car by his best tie. Seems as if it wasn't a soft landing either, something about armor plate."

"How many shots fired?" Gladys stifled a laugh.

"Three, two hit the car from above and left at principal target, probably from the church roof. Third shot, couldn't tell direction. Maybe covering fire from across the street. There might be a second shooter. I guess we're not going to the cemetery," Anson concluded.

"That will have to wait. Not advisable, he might draw fire, cause civilian casualties," Gladys acknowledged.

Inside the church, Bertha sloughed off her choir robe, pulled out her gun and showed her shield. She went about restoring order and creating an evacuation plan. Joel Schwartz led the agents on their pursuit of the shooter in the tower.

Halloran began cautiously moving around as if making for the car door, again. "Sir, don't get out," Anson practically yelled over the seat. "Car's locked, it's bullet proof. Motion sensors all around. If we move off, or if you get out, we could stretch our forces on the ground."

"Motion sensors, did you have that done? What else?" Halloran was immediately attentive.

"It came this way. It was a general's car. Special glass. Custom suspension. Undercarriage reinforced. Drives like a tank, corners like a sidewinder. It's a pursuit car on steroids. Minor modifications only, sir. Honestly." Em and Halloran looked at each other doubtfully. Seeking a diversion Anson continued. "We're armed, too. Weapons lockers under the seats." He raised up a gun that looked like a compact semi-automatic short rifle. "Would you like one, sir?"

"What have you got there, Lieutenant?" Anson passed the weapon over the seat. Halloran took it readily.

From the byplay, Em guessed their words could be overheard by their command center, but she suspected not seen. Taking the opportunity of the distraction, she ran her hand under Halloran's coat, across the small of his back.

Instantly alert, Halloran looked her straight in the eye and mouthed the words, "Not now!" and went back to his conversation with Anson. Em worked her hands down his sides under his jacket to find the holster she thought might be concealed there. To stop her from finding his gun, he pressed her arm firmly against her side. "Not there either," he said aloud. "Keep your hands to yourself."

"You both have one. How am I supposed to defend myself? I don't have a gun," Em asked as she struggled with his jacket.

"Can you even shoot? Get your hands off my holster. You're not supposed to be armed," he replied with asperity.

Snickering came across on the open channel. Anson had a hard time holding in a belly laugh. His dignified and seemingly detached commanding officer had been reduced to arguing with a woman, and not winning, like any other poor son of bitch.

"I never said I wasn't armed, I just don't have a gun. How hard can it be? Point and shoot!" Em protested.

After her performance with the hunting bow a while ago, Halloran wasn't sure she couldn't do that. Caution was clearly advised.

"Whatever it is, keep it to yourself. Let me handle this. Stay down."

Em gave him a look of apology. "I'm sorry I hurt your leg."

Through the channel came the voice of McLaren. "Second sniper nest located on building roof opposite church. Bird is still in the nest. Repeat, do not exit the car. Sniper is in place."

"Description," Halloran queried.

"Sniper appears to be female, small stature, medium height, straight black hair. Blue dress, high heels. Maybe Asian."

"You have the tranquilizer darts?" Halloran replied, tone of command in his voice.

"Yessir, as ordered," McLaren said reluctantly.

"Fire at will to disable only."

"Understood." A pause followed. "Got her, sir. But she's getting up. Heads down!" McLaren barked. A wild shot popped in the air.

"Give it a minute," Halloran's voice implied patience needed.

"Upps, she's down now, sir. We'll bring her in." McLaren was relieved. Cornering a trained sniper was a most dangerous action. McLaren lost men to one, either injured badly or killed outright and had no wish to see a repetition. The darts were useful after all. Halloran had given all agents the lecture. *Dead men tell tales only a pathologist could love.*

"How's the church roof assault?" Halloran called for a report.

"Still in pursuit, he's down out of the tower and onto the roof. Witness was correct. We have him cornered at the far end away from the street," reported Schwartz.

Em stirred beneath the man in the superior position and gave a wriggle down below.

"What are you doing?" His attention was captured by

her attempt.

"Just straightening my spine, I landed kind of hard on it." She grimaced, and he rolled slightly to the side to let her settle back down more comfortably. In that space of time, Halloran realized she was making no move to throw him off as she had unceremoniously flipped a similarly circumstanced geology professor onto the grass. She watched the realization dawn in his eyes with a hint of a smile on her face, Mona Lisa's inspiration.

"We'll talk about it later," he said to her in an undertone that gave her the sensation of warmth and excitement, way down deep.

———————

In the Control Center, Garvey hung over Gladys's shoulder, listening. They watched poor quality video sent by a camera on the helmet of one of the roof team. He motioned to Gladys to put her microphone on mute. "Did I miss something? Are they married? They act like they're married."

Gladys laughed. "What would you know about that?"

"What did she mean by weapons, 'None I care to disclose?' A woman who carries all those knives, the darts, and a slingshot could turn anything into a weapon. Not good for this situation of course, too limited range."

"Probably why she was going for his gun, dummy. I wonder where he's keeping it. Professional curiosity. I'm just saying, we keep this girl around and Bertha's going to have to come up with body armor to protect that shin of his. Can't have the boss out in the field taking cheap shots to the leg."

"Saved his life," Garvey said.

"This once maybe. Anybody else gets onto it, he's in for trouble. 'Course he could stay in the office." Gladys's tone of voice was resigned.

"Getting him to stay behind his desk is a lost cause and

a half, my friend." Garvey and the rest of the staff were fond of Gladys. Although confident of her leadership, he was alert to ensure she had everything she needed without having to get up.

"Go back to your desk, Garvey."

"Yes, ma'am, sir!"

"Shooter fell from the back edge of the church roof. Ambulance needed," announced a female agent's voice on the open channel. "He's still moving."

"We will call it in. Proceed with caution. Secure the area." Gladys shifted her position in the chair and stretched out her legs to ease her back. The sooner she got that renegade Anson trained, the sooner she could go off on maternity leave which felt as if it was quickly approaching.

———◆———

Gradually untangling themselves, Em and Halloran attempted to regain their seats. It was not a dignified process, with Em trying hard not to bump his shin. Em came up first and was staring with rapt attention out the back window of the car at the church's bell tower. She reached over, grabbed the sleeve of Halloran's jacket.

"Something's wrong! How many people are there on a hit team? I think there's another one in the tower! Three shots, three shooters."

"What are you saying, woman?" He swung around on the seat next to her, keeping low. Two heads, close together, eyes only above the back seat, gave minimal silhouettes.

"The light and movement I saw came for the top of the tower between the crenellations. Look at the louvers covering the windows of the bell chamber below. When we first arrived, the slats on the front window were collapsed at the left side. Now, look, there are slats down on the right side, too, could be for a better angle at the car."

"Dammit all. The tower was supposed to be secure. It was searched and sealed."

"You have to get them to search the bell tower all the way down to the cellar. There could access from the tower roof."

"Anson, relay that to Joel and Cardozo."

As the trio in the command car watched, Agents Cardozo and DeCarlo on the church roof, dressed in Swat tactical gear, threw a grappling hook up through the battlement at the top of the bell tower. Armed with a crowbar and a fire axe, they went up and over onto the bell tower roof. The sound of wood chopping carried across the street. The agents on the tower roof stood back, one dropped a small object. A muffled explosion sent clouds of dust and smoke out through the louvered windows. The agents on the tower roof flattened themselves against the side walls. Shots aimed upward flew past them. Agent Cardozo who threw the tear gas grenade motioned to Agent DeCarlo to cover his ears as she tossed another grenade into the bell chamber. The grenade set the church bell vibrating with a deep booming strike tone followed by a penetrating hum one octave lower.

"What was that?" Em asked, her ears ringing.

"Stun grenade. That should do it." Halloran approved.

"I would not like to be in a stone tower with one of those, sir. You know, I was afraid I signed on to a cushy civilian job. I'm going to like this. Nice going ma'am. Glad to have you along." Anson, ex-Army, was grinning.

"We have a third shooter. Disabled by the shock and sound. Need another ambulance. Good call from command. Thanks," a determined woman's voice was heard on the open channel, Agent Amy Cardozo. Cardozo had been a promising young lawyer who lost her job, downsized out of a prestigious law firm. On days like this one, she didn't miss the courtroom one bit.

Halloran turned towards Em but didn't look at her. The strain on his face began to ebb. "I'll say thank you, later," he said quietly.

"You're welcome. Can we sit up yet, this thing's…"

"Uncomfortable, I know. I heard you. Tell Bertha when you see her."

Anson collected the extra weapons to replace them in the locker under the front seat. Keeping low, Em leaned back against the leather. Eyes, closed, she took a deep breath to relax. *I wonder, just what do they have in the locker underneath the back seat?*

When the all clear came, Em and Halloran were feeling more closely acquainted but not exactly at ease. As they emerged from the silver car, agents formed around them. Halloran reached down to give Em his hand. With her hair wildly out of place, Em's skirt was creased down the front, her sweater had lost top buttons and the bustier showed above it. Halloran's tie was jacked to one side, and his lapels were crushed. No one appeared to mind.

The mourners were gone, evacuated through the vestry. All activity now centered on evidence collection. The shooters were on their way in ambulances to be treated and held for questioning. By her side Halloran stood near the car taking verbal reports. Andy Vargas and his partner Rankel came to show cell phone pictures of the shooters. Em identified one as the assailant from the alley. Leonard's partner also identified the picture as a confidential informant who worked the last case. Two assailants remained unidentified.

Looking around, thinking herself unnoticed, Em began to ease her way towards the church doors.

"Miranda. Don't wander!" Halloran hadn't turned or missed a word of his interview with Joel Schwartz, who smiled.

"I was just going too… it's riding up again," she spoke so only Halloran could hear her.

Inclining his head for a private word, he turned towards her. "Get back in the car. See if you can fix it. We'll be leaving in a few minutes. Stay in the car. Please."

Ought to be safe enough in the car, was his first thought. On second thought, he remembered her curiosity and the weapons lockers under the car seats. A nod brought Anson straight to him. "Give her a few minutes alone in the car, then get in and stay with her. See if she needs anything. Keep her out of trouble."

Anson wondered aloud. "Exactly how am I supposed to do that?"

ON THE ROAD AGAIN

When Halloran finally climbed into the back seat of the new used general's car, Em was sitting in the opposite corner. A relieved smile played across her face, ready for a more comfortable ride back to the office. She'd managed to wriggle around enough to unsnap the bustier and pull it down. Ever observant, he noticed the missing top buttons of her sweater and the soft curves underneath. As he sat down, he pulled his right leg in carefully, appreciating the leg room of the back seat.

"Alright, Anson, let's go. Don't fly low," which is exactly what Anson planned to do, to take the new car out on the highway and open it up.

"A driver has to know his vehicle's capabilities after all. Could we arrange a few laps around the track at Lyme Rock instead, sir?"

"Hi oh, Silver!" Em joked.

"Don't encourage him." Halloran smiled for the first time that day.

Em lowered her voice, hoping to keep their conversation between themselves. "You risked your own life today to draw out the man who killed your friend, didn't you? Are you feeling better now?" By this she meant to ask if it helped to relieve his sense of deep regret at Leonard's loss.

Looking at her with steady grey eyes, well set over high cheek bones, he nodded. "Yes, surprised by who it turned out to be though. His own CI. Pete must have figured it out or been too close. That would explain why he pulled his gun on the informant in the alley. Seems Reid was working both sides against the middle. He gave Pete information on one operation, provided to him by rivals, who used us to eliminate the competition. They knew when the next raid would be and arranged to have Pete killed during it." With a deep sigh he said, "It gets personal sometimes, they know who we are and what we can do to their business."

"You know, I wondered about that. Sherlock Holmes and Moriarty. A CIA station chief killed in Syria, I think it was, several years ago. The third plane on 9/11 flying into the Defense Intelligence Agency wing of the Pentagon."

"Some things go without saying."

"Your leg, did they try for you first?"

"You've got me there. Yes," he said as he stretched out the injured leg.

"It would appear that way now. Would have succeeded, too, but Andy Vargas and Rankel showed up. Andy jumped off the dock and pulled me out of the water. Rankel chased down the woman who threw me over, and she will be serving a good long and well deserved sentence."

"Is this afternoon payback?" Receiving no answer Em asked, "Will you tell his wife?"

"Yes, we served together in the Navy out of college. I recruited him to join us. He wasn't a man for a desk job." Pain and loss showed in his eyes, but they were still and steady.

They sat in silence for a while, each lost in thought. As before, Em chose to break the silence.

"You know the older I get, the more I observe people in the corporations, the more I see that experience matters. People who have good abilities, who've been doing the job well, develop an instinct for the right and the wrong way to do it. Sounds simple, but the more specialized a person becomes, the more difficult they are to replace. People aren't widgets. Individual determination, skill, abilities and just plain guts make a difference. In corporations, casualties are more likely to be an internal affair. It's career assassination done by the numbers.

"There's a Pennsylvania Dutch saying, 'We grow too soon old, and too late schmart.' You need to be more careful, so you can continue to lead the team. Your experience got you the position. Don't risk your life easily. Peter Leonard's family would agree with me."

She reached over and ran her hand across his. He grasped her hand in his, and they sat together hand in hand for the rest of the ride. Anson hit eighty before Halloran said, "Speed limit" to him.

"Am I going to have to be a witness in court? I don't think that would be good for my new business. Just research only, you know, someone writes it, they publish it, I find it and compile a report. No guns, no muss, no fuss."

"No bows and arrows like last time?" joshed Halloran.

"I want to be known for *excellent* research. Not my marksmanship, or lack of it." Em contemplated the many ways her carefully reasoned, meticulously documented business plan had gone badly awry. *What should be the appropriate hourly rate for being shot at and forced to wear an awfully tight bustier?* she wondered.

"Then stay home, and stay out of Professor Kirbee's case. You won't be needed as a witness in this morning's incident. It's clear cut. Giving a defense attorney the chance to question you might lead to matters best left alone. There are questions we would like to go unanswered right now." Halloran flexed his fingers over her hand, back and forth in a truly pleasant way.

One amused look telegraphed her thought to him. *That's not going to work on me.*

"Be more careful." Halloran laughed. "Try to stay out of trouble. Call if you need backup. Do not pick up a gun without training. You're liable to hurt someone you don't mean to, including yourself."

"Stick to your computer, little girl?" Her tone was arch.

"I have heard it said with a computer and a connection, you could be termed armed and dangerous."

"Let's see, are we almost there? I could use a ladies' room and a latte." Em decided to move on past that interesting subject.

"Anson, it's not necessary to rocket through local streets. Slow down. No civilian casualties or near misses. I don't want to hear about it from New Haven Police Department."

Anson took the intervening streets at a more sedate pace, but not slow as if on patrol. That, he judged, would be bad. Better to coexist with the neighborhood.

The silver car came to a sharp halt in the parking lot behind the café that masked Halloran's extensive federal office. Em felt as if she were deplaning as Halloran extended his hand. "You can go in the back door of the café. Go up to the second floor Employees Only entrance. We'll meet you at the desk." Halloran gestured for her to head on along and watched thoughtfully as she crossed the macadam, stretching her shoulders as she walked.

"Afraid she'll take a hike on us, sir?" Anson surmised.

"She's certainly capable of it. With women, you never know. Especially that one."

6
BACK AT THE OFFICE

———◆———

EM HEADED TOWARDS the back door of the café with seeming obedience. She intuitively felt several pairs of eyes on her back. Once inside, her reception was different than anticipated. The blonde waitress guarding the dining room looked up, smiled and nodded. José, the counterman, spotted her and touched his forehead with a casual suggestion of a salute. It appeared news traveled around the home station quickly. Em wondered why she was not taken in through a door from the parking lot. Surely their uninvited guests were not brought through the café. It occurred to her suddenly, they might have no uninvited guests here, at all.

In front of the Employees Only door on the second floor, Em looked up and to the left as on her first visit. The air lock door slid open. Once inside, Em again had a sense of air swirling around her and air being exchanged, perhaps as many as four times. Garvey's voice greeted her by name and let her know when to place her hands on the blue lighted shapes. Em expected to be met by Garvey and Halloran behind the desk. She wasn't prepared for the welcome committee that greeted her. Lined up behind the desk Gladys, Bertha and Joel Schwartz faced her, with Halloran and Anson behind them.

Bertha yelled, "Way to go, girl!"

"Come on in, ma'am. Don't just stand there. You know

the drill. Drop the little bag of yours on the desk scanner. What have you got in the vest? Too thin to be knives." Garvey was professionally amused.

Em had the grace to be embarrassed. "Crochet hooks." While fighting to adjust the bustier in the car, she had forgotten to remove them. Hoots of laughter and catcalls greeted this. Halloran scratched his chin and shook his head.

"Well, you'll have to take them out, right here, right now." Garvey grinned and drummed his fingers on the desk.

With a less than gracious face, she reached first with one hand, then the other, down under her black sweater into the long narrow pockets she'd created on the vest under each arm pit. Out came one steel crochet hook at a time, quickly and easily, and were planked down on the desk. "I'll want those back," she told Garvey defensively.

"Clear now, for the time being, that is," Garvey said. "I'll think twice before sitting next to a lady crocheting on an airplane."

"Miss Marple rides again," Halloran muttered at her.

"I'd take it as a high compliment, but Jane Marple was a knitter. People underestimate the abilities fine hand-work takes, the ability to read a pattern, to understand the techniques and to execute a complex pattern with dexterity. Takes brains, takes skill, takes concentration, and it takes imagination." Em grinned at him.

Joel Schwartz stepped forward to shake her hand. "We will need you to make a statement for the record, with my assistant V.J. Agarwal, who was not present this morning."

"Yes," exclaimed Bertha. "Tell us all about it! I can't wait to hear it from the source."

"Can I get out of this thing first?"

"What are you calling a thing? That's a first class, custom-made one of a kind model. Right this way, lady.

We'll have her back in a few." Gladys and Bertha took Em off down the hall towards the Armory.

As soon as the women were past the glass doors, Halloran turned to Garvey. "Got it this time, sir. Oh yeah, good bio-sense, last time the latte and the cannoli confused the sensors. This time, she's nice and sweaty. It's good for the sensors, clear and distinctive." Halloran was quite aware of Em's distinctive bio-signature, first hand, and just looked at Garvey, who misinterpreted the look.

"Okay, sir, a lady-like dew. Now all we need is a retinal scan."

"Good. We'll get it if needed."

"Glad to have you all back in one piece, sir. You had us concerned. A three person hit team's pretty impressive." Garvey looked worried, an unusual expression for him.

"Yeah, I thought so too, Garvey. And expensive. Not just three guys they found in a bar out for a good time. Keep a sharp eye out on the café and the rooftops. Let's make sure no one's followed us home." Halloran was considering the higher visibility of the new silver staff car.

"Right, sir." Garvey, head of building security, went to work immediately with cameras controlled from the desk. "I'll tell the duty officer. She can send out an alert from the Armory."

Halloran took himself off in search of coffee and sandwiches.

BACK IN THE ARMORY

An Armory may seem like the last place for a women's conference room, but such is life in the world of equal opportunity. Em sat on a high stool, right next to Bertha's workbench. A look of puzzlement and concern was on her face. "Something feels wrong about the funeral." Bertha and Gladys looked at her. This was only Em's second brush with the reality of their jobs and they had misgivings. "How many people on a hit team?" she asked them.

"Three usually," replied Gladys.

"What are their functions?" Em was in pursuit of knowledge she did not possess.

"Functions? Functions? They're out to shoot somebody dead." Bertha was not following this.

"We saw three people out in front of the church, right? Shouldn't there have been a spotter inside the church to give them notice when we were coming out and which door we would be using? Suppose he and I went out the side door instead of out the front door with the crowd? What would they have done then? They had two snipers in the tower, one pointed front and the other pointed in the other direction." Em paused to observe her audience's reaction.

"I see where you're going with this now." Bertha nodded her head thoughtfully. "A good sniper needs to set up a shot, without a spotter it might be too rushed."

"There's a piece missing. Sitting in the pew, I felt someone behind me staring. It was ...creepy. Did you ever have the hairs on the back of your neck stand up? You can't do that on your own if you try. It's some sort of primitive survival thing." Em shook her head and a shiver ran up her spine. Her shoulders shook so both women could see it.

Bertha said in a low voice, "And you got that feeling sitting in the pew?"

"Oh yeah. I turned around to look several times. I couldn't pick anyone out but it felt like directly in back of me, maybe a few rows behind."

"Bertha, you were up front on our side of the church when you sang. Did you see anything unusual? Anyone unusual?" Em's sharp gaze focused on the Armorer, trying to read her expression for a clue to what she might have seen.

"I didn't see anything myself, but I can do you one better. We can look at the video! Hard to sing and investigate at the same time." Bertha chuckled.

Gladys said, as she hoisted up from the ergonomic chair, "I'll get the media conference room set up."

"You and I are going to see Mr. Halloran, Ms. Huber. Get dressed lady! I don't know what you thought you were going to do with those crochet hooks, and now I'm afraid to ask!" Bertha sighed audibly.

"But …" Em started to express concern.

"We'll get you whatever. He ordered lunch from the road. Everyone knows you have to eat after a funeral. Emotionally draining, that's what it is. Got to keep up the blood sugar. Got a sugar issue myself." Bertha hustled Em down the hall with Gladys taking her time following after them.

Halloran was seated at this desk, a half-eaten ham and cheese sub and coffee in front of him.

"Yoo, Mr. Halloran, we've got a lead for you. We've been discussing the operation this morning. We've come to the conclusion Ms. Huber and I should go over the video from this morning to see if we can pick anyone out of the crowd." Bertha's tone showed she was confident of his response.

"Okay. What brought this out?" Halloran asked.

"When we were sitting in the pew next to Mr. and Mrs. Schwartz I could swear, I mean I felt like someone was staring at my back in a bad way. Did you ever have that?" Em asked Halloran. "Like survival instinct. That's why I grabbed you so fast when I saw the flicker of light in the tower. I was on edge already," Em explained her speedy reaction.

In her eagerness to express herself she leaned towards

him while he was trying not to look too hard at her breasts, each decorated by a perfect little nipple bump. The bustier was no longer in place, and neither was any other form of support. Em had only a camisole on under her silk blouse, and the lace edge peaked out of the neckline.

Halloran looked up at Bertha's determined face. "My camera would be the perfect height to see over your heads and behind you."

"Go!" Halloran said. "Have Gladys run the programs for you. She should be training Anson."

"But not today! The three of us is enough," Bertha cautioned.

"Very well," Halloran said and thought, *Ladies' day at the races.*

Walking quickly Bertha guided Em out of the small office. "We'll get lunch to take with us."

At the small media equipped conference room, Gladys entered the code into the key pad by the door and pressed her thumb onto the reader. The door lock popped open. From a specially designed case she removed a thin laptop and placed it on the conference table facing a wall mounted flat panel screen. Several cables and a surge protector emerged from the laptop bag to be connected. "The new printer is in the console," she said.

With a nod Bertha opened the console, pulled out a shelf containing a small high speed printer and cabled it to the laptop. A cable went into a wall jack which required a code to be entered into its cover to be live.

As technical support Gladys sat in front of the laptop flanked by Em on one side and Bertha on the other. Sandwiches, several bags of chips, a plate of pastry and drinks came into the conference room with them. Em had captured a plate of chocolate chip and oatmeal raisin cookies and placed it in the center of the table.

"I can use the electronic white board to show you

how I think we can narrow down our search." *It's like being back on familiar turf, like the corporation,* thought Em. *I just have to remember to lock the castors so this one doesn't roll away from me, again.*

With a black dry erase marker from the ledge of the freestanding white board in one hand and a water bottle in the other, Em drew the floor plan of the church, the tower, the cars parked in front and the building across the street from a bird's eye view.

"Okay, one side of the bell tower joins the church so they could see the front and along the building past the side door. The tower was sealed, so they probably climbed up and over and broke in from the roof. The third shooter set herself up on the roof of the building across the street to aim directly at the front door of the church.

"No wonder people worry Lee Harvey Oswald wasn't acting alone. This is like serious determination here." They considered Em's diagram as Gladys and Bertha munched sandwiches and chips. "The distance to the target is close. The window of opportunity is narrow. Even with three of them tracking him, he stood there to give them time." Staring at the diagram, remembering how it felt to see Halloran so exposed as a target, she frowned, her brow furrowed deeply.

"And you pulled him out of the way just in time?" Bertha observed the intense look on Em's face and tried to change the mood.

"Ye-es, but if I were going to all this trouble, I'd sure have someone inside to tell me which door he would be using to leave. One bad shot and you lose your target. Not that I know anything about planning this kind of thing," Em said, deprecating her own insight.

"You're doing fine so far," Gladys responded, reaching for an oatmeal cookie.

"Pass me a bag of chips? Thanks, Bertha." Em continued her thoughts out loud. "Now these are the rows of pews. We were in the third pew on the right side. Bertha, you sang from up here behind the lectern."

"That's right. I had a clear view of everyone, and I panned my camera around slowly on purpose as I sang to get everyone," Bertha confirmed.

"All the digital videos from this morning are loaded on the server so we can show them on the wall monitor. I have the file from Bertha's camera ready to go." Second oatmeal cookie in hand, Gladys browsed through the list of videos displayed on the laptop.

"Bear with me here. What I felt came from in back of me not from the left side of the church. Also not from the two rows in back of me, the people were families, kids or older people. We can leave them out." Using a blue dry erase marker Em drew a square around the pews from the sixth row to the last row and turned to see if Bertha and Gladys were in agreement.

"Good, let's capture this before we go any further," Gladys remarked. "Whiteboard please." Bertha cabled the whiteboard to the printer and the laptop. "Hit print, Bee!"

Bertha located the print button on the whiteboard and the high speed printer hummed to life.

Finding a red marker Em returned to the whiteboard with a flaky Italian pastry shaped like a scallop shell in her hand. "Boy this is an old whiteboard. No wireless connection?"

"Second or third hand government issue. But it still works." Gladys laughed. "Garvey hates the thought of any more wireless signals to jam. Leave it to him and we'd all be using tin cans tied together with string."

Em took a bite of pastry and gazed at her drawing. "Okay, so based on my observations, the angle I could turn around without appearing to climb out of the pew is this. Here are the angles of my range of motion. Wherever I couldn't see, we look for the spotter." In red she drew a shape like the truncated pyramid on a one dollar bill that extended from the sixth row of pews to the back of the church. "The last three rows are probably too far back for good visibility. So I'm going to draw a line in front of them. Make sense?" Em asked.

"So now we have the most likely position based on intuition and logic," remarked Gladys.

"Probably either dead in the middle or right behind us. This quadrant is the prime area. If I had to bet, I'd say towards the center aisle. I know facial recognition takes time, so if we can narrow it down it might speed up things."

"Hit print please," said Gladys as she typed notes into the laptop.

"Gladys, can you find a straight shot of that half of the congregation? Should be a few good ones, I'm handy with a camera when they let me out of here to do anything." Bertha chose another half of a sandwich instead of cookies or pastry.

Em asked, "When you find a good shot, can you freeze it and copy it to a file so we can edit it?"

"Yes, give me a minute." The flat screen on the wall lit up with a moving image of the congregation inside the church. The diverse group of mourners composed of church members, neighbors, relatives, teachers, friends, and of course, various work colleagues of both Peter Leonard and his wife packed the pews tightly. Children were wedged in. It made individual identification a challenge. The women focused their attention on the screen. Lunch was momentarily forgotten.

"There, that's a good one," Bertha exclaimed. "See, I'm good!" The camera was carefully directed and moved at a speed that enabled Gladys to produce clear still images.

"Okay, I'll go back, freeze it, make a copy to save and one to edit. I'll brighten it up first." It took Gladys a few minutes to Photoshop the image to increase resolution to her satisfaction.

"First take us out of the picture. See what I mean about the people in the two rows directly behind us?"

"Yes. It's Pete's kids, their friends and parents, not likely candidates," agreed Gladys. "You know he was a trustee of the church, right?"

Em stood up to point out people to be cut from the image and tripped over one of the cables. The cable yanked the laptop across the table, and Gladys made a dive to save it.

"Honey, we have a laser pointer for this. Top right-hand drawer of the console." Gladys repositioned the laptop.

Embarrassed, Em reached into the drawer, pulled out a silver tube like a short wand, pressed a button and pointed a beam of bright red light towards the wall. "Cool, this could be fun."

"Or not, please be careful not to point it at yourself or anyone else." Gladys worried about injury to vision.

"I apologize, I do know that, I was only kidding. Must be the sugar rush." Em was contrite.

"Come back here and sit down so we can all share the pointer, lady. And we don't have to worry about you breakin' your neck on government property. I hate those accident reports. The paperwork will kill you." Bertha laughed.

The first five rows were cropped out. "We're losing some people off the sides. You want everyone in the middle, right?" Gladys asked.

"Yes, we can eliminate the kids and the grandparents." Em pointed out three or four people for Gladys to crop out. Working row by row they eliminated unlikely suspects.

"Pass the little bitty light saber to me. I see some people there I recognize. People from other agencies Pete worked with in the past." Bertha used the laser pointer to designate five more people including a young couple who Em had taken for sweethearts, a man with dread-locks and a shifty looking thirty something man with straight dark hair slicked down on his head.

"Are you sure about the last guy?" Em asked dubiously.

"That man is a top DEA agent. You do not want him after you. He likes looking that way. He cleans up nice though. Not a bad dancer either," Bertha remarked.

"My turn," said Gladys as she cropped out two more women and a man with shaggy sandy hair over his eyes and a droopy mustache. "These are local detectives."

"The last guy, Detective Nilsson from New Haven Police, isn't it? Was he sitting next to Nancy Dombroski?" Em scrutinized the faces left on the screen.

"Yeah, but we already cropped her out. Friend of yours?" Bertha inquired.

"Yes, she is. You know, if there really was someone inside, he or she has chutzpah. There are enough armed law enforcement people here to quell a street riot. Must be someone who is confident they won't be recognized." Em concentrated on the remaining images, one by one, in order, right to left, front to back, until her eyes returned repeatedly to one man's face. *It's the look in his eyes, and something else about him drew my attention.*

"Gladys, the guy in the eighth row, three people in from the center. Can you copy him out and enlarge the picture so we can look at him closely?" Em felt she was getting close and shivered.

"He's staring straight ahead, not a funeral kind of look, looks mad. He'd give me the chills if he was staring down my back," Bertha judged.

"He did," replied Em. "Look at his suit."

"You don't like his suit? Looks *fine* to me, if you know what I mean," Bertha eyed the image appraisingly.

"Exactly my point, Bertha." Em sounded sure.

"Hold on, let me get it sharper for you." The image changed several times on the screen.

"Okay, best I can get it," Gladys triumphed. This was a talent she enjoyed using. "I'll send this out for facial recognition right now."

"Look at the lapels, Bertha. The suit looks like a European cut and an expensive one. See how well it fits his shoulders. Could be custom made."

"Yeah, I do see and the shoulders aren't bad either. He works out. Looks like that new James Bond guy."

"Conservative cut, British maybe. I wouldn't know Savile Row if I fell into it on a dark night. But who wears a European suit to an American policeman's funeral? You might want to try Interpol, Gladys." Em was not about to let this one go, the effect of the shiver down her spine stayed with her.

"I can have the analysts do lots of stuff you don't even want to know about to see if we can find this guy." Gladys grinned knowingly. "Matter of fact, I'll send them the whole bunch from the church just in case the Euro here isn't our man. Looks like a banker to me."

"With my luck, he'll be MI6." Em groaned.

Gladys's mobile device vibrated. "Em you have an appointment with V.J. Agarwal. He's been texting me for twenty minutes. I've been ignoring him 'cause I'm having so much fun here with you two."

"I'll take her out to V.J.," volunteered Bertha.

"I think we'd better take these in to the boss. Can you make good copies of the photos?"

"They are printing at my desk as we speak." Gladys smiled.

"I don't care how he found her, I think we should keep her." Bertha laughed that special deep laugh of hers.

Bertha retrieved Em who regaled an anxious to hear everything V.J. Agarwal with all the details she could remember about the morning's events. V.J. was looking pleased, but Em looked worn down.

Gladys waved to them. "He's off the phone, get in there

while the getting is good!" Long gone were the days when an assistant could play gatekeeper with the phone and hold the boss's calls at will.

Bertha and Em walked into Halloran's office and sat down in front of his desk. The flat screen on the wall showed the whiteboard diagram of the church. A pile of 8" by 10" glossy photographs were on the desk in front of him.

"Good job, ladies. This man looks familiar. Analysis is running his photo now." Halloran turned two photos around so Em and Bertha could see them. "This is the man you picked out, and this one was taken from across the street right after shots were fired. He's standing outside the church doors looking towards the cars. Bertha, your back is to the car, you're directing people back into the church."

"Damn, that's him? That one did not want to go back inside the church. I had to practically drag him."

"Trying to get away?" Em conjectured.

"Could be so," returned Halloran.

A chime sounded from Halloran's workstation. "It's from Analysis. They have an ID from Interpol, Liam Robert Innes. British-American. Scotch mother, American father. Home town is Glasgow. Known in this country as Bobbie, in England as Liam."

"After the fiasco this morning, if I were him I would get out of Dodge. He's got to be aware there's a chance he would be recognized, or one of the three will talk eventually," concluded Em.

Bertha watched them with growing amusement. She hadn't missed Halloran's interest in Em on their last visit to his office.

"Does he have connections back in Scotland? You might have the police stake out his favorite local pub. See if he turns up any time soon," Em suggested.

"Worth a try." Halloran respected both good analysis and good hunches, which in his estimation made up intelligence. "I have a friend over there I can call. Ms. Huber, you need a ride home. Call us if inspiration strikes you again." He smiled. Bertha looked from Em to Halloran and raised her eyebrows.

"I'll have Anson drive you home. Tell him…"

"Speed limit. I know." She chuckled tiredly.

7

CONNECTIONS

———◆———

"I'M TELLING YOU. You don't want to do this again."
The well-tailored man, Liam Innes, spoke into his
satellite phone, glancing around the city park to ensure
no one was close enough to hear or see him. "Halloran
had a female bodyguard. We missed that. He was treating
her like his companion. She was throwing eyes all around
the church. I thought she was looking for some friend."

"Did she make you?" The voice on the other end of
the satellite connection asked in a lightly accented voice.

"No, I was sitting directly behind them several rows
back. Most difficult spot to see. She walked right by me
on the way out. No recognition I could detect."

"Then why do you think she was a bodyguard, was she
a big woman? Did she look armed?" his business partner
asked.

"No, rather average size for an American woman, not
armed that I could see. But when they had a good clear
shot at him, she looked up at the bell tower. Must have
seen something because she wrestled him into the car
and held him down. Professional."

"But not armed? Girlfriend like that, hmm. We know
he likes women." There was a laugh at the end of the line.

"You gotta give this up if you want to keep the operation going. Your girlfriend is in jail, she's not dead. They
caught her when she tried to kill him last year. I barely

got the boat away from the dock. It's a risky business we're in. Now he has captured three of our, shall we say, temporary employees. They are alive. It's not good. One of them is bound to talk," Innes surmised.

"They were supposed to succeed or die trying," his partner said rapidly.

"You mean get killed by the feds in the attempt? It didn't work out that way."

"I made a promise," the accented voice protested.

"Forget the damned promise. This guy's connected. Old Navy buddies. You want SEAL Team 6 to visit your house, maybe? They don't care where you live. The commander in Washington says 'Justice' and it's all they have to hear."

"Okay, okay, but I'm not forgetting." This was followed by *sotto voce* curses and imprecations that Innes ignored.

"Nobody forgets anything in this business. Do it the American way. Hire a high priced crook of a lawyer. We got plenty of those here. He'll get her out in no time. I'll get you some names with good jail house recommendations. Then you got to get her out of the country because they'll be hanging on every breath she takes looking for you. Getting her out shouldn't be a problem for you, right buddy? Set her up somewhere nice, an island maybe. Good tax shelter." Innes, alone in the park, was growing edgy, long phone conversations could be a bad thing.

"As one business partner to another, I'm telling you, you gotta be smart to survive in this business. I'm heading out. Scotland is beautiful this time of year, any time of the year. And we have business to do there." Innes signed off.

8

AFTER THE STORM – VISIT TO THE FRED

"MOM, HAVE YOU heard?" Deanna rushed into the living room. The wind slammed the door behind her. She carried an armload of cushions from the patio chairs and garden benches. In her trip around the yard, she'd gathered up a bucket of garden tools and gloves, a kneeler and stowed them in The Fred, their composting outhouse and tool shed.

Sandy turned the Adirondack chairs over, leaving them upside down on the lawn. On hands and knees she tied the gauze nets tightly around the blueberry bushes to keep birds from stealing the berries. A clever bird might find its way up under the nets.

The wind blew along the ground, turning the leaves of the trees and bushes over to show their silvery undersides, a sure sign of impending rain. The tops of the trees tossed in gusts of wind, but no rain came from the thickening grey clouds, the headwinds of the storm.

A good-humored debate raged, what to do with the shade nets covering elder daughter Celina's special crop. Celina's garden plot in a sunny corner grew medicinal plants and herbs. Em made her promise not to grow anything toxic. Many plants were unfamiliar, some looked downright strange. One smelled so badly they refused to weed around it. The plants under the nets were different. Celina was investigating a folk remedy for snake bite and grew Connecticut Broadleaf Shade Tobacco to obtain tobacco juice. Deanna and Sandy decided to leave well enough alone.

"We're in for a storm. It's coming up the coast faster now. They think it will hit Long Island." Em had just returned from last minute errands. "I managed to get more batteries and cash. We needed fresh gas. The lines at the gas stations are starting. It took me longer than I planned. I had to go into the bank to get cash because the ATM was already tapped out."

"It's early season so it's not a strong hurricane yet. I hope only light wind and a good rain." Em tried to be optimistic.

"Huh, that's not what the Weather Channel said. We can feel it out there, Mom. It's a warm, gusty wind coming from the south." Deanna's hair was blown into twisting strands around her ears. "The clouds are moving faster, heading north. The birds are all in the trees, hardly any flying. How's Genny?"

"I tested the generator this morning. It was hard to start, but I did get it going. Damn thing's as old as Methuselah." Em shook her head. They were lucky to have it, and she would not be able to replace it any time soon.

"The Smithsonian can have it when we're done with it," Deanna said airily.

"At least we didn't have to rush out to buy one. I hope it's willing to start again if we need it," Em replied. Like many of the Spring House's tools, the generator was left in place by a succession of owners.

"We're charging our cell phones and stuff now."

"Good." Em dropped her bag of last minute purchases including snacks, instant soups and dried pasta meals on the kitchen counter. A line of charging devices were plugged into a power strip. She added her own cell phone to the lineup.

Sandy returned, she'd lashed the garbage cans to the woodpile. "No one took the bread out of the bread machine, Deanna. I'm going to take the clothes out of the washing machine."

"Mom, will we be able to leave for Texas?" Deanna looked apprehensive.

"The weather should clear by then, and you will be flying inland away from the remains of the storm. This storm is spreading out along the coast. We know it's been to New Jersey already — look at the Jersey fly on the window screen." A large mosquito like creature standing an inch and a half high rested outside the kitchen window.

"I'm going to take a shower and wash my hair now." Sandy waited until Deanna was in the kitchen with her mother to say this. She had one foot on the staircase ready to run up.

Deanna had forgotten this and was about to race Sandy for the bathroom when Em stopped her.

"Time to back up the computers. She'll be quick. Go on, get started. We still need to fill the jugs with spring water for neighbors and friends who might be without water. Let's do it before we shower." Em hoped there would be time for her to shower before the storm began in earnest.

Deanna dragged out four laptops and placed them on Em's desk in the living room. She began systematically running back up on each one. Ash came to sit next to her. The black cat complained in cries like a cranky two-year-old child. Without a cat door, he was at their mercy. Her older brother Joshua insisted it was a security hazard for the Spring House. But Ash had a long memory and resented having to ask to be let out.

"See if you can't find Cleome. I haven't seen her since this morning. Where does she go when we can't find her? I wonder. Please let the yowly beast out, Dee. The

weather is making him nervous." Cleome, their elegant
Siamese house guest was the pampered cat of Em's missing client Professor Frank Kirbee, who entrusted her care
to Em before he disappeared.

"Me too, Mom. The weather on cable makes it sound
so ominous. You never know." Deanna was looking distinctly uneasy. During her early childhood, the weather
in New England had been quiescent. The hurricane season meant little to her until recent years. Her mother, on
the other hand, remembered the dread of coastal com-
munities. In her own childhood, coastal storms sent the
surf inland and turned the rivers into floodwaters that
devastated the centers of the towns in Connecticut river
valleys.

"Cleome's not around, Mom." Deanna let Ash out to
take a cat hike.

"Did you check under the Fred? She seems to go off
in that direction."

"Nope, she's not under the outhouse or in it. It's starting to rain, though," Deanna saw the large splotches come
down. The leaves were showing the first gloss of rain.

"Better get upstairs and take a shower. A short one
please. I'll get supper in the oven."

The kitchen matches came down from the cupboard.
This was one of the few times they were glad the stove
was so old it had no electronic ignition and required a
match to light it. As long as there was gas in the tank, they
would have hot food. Macaroni and cheese went into the
oven to heat. Leftovers in the refrigerator were purged
that morning. The freezer was reorganized to hold plastic
containers of water to be frozen into blocks of ice. The
fridge was turned up to get everything nice and cold.
Loss of power was common along the tree lined country
roads. Service was restored to more densely populated
areas first. They often had to wait for hours, even for days.

"Bring down the sleeping bags. If the wind is strong

we'll need to sleep in the living room away from the windows." The tall trees standing on the ridge to the east of the house were a concern. Powerful easterly circulation could land branches, even whole trees right down to the root balls on the ground, all pointing in a westerly direction, all symmetrically arranged like fallen dominos. A less organized storm could blow falling limbs any which way, which was scary as well.

Sandy and Deanna vacated the bathroom for Em to shower and quickly wash her hair. At her insistence, they filled the bathtub with water for emergencies, although it would leak away gradually. The girls filled their three tin camp fire buckets from the bathtub tap. Em filled a large plastic bucket for the downstairs bathroom. In times when there was not enough electricity to power the well pump, (the generator being persnickety) they had a saying, once illustrated by Deanna and posted on the bathroom door. "If it's brown, flush it down, if it's yellow let it mellow."

By the time Em finished her shower and dried her hair, it had grown surprisingly dark, as if dusk had come early. The wind increased in velocity and plastered leaves against the house. Back in now, Ash lay curled up on the hall rug waiting for her. Still no sign of Kirbee's Siamese house cat. Down in the living room, the girls watched local weather, and the news was not good. They decided to eat an early dinner although it was only 5:30 p.m. As they ate salad, fresh bread and mac and cheese, the sky darkened further. The wind and driving rain hurled forest debris against the house in strengthening waves. Branches snapped and fell, thudding to earth in the woods surrounding the house. Smaller branches were carried away in the strong gusts.

Em set a lantern with fresh batteries in the middle of the table. Deanna and Sandy used a battery operated pump to inflate two air mattresses. By right of age Em was always awarded the Stickley couch. Dessert of ice cream and berries was eaten in front of the TV as they watched the storm on radar until after 8:00 p.m. when the lights first dimmed and then came back up.

"I'm going to brush my teeth," Em announced. "Please check for Cleome." But the Siamese cat was nowhere to be found. "Damn that cat, where can she be? I lose his precious cat and Kirbee will never forgive me." And to herself she said, *If the man is still alive.*

Em had no sooner finished brushing her teeth and was spitting rinse water into the sink when the lights went out completely. She finished flossing by the beam of the flashlight kept in the bathroom for occasions like this.

In the living room, Deanna turned on a lantern and pulled out a deck of cards. She and Sandy began a serious game of War. Their emergency radio carried storm news and the worst was expected soon. It would coincide with high tide, never a good thing. The wind continued its assault on the coastline, driving in higher tides. It shook the storm windows of the Spring House until it seemed they might break. In the dark, the tops of the trees bent down, their branches punching back against the wind as if trying to right themselves.

Using a tiny book light, Em was reading a mystery set in Scotland when the first branch hit the roof, bounced off and fell past the living room window. She drew a deep breath, they still had several hours of storm to ride out. Rain coursed through the gutters, rattling them so loudly they thought sleep would be impossible. But there was only distant thunder. The increased activity of the day and the intense early darkness led them into sleep.

Several hours later, the security system awakened Em and Sandy with a constant regular beep. Battery backup power had been expended. Em roused herself to perform the system shutdown routine, which would not please Joshua one little bit and could not be helped. It was too early to fight the weather to go to the barn to start the generator. It seemed unlikely an intruder would take the opportunity of the storm to find the Spring House, much less attempt to breach it. On a visit to the downstairs bathroom, she stayed well back from the kitchen windows. The winds wrenched the trees back and forth. Small branches hit the windows and the sides of the house. The wind's direction had already changed. The storm windows on the northeast side now rattled, one in particular.

As Em returned to the living room, she heard a rushing sound like a great whoosh off in the woods above the house. The ground shook with the impact of a large tree falling. She stood stock still and let out a sigh of relief. The tree must be up on the ridge, too far for its top branches to reach the house. Not long after, a branch blown from the top of a younger tree met the roof over Em's own bedroom, crashed down to the ground and dragged the gutter with it. About 3:00 a.m. the storm subsided into bands of rain, by dawn the tail winds ceased.

In the morning, they discovered other trees had fallen, all in parallel, but none close to the buildings. When the clouds broke and light found its way into the living room, Em got her first look at the close call. The lawn was littered with leaves and branches, many were dead branches pruned out of the trees by the high winds. The dry branches would provide kindling and fuel for next winter's fires. The blueberry nets were pulled towards the west and hung like sodden shrouds around the bushes. The tree top that hit the roof tore the gutter off at the corner which would need to be replaced before the next heavy rain.

To their surprise, Cleome sat on the porch outside the living room door waiting to be let in for breakfast. The cat looked poised and not all that wet. A wet cat is usually a disdainful beast until it dries out. Cleome hopped into the house and went directly to her bowl, passing Ash on his way out.

The last of their eggs went into breakfast and Em had tea and toast ready when the girls crawled out of their sleeping bags. All managed a decent night's sleep in spite of the turbulence around them. Em looked down at the contented Siamese cat scarfing her special cat food and said aloud, "The curious incident of the cat in the storm. I wonder…."

Deanna followed her mother's gaze and began to sing a spirited version of, "The cat came back. Cleome came back the very next day…"

During breakfast, the radio reported widespread power outages. The storm brought down wires all over central Connecticut. Their electric wires were strung between telephone poles due to bedrock and rocky soil. The number of customers without power numbered in the thousands, although not quite a record high.

Em groaned aloud. "I guess that means I have to go fire up the generator to keep the refrigerator running. Two hours on. Two hours off. *No TV.*" Once dressed, she threw the switch in the hall closet to take the Spring House off the power grid and turned off several light switches.

"At least we still have the wireline. It's on backup power. I can tell because the dial tone is fainter," she remarked with the kitchen phone in her hand.

As soon as her mother left the house to cross the road to the barn, Deanna looked across the breakfast table at Sandy.

"I have an idea. This is going to be fun."

"You mean cleaning up the yard again? Always lots of laughs," said Sandy, often a reluctant accomplice to Deanna's pranks.

"Not quite." Deanna ran up the stairs and into the attic to begin her preparations. The sun was struggling through the remaining clouds.

Em wrestled with the aging generator. Her foot braced against the base, she pulled the cord repeatedly to get the engine to turn over. When the generator sputtered and finally kicked in, the old wooden barn shook. Em threw the switch to send power over to the house. The security system began to recharge, by the time she reached the living room, its lights were blinking, ready to be rearmed.

Meanwhile, up in the second floor hallway, Deanna opened two windows, arranged a set of sizable old speakers in front of them and made haste to cable in her CD player. She found the track she wanted and waited, biding her time for the right moment. When the sun finally broke through the clouds, she turned up the volume to blast an original recording of the Beatles "Here Comes the Sun," down towards their neighbors in the valley below the Spring House.

In the kitchen Em yelled, "Deanna!"

Down the road in the farmhouse kitchen Mireille said to Philippe, "Sounds like Em has power at the Spring House."

"Well, I'm glad somebody does. What are we going to do with all this ice cream?" her ever-loving husband replied.

On the second day after the storm, rumblings and grumblings were heard from the upstairs bathroom, and the door burst open. "There's no more water in the bathtub to flush the toilet. The rest of it drained out last night. I'm going to the Fred!" Deanna exclaimed with an over-abundance of feeling.

"Calm down, Sarah Bernhardt. You don't need to go to the outhouse. You can go down to the cellar to the spring and haul a bucket of water upstairs."

"Not happening, Mom."

"Okay for you. The keys are hanging in the hallway. Take a lantern. Use the broom for spiders, first."

The Fred, more usually referred to as a john, was an old classic clapboard outhouse, complete with quarter moon shaped vent cut into the door, its vent pipe properly oriented to provide draught in the northern latitudes. It was the requisite fair distance and downhill from the backdoor and stood towards the edge of the woods, out beyond the grape arbor. Screened by a tall long growing lilac bush, the shingled roof was visible from the house. The outhouse was maintained all these years as a convenience for working in the yard and for hikers on the old lumbering road that ran into the woods behind it.

In most recent years, the Fred was kept locked. Local kids, who often made use of the facility, blew it up one Fourth of July with cherry bombs. In rural New England, old traditions died only when the suburbs encroached. Early Yale College records described the discipline meted out to students who blew up a "necessary house with gun powder," giving a totally American spin on the phrase "gunpowder plot."

Previous owners renovated The Fred, converting it from a two-hole outhouse to one seat. They gave it a small deck and added a composting toilet. Garden tools were stored in compartments built into the side. Supplies were stored on overhead shelves. Reading material took the place of the proverbial Sears Roebuck catalog in the rack by the new seat in the tiny throne room. A small square screened window could be closed by a green wooden shutter. A long hook designed to suspend a planter held the lantern that was necessary after dark. Spider paradise, also home to Daddy Long Legs in numbers, it required a thorough look before seating oneself in comfort and privacy. Great thoughts could be had there, as well as mosquito bites in season.

Deanna returned through the back door. "Ma! Someone's been visiting Fred! The door wasn't locked."

Locking the Fred was a new thing. Certainly its original lock could be opened with a skeleton key from the local hardware store. Or perhaps simply opened with a credit card or dull knife blade.

"We probably just forgot."

"No, Mom," Deanna replied with exaggerated patience. "They changed the toilet paper, too. It's the expensive quilted kind. The kind you never buy. Look!" she said displaying a sample of two sheets of TP that were obviously thicker than the house brand. "It's even in the plastic bin we use to keep the extra rolls. And, the Fred's really clean, no spiders and the hand sanitizer and cleaning wipes have been used. You'd *like* the change in reading material, too. Look what I found in the magazine rack. *Solar Life*."

Em browsed through the magazine, from back to front, articles covering current residential solar applications, ads for products and books on converting to solar. There was no address label on the magazine, possibly bought at a newsstand or bookstore, and it was last month's issue.

"It's a neat man. He leaves the seat up," concluded Dee triumphantly. Of course it was indisputable proof of an alien invasion in the Fred.

Sandy and Deanna looked at Em who said, "Well, well, well…I'll take care of this. Nothing to worry about."

"Who is it, Mom?"

"Oh, probably one of the neighbors got to it before we did to resupply. That's all. It's hiking season." Em was not looking at her daughter as she spoke.

Deanna looked at her mother and rolled her eyes. "Yeah, right."

9

FIRST DATE

———◆———

"EM, I ASKED you to come in to the office today to thank you, for yesterday." Michael Halloran paused. They were seated in his office, and he was approaching the hard part. "I'd like to invite you to go to dinner with me, by way of thanks."

Halloran watched her reaction carefully. Em's eyebrows shot up, and she looked at him quizzically over his desk. She hadn't fled the room screaming yet but looked at him with a curiously searching gaze she tried to hide, which made him feel the need for reflective armor.

"What do you have in mind, may I ask?" There was a hint of something off in his demeanor that warned her there was more to this invitation, especially coming so soon after the funeral. Too soon, in her opinion, to be a purely social invitation.

"A good dinner, and uh…." He looked back at her. "Some investigation." *Why do I feel as if this woman is trying to read my mind?* he wondered.

"Into Hussein's murder?" When he didn't respond readily, she said more quietly, "Into your friend Peter Leonard's death?"

"I'm not sure yet. Could you go for some dress up?"

"Oh! How formal?" Em's mood brightened with visions of being escorted by a tall very presentable man.

"Not that kind of dress up." Halloran hid a wry smile.

"We will need to go in character."

"It's not Halloween, a masquerade ball?" Em held out hope.

He shook his head, no. They stared at each other over his desk.

Em tried again, "Character? Whose character?" Suddenly suspicious, she held her hands together in her lap, and re-crossed her legs.

"Mine, or one for me and one for you," he replied, realizing negotiation was required from the face she made at him.

"You asked about undercover. This is an opportunity. Yesterday you suggested checking Liam Innes's favorite bars. That started me thinking. We checked Pete Leonard's logs and case notes for the weeks before the shooting. We found nothing for Thursday evening when you saw him in the alley, or for Friday evening, and all day Saturday."

Here's the buildup, Em thought, *to engage my interest*, and inclined her head to indicate willingness to listen.

"Pete was extremely conscientious about reports. But, like most of us, he could be several days behind entering notes if he was extremely busy. I asked his wife, and she remembered easily Pete worked both evenings and was home earlier on Thursday, before midnight. On Friday, he came home later, after 1:00 a.m. with beer on his breath. He'd given her a beery kiss when he crawled into bed with her. She choked up after telling me that but was able to say Pete was home with the family all day Saturday. That weekend he made and received a number of phone calls."

"Oh dear. Poor thing, she must be so stricken," Em said, and thought, *so is he.* Grief showed in his eyes, they seemed a deeper grey, and the circles beneath them darker.

"It's one thing to know the risks, one thing to be the person who confronts them, and another to be the person left behind when the worst happens. Now the task is to find out why. We can use your help."

Em sat and said nothing, which Halloran took to be a good sign and proceeded to outline his proposed course of action.

"You seem to have a good memory for faces, not everyone does."

Em nodded in agreement.

"Not all the faces are clear on the surveillance video from Bertha's camera. The images are flat and can be harder to identify, especially people in the back pews. We were lucky Innes was closer to us."

"Right behind us," Em spoke with regret.

"Probably no accident. Time to go investigate and I would like you to join me. We go in with certain modifications to our appearance. It is not without risk," he concluded.

"More or less than going to the funeral with you?"

Halloran scratched his chin. "Hard to say, maybe about the same. Hell, we thought we were relatively safe to have you go with us then, too."

Em crossed her arms. "So when do we go?" and thought, *some dinner date.*

"How's tonight? It's an active investigation." He sat up and tucked the sore right leg back under the desk.

An evening of adventure was worth considering. Sandy and Deanna were at a beach party. An afternoon playing beach volley ball at a friend's cottage on Long Island Sound was to be followed by a cookout on the beach. It would last well into the evening. Timing couldn't have been better. Em was a free woman. Only a simple phone call to Deanna was needed, so her daughter wouldn't call out the cavalry if Em was not home when the girls returned.

"You will have to tell me how to dress." Em wondered idly if a clothing allowance came with her contract with

Kirbee. "How are you dressing?" She grew impatient for details.

"I told you I am going in character, an older sports jacket, glasses, things like that."

"That is not extraordinarily helpful." *So much for my visions of a long dress for an elegant evening soiree.* "Where are we going?"

"To a bar. I'll let it be a surprise. How would you feel if I gave you a spray to change the color of your hair?" He gave her a conspiratorial smile.

Although his smile produced a flutter she replied, "I'm not dyeing my hair."

"It washes out. Burgundy highlights?" Halloran looked at her critically. "Maybe change the style. How good are you at makeup?"

"Reasonably good, why?" Em tried not to be offended by this and controlled her tone.

"Give yourself a different look, hair, nails, makeup. Choose something you wouldn't normally wear but you feel comfortable wearing. Same for clothes, casual for bar hopping." A wider smile appeared. "But it will have to be different too, for this special occasion. It could be a long leisurely evening."

Here, she swore he smirked at her.

"We'll ask you to use your eyes, take a careful look at everyone in the bar, especially the men. But, we don't want them to focus on your eyes. Wear something distracting. But don't go all Mata Hari on me."

"How distracting? I'm not going as tart for dessert." She huffed at him, still unsure whether to be offended or not. Intelligence gathering, as she previously practiced it, was confined to a desk, corporate conference rooms and telecommunications technology of an advanced and interactive sort, with hazards to career only.

"I wouldn't ask you to do that. I said something you feel comfortable wearing, but more eye catching. Down in front, maybe? Away from your eyes." *How much more specific could I be*, Halloran wondered. "I can promise you drinks and a good dinner." In a moment of true inspiration he said, "The desserts are exceptional, chocolate, cream things and fresh fruit. I'm fond of the rice pudding." This surprised her.

"You've been there before?"

"In character, yes. The owner is an old shipmate of mine. Comes in handy for both of us." As he replied, the corners of his eyes tugged up. It was not quite a true smile.

Since no further explanation was forthcoming, Em said, "Something distracting?"

"But in reasonable taste." He thought he had her. "Create a character for yourself you can maintain throughout the evening, and be able to hold it even when we are alone and you think no one can hear us." He paused, and receiving no objection continued. "Good then, five-thirty, I'll pick you up at your place."

On her way home, Em gave considerable thought to creating her character and decided to wing it. Everything in her closet must be in her own recognizable taste. Closet raiding at home was out of the question, nothing the girls wore would fit her. There was a black skirt from her closet that could be shortened, although now tighter than she considered appropriate for day wear. A sense of corporate decorum died hard.

Ransacking the habitual stock of coupons in her bag, Em located one for twenty percent off and drove to a chain clothing store. Cruising sale racks of off season blouses, she found a designer watercolor print of vibrant red and dark purple on white. The blouse featured a draped neckline. Em tried on the blouse, reluctantly noticing it was one size too small. The neckline dipped nice and low. *The sleeves are too tight.* Em's days at the gym had given her not only a heart shaped behind but toned arms as well. She sighed at her reflection. *The sleeves will have to go, how sexy were long sleeves anyway? Red attracts men, if I believe a recent Internet article, and it does explain their reactions.*

Pleased with her selection, time in mind, Em trotted off towards the checkout counter. Coupon in hand, her path led by the Jewelry counter. It struck her, *I am about to make the same mistake the imposter Marla Eisenstein made and wear my own jewelry.* So much for going to your favorite store, she realized too late.

From the display of good quality costume jewelry, Em choose a pair of twisted gold toned hoops. Showy enough for evening the earrings were hardly capable of diverting attention from the main attraction below.

Alone in the Spring House, Em retreated to her bedroom with the new purchases and a well-appointed sewing basket. She used a small sharp seam ripping tool to remove the sleeves of the blouse and basted the seam back around the arm holes. In the name of frugality, she determined not to cut off the hem on the black skirt but to turn it up several inches farther. With quick long stitches, she shortened the skirt leaving an opening several inches long in the front. To change her height two inches, she resurrected a pair of black shoes with solid heels that could easily be worn without stockings.

Looking at the bedroom clock, she saw it was time to get a move on and get dressed for the occasion. Then, she did the unspeakable. The condition of Deanna's room was highly variable, and this was not a good day. By stepping over several days of used clothing on the floor in her daughter's room, she approached Deanna's dresser. Spread across its top were the newest shades of nail polish and lipsticks to match. The black and dark purple shades were too much for her older "character", so she used a new mauve shade. With a selection from the dresser, she gave herself a manicure, shaping her nails to sharper points and painting them with color. Fanning her wet nails, Em went in search of her daughter's curling iron. Luck was with her, a small black beaded bag hung from the doorknob, and she tucked it under her arm.

Once showered and shampooed, Em set about doing her hair and makeup. Making sausage curls around her head without singeing her ears was a serious challenge. She did manage to give herself a burn on the tips of her fingers. More than once she wished Deanna and Sandy were there to help her. When convinced her hair was dry, she sprayed on the burgundy highlights Halloran gave her. She stood back to admire the effect. *Well, this is certainly different. I hope the girls don't see me like this. I could tease the federal agent. Or, maybe I should be careful with that…*

Now the fun began. Em always enjoyed painting her face. She stared at her reflection in the bathroom mirror. *My eyebrows definitely need a do.* With no time or budget for a salon wax, she located eyebrow tweezers and went to work. First shaping one brow and then the other, she worked until they were slender and matched on both sides. It was no easy feat.

Using her own cosmetics, because *who in a bar will know or care if my eye shadow colors are out of date*, she spent most time on her eyes. Dusky mauve and grey blue would suffice. She dabbed cover-up cream on her few small facial moles. With liquid eyeliner, she subtly changed the shape of her eyes and the perceived distance between them. Acting in school plays and doing her own makeup certainly had unexpected benefits, even years later. Mascara was never her favorite as one black smear across the bridge of her nose proved. *Oh, Lord'amercy.*

To avoid ruining her finished makeup, she shimmied into her shortened skirt and gently pulled the now sleeveless blouse over her head. The skirt looked as if painted on, and the blouse clung to her breasts in all the nicely rounded places. The neckline hung low, giving an occasional peek of black lace bra. Powder from hairline to bra line, and two shades of blush used to shape her cheeks finished the makeover. Mauve lipstick glistened on her lips. For the fun of it, she took the mascara wand and gave herself a decorative mole. Her bangs drooped down over one eye, and a few bobbie pins were added for good measure. *They are so useful to have, and you never know when you might need one.*

Em stood in front of the full length mirror on the bathroom wall in wonder. The image reflected was not quite her own. "If I ever looked like this when I was married to Huber, I'd have had to scrape him off me," she said to her reflection.

The transformation took longer than anticipated, and she stuck her feet into her shoes and rushed downstairs. She turned her bag out for the needed items to put into the beaded bag, an inhaler without the prescription label, a small knife, her driver's license, one house key, a credit card, lose change, cell phone and a lonely twenty dollar bill. Em left the gum and the Jolly Ranchers candies and the empty wrappers as "pocket trash" that agents use to make their false IDs seem legit. Lipstick and compact went into the beaded bag. Sitting at the kitchen table, she flipped over her hem, stuffed her license and credit card into the opening she created when she shortened the skirt. The house key got tucked into the small pocket at the waist. *Women's clothing offers fewer opportunities for concealment. If they strip me naked,* she reflected, *I'm done for anyway, so I'm not going to worry about my skirt.*

A car of intermediate size carrying no maker's name pulled up in front of the Spring House. Em later referred to the color as 'honey beige,' to Halloran's consternation. The car gave the impression of weight and speed, although Em could not say why. The license plate was a scramble of letters and numbers, which made no sense.

Connecticut license plates had structured sequences of letters and numbers, and for the knowledgeable, could be read for approximate date and DMV issuing office. Em surmised, *That license plate number is, most likely an untraceable dummy.*

Halloran remained in the car, waiting for her to join him. Em attributed his reluctance to get out to the discomfort of his injured leg. This was wrong, she saw it the instant she climbed into the front seat. The person in the driver's seat was Michael Halloran, but she crowed when she saw him.

"Aren't we a pair? Let me look so I'll recognize you." Em laughed at him merrily.

Well prepared for undercover, his pepper and salt hair was now jet black on top and white along the sides. It stood up in short spikes. His skin tone usually seemed a warm olive with his light grey eyes now it was set off by dark brown eyes. Americans recognized each other's ethnicity without thinking, and he managed to change that perception subtly with contact lenses.

Em spotted a pair of dark plastic framed glasses on the console between them. She continued to scrutinize his face, and Halloran found he liked it. The scar in his right eyebrow was no longer visible.

"I didn't realize you had a scar up over your left eye." A thin straight white scar line extended from the corner of his left eye to his hair line.

"I don't. It's a stick on. One way to create a new identity."

"Eliminate the real scar with what, eyebrow pencil? And create a new one?" On impulse she said, "Smile."

He grinned widely, revealing teeth a different shade and not quite the same shape. She moved in closer to him, close enough to see teeth that had received an artful shading.

"How do you get that off?" she queried, staring, head

cocked to one side.

"Gargle with the mouthwash and it comes off."

She continued to study his face, it seemed she was not looking at Michael Halloran, but at a relation, an ancestor.

"How do I look?" A "say cheese" grin on her face, she was ready for his review.

"Nice makeup. Show me the side. Pretty," he spoke in a business-like voice. "Hair's good, too." Long fingers reached out to run through the curls on the sides of her face. It was a short reach.

"You're messing up my hair!"

"That's the general idea. More casual. Better."

Giving a gentle shrug, Em slipped her thin lacy shawl off her shoulders, revealing her blouse. "This okay?" she said innocently. "Distracting enough?"

Halloran burst out laughing. "Take it off! Take it off right now!"

"You don't like the blouse? You said you wanted me to provide a distraction." Impish words dripped with saccharin.

"What is the spot on your …. your chest? Eyebrow pencil?" He indicated the dark spot Em had drawn well down on the curve of one breast, visible as her blouse dipped low.

"Mascara. Stop laughing. I was going to make it a little heart."

Halloran forced himself to speak coherently. "It's smudging." He handed her a tissue from the box on the console. "No Mata Hari."

Offended, she argued, "I'm not naked. You can stop laughing now." Mata Hari, a WWI German spy, was rumored to have disrobed before robbing an embassy safe, to give herself an excuse if she was caught in the act, so to speak. Em spit on the tissue, looked down, her cheeks flaming, and rubbed gently to remove the spot.

"Over the top, right?"

Halloran looked at her for a long moment, "You look lovely, quite distracting enough without it. No need to gild the lily."

Accustomed to grey eyes that changed with light and his thoughts, that helped her sense his emotions, she was unsure. Em looked into his eyes, the unchanging dark brown was so different for her.

"Now tell me what you have in your purse."

Dutifully Em showed the contents of the beaded bag and mentioned most things she concealed on her person. To men, underwires in bras could not be considered potential tools, or weapons, so hardly worth disclosing.

"Are the card and license shielded? No. Well, probably not alright for tonight. Leave them in the car. The cell phone is a definite problem," Halloran asserted.

"What if the girls need me? They're at a party at the shore," Em objected on the grounds one could never tell what might happen at a college party.

"We can monitor the line for you and forward a call to a re-useable phone. Take this one." A smallish generic looking cell phone came out of a compartment in the console. He gestured to her to hand over her phone, license and card, and placed them in the shielded compartment.

"What, no iPhone? I know, budget cuts." Not fully understanding the capabilities of the miniature device, she looked at the small phone in dismay.

"It looks cheap. But don't underestimate it, and whatever you do, don't lose it. It's hardened, waterproof, and has secure satellite uplink. Among other things. We've been in your driveway long enough, and we have a drive ahead of us."

Using the custom hand controls which allowed his right leg to be at rest and out of the action, Halloran guided the car in a U turn and headed north up a winding side road. He tapped his collar and said to it, "We're leaving now." The drive took them along a narrow river road that wound its way north through residential countryside and crossed a dam at sharp right angles. Em recognized the road.

"Who are we this evening?" Em finally thought to ask.

"I'm known as John Michaels, business man with questionable and flexible interests. Who would you like to be? Pick a name for my new administration assistant and companion out for a date. You should be able to bring it off, since you don't carry a gun." Halloran visibly suppressed a smile.

"Oh, do you think? Sounds phony. I could be your gun moll, Betsey Dain," she volunteered.

"It's meant to be difficult to trace, Miranda. We're not making a gangster movie, we're going out on surveillance detail. And for a good dinner." He glanced sideways at her.

"So, tell me where we're going, and what I'll see so I don't totally freak out on you when we get there." Her threat worked a charm.

Halloran sighed and began, "We are going upstate to a well-known bar close to the large estates in the area. Regulars are locals, household staff, chauffeurs, high paid personal assistants, bodyguards and the occasional tourists. The bar and the food earn stars because these people are used to it. What you won't see are the undocumented people who work around the estates. It serves as a good listening post."

"Like the Brass Monkey Bar during World War II?" Em conjectured.

"That was quick, Em. I'm guessing, yes. The rich, famous and infamous jet in and out of this country at any number of spots in private aircraft. If we want to know who is in town, we count the employee noses at the bar. Occasionally you will see the famous names themselves.

Try not to notice. No one else will."

"Sounds fascinating, what's my brief, who am I looking for?" Em was all attention.

"We have reason to believe Pete was in this bar on Friday evening, maybe to meet someone, or looking for information. I am going to try to find out why, and you are going to see if you recognize anyone."

"Celebrities included?" she joked.

"Don't exclude anyone, the chef, the house guest, the gardener or the lady of the house." Halloran's eyes narrowed. "We don't know the extent of this organization yet. The famous, the near famous and their hangers on are vulnerable to pressure in ways the average person is not."

"Oh, I see, hijinks in high life. This operation requires a healthy bankroll," she affirmed, thinking of the cash thrown down for Marla's four day stay at the Alcorn Inn.

"If someone approaches me, I'll let you know if we need privacy. Be a good moll, Betsey, and go to the ladies', okay?" He chuckled.

"Alright, boss. Should I have a wad of gum in my mouth?" She watched as he drove with the precision gained through training and practice. Em felt no need to refrain from humor or questions and supposedly helpful comments. Pulling his leg was not out of the question.

It surprised Em that they pulled off the road into a wide driveway in front a disused building. The rusting sign said, "Eddie's Garage, Repairs and Removals." As the car neared the building, one of the overhead doors raised silently, and Halloran drove in. Inside the garage, everything was clean, organized and apparently in active use.

A short lean man with slicked back black hair in a slashed motorcycle jacket stood next to a disreputable maroon Civic.

Halloran pulled up and got out of the car. "Evening, Leroy. Come on out, Betsey Dain. This is our driver." The tight black skirt was working its way north up her thigh, Em emerged from the car carefully.

"Sir," replied the head of their motor pool. "Nice duds, ma'am."

"You, too," she replied, assuming correctly that Leroy was also specially rigged out for their leisurely evening.

"Yeah," he enthused. "I found this jacket in a thrift store, hung it up and took a switch blade to it to make it look like I'd been in a knife fight with a right handed assailant. Then I took it to the tailor to have many more pockets put into it. You can't tell, can you? The guy's a genius."

"Impressive, do you always dress up like this?" Em surveyed Halloran in a short sports jacket, who now held a plain bentwood cane.

"Only on assignment, well, some of us anyway. Leroy likes to confound his most respectable father," Halloran remarked.

"Gives my old man hives. Ready when you are, boss," Leroy growled out of the side of his mouth, in character, as he moved towards the rusting Civic.

"We're going in that?" she exclaimed.

"I beg your pardon, ma'am. It's been totally rebuilt and will do zero to sixty in …." Leroy was affronted.

"No offense meant. Do you have a *nom de guerre*, too?" Em was quick to say.

"A what? You mean like an alias? I'm Jones the Driver. Sometimes he," indicating Halloran, "forgets on purpose and calls me Martinelli. I have to remember to answer to both."

"Okay, let me get this straight in my head. I'm Betsey Dain, office assistant to John Michaels, the boss, and you are Jones, the Driver, alias Martinelli. I'm good to go." She opened the car door and climbed into the back seat. The two men looked at each other over the car roof. Jones the Driver shrugged, and the men took their places for the shorter drive into the wilds of fashionable upstate Connecticut.

Twisting two lane roads through farms and over bridges that crossed and re-crossed wandering rivers brought them to the main street of a small town that breathed money. Colonial era homes lined the main street with small front gardens surrounded by white picket fences, and farther on, early twentieth century mansions. The in-town estates of the wealthy were hidden behind high, finely crafted dressed stone walls. Here was New England colonial style architecture on a grand scale — columns, porticos and tall, stout redbrick chimneys visible above gated walls.

Halloran could see from Em's changing expression she knew where they were. When Jones parallel parked the car on the main street, she looked at her companion.

"This is your idea of bar hopping? Will we have time to hit the used book store down the corner first?"

"What exactly would Betsey Dain buy in a rare book store? Tell me, I'd be interested to know." Halloran had a smile on his face. "Time to get into character and stay there for the evening. You and I are the shills, the showy part of the act. Jones here is our postman, collecting and distributing mail and keeping a weather eye on us. He'll do most of the work this evening. The regulars know him as my bodyguard. He'll be sitting in the bar if we need him."

Together the three of them walked down the sidewalk paved with three foot square slate stones that rose unevenly at the edges towards a bar and restaurant with tall windows that looked out onto the main street. The driver opened the front door for them, and Em pulled a face at Jones as she walked by him. She was not used to personal service.

Jones, for his part, issued a hope the boss knew what he was doing taking this particular sassy civilian female with them. Keeping tabs on both of them was an assignment meant for a detail of two, at least. He was relieved to know Vargas was positioned in a car down the street and Rankel would be mooching around somewhere in the back.

Em was anxious to revisit the bar she remembered from rambles with Huber early in their marriage. Dark wood, light stucco walls decorated with authentic beer and wine memorabilia, advertising posters, illustrated beer trays, branded beer mugs and the occasional antique beer stein decorated the interior. The long bar, backed by a mirror, retained a solid brass foot rail. A pleasurable atmosphere was composed of yeast, hops, spicy beer nuts and good cooking.

An early twentieth century British advertising poster with the slogan "My Goodness, My Guinness" hung close to the doorway. She was about to ask Halloran if he thought Dorothy Sayers, as an advertising copywriter, might have written the slogan herself. Then, Em remembered abruptly Betsey Dain would most likely not have a clue about the famous English mystery writer.

John Michaels and his driver were recognized immediately by the bartender, the wait staff and some of the regulars as well, who gazed curiously at the new woman entering with them. Michaels and his guest were shown to a table at the back of the dining area, against the wall. Jones sloped off to take a small table in the bar, chosen so he could see them, the customers in the bar and watch the door.

The waiter stood attentively, waiting patiently. Michaels ordered a Belgian beer, not his usual. After brief consideration, Em looked up from the extensive list of wine and domestic and imported beers and said, "Cuba Libre, light, with a slice of lime. Do you have a good Amber rum?"

The young waiter looked first at Michaels who nodded,

and then at his companion. "We have a special *Ron Anejo*. We keep it under the bar. I think you will be pleased."

Betsey Dain gave Michaels a foxy little smile. They were seated next to each other, both with their backs to the wall. Appetizers and drinks arrived so quickly she wondered who the hell Michaels was supposed to be. The bruschetta appetizer disappeared from the large oval plate with remarkable speed, and Michaels needed to make a fast grab for the last piece. Betsey Dain outpaced him for the crisp slices of Italian bread topped with chopped tomatoes, fresh herbs and artichoke hearts.

"Have what you like for dinner, I'll write it off as a business expense against the Walker account." When their waiter arrived, he ordered mesquite grilled trout, and she ordered linguine with shrimp, baby scallops and lobster chunks in a light sauce of garlic and white wine.

"Close to a full house tonight, sir. Dinner will be a few minutes. Please enjoy the garden."

Trying to carry on with small talk, Em carefully focused her attention between the patrons in the dining room and the bar. In her mind, she divided the rooms into quadrants and searched each section thoroughly between compliments on the excellence of the rum in her Coca Cola. She decided Betsey was smarter than she looked, no surprise there. On the subject of rum, she was positively learned. Betsey regaled Michaels with everything Em knew about the subject. Once finished with the surveillance task, she commented with what she hoped would pass as a girlish giggle. "You know, I'd swear half the men in here are carrying guns and some women, too. We'll be all prepared for a Zombie Apocalypse."

Now, this was trying Michaels's patience, who had a limited tolerance for constant chatter in any character, and it was time for a change up. "Leave your shawl, let's go out in the garden."

Em assumed this meant they needed to check on the

people who had chosen tables in the garden for drinks or a quiet dinner.

10

GARDEN PARTY

———◆———

EM DRAPED HER shawl over the back of her chair and shot a hasty glance at Jones who was fiddling with his coaster. A hamburger stacked high with bacon, lettuce, cheese and a fat slice of red tomato sat half-finished on the plate in front of him. A mound of steak fries covered in melted cheese was nearly down to the ground on a separate plate. He appeared to be working on his second beer, although this was not actually the case. It was a carefully staged illusion, like the rest of his performance that evening. Leroy/Jones the Driver never drank on duty. By arrangement with the barman, his beer was deep golden and non-alcoholic masquerading under a quick label change done behind the bar.

To Em's dismay, Michaels was not the gentleman, and her chair scraped on the floor as she rose without his assistance. Michaels was engaged in signaling Jones and the waiter, he and his lady guest would be out in the garden. With an arm wrapped possessively around Betsey's waist, he paraded her out through the sliding doors to the paved yard behind the bar.

Still seated, Jones turned, obviously watching Michaels and the woman with him, as a bodyguard, his bar mates would expect no less. Then, in a nonchalant sort of way, Jones positioned himself at the end of the bar closest to the sliding doors leading to the garden.

The barman approached Jones, asked for his next order in a friendly and familiar way, reached under the bar, placed a coaster on the bar and opened a bottle labeled Coors. He placed the beer on the coaster and topped it with a chilled glass. Jones carefully pulled the coaster and beer off the bar. With dexterity, he palmed a square of paper lightly adhering to the bottom of the coaster and deposited it into one of the custom made pockets behind a slash in his jacket. He took his beer casually back to his table.

Leroy won the role of Jones the Driver, not only because he could drive hell bent for wheels, but because of his childhood preoccupation. Little Leroy was obsessed with magic and especially sleight of hand, and this now translated into spycraft. Robert Mulholland, the CIA's consultant illusionist, would have been proud. Leroy read a purloined copy of his book. It wouldn't due to buy it openly. Since the color of a feather in his fedora, or the chrysanthemum in his button hole could no longer be used as the book suggested for recognition signals, Leroy shopped carefully. His black tee shirt had a narrow red ring of color around the neck edge.

As Jones, he hoped to pick up three more reports and to pass out as many assignments this evening. Certain questions to informants were more pressing than others. Sometimes, contacts could be difficult and having everyone show up at the bar at the same time was not either doable or wise. The old saying, "There's many a slip between the cup and the lip" was certainly appropriate for their bar room meetings.

Out in back, the beer garden was surrounded on two sides by clipped boxwood hedges that reached above Michaels's head and on two sides by the brick walls of the building. A latched gate led out to a parking lot. Large European style terracotta urns filled with bright summer flowers in pink and light purple were placed between the metal chairs and tables. Only a large mixed group of twenty something folks caroused happily at the far end of the garden.

After studying them carefully, Em found nothing other than a generational resemblance to her adult children's friends, although more affluent. She turned back towards Michaels, who stood quite close to her, unexpectedly close. One look at him told her he'd dropped out of character and Michael Halloran stood smiling at her.

"How am I doing," she asked softly.

"Just fine, Betsey," he snaked an arm around her and drew her close, ostensibly for a more private chat.

"Only one person looks even vaguely familiar. It's a woman with a kind of unruly mop of hair and tons of makeup." Raising her head, tilting it coyly, she spoke into his ear.

"Oh, that's alright." Turning towards her, he tugged gently at the curls by her cheek. "I like it better down."

Giving a sideways look at his raised hand, a bit of a smile puckered her mouth with humor. And then she looked back up into his now intensely brown eyes. With an injured leg, Halloran couldn't dance, and neither could his alter ego, Michaels. So they made do with a full body clench in the lea of the boxwood hedge.

"A man can have several reasons for going out to dinner. Work is one tonight and the other is you," he spoke, voice both warm and hard to overhear.

"Really? Me?"

"Yes, really. Garlic, I like it." Halloran interrupted her with a firm smooch on the lips.

Em gave a surprised and intimate laugh, not at all a girlish giggle, and wrapped her arms around him under his jacket, feeling firm muscles. Little wet kisses were placed below her ear, and lips worked their way down her neck. Once they found her collar bone, he headed further downward. Em arched her spine, her chest came forward, and she drew her head back to look down. "What are you doing? There are people here, someone will see us…." Her words caught between breaths.

"Nice blouse, it's been distracting me. Nobody in this place sees and nobody cares who brings who. They all develop amnesia the minute they are out the door. Not a problem." Not rebuked, he continued nuzzling.

"That's why you brought me here." Em gave her best Betsey voice.

"You got it, Sweet Cheeks." Michaels gave his one sided smirk and tickled her ribs fondly to get a laugh. This was taking things much too seriously for him.

Grinning back, teeth showing, she thought, *Michaels may call Betsey "Sweet Cheeks," but just let Michael Halloran try to call me that.*

Unmistakably, Em and Halloran had things on their minds other than a good dinner. They stood staring into each other's eyes when the waiter found them in the garden. Em was feeling damp from Michaels's attentions. Especially in character, freed from restraints of office manners, Halloran created a longing in her. Face reddened, she realized she held him longer than quite necessary and had discovered he was carrying.

With a nod to the waiter, Michaels maintained his snug clinch on Betsey, who settled her cheek on his shoulder. His free hand ran through her hair and tugged at the curls at the nape of her neck.

"You're ruinin' my h'expensive hairdo, suh!" She picked up her head, sensation tingling along her spine. "Feels good."

"We need to go in for dinner. I still have work to do. Later." Michaels slipped his arm around Betsey's waist proprietarily to steer his moll back to their table.

Though sorry to leave his embrace, Em was glad to see her dinner arrive with savory chunks of lobster, shrimp and scallops over handmade linguine. After all, as she advised her daughters, food is the next best thing. Em took a long drink of wine, hoping it would help her to digest. The bar seemed to be growing warm, even warmer since their return from the garden. Dinner was a quiet meal. Em observed each new arrival in the bar. One man piqued her interest, medium height and build, short blond hair and central European, perhaps Slavic features. The cut of his suit also suggested European origin. Although she did not recognize him, she saw her companion's eyes flicker when the man chose a table and sat alone with his beer and bratwurst until they finished their plates. In character, Betsey was sitting, hand resting on her cheek, all attention seemingly on Michaels when the man approached the table.

"Lev, have a chair. Betsey, didn't you say you needed to … "

Snapping to attention, Em remembered her brief. In her best Betsey accent she replied without missing a beat, "Oh yes, I do. I do need to go to the little girls' lounge. Nice to meet you," she added although she had not been introduced. In seeming haste, Betsey left the table and made her way cheerily through the bar carrying her beaded bag. Best not to forget the lipstick, Betsey would never do that, and Em would never be without her pocket knife. She guessed Betsey would strut her stuff if she found a ready-made audience composed of a bar full of men. Especially as they were appreciative and diligently working their way to intoxication on the best quality domestic and imported beer and liquor. In her progress, she gave Jones a big stagey wink as she passed his table. Bar flies and table hoppers gave Betsey the eye as she walked by and turned into the short hall leading to the restrooms and ending in an emergency exit to the backyard parking lot.

The ladies' room proved to be acceptably clean and had the air of one less frequently used than the men's across the hall, which gave off a decided pong. Em made use of the facilities and returned to the two side by side sinks. *I wonder how long I should stay away from the table.* Em washed up and made quick faces at her reflection. Her makeup had begun to slip, she looked more like herself and less like Betsey. Working to refresh her makeup, taking too much time doing it, Em did as Betsey most likely would do. She was putting the finishing touches on her lips with Deanna's mauve lipstick when the door swung open.

The woman Em noticed with the big hair and thick makeup came into the ladies' room briskly and made sure the door closed solidly behind her. She checked the stalls as Em watched her out of the corner of her eye. *She might be checking for a good seat. Not the case.* The woman came towards Em, and she turned the faucet of the sink on full blast gesturing for Em to do the same.

"I'm Evie. There's a line to see him tonight. The place is too full. They're an edgy crew. I can't stay and I can't get near him," she spoke in a low husky voice reminiscent of Marlene Dietrich.

"Oh, and who would that be?" Em put on Betsey's voice and attitude.

"You know who. Nice work at the funeral by the way. We appreciated it. Protecting him must be a bitch."

Em rolled her eyes at Evie. There could be no mistake, she was referring to Halloran.

"Be careful out there. They are a tough crew tonight. Too many alphas in one bar room. Something set them off. Several are packing to head back into the City." By this, Evie meant New York City.

Evie reached for the paper towels, dried her hands on one sheet and passed the other to Em, who noticed it was unevenly folded.

"Nice to meet you. Here's an extra." And in a barely audible voice Evie said, "Don't get it wet unless it's an emergency." With a quick smile, Evie turned off the faucet in front of her and left as quickly as she had come.

Standing still for a moment, paper towel in one hand and lipstick in the other, Em handled the towel carefully, opening her hand, allowing the fold to separate enough so she could see a white square of folded paper. It appeared to be sealed around the edges. Her first impulse was to put the slender square of paper into her beaded bag, but her intuition stopped her. It was too easy to relieve someone of a purse.

Mindful of the caution exhibited by Evie, she used the paper towel as if wiping drops of water from the perfectly dry front of her skirt. Em brought the towel out of view below the counter top. Reaching down, she flipped over the hem of her skirt and quickly slipped the white square into the hidden pocket. She straightened up and used the now empty paper towel to wipe the water splashed from the basin. Another towel from the dispenser finished the job around the sink. Both damp towels went into the trash.

After a reflection check to her satisfaction, she looked more like Betsey again. The beaded bag's narrow strap slung over her shoulder, she pulled open the ladies' room door. She stepped out into the hall smack into a rather unkempt man, a head taller than herself whose face needed a serious meeting with a razor. The current style of a two-day beard succeeded in looking shabby on him. The jacket wanted a good cleaning and his breath exuded yeasty beer and spicy beer nuts. She stood stock still, frozen for the moment, to take in his appearance before the man lurched forward. More drunk than not, the man blocked the way to the bar. She felt a flash of adrenalin and squared her stance, aware his larger body must hide her from sight of those within the bar.

"Say now, you're a pretty thing. What do you do for Michaels?" His speech slurred. With malicious intent, he moved closer, within arm's length.

Em drew back, raising her arms to fold them lightly in front of her body. "Let me through," she said evenly. "You're drunk."

"Not so fast, meet a friend in there? The broad in a grey suit, she give you anything?" His voice carried an undertone of menace and was no longer slurred.

"I don't know what you're talking about, get out of my way." Em tried to force her way past him along the wall. The man shifted to counter her move. This was not going well. She could scream, but keeping Halloran's mission for the evening in mind, she chose not to. Em raised her open hands out in front of her, making a V with her fingers to keep him back and at bay.

The drunken man stepped forward into her space. She attempted to repel him with two hands planted firmly on his chest. The smell of cheap beer and a rotten tooth affronted her. As she pushed him away, he grabbed one of her breasts.

"You're going outside and you're going to answer me!" he spoke harshly into her face.

Now, most people have the sense not to corner an animal, even a domestic pet. Why this man thought it was a good idea to corner Betsey, only he knew.

Her stomach churning, Em drew back one hand and drove the heel of it upwards as hard as she could under the man's chin, slamming his head back and knocking him against the opposite wall. The errant paw let go of her breast. With her other hand she grabbed his throat under his jaw in a strong grip and squeezed. The man gagged in shock.

"Nobody touches me!" Em exclaimed. With her right foot she stamped the chunky heel of her shoe down as hard as she could on his instep. He tried to yell in pain but could barely draw breath, and it came out as a sound like a deep gargle.

Hearing the commotion from the hall to the rest rooms, Jones came to investigate and arrived in time to see Betsey with her assailant jammed up against the wall.

"I'll tell you what I do for Michaels. I file things. Lots of things. When I'm done no one else can find them. It's job security. And I've never seen that other woman before." It was the truth. Em said this easily with conviction.

"Betsey, you can let him go, I'm here," Jones called out to her.

"It's a ladies' room. We all get to go there whenever we want to. Understand?"

At this point, Jones took the better part and went for reinforcements. The seasoned agent turned tail and headed back through the bar where the regulars were beginning to show interest.

In close conversation Michaels and Lev were still seated at the table. Jones got to within ten feet before saying, "Boss, you gotta come. Betsey's got some guy by the throat, and she won't let him go."

Lev looked up at Jones then remarked to Michaels, "American women, so much variety. Good help is hard to find, my friend."

"Yeah, and the good ones can be hard to control. She's good with me," he said with a leer, still in character. "But this one can be, let's say unpredictable. Even dangerous when provoked. Are we done?"

Without a word, but with one slight nod, Lev made his way back to his table. Michaels picked up his cane and walked with surprising speed, in spite of his limp, through the bar to the hallway entrance. Jones took up a position behind Michaels in the bar, with a view to both his table and theirs, in case the rumble in the hall was a diversion.

"Betsey, darlin', let him go." Michaels was both concerned and amused. He let it show on his face.

"He *grabbed* my tit!" Betsey protested. "He deserved it."

"Maybe so, but he needs to breathe. Let him go, darlin', we're here. Step back behind me."

The tall man was swinging his cane. Michaels sounded unperturbed. Em knew he was armed. She made a sound in her throat like a female growl. Truth be told, she had no exit strategy except to cut and run, so getting behind him sounded like a good idea. She released the vise grip on her captive, whose eyes were bulging. He gasped loudly as she scooted away behind Michaels. They stood together, her hand on Michaels's arm, watching as the drunk attempted to recover.

"Bitch broke my foot!" he yelled hoarsely at Michaels.

"You're damned lucky she didn't break anything else. Never touch her again. I wouldn't like it."

Unsteadily the man started towards Michaels in anger. The cane came up smartly and was driven into his stomach. It was well aimed. They could see the gorge rising to his mouth.

"Leave now. Out the back," Michaels commanded. When his target delayed, Michaels poked him sharply twice more. With unsteady steps Betsey's assailant turned towards the exit. The door was already ajar when he pushed it open.

"He grabbed me and tried to force me out the back door," Betsey said aloud, conscious they now had drawn onlookers from the bar to the end of the hall.

"We'll talk about it later," Michaels said as he grasped her arm.

"You always say that, and we never do," Em responded in the character of Betsey. "What is that awful noise?" Sounds of deep heaves coming from the back of the building filtered through the partially open exit door.

"Something he ate, no doubt. After you, darlin'," Michaels replied, managing to control a grin. When Em hesitated, he said, "We're not done. You'll like dessert. Have something to drink with it. You look like you need a sugar rush, and a good stiff drink."

The distance down the hall was short, Em stopped to prepare herself for her entrance into the bar. She tugged her skirt back into place, pulled down her blouse and shook herself like a feisty hen with ruffled feathers, glaring around the bar as she did this.

"Way to go, lady," one of the regulars yelled from the end of the bar. Cheers rang out.

Em looked around the room at the smiling faces and burst into a relieved grin.

"Buy you a drink!" a burly man offered.

"I'll have a Long Island Iced Tea..." she began.

"Betsey," came a warning voice from Halloran, who stood directly behind her.

"Rain check! Rain check!" Betsey addressed the men in the bar, gave a little finger wave and let Michaels guide her to their table accompanied by laughter in the barroom.

The waiter appeared as if he rose up through the floor right in front of them. "Dessert? Drinks are on the house, ma'am. Our apologies. The bouncer has the night off. We don't usually need him this early on weekday evenings." Michaels ordered his rice pudding. Betsey ordered tiramisu and an Irish coffee. And, she asked the waiter to put something special in her coffee. The waiter grinned, said, "Can do, ma'am," and disappeared as quickly as he arrived.

When they were alone at their table, Em said quietly, "I'm sorry if I embarrassed you."

"Embarrassed me, hah!" Michaels laughed out loud, and it was not a cultured laugh either.

Oh, give him an Oscar, Em thought. *He's not bad.*

More quietly he said to her, "I think you've established Betsey as a character they will remember here for quite a while."

"What about...."

"It will be taken care of. Enjoy your dessert."

And she did enjoy it. The Irish coffee arrived with the best Irish whiskey, and a tall head of whipped cream accompanied by the legendary house tiramisu. Betsey was more relaxed and certainly mellower when she noticed something odd. Jones had made an arrow on the table in front of him using empty beer bottles and glasses. To Em it looked like a trail sign pointing to the door.

"Finish your coffee. We're going," Michaels said in an undertone as he raised his hand to call for the check. Cash came out of his pockets, small bills he used to pay for dinner and a generous tip.

"Move now," he instructed Betsey who pasted on a wide smile, picked up her beaded bag and wrapped her shawl around her shoulders. Betsey plowed the path through the barroom crowd, followed by Michaels, with Jones in rear guard.

Once on the sidewalk outside, Em paused to look up at the sky. "Beautiful evening." Away from any large city light sources, the sky shown deep black with bright points of light, with subtle variations of color visible in the atmosphere.

"Keep moving," Halloran held her arm and hustled her down the uneven paving stones to the waiting Civic.

"What was that about?" she asked him as soon as they were in the car, but the two men were looking back at the entrance to the bar. She followed their gaze to see several men hit the street, all leave alone and head in separate directions.

"Rats are disembarking, boss," sneered Leroy in Jones's voice.

"Yes, they are following our lead. The resident State Trooper is on his way." Halloran laughed his own laugh. "Pull around the corner and stop." An earbud came from a tiny compartment on the hilt of his cane, and he stuffed it in his ear. "How did you do, Jones?"

"I only made contact with two, sir." Leroy sounded disappointed.

"And I was only able to meet with Lev, who had an interesting tale to tell us." Halloran explained this for Em's benefit. "He's a successful businessman in his home country, but he worries about political stability. He's established residence here so his kids can go to school, and the wife can go shopping. In his travels he hears things. Sometimes our friends and business acquaintances tell us things they think we should know. Once in a while we can act on them, and regrettably sometimes we cannot. Then they have the frustration of telling us, and later saying, *We warned you.*"

"You can say that again," Leroy agreed.

"Evie gave me something for you, does that count?"

"She did?" Halloran reacted with surprise.

Em flipped over the hem of her skirt and worked it to extract the small white square of paper, which she placed in Halloran's outstretched hand. "Why did she say not to get it wet unless it was an emergency?"

"It's rice paper, Em, it dissolves completely in water if you need to get rid of it fast," Halloran informed her.

"Spit or piss will work, too," contributed Leroy. Halloran looked at him sternly. "I'm just saying, boss, other things will work in an emergency."

Em laughed in relief. "I'm glad I stayed dry," and she continued to laugh.

"Cool, look at this!" Leroy had leaned over the seat to watch Em. "We'll have to tell the evidence courier. She's a hider, too."

"Evie say anything else?" Halloran inquired. Taking Em Huber with him on what should have been a routine op turned out to be more fun than Amateur Night at the Opera.

Em cast her memory back. "She was careful to run the water full blast to make it difficult to hear her speak. She warned me to be careful, the crowd was rough tonight. She mentioned seeing me at the funeral. Her makeup was different then. She needs a makeup consultant. It looked like it was troweled on tonight. Is she always a woman?"

The men exchanged a look. This was a close guess on such a short meeting. Halloran replied, "Mostly, with her height and build it's easy for her to pass as a man if we need her to do it. The heavy makeup tonight was to hide the sunburn."

"She came back from her last assignment, a stakeout at the beach, looking like a boiled lobster," Leroy added helpfully.

"Thank you for this, Em. We're still missing one, and that's not good." Halloran was listening to the voices from his earbud.

"The bartender said Pete Leonard was here Friday. The subject he was watching hasn't reappeared since. They think he's blown town. I think I'll ask him to switch the labels on my beer to something more expensive. I know it won't help the taste, but I can dream, can't I? At least the food's good." Leroy surely didn't mean to give the impression he didn't like this gig.

"Rankel says Evie got away clean out the back door, thanks in part to Betsey's delaying action," Halloran told them.

"He knew about Evie, asked me if she had given me anything. What happened to that guy?" Em asked in mock concern.

"Rankel took charge of him. He's turning him over to the state police to dry out and get medical attention for his foot. Seems he tripped and fell hard. Rankel will ask them to hold him for us to question. He is involved enough to ask if anything was given to Betsey. Hmm. I'll assign Rankel and Vargas." Halloran stretched his right leg over onto Em's side.

Leroy leaned over the front seat, his earbud now back

in place. "Rankel says, *Nice going!* ma'am. He found the guy tossing his guts up in the bushes by the parking lot. Says they'll have to bury it." He paused. "State police are going to hold him on charges of drunk and disorderly, disturbing the peace and barfing in a public place. Apparently heavily frowned on in this community."

"As soon as Vargas and Rankel are ready, we can go back to the garage. I'll take Miss Betsey home from there." Halloran reached over and squeezed her hand. "Good job, for a newbie. Tell us what happened in the back hall while we're waiting for Rankel to finish up with the police."

"Well." Em took a deep breath and began her narrative. "I hid the paper in my skirt and went out into the hall. The man came towards me kind of fast and stopped short in front of me. I didn't have a good feeling about it. He exaggerated being drunk, and wouldn't let me get by him. It scared me."

"Not a good strategy, obviously," stated Halloran.

"No, it wasn't. He tried to get me to go outside, and he grabbed my chest."

"He what! Did he hurt you?" There was steel in Halloran's voice.

"I panicked. That's when I hit him and grabbed his throat. Then I was mad, so I stomped on his foot. And if 'Jonesy' hadn't come along I had some other ideas from class."

"From class? What class?" Halloran and Leroy were looking at her in amazement.

"After that, uh, problem in our backyard, the girls decided we should take self-defense classes together at the gym. I've had a few lessons before this. It was pretty basic stuff, and he didn't fight back."

"Because he had too much, and you were choking him so he couldn't get air," Leroy interrupted.

"I don't think he was well trained, certainly not military," Em concluded. "Maybe more cheap help. Anyway, our new house rule is, if anyone lays a hand on you and you don't want them to, whatever damage you do is okay. Provided it's not permanent or irreversible, that is."

"A little knowledge is a dangerous thing," Halloran remarked dryly.

Leroy muttered, "In her case more than a little dangerous. Rankel and Vargas are ready to go, sir."

"Take us out, Mr. Jones."

It had been an entertaining evening, and one productive of intelligence as well. At Eddie's Garage Halloran and Em changed cars to continue back to the Spring House. In Halloran's own car, Em wrapped her shawl around her shoulders and tried to think through the evening, to commit to memory the events, her impressions and observations. Some of it made her laugh quietly. When asked her why, she responded, "I can't believe I did that."

Relaxed, Halloran smiled with warmth she could feel and acknowledged Betsey had been a surprising dinner companion, and it had been one hell of a first date. Mind wandering, she grew conscious of his presence in the driver's seat next to her, the set of his shoulders, his hands on the wheel, the line of his thigh.

The drive home led through the back country roads, numbered routes which changed direction at a variety of intersections as they wound through small towns built on the rocky hillsides of the Housatonic River Valley. The zigs and zags of old numbered routes presented peril of a wrong turn at every corner.

Coming through the last town in front of a local bar young drinkers were laughing and shoving each other. The next corner took them towards the level crossing of railroad tracks just as the warning lights flashed. Parked at the level crossing behind one other car, they waited for the train, its horn sounding way down the track heading towards New Haven.

Halloran reached over for Em, who settled against his shoulder as they watched the southbound train pull through the crossing. Lips brushed her forehead. Reaching up to nibble his chin, apparently a favorite move, Em encouraged him to kiss. Not a man to often miss a cue, they were soon tasting each other for the second time that evening and hoping for a long train. The train passed, and it took a horn blast from the car behind to separate them. "Damn teenagers!" remarked the old fellow in the car behind them to his wife.

Conversation was only a word or two, here and there, with soft laughter, for the trip across town, down to the country road and home. Halloran pulled his car onto the cobblestone apron in front of the car barn across the country road from the Spring House and turned the engine off.

"Thank you for dinner, I enjoyed the evening," Em began before Halloran cut in.

"Dinner was fine. Quite memorable. I enjoyed the railroad crossing more." Again he reached over, and she met him on his way, sliding as close as she could. The backs of his fingers stroked her cheek, his kisses were warm and lingering and covered her lips and cheeks, teasing her. She returned his kisses with pleasure, chuckling when he tickled her with an end of day beard. Her arm reached under his jacket and around the back to hold him close. Not to be out maneuvered, he leaned back in the seat, bringing her along with him.

The hand that caressed her cheek slid down her side, and not meeting resistance, wandered around front to rub the side of her breast. Her body moved away from him enough to give his hand the purchase it sought.

A pause gave Em the chance to say, "You know, it really is the same whether it's sixteen or sixty. All we need now is a pickup truck with a bench seat." He gave her a gentle squeeze. She laughed a low sweet sound like water running along in a brook.

"Except I know what I'm about now," he said with a catch in his voice. As she laughed, he reached under her top, and with an easy movement undid her bra. "Very nice blouse." Halloran ran his hand back around front, all before she had much of a chance to react.

"Smooth move, fella." Em breathed as his hand fondled her breast.

"Enjoy yourself." He was enjoying the mixture of welcome and shyness in her voice, her sighs and her touch.

"At sixteen I didn't have much of a clue. But, by twenty-one, a pretty girl has heard plenty of lines. 'Just lie back and enjoy yourself' has got to be a classic."

"Are you sassing me, woman?"

"Yes, always." The early beard on his cheek lightly grazed her fingertips. A languorous stare, breathing each other's air for what seemed to be an age, ended with a quick kiss.

"You'd better go inside before I get the rest of your clothes off you."

"What makes you think I'd let you?" Em played her hand across his shoulder and down his arm.

"The way you look back at me when I look at you. How it feels when we touch each other, even lightly. The way I feel around you, the way I hope you feel about me. Take the time you need. Tell me when." A low pitched, mellow man's voice with gravel to it sent a rush through her, a tight feeling cinched around her heart and it gave a jump.

A man who spoke so little, gave directions in clipped phrases, who seemed so in control of himself, surprised her. In the dusky moonlight, taking in his scent, that unique personal chemistry, she admired the half-light on his face, eyes darkened, the lines of cheekbones and fine square jaw. For a woman who could concoct a ten minute rant on any given subject at any given time, she could think of nothing to say. Breathing slower and deeper, all senses enlivened, she could feel his heart beat strong and steady under her breasts.

Considering then deciding, she placed her cheek next to his, and softly said, "Fine with me."

The muscles of his face scrunched up into a smile that sent happy anticipation through her. *Certain males of the species make you feel warm and wet all over,* Em thought. *It was not like the immediate reaction to landing flat on my back, jumped by a hot and sweaty geologist. It's the sense and feeling of being lured, enticed and then drawn into intimacy. Who's evolved?* she thought. *This is a man with designs on me. Do I want that?*

This is a game of strategy two can play, Em figured. She licked her lips to wet them, then lightly kissed him below the ear, working her way up to nibble on his earlobe, tugging it gently between her teeth. Halloran responded to the provocation. When she paused to breathe, she was rewarded with a kiss that began gently and grew more ardent as their tongues found each other, as he took it deeper. The kiss left her breathless. The bit of a tang, the taste of him was exciting in itself.

It left Halloran smiling.

"Go on now." One more stroke to her breast, and he watched her eyes close slowly in pleasure. "Want that hitched up again?"

She signaled ever so slightly, no, eyes half open. They lay, feeling hearts beating and chests rising and falling, bounds of instinct and affection twining together. Halloran touched her cheek, ever so lightly brushing her face with his thumb below her lips.

"I have work tomorrow. I'll walk you to the door."

"Not if you want to go home tonight." She laughed and pulled herself up. "To be continued?"

"At your pleasure, m'dear." The low notes of his voice

gave her the feeling of the warmest of chills.

Feeling considerable reluctance, Em got out of the car and crossed the country road in the cloud scattered moonlight. With only half a mind, emotions engaged elsewhere, she unlocked the Spring House door, turned on the light, and typed the code into the security system.

Once inside her kitchen, she stood and sucked in a deep breath. It seemed to go down all the way to her very toes. Memory of his scent clung to her and the feel of his touch followed her into the house. These haunted her thoughts that night, all night, and woke with her in the crisp, clear morning. Truly remarkable what a tonic new love and desire could be.

Back in the car across the road, Halloran watched her softly curved shape and the ease of her walk. Not the graceful walk of a dancer, she possessed a limber grace, the result of a lifetime of activity. Halloran stayed as the lights went on in the kitchen and living room. A patient man, a calculating and effective hunter, he was not given to let impulse sway him. *This woman*, he felt as well as thought, *I want this one*. It was as simple and basic as the longing to see and feel, to have and to keep, for himself alone.

A successful advance was a pleasure in itself, but he considered trying to walk it off down the road in the half light. Resolutions taken to foreswear women vanished without regret. As he pulled his right leg in, it throbbed enough to change his mind about the walk. Instead, the dedicated man pulled out his satellite phone to check messages. One or two were enough to dampen any ardor, but not enough to remove any thoughts of renewing it and the sooner the better.

PUB CRAWL

Several days later, in a pub down a narrow side street in Glasgow, an old neighborhood regular returned. His thirst got the better of his caution, as it has many a man. "Liam" had been in Scotland almost a week, and no one had shown any particular interest in his coming. Working out in the flat didn't satisfy his thirst for a good ale, a woman or his penchant for a competitive game of darts.

As he sat at the bar jawing with the rather attractive person next to him, another man came up behind him and said, "Liam Robert Innes, you are under arrest for the attempted murder of a federal agent in the State of Connecticut, USA. We have received a request for your extradition. Looks like you're going back."

"Bloody Irishman!" Innes jumped from his bar stool. Four strong hands were waiting for him and the female constable who sat next to him did the honors with the cuffs.

"Yah, he called himself and he wasn't half happy with you, lad!" replied the Glasgow detective, who was formerly Royal Navy and a longtime friend of Michael Halloran's.

11

TEXAS BOUND

———◆———

DEANNA WAS IN tears, the kind that run down the cheeks in great sorrowful streams and provoke a good case of the sniffles. Sandy went searching for Em, who was in the Spring House kitchen in the afternoon kneading dried cranberries into a ball of yogurt scone dough.

"He says we can't go to visit him in Texas and Deanna's crying something awful." Sandy was not easily upset. "Please come upstairs."

"What happened?" Em finished kneading the dough. "What on earth did he say to make her so upset? She usually adores her father," Em said through her teeth. She divided the dough into two pieces and formed them into balls.

"She said he has someone else staying with him, and it won't work out for us to come down to visit any time soon." Sandy's face fell, her own parents divorced years ago. She had seldom seen her father since. While staying with the Hubers, Travis Huber had become at least a partial substitute for her own father. Now it seemed to her both she and Deanna had lost their fathers.

"Is it Brigitte? I thought she was married. Is she back?" Em patted the dough into two thick flat rounds and placed them on a greased baking sheet.

"No, it's some other woman we've never heard of. Not

a person he wants to meet us apparently. Maria's threat-ened to quit, too. Deanna's too upset. We were looking forward to going to Texas before starting back at college again."

Em brushed the scones with beaten egg white and sprinkled them with a mixture of cinnamon and sugar.

This was now sounding serious. Maria was the house-keeper for the Huber family home when her husband's mother was still alive. Unprintable, uncharitable, most probably mostly true thoughts about her former spouse, the father of her children occurred to Em.

Using a long sharp knife, Em cut through the scones to shape individual pieces. She wielded the knife with more than usual vigor.

Though visits to Travis Huber in his new place was fraught with worry, Em always encouraged her children to visit their family ranch in Texas, The saving grace at their father's was his housekeeper Maria. Since she first married Huber, Em and Maria had a history of recipes and family stories swapped in the kitchen.

"Okay, you know all is not lost, right?" The loaded baking sheet went into the oven. Em had a plan B. "We have fifteen minutes to convince Deanna the world has not come to an abrupt and untimely end. I'll make a phone call." Em picked up the wireline phone, tapped a long familiar number and waited for an answer.

Down in Texas an elderly woman pulled off her gar-dening gloves to reach for her portable phone.

"Aunt Marlene, how're you'all down there?"

"Why dear, we're fine, just fine. There is something I've been wanting to talk to you'all about. But it can wait. You only call on holidays and when you need to talk about family things. Is it that nephew of mine giving you a hard time again? I'll shave his tail for him if he is."

"Oh, Aunt Marlene." Em felt her throat go tight and her eyes begin to sting. "It's Harley. Deanna wanted to come down to Texas to stay with him for a week before she goes back to college. She called him an hour ago. Honestly, it's a good thing he's in Texas, and I am not. He told her she and Sandy can't come to visit him because he has another woman living with him, and he's not ready for her to meet his children."

"God Almighty! That boy goes from bad to worse. Your Uncle Bob would have no patience with this." The elderly woman paused, jabbed at the air with her gardening trowel in a menacing way. "What can I do for you, dear? The girls can come right down here to me. We can go shopping and riding. If they get too bored without the Riverwalk, I can take them to Austin for music. Did I tell you I have a new horse?"

"It would be wonderful, I was so hoping you would offer. I'll buy the plane tickets when you've decided on dates," said Em gratefully.

"No, I'll have none of that. Harley should pay for his daughter's visit. I'll send you the tickets." Marlene was already figuring out how she could deduct the cost from Harley Travis's salary, or better yet his annual bonus. After all, he did work for the family business now, which gave her considerable leverage. A pleasant thought occurred to her, *How they would like flying Business Class?*

"So that's settled. Being eighty, it might be time to think about riding out by myself a little less. A friend suggested I get a carriage. Actually it's more like a cart, so I needed a carriage horse to go with it. Let me tell you about Brandy, he's a retired five gaited saddle horse, a rescue actually. Some unscrupulous trainers do things to those poor horses' legs to get them to pick up their hoofs high for the show ring. The skin above Brandy's hooves is quite scarred. He wants to be a barn pet now. So handsome, a beautiful flowing tail, he descends from one of that breed's best I believe, a horse called Wing Commander. He's very sweet. The girls will love him, and he just loves to pull a little cart."

"Sounds like a great idea, I didn't know you drove."

"If you can ride you can drive, it just takes guidance and practice. And a good horse. Would you like to come with the girls dear? We'd love to see you, too."

The scones came out of the oven golden brown and fragrant. A kettle of spring water was coming to a deliberate boil. The teapot was in readiness with Earl Grey tea leaves inside awaiting their bath of boiling water. Em poured the boiling water into the teapot, preparing tea for three.

"You know, I've started a consulting business. I have a project that I can't leave right now." Em winced, this was not exactly the full truth. "Another time, maybe around the holidays. You said you had something you wanted to talk to me about?"

"Oh yes, Billy Hafner called me this week. Seems they talked it over and they want me to run for state representative. Now isn't that the thing? I told him I was too old and too honest."

"Marlene, I think that's what they need. You would be great. I think you should do it."

"Well, well, I'll think about it then. Could be fun, not much real work Billy said. Can that be right?"

"I don't really know, I sort of hope not," replied Em.

"Once, a long time ago they asked Bob to run for Congress, but I talked him out of it. You know how he was. In politics once his mind was made up there was no talking him out of it, and no compromise. Now that's not good. Men are like that when they get together. Someone always has to win and someone has to lose or they're not happy. Bob wasn't like that with me and our daughters of course."

After a moment of reflection Marlene continued, "But it won't have been a good thing, not compromising, when you're making decisions for everyone all at once.

If he was in Congress, if it was up to him, the Navy would never have another boat. The Army could have all the tanks and whatnot they wanted and the Air Corps any plane. But no boats. He used to say they were too damned big and too expensive, and when they sink every sailor on the boat dies. You'd think he'd never been to Galveston, never been out on a boat — if you didn't know several of his boyhood friends died together. An enemy submarine torpedoed their troop ship. Never got over it."

Em paused and thought before she spoke. The elderly woman's reference was not exactly clear. Uncle Bob had an aversion to the Navy. "Actually, I do understand. My father told me about sailing from North Africa to Bombay through the Suez Canal, out into the Indian Ocean on an American troop ship in a convoy. Submarines tried to sink their ship. He said it was the most frightening thing he'd ever been through in the War, and his former post in North Africa had been under attack by Rommel's Afrika Corps," Em reminisced.

"You know Bob was a war hero. He came home with all sorts of ribbons and medals, but he said nothing like that could make him feel good about war. The dear man just put them in a drawer and wouldn't wear them except on Veterans Day when they made him speak."

"Talking about World War II, I've recently had dealings with a federal agent named Michael Halloran. Apparently he spoke to Uncle Bob about gold bars before he passed away. He even attended his funeral, where I first met him. He asked me if I knew anything about them."

"And what did you say, dear?" the elderly lady asked quietly.

"I repeated what Uncle Bob said at dinner before I married Harley."

"Your uncle warned me, he is a man who won't give up. If he asks you again, you can say I gave you my word

I have never seen gold bars, either Nazi or American," came the reassuring voice of the most respectable elderly woman.

"Now, Mexican gold, is another story and we don't have to go into that one. What belongs in Texas stays in Texas." Marlene smiled to herself down on her veranda among the flowerpots where no one could see her.

"Very good, thank you, Aunt Marlene."

"Thank you, dear for reminding me. There's something I promised to do for Bob."

"I think you should run for office, Aunt Marlene. You remember so much so well, but it doesn't stop you from making reasonable judgments. You would be an inspiration to all the women in the family."

"That's as may be, but I was not in battle. I guess those of us who stayed home can't know or be responsible for what happened then. I'll call Billy to discuss his offer. You send the girls down. We'll cook, we'll eat. I'll teach them to drive the horse and the little cart. And we'll talk politics.

"Oh, and deary, you can leave Harley Travis to me." Em thought she heard the distinguished head of the family laugh softly to herself.

"You know, Deanna met a boy when she was out riding the last time she was at the ranch. She is looking forward to possibly meeting him again. Do you know him?"

"Indeed I do, Sam Johnson's grandson. But dear, I wouldn't place too much on that one. He's a nice enough boy, but he's going to Law School. He's going to spend the rest of his life in an office doing other people's business very well. My niece would be running circles around him in no time. Deanna needs someone with more in the saddle than that boy. That's my opinion, of course." Aunt Marlene sounded quite definite.

Being Deanna's mother, Em hesitated. She was not

about to ask what exactly their aunt meant by "more in the saddle."

The conversation closed with relief and many thanks, and a fleeting feeling of pity for Marlene's errant nephew. Em called Sandy's cell phone to invite her and Deanna downstairs for tea. When they arrived, good news greeted them. "You've been invited to go stay at the ranch. You'll never guess. Aunt Marlene has a new rescue horse and she's wanting you to meet him. He pulls a cart. She'll take you shopping. If you get bored, she'll take you to Austin, and you know what fun that is. Deanna, you can practice your barrel racing. Just please promise me you won't let Aunt Marlene race you!"

HARLEY'S SHENANIGANS

Sam Houston Johnson and his grandson Nathaniel were sitting on the porch one evening, enjoying the fine breeze and the smell of clean Texas air. The Bluebells were in bloom in the park of which Lady Bird Johnson was so fond. The Bluebells made the *New York Times* in a short article to let the folks up north know it was time for a visit. Mrs. Johnson was no relation to Sam and the boy, but you never know. They finished discussing politics, and the state of the world, and the conversation came around to women.

"Watch out for that one, son." His grandson had been giving his eyes to a young woman he'd met out riding who was staying with her aunt Marlene Albrecht down the road. "She's Trav Huber's youngest girl, Deanna. Takes after her mother, Em. Woman like that'll spit fire and nails at you if you get her mad. But if you're good to her, ain't nothing sweeter. Won't walk out on a man like that blonde did on him. Huber gets the divorce and is all ready to settle in with the trophy. Bergeet or something like that. From France or Sweden or some such place. And then she gets a better offer from down the road and takes off. She's the one married to old man Schmidt. Rich bastard. Can barely walk, I heard." The grandfather's smoker's voice was deep and gravelly. He scratched the bit of grey stubble on his chin.

"Doesn't sound too bad, Grandpa. She rides well. Likes a good Quarter Horse," his grandson noted with appreciation for a young woman with a good seat on a horse and a nice ass to go with it.

"You haven't heard it all. Em, his wife, comes down for a visit with my friend Bob Albrecht, who wasn't doing too well at the time. This was right around the time that they got the divorce. Trav Huber gets himself all looking like New York, and when the wife sees him, she takes to yelling at the top of her lungs. Housekeeper Maria heard her plain enough. 'Harley,' she still calls him Harley like he was a kid. 'What happened to your nose? It's all straightened out. You are so thin. Were you sick? What did you do to your teeth? Don't grin at me like that. Where are your boots? Are those Italian loafers? Do they do that in Texas? You look like a damned Brooks Brothers ad.' Now she shouldn't have said that, but I guess she was in shock."

"What's all this got to do with Huber's daughter, Deanna?" asked his grandson trying not to laugh.

The older man nodded. "Son, if you can't stand the spice, don't eat the chili."

HOME ON THE TEXAS RANGE

Marlene Albrecht had decided, and once she decided anything it was as good as fried and done. She was running for public office. Plane tickets were purchased. Then she let the family know she would be announcing her candidacy for State Representative on Wednesday and wished Deanna and Sandy to be there. This was four days before the planned departure for Texas. They needed to quit work early and pack quickly. The girls were not sorry to be away so soon but expressed regret Em could not be persuaded to join them.

Em had other ideas and was glad to think the girls would be out of harm's way for a while in Texas. Relief was to be short lived. Em considered items they might need that in safer times travelers could pack in their luggage. She put together a box of nail clippers, nail files, pocket knives (safer that way), a letter opener, talcum powder, foot powder and a First Aid kit, which was the perennial accompaniment to any of Em's travels. The box was rushed off to the Post Office in time to arrive before Deanna and Sandy would touch down in Dallas.

Early on Tuesday morning Em drove the infrequent flyers up to Bradley International Airport north of Hartford. She saw them through security with relief and watched their plane depart from the observation deck. The drive back to the Spring House was as smooth as any was likely to be through the Hartford interchange at rush hour. Though challenged by a Range Rover, Em prided herself on her ability to avoid being driven onto one of the wrong exit ramps.

With forethought, Marlene reasoned special flight insurance might be in order. She was wary of uncivil behavior two young and attractive women might experience. They would be flying on their own out of Hartford, Business Class, in the company of corporate road warriors and the well to do. Marlene called the airline of her choice. The prospective candidate for State Representative explained the situation to the airline representative. Her niece and her friend had recently been subjected to a home invasion and were likely to be skittish. If the cabin staff might be especially careful of any approach to the young women, she would be grateful.

Deanna and Sandy were casually dressed for travel. When boarding with other passengers, they were rather surprised at the location of their seats and the cordiality of their welcome. The cabin staff found them unassuming and funny. The two young women were met, at Marlene's behest, as they deplaned in Chicago and taken to a lounge for lunch. In due time, they were collected by the driver of a small cart who loaded their carryon bags and gave them a lift to the St. Louis bound plane. In St. Louis they were again retrieved and driven to the plane for Dallas.

On the air route to Dallas the tenor of the passengers changed. Men in cowboy boots, retired Air Force officers, and corporate types were more respectful. They were also better mannered than the businessman out of Hartford who had tried to force an acquaintance first with Sandy and then with a huffy Deanna. When the other passengers heard Deanna welcomed as Miss Huber, niece of Mrs. Bob Albrecht, knowing looks were exchanged.

Deanna and Sandy had a pleasant final leg of their flight with good conversation. Not one of the other passengers attempted to play footsies or kneesies with them, or tried to buy them those chintzy little airplane drinks. Not a single person leaned in to set their gaze over Sandy's shoulder to see how far down they could view. On landing, no one tried to play keep away with Deanna's carryon bag stored in the overhead luggage bin. Friendly assistance was given unasked. They made it down the passageway without a single ass grab, and no one attempted to play bumper cars on the way.

Marlene Albrecht herself met Deanna and Sandy in Dallas at the airport with her campaign assistant Millie and her driver in tow. Now Marlene only drove herself when she felt no one would notice. The crowd at the airport with good manners and respect for her age, parted like the waters in front of Mrs. Albrecht as she walked through with her growing entourage. Enthusiastic greetings were exchanged, and their luggage was collected by the ranch hand turned driver. The girls, most especially Deanna, confessed to being both hungry and thirsty. A coffee and pastry stop was arranged before they even got out of the airport for the drive home where the ranch's famous barbecued ribs were awaiting their arrival.

Early the next morning everyone in the ranch house was up and dressed early. Breakfast was huevos rancheros eaten quickly in the kitchen. Marlene fussed over her driver who showed up looking too much like a chauffeur in his best suit. He was sent back for a sport jacket, which he borrowed. Sam Houston Johnson arrived with his grandson Nathaniel and several other worthies of the party. All set off for the Community Center where the announcement of Marlene Albrecht's candidacy was to be made to friends, supporters and all members of the Press who the party could entice to attend an event early in the morning.

Only one of Bob and Marlene's daughters could attend. She came in a flurry, with her hair flying and had to be combed out before she could stand on stage next to Deanna, Sandy, Sam Johnson and Nathaniel. Marlene's speech was a carefully crafted statement mixing her views and affirmations of the character of the Great State of Texas. In summary it expressed her priorities for education, safe schools, respect for the ecology of the Texas range, Blue Bells, and watch out boys you need to keep it honest in the capitol. Much applause followed, with hand shaking and flowers for the new candidate. No babies were kissed at this event as that would seem to be the prerogative of campaigning male candidates.

A reception followed at a local family restaurant that

brought the younger folks together, which they enjoyed. At the head table the politicos plotted strategy for the next campaign event with gusto. It was an enjoyable event for everyone and a novel one. Except Deanna couldn't help but notice Nathaniel's growing partiality for Sandy. Her dear friend and frequent co-conspirator was now introduced as Miss Allesandra Waitely.

12

LOVE NOTES – HOT TUB

———◆———

EM LICKED THE milk chocolate from her sticky fingers. The girls were away visiting Aunt Marlene in Texas. She had the Spring House to herself and invited a friend to keep her company. Em wasted no time. It was Wednesday evening, Marlene Albrecht announced her candidacy that afternoon.

"Isn't this against policy or something?" Em was finishing the gourmet S'more, a jumbo toasted marshmallow resting on the classic graham cracker, topped with milk chocolate and homemade red raspberry sauce with whole berries.

"Maybe, probably, although you're not a witness in any active case. You didn't witness the murder or the theft. You didn't see who shot at you. Besides, we would not want you for a witness. If you took the stand, they could ask you anything. You'd tell the truth, right?"

She nodded, wiping the raspberry sauce dripping down her chin with her napkin.

"We won't want that, and neither would you. How would you like to tell them in open court what you did for your client, and what you did previously for the corporation?"

"Oh, there's a thought, isn't it? I was careful. There was nothing illegal in my work. Just a little more creative than most."

"I've heard that before. Creative, good one. The CIA gets creative too, or so I understand." Halloran was enjoying dessert, as he had dinner. Earlier in the evening, a light rain sent them into the living room after grilling shrimp over mesquite chips. Once inside they loaded up plates with new potatoes in rosemary butter and fresh peas with mint. Em drank a Finger Lakes Riesling. Halloran opted for one of her son Joshua's bottles of Sam Adams. He swore it called to him from the fridge. They were sitting comfortably on the wood frame Stickley couch in front of a small fire of windfall branches built to toast the marshmallows.

"Do you think this is early to be doing this? You've heard of the ten date rule?" she asked him. Halloran acknowledged he had heard no such thing, he preferred to make his own choice of time and place. Slipping his arm around her, she moved closer to him. He licked the last little bit of raspberry sauce from her chin with a wet kiss. He proceeded to nibble on her cheek, making her laugh softly in his ear. Halloran, gently, ever so slowly ran his hand down from her neck to her breast.

"Let's see, first at the office, then you yelled at me on the phone about getting shot at in the canoe," she mused.

"Hardly a date." Halloran enjoyed the feel of the creamy silk of her blouse and the scent of lavender from her hair and skin. The silk blouse was designed with a generously draped neckline and came off so easily. Em lay back on the soft leather cushions. The silk blouse dropped to the rug, leaving Halloran's lips free to explore her neck and down across her collar bone and his tongue to tickle that little indentation we all have between the bones.

"Then we spent the afternoon together at the rent party, and I got to know you." Em was forced to take a breath as she felt her bra released, eased down and off as he continued nuzzling and nibbling at her. Halloran raised his head, smiled at her, and finding no censure, slid his hands down to caress both breasts, no favorites yet, both soft and warm in the slight chill of the evening.

"You freed the ladies. They like it."

"Do they indeed." Taking this as permission for further liberties, his mouth followed his hands down to a lovely pair.

"I can't think when you're doing that."

"Don't think. Enjoy. I told you before." He felt her hands press firmly across his upper back exploring right up between his shoulder blades.

"Then... and the office visit. We went to the funeral I …."

"You pulled me down on top of you. Did you enjoy that?" He looked up and caught her smiling at him. "You did enjoy it. I took you out to dinner." His hands were still busy. Her eyes were beginning to lose focus.

"You kissed me in the tunnel. There must be at least seven."

"Close enough for government work, I'd say." He had no patience to wait for her to find three more excuses to make love with him.

She began tugging at his pants in a determined effort to remove his belt. Mindful he should be removing certain items carried for personal security first, he gave her a long, lingering tongue in cheek and everywhere else kiss, and said, "I think we should get a room."

She ran her hands up his arms. "I happen to have one handy. Only a single bed though."

"Any port in a storm," was his reply.

"Grab your gear, sailor. Let's head upstairs," she said and returned his kiss with fervor that pleased and surprised him. Hands placed on his cheeks she drew his mouth to meet her own. The start of a new beard on his face intrigued her. She wondered how it would feel all over and rubbed her face against it, then nipped his ear. "Ready, set, go!" she whispered.

Halloran picked up the black satchel he'd brought in with him.

"Come prepared?" she asked in a low husky voice.

"Scout's honor," he replied with a short laugh.

"Me, too."

The branches in the fireplace were burning through, the fire was almost out. Feeling like a very naughty lady indeed, blouse over her shoulders, she led her more than willing companion up to her bedroom at the end of the hallway, facing the woods. Pointing out the bathroom on their way down the hall she was excited, and nervous, and so pleased with him. Also astonished, it must be said, at her age.

Once inside her bedroom, Em lit a small light on a nightstand. She tossed her favorite blouse of rich cream colored Indian silk on a rocking chair and stood smiling at the tall man, her chest forward, the way women do when they're flaunting perfect breasts. Em's jeans were long gone. Halloran was not unappreciative, but he had a few things of his own to remove. Fascinated, Em watched him take a hip holster with a small gun from his belt. Next he reached down to his left ankle to pull off a black nylon holster held secure by a wide woven strap.

"Can I help you with those pants now?" She crossed her arms under her breasts. Getting this man into bed was turning out to be an education in self-defense, and a major undertaking. "Can you take your socks off while you're at it?" she asked, an arch tone in her voice.

"In a minute, Em, in a minute." He pulled up one sleeve to tug off a black arm band containing a knife and a few other useful tools. The arm band along with one of the guns went into the black satchel, which he habitually kept in the car for business emergencies.

"You are safe with me, you know," she told him and fiddled her fingers against one elbow, pretending impatience.

Glad she was taking this process calmly, he crossed the room towards her, placing the holster from his belt on the nightstand by the bed. Reasoning she already knew where he wore most of the weapons, he was not about to go hide in the bathroom like a nervous kid on a first date to take them off. Aware of her aversion to guns, he had chosen smaller guns from his personal arsenal. Halloran's preference for duty weapons were significantly larger, heavier, and potentially scarier.

Hesitating, he came into her personal space, stopping within inches of her. She reached down and with determined effort got his belt, his pants, and his shorts off in one motion.

"You can take your socks off now, sir." She stood openly admiring him as he reached for his socks, one at a time, leaving on a wide black nylon band covering half his right shin. Em, naively, thought it was only a brace for his sore leg. Nice clean limbs, hairy legs, a tight butt. She'd given considerable time to contemplating the male form as a younger woman. *Some things never get old,* she thought, *and admiring a man naked is one of them.* It was as he turned back towards her that things began to grow more interesting still.

How they got the rest of their clothes off, Em could not later remember. She knew she must have gotten all those buttons on his shirt undone, but her first clear memory was slipping between the clean sheets, windblown and smelling of fresh air and sunshine, with Halloran right after her. It seemed so very different, new and exciting, after the last several years of obligation and routine with Huber.

Still she was wary. "Can we agree not to ask each other questions we shouldn't answer?"

Halloran was playing around her right nipple with his tongue while fondling her left breast. He thought for a moment but didn't stop. "We can try," he replied, thinking the sooner she stopped talking, the sooner he could get her to play with him. The lavender fragrance of her hair, the taste of her skin, slightly salty, and the personal essence of her scent were most pleasurable. Her yielding softness and gentle warmth were seducing him effortlessly.

"Like no questions about Uncle Bob and bars of gold. I don't think he had any."

He came up for air and let his fingers do the walking. "I think he knew where they are." His hands rubbed her sides over her ribs, working their way downward in a steady progress.

"Is that what you think this is about? Gold bars?" he asked. A pair of grey eyes looked up at her from between her knees "Could we not talk about work. Relax and enjoy yourself." Clearly, it was time for another strategy. First with stealthy gentle fingers at her waist, then with his tongue on her tummy, just above the rumple, Halloran teased.

"Stop, you're tickling me!" Em laughed.

"Ticklish, are we?" *I've got her*, he thought.

"Yes, very." This incited him to more creative efforts until Em was laughing out loud and squirming beneath his hands.

"You are a fresh man." She gasped.

"Glad you think so."

Not to be outdone, Em wriggled down, reached around, practiced a move learned early in her dating life — men are ticklish over the kidneys. She soon had Halloran rolling around on the narrow bed, playing with her as if they were two teenagers in love. The antique wooden bed creaked and groaned, hopping around on four legs as if it had come alive. No one noticed though. Halloran could barely get her settled down enough to let him make serious love to her.

Startled by a particularly sharp crack from the bed

frame, Em came out on top, stopping for a moment to catch her breath. Halloran lay there, enjoying the feeling as her chest moved up and down against him, plotting his next move. She laid her head down, the hair on his chest was dark and curly with a few white hairs interspersed. Em smoothed her hand across it. She was not fond of the hairless Chihuahua look for men, which was a good thing in Halloran's case. Unconsciously placing her face towards his arm pit, Em's senses savored his male presence, taking in his scent and storing it away in memory with the pleasure it invoked.

Feeling skin on skin was an excitement for both of them, but being a man, he liked to look at what he was doing as well. Getting her to turn over on her back and let him take her was the challenge. *Easy does it*, he thought to himself as he began to run both hands down her back, up and then down again. She made a sound like a soft purr of pleasure. Encouraged, he reached down further, and massaged her buns, and found them nice and firm. Good workout at the gym, no doubt.

"Nice bun rub," she murmured. Em's approach was to let Halloran show her his stuff, with encouragement along the way. She found she could guide his hands and encourage his touch with the slightest of movements.

"How about some, uh…"

"Time to roll over?"

"Yeah." He gathered her into his arms as the bed was narrow. Maneuvering together, with laughter, they changed positions, avoiding stress on his sore shin.

The rain that began in the afternoon as showers was growing harder by the minute. Thunder rumbled from the northwest. Large raindrops splattered against the windows and thrummed on the roof.

"Did you know in India, it is believed rain is an auspicious time to make love?" She ran her hands down his back and sides.

"I didn't. Do you think this is an auspicious time?" *In other words, are you ready, lady?*

"Are you a careful man?" she asked.

"Always," he said in a quiet voice. *Here we go, final negotiations*, he thought.

I'll bet you are, she thought to herself, *always careful and always armed.*

"You must know the old saying, 'Don't go out into the rain without your rubbers.' I have a present for you. I didn't know what size to buy, so it's a medium." Her voice was apologetic about the size, because, from what she had seen he was a man with substantial understanding. "Here's a little something else." She handed him a tube. "For the older woman who is no longer Niagara Falls, but who likes to be nice and wet."

He was a gentleman, he accepted the gifts from the clever girl with thanks. "There is something I'd like to do first to please the lady. Let me know how you like it." He backed off and sat between her knees, rubbing the inside of her thighs with his hands. He leaned down to kiss her thighs, his five o'clock shadow providing an intriguing friction. For a man of fewer words, he proceeded to prove how adept he was with his tongue, which did please, until he stopped short.

"Oh?"

"It's alright, sweetie, I'll be right with you," and he certainly was ready. Halloran was not only a man who could hold his liquor, he could hold on as Em squeezed him tight. Her breathing deepened and slowed until she moaned quietly in his ear. He did this with patience, and ardor, and skill, and was rewarded with a full partner who was hungry for his touch, warm with feeling, soft and responsive.

She held him in her arms as he curled his body around hers until she encouraged him to come to rest between her breasts. There, she let him fall quietly asleep as she hummed the familiar tune to "Chili on the Table," softly to herself.

Halloran had an old-fashioned taste for women with large soft breasts and some meat on their bones and generous temperaments. His ex-wife Gillian was compulsively, obsessively thin, possibly because towards the end of their marriage, she drank at least one meal a day. After that his next serious relationship with a woman lasted five years. She made him get dressed and undressed in the bathroom, and was quite demanding in all things. Em Huber was so much more of what he had been looking for, without realizing how much he had been longing for it. It was good to be welcomed, to be shyly admired in the buff, to succeed in pleasing and to feel affection returned.

HOT TUB

Sunlight brightened the curtains. Early morning bird song and squabbling, accompanied by the incessant sound of chain saws, found their way in the second floor bedroom window. Cleanup from the previous week's severe storm was in progress early on a Saturday morning. Hurricane force winds and heavy rains had given the southern New England coast a good scouring. Shoreline cottages that stood too close to the high tide line were damaged, their foundations were pulled out from under them. The marshes along the shore flooded by storm surge and waves and filled with sea water farther inland than they had ever done in the memory of most living residents. Many of the younger residents had never experienced a true "hurricane season." Personal belongings surfaced and were beached all along the shore. The Coast Guard patrolled the shoreline to forestall looters who took to raiding by boat. Large trees washed down the rivers, came ashore briefly, to be carried away again at the subsequent high tides. Other things washed ashore too, that were meant to be forgotten.

Em rolled over in bed, reached over Halloran's warm back, taking in the scent of a sleeping male. She ran her hand over his back, around to his chest, and rubbed her cheek against his shoulder. His hand covered her fingers and held them. She wriggled closer.

"Watch out for the leg."

"Oh Halloran, are you sore this morning?"

"Yeah," he said shortly. "Stiff."

"Is that a good thing?"

"Not when it's my leg."

"We'll have to do something about it."

"What did you have in mind?" he said, a reservation clear in his voice.

"How about a good long soak in a hot mineral bath? It works wonders for me. Think of the Roman Baths." Em rubbed his chest.

Halloran knew well enough by now to know not to ask if she was joking. Em's bed was narrow. She carefully moved her leg up and over his injured right leg and eased herself out of bed.

"Are you okay for a few minutes? I'd like to run down the hall, take a quick shower, then I'll run you a hot bath."

"Honey, I'm not going anywhere fast this morning." Thinking twice, Halloran rolled over and smiled at her worried face. "This happens when I spend too much time standing or climb too many stairs. It's just stiff, not a problem from last night's, uh, last night."

"Good to know. I'll come get you when the tub is ready." Halloran closed his eyes and settled back into the middle of the bed. Good to have company, but good to be able to stretch out, too. He watched with one admiring eye open as she selected two robes from the closet and slipped one over her body. Em turned towards him and caught his look, winked at him, and placed an Egyptian cotton robe, relic of a more prosperous time, on the foot of the bed for him.

As she headed down the hall, he remembered his grandfather saying, "If I ever get too old to enjoy looking at a pretty leg, I want to be dead." Mike Halloran was feeling quite the opposite. It had been a good while since a pretty woman had taken him to her bed.

Em showered quickly, enjoying the pelting of hot water, but cut the shower short to save the hot water. Here in the large family bathroom, she turned on the hot tap in the old ball and claw footed bathtub. The faucet was small, the tub a deep one, so the bath filled rather slowly. Thinking it might be a challenge for Halloran to step up to get into the tub gave her a moment of concern. From its place in the corner she dragged out a low wooden bath stool to use as a step.

To give him the house special soak, she headed down the stairs for mineral water to add to the bath. She grabbed the spring room keys from the peg in the hallway. The cement cellar stairs were cool on her feet. The stubborn wooden door was swollen by the damp from the recent heavy rain. With an effort she hauled it open and switched on the overhead light. A rush of cool, damp air greeted her.

The light shown on the spring water that streamed down the bare rocks into the natural stone bowl. The splash and babble of the water down off the rocks was as loud as she had ever heard it. In the background, coming from the rock face was a piping sound that made the walls of the spring room vibrate with a kind of music. It was almost overwhelming first thing in the morning before coffee. Times like this had earned Wintergreen Spring a place in stories told by many generations about a singing spring.

Selecting two good sized metal pitchers from the array of jars, jugs, vases and various other containers on the wooden shelves, she approached the spring cautiously in her bare feet. Kneeling by the holding tank, Em filled the pitchers from a faucet at the base of the tank. Since the water would not be used for drinking, but for bathing, she hoped to capture minerals that sank towards the bottom of the tank. Rising, she took a chipped enamel cup from its hook by the spring, rinsed it, and filled it directly from the flow off the rocks, as was her custom for a morning pick me up.

On her way towards the spring room door, she paused by a large ancient pottery amphora graced by a sizeable funnel shaped spider web. A devastatingly large brown spider crept out around the neck of the jar, front legs twitching. "Good morning to you, Ariadne." Em addressed the spider in quiet tones, and thought, *Here I am eye to eye with an arachnid. Does she know I won't hurt her? Professor Martin guessed they understand tone of voice and interpret our movements, our body language.* The desiccated carcasses of Ariadne's prey were scattered under the funnel of the web. Em was not tempted to clean them up at the moment.

Turning out the light and locking the spring room door presented a challenge to Em as she hefted two water pitchers. The key ring was replaced onto its peg in the hallway and she continued up the narrow stairs to the second floor bathroom. The water in the ball and claw-footed tub was over half full. Leaving the pitchers by the tub, Em returned to the bedroom to roust Halloran out of bed and to coax her new lover into the hot tub.

"Okay, time to go soak, fella!" A groan came from the bed. He looked rather scruffy, short hair standing straight up, five o'clock shadow going from cheekbones to collar bones. "Really, it will do you good. It always makes me feel so much better." She paused. "Can you get up?" she inquired.

"Yes, woman, I can get up."

"Come on then." Em tossed him the robe and stood combing her hair in front of the mirror, her back to him. She placed herself so she could surreptitiously watch him as he cautiously swung his legs around and wrapped himself in the robe. Together they walked down the hall to the bathroom. Halloran walked gingerly on the right foot.

The bathroom was pleasantly warm and steamy. The water in the tub was the perfect height to soak a grown man without sending a gush of water over the edge. Halloran watched skeptically as Em poured the two pitchers of spring water under the flow of hot tap water. She inhaled a whiff of the steam as the scent of the water changed. It gained the tang of the red clay and basalt through which it flowed underground.

"Some people say you can smell the minerals, to me it does smell like iron in the water. This spring water is from the bottom of the holding tank. The minerals settle down towards the bottom." She tested the temperature with her elbow. "Great. Like it hot? Can I help you get in?" This of course, was entirely the wrong thing to say.

Halloran stood his ground on the bathroom rug. He looked at the tub and he looked at Em, then dropped the overnight kit on the wooden bench.

Em chuckled at his expression. "Irishman. You can take off your robe. I saw it all last night, and I don't think it's changed any this morning. There's oatmeal soap, so you don't have to come out smelling like lavender."

"You're mothering me," he protested.

In a soft Irish brogue Em replied, "An' it's a silly arse of a man you are if you think that's what I'm after being." She was indeed admiring his arse, at the time, and wondering when she might have a chance to see it again.

"You sound like my Aunt Mary."

"An' she was your favorite aunt, was she now? Com'on, you'll be a better man ahll the day long for a good soak in yon tub. Me great Aunt Kayte was Irish, an' she left that side o' the family with her good nature, blue eyes and the freckles."

Halloran shot her a look and dropped the robe without ceremony. Spotting the grab bar on the wall, he used it to ease himself into the water. Em tried not to take obvious notice of the two long jagged branching scars that ran around his knee and trailed down his shin almost to his ankle. The scars were raised red and looked fairly recent. *Compound fracture*, she thought, *a nasty injury*.

"Like oatmeal for breakfast, tart cherries and walnuts?"

"I'm Irish, I was raised on oatmeal." A look of pleasure crept across his face.

"If you're good to me, I'll make you the soda bread," she said with a soft lilt in her voice.

"Feels good. Go along with you, woman, and let a man soak in peace." Eyes narrowed, a gratified smile spread across Halloran's face. He had every intention of being very good to her.

Laughing softly to herself, Em closed the bathroom door behind her. As she turned towards the stairs, he burst into a hearty laugh. Minerva, the generously blessed, topless mermaid painted over the door, waved her girlish hand at the occupants of the tub. She often elicited a good laugh from those seeing her for the first time. A long time ago a guest of Professor Martin's, two sheets to the wind, claimed he'd made an indecent proposal to Minerva, and she never waved at him again.

Em retreated to the kitchen to fix breakfast. Into the saucepan she poured spring water from the fridge, added brown sugar, cinnamon, dark dried Michigan cherries, a pinch of salt and the oatmeal. While the oatmeal cooked, she chopped California walnuts to add. Water boiled in the kettle for tea. She added little pellets of loose tea to a simple white teapot and poured in the boiling water. Leaving the tea to steep and the oatmeal to settle, she took the stairs to see if Halloran was ready to come on out.

When she came to bathroom door, she heard a cell phone ring followed immediately by a string of muttered curses from the tub.

After the briefest knock, she opened the door. "Hold on, I'll get it for you. Breakfast is ready."

"Okay, it's in my bag. I can't reach it from here."

"You're looking better already." In truth, he was. His smile was relaxed, not drawn as it had been when he'd first walked down the hall. With one hand she dug into his bag, carefully avoiding the gun found there. "Here you go, your cell. I wrapped it in a wash cloth to keep it dry. Do your back?"

"Damn it, it's work." He waved the cell phone at her. "I'm attempting to take a day off. Not planning to go in. Where am I? I'm taking a hydrotherapy treatment. In a hot tub of mineral water. No, I am not kidding. My leg's stiff this morning so I'm taking therapy." Em laughed softly, he waved her out of the bathroom. As she left quietly she heard him say, "Send the team, I'll meet them later. I know I'm not home, why did you send them there?"

Em closed the bathroom door behind her, and laughed. *Hydrotherapy, I'll have to remember that one. Maybe we should take paying guests.*

Her guest was enough restored that he climbed out of the tub all by himself, dried, shaved and dressed in record time.

Breakfast was served at the small table by the window in the kitchen. Em poured the tea. "Try it," she said. "It's Chinese, it was my grandmother's favorite." She waited until he tasted and commented it was indeed fine. "Imperial Gunpowder. It was a gift from friends," she added quietly with a secretive smile.

He hesitated to think, *how did she manage to get anything "Imperial" out of China?* and decided that some questions were best not pursued.

"I need to get into the city for a while. Something's turned up. It may not take all day." There was a question in his voice.

"How does free range chicken, baked with new potatoes, carrots and peas sound for dinner tonight? They're small but, boy, are they tasty chickens. Mixed berry pie for dessert," she offered. "I have plenty to do around here for the afternoon. Dinner around 7:00?"

"I could leave my bag here."

"Yes, Irishman, you could."

13

LOCAL TRADITIONS DIE HARD

———————

THURSDAY AFTERNOON HALLORAN returned from the city, tired, puzzled and anticipating a good dinner. The weathered grey barn door was open, and he pulled the car right in. Although the barn did not look to be up to the standard of the usual suburban garage, he preferred the car in a more secure location than right out on a country road.

Fewer phone calls came from interested neighbors when he stashed his car in the barn next to the aging van. Mireille, whose farm house was down the road and had a good view, called Em in the afternoon to say, "See you had company last night!"

Presuming it would be more discrete, Halloran rang the front door bell. He stood more or less patiently on the stone doorstep waiting for Em to come down the hall from the kitchen to let him in. The bag he was carrying was awkward.

Em ushered him into the front hall before demonstrating how glad she was to see him, and he responded in kind. *The man certainly has a way with him, as the saying goes,* she thought.

"I'm so glad to see you, I didn't know whether you'd come back." She blushed and seemed shy to reach out for him.

"Why? I left my bag here. I said I'd be back. If I was going to be late, I would have called you, Em." Halloran looked clueless.

"Well, after the first night, I wondered if it would be only that. I don't do one night stands at all and..."

"Not on your life, sweetie." The grin on his face widened farther than she'd ever seen it. "One good, really good night deserves another, and then another…." This was spoken as he leaned in for another kiss.

Halloran's five o'clock shadow was fast turning his face into sandpaper. A day at work with a trudge across the salt marsh at the head of New Haven Harbor gave him the unmistakable tang of urban seawater. He nearly dropped his bag on the slate tile of the hallway.

A soft stretchy top sorely tempted him to reach behind her, pop the hooks on the bra to feel lovely softness. Instead he stooped to put his bag down on the slate, and used the opportunity to run his hands back up to her firm derriere, which he clasped in his hands, pulling her towards him. Em gave in to instinct so long dormant. She was very glad to see him and gave him a passionate kiss. Halloran was a trained diver and could seemingly hold his breath forever. Em needed air first. Halloran had received complaints in the past about duration and asphyxia, so he relinquished her mouth easily when he sensed her need. It was a mutually satisfying moment.

Gym toned buns are well worth the effort, Em reflected.

Halloran was appreciating a nice bottom with an encouragingly firm grip. From there he could see the Stickley couch in the living room. If he weren't both tired and hungry, he would have encouraged a visit.

Feeling warm all over from the tone of his voice, the look in his eye, Em considered letting dinner cook itself when they parted from a lingering kiss. Fortunately for the free range chicken in the oven, Em brought the enticing smells of dinner with her to the front hall. Halloran let it be known he was more than ready for a taste of a well done bird, dessert and love making *aprés le dejeuner*. Always the thoughtful guest, the bag deposited on the floor produced a nice bottle of port wine, a six pack of Harpoon IPA for himself, and a six of Sam Adams for Joshua Huber's next visit.

"What, no Guinness?" Em quipped. Halloran let her know their prime suspect had been apprehended at his local pub in Glasgow, half way through a Black and Tan.

"In honor of Innes? No way! Some other time maybe." Halloran put the beer in the fridge, except for tucking one in the freezer to chill. Em sent him into the living room to sprawl out on the couch, with his right leg elevated, while she finished setting the table.

"Deanna called while you were out. It seems the boy she had her heart set on seeing again developed an interest in Sandy, and she returns it. I wish Deanna was better at being a good sport about things. She says she's trying, but it sounds to me like she's sulking at home with Aunt Marlene this evening. Sandy's new friend has asked her to go for a moonlight ride. You know I can't say that Aunt Marlene didn't warn me." Em waited for an acknowledgment her guest was listening to her.

After a pause, Halloran caught on, a response was expected from him and said, "About what?"

"About Deanna needing someone with more going for him than the Johnson boy, who she said was going to spend his life in a lawyer's office. I think Deanna needs an older boy myself." Em laid out the silverware on the dining room table as she talked.

"Funny thing is, Dee thinks Sandy would be better off with Swamp Thing. Lucas is his real name, and he tried some moves on Sandy before she was ready. I came home, found Sandy defending herself. Dee calls him Swamp Thing because, in retribution, I threw his sneakers into the vernal pool down the hill. But, he apologized

effectively and still comes around. Something about per-
severance and love triumphing in the end. Sounds like
she's done her homework for a change. Shakespeare has a
lot to answer for if you ask me," Em pronounced waving
a spoon.

Halloran laughed at Em who made a face at him over
the table. "I was thinking you are probably right. Someone else, somewhat older, not easily intimidated, smart
enough to let her have her own way once in a while, but
not too often," he joked.

"Are you thinking of Anson?" Em caught on quickly.
"I thought we decided to let them work it out on their
own."

"So we did. Dinner ready? I'm half starved."

Just about ready to snap out a request for help carrying
plates to the table, Em thought better of it. Learning to
read the expressions on Halloran's face and to listen to
the tone of his voice, pleased her in ways she hesitated
to mention. Especially the low notes of his voice seemed
to resonate somewhere south of her navel. That evening,
his face held a concentration he was having a hard time
hiding. The abstracted look and the restraint in his voice
telegraphed disturbance of mind.

Getting a man to talk about feelings, well, Em had
given that up as a lost cause with Huber. With Michael
Halloran she'd learned that she could wait for it to be said
when he was damned good and ready to deal with it and
not before. But he would talk, and simply say what he
was thinking and feeling, without flourishes and without
all the elaboration Em herself might give.

The table was set with her favorite earthenware dishes,
the ones too heavy to be practical for everyday use. She
brought out the herbed chicken baked with new potatoes, sweet potatoes and carrots in a casserole dish and a
small earthenware bowl with fresh peas from her garden.
Fresh spinach salad with cranberries, mushrooms, red

onion and sliced almonds came to the table in a beautifully simple glass bowl. A small pitcher of yogurt chive dressing accompanied the salad. Thin green beans steaming and dressed with fresh butter were set on a hot pad. A pitcher of spring water, a bottle of New York State Riesling for Em and Halloran's half chilled bottle of Harpoon joined the food on the table.

The free range chicken was one succulent bird, enough for the hungry pair to split between them. Halloran ate his veggies with more relish than he anticipated. When they were nearly finished with the meal he sat back in his chair, stuck his right leg out straight under the table. Em knew enough to dodge the move effectively now. One solid kick on the shin from the man's long leg was enough to teach her to react quickly when he started to move. Halloran looked at her and smiled, showing himself well satisfied with the meal and the company.

"I have to tell you, something turned up today," he started the conversation slowly.

"I wondered what you had on your mind." Em sipped her wine thoughtfully.

"That obvious, is it?" He sighed and thought, *I've got to do this*.

"Kids playing alongside the river above the Interstate Bridge, where the river flows into the harbor found a block of cement with an arm and a leg hanging out of it."

Em felt her stomach drop.

"Looks like the storm surge carried it up out of the channel onto the bank in the marshes. It's Dornefield's body and the gun used to kill Hussein was in the cement with him." Halloran told her this in a just the facts voice.

Em's face held a look of surprise, "It washed up on the north side of the Bridge?"

"Yes. That's where it was found," he replied patiently.

"Talk about amateur," Em exclaimed.

"Say again," Halloran asked pointedly, thinking she

must be in shock and denial.

"Honestly, this is not up to local standards. No one around here would do that."

"Too morally upright?" he asked, sarcasm in his voice.

"Not stupid. The whole point of a cement overcoat and a trip to the harbor is that what goes down never comes back up." Em was exasperated. "Most people who do this sort of disposal would realize cement doesn't only need to dry, it needs to cure for a while so the salt water won't corrode it. You said it showed arms and legs when it was found?"

"Yes. I did see it myself, not a pretty sight."

"You know, it might be someone from out of town or even further, it's almost un-American. Do you remember the first *Thin Man* movie with William Powell and Myrna Loy? The thin man is the scientist who ends up in the cement. It's part of our national folklore from the 1920s and 1930s." Em waited to see if Halloran would pick up her train of thought.

"Good movie. I hadn't thought of it that way. What are you getting at?" Halloran took a last swallow of his Harpoon.

"You and I can go play Nick and Nora Charles later. The cat can play their dog Asta." She laughed. "Ash is never type cast.

"But seriously, the location is all wrong, too. What genius would land a hunk of cement in the shallower waters above the bridge unless they only had a truck and were in a hurry? They probably backed up the truck at night and dumped it in thinking the water would hide it." Em certainly had Halloran's attention.

"So what's your take on this?" Halloran asked. "Analyze it for me."

"Okay, my mother told me.... Stop laughing, Michael. She grew up here and she thought I should know things. During Prohibition the cutters used to sail into the harbor on dark nights. They unloaded the whiskey at the foot of one of the streets on the west shore. When they left they would take out anything that needed to go. If it was cement-coated, they would dump it in the deep mud on the west side of the harbor. The ship channel is on the east side. No one in his right mind would dump anything in the channel for the Army Corps of Engineers to find the next time they dredged the harbor."

Halloran nodded his head. "So much for local knowledge. Our Coast Guard contact said about the same thing."

A thought struck Em. "Oh dear Lord, they don't think I did it, do they? I mean I did educate him briefly on the local customs here. After I shot him."

Halloran's grey eyes sparked with Em's brown eyes. "Not hardly. Dornefield told everyone who would listen about what you said, especially his lawyer. No, I think you could have shot and killed him when he was holding a gun on me. If you wanted him dead, you'd do it yourself."

"Thanks for the vote of confidence, I think. But seriously, they don't think it was me?" Em looked sheepish.

"We do have reason to believe it was done by others. To our surprise a high priced New York lawyer arrived in a chauffeur driven limousine. The lawyer got Dornefield out on bail as you know and took him out for lunch. Restaurant wouldn't make Zagat's but it's not known for trouble, and it's not on the west shore. It's right downtown. Lawyer and client go in together with a plain clothes officer following them."

"Anyone I know?"

"One of Detective Nilsson's New Haven officers who needs a lesson from Vargas," Halloran admitted.

"Lawyer comes out. Client gets up from the barstool. He's alone and heads to the back of the restaurant towards the gents' and was never seen again. Patrons and staff all say the same thing. There is a backdoor to a parking lot."

"He probably believed they were going to help him hide out. And the lawyer?" Em was not happy.

"Gets into the limo and is driven back to his office in Manhattan. That was the end of the story until the hurricane scoured the ship channel." Halloran contemplated his empty beer bottle.

"Maybe he asked for more money. Kidnapped and murdered to keep him quiet?"

"One would think. He had a hell of a mouth once he got going. We didn't have him long enough for a good questioning," said Halloran regretfully.

"Done here but not by local talent. Guys in a rush, with no boat," Em profiled. "Maybe too young to know better or from way out of town."

"Speaking of local talent, seems as if they were as offended as you are. Vargas made the rounds, seems no one asked the local mob permission to operate here. Such sloppy work gives the place a bad name."

"Do they know who did it?"

"Vargas says not, at least not right now. We're checking New York and points west and down to Jersey."

"We have a second accomplice. The numb nuts who can't mix cement. And someone to help with the heavy lifting, cement isn't light. I'm thinking the brains are elsewhere." Em was still in profile mode.

Halloran could see the thoughts tumbling through her mind and was relieved she was taking it with equanimity and wouldn't be startled by the impending news coverage.

"Dessert?" he asked hopefully.

"White chocolate mousse. Before or after?" Em, across the table, looked into his eyes and smiled. "We could go play Nick and Nora first."

"How do we do that?" Halloran could feel the temperature rising.

"I go slip into something long and silky and look absolutely gorgeous, and you come along all dashing and
daring and take it off," she proposed.

"Is it nice and tight around the bottom?"

A true grin lit her face. "Honey, the mousse can wait."

———◆———

SATURDAY NIGHT SPECIAL

———◆———

Halloran came for dinner Saturday evening intending
to stay for lunch on Sunday. Progress on the case was
speeding up, not tailing off as some cases might do with
passing time. Em's client Frank Kirbee was off the grid
but hadn't turned up in cement, which was a good sign.
Significant parts of New Haven Harbor had been dragged
at Halloran's request. The assumption that the block of
cement containing Dornefield's body was dumped from
an old pickup truck was correct. A reluctant witness had
been found through Vargas's diligent field work. The witness was persuaded to talk about his late night ramblings
along the tall grass of the marshes above the Interstate
Bridge.

In the evening Em and Halloran had dinner out in the
rock garden. To the delight of the cats, Halloran grilled
salmon over a wood fire laced with mesquite chips. Em
brought out bowls of basmati rice mixed with wild rice
and fresh peas. Cleome and Ash begged the tail end of
the salmon and lazed away happily after their supper. Em
produced a bottle of local wine and tried to persuade
Halloran to join her in a glass before he selected another
Harpoon.

They found themselves on the teak bench, arms
around each other. The evening was growing cool, all
around them the insects of the night were coming to
life again. Em loved the night sounds in the country. She

liked to sleep with her window open to listen. Joshua of course frowned on this from a security standpoint until he understood he could use that to his advantage. The sounds of the woodlands, the gathering darkness and the wine, things were becoming mellow. Em began to fantasize about how the long green grass of the lawn, still warm from the sun, might feel on her back and whether she might share a romp there with her dinner companion.

"What?"

"Huh?" Em startled.

"You looked far away there for a minute." Halloran finished off his beer. "What's for dessert?"

"Flan. I was just thinking." She smiled at him

"With you that could be a dangerous enterprise." Halloran was intrigued.

"I don't know whether we know each other well enough for me to share certain thoughts with you," she demurred.

"Try me."

"I was wondering. See the nice green grass over there in the backyard?" Em indicated a particularly lush patch on the upper reaches of the south facing lawn.

"So? Don't tell me the grass is greener over the septic leaching field." Halloran found it funny.

"It's not the septic field, that's on the other side of the house, downhill. You are an impossible man."

"Then what?"

"I was imagining how nice it would feel to have a roll in the grass together." She paused to see the effect of her words. "Naked," she said softly.

Halloran raised his eyebrows and laughed under his breath, "You are a most surprising woman."

Em paused and bit her lip, gazed out into the woods. "Oh, now that I think of it, I'm not a lucky one."

"Second thoughts will get you every time, Em. What

is it now?"

"With my luck, we'd just about get all nice and bare naked and comfortable. Can't you just feel the cool grass a little damp and dewy, and the night air on your back side? And then a troop of Boy Scouts lost in the woods finds the backyard and parades through it to the road."

Halloran let out a thoroughly bench shaking laugh. "I don't think it's likely…"

"Oh, but they do get lost. They have tramped through the backyard. They have a rustic camp over the hill."

"Alright, if you say so, Chiquita. Let's go inside. I can wait for dessert."

———◆———

The wireline phone on the bedside table rang, loud, shrill and unexpected at 2:30 that morning. Em startled so sharply she rose up to land directly on top of Halloran in an attempt to reach the phone.

"Something's happened. I can feel it." Em grabbed for the phone nearly skinning his nose in the process.

"Calm down Em, you don't know that yet."

"Hello?"

"Mom, Sandy's been kidnapped!"

"Kidnapped? Lord in Heaven. What happened?"

Halloran mouthed, "Speaker." Em hit the speaker button on the phone she'd bought to use for conference calls.

As they listened Deanna spoke, her voice breaking. "Sandy went over to the Johnson's ranch for dinner and a moonlight ride with Nathaniel. They went out on the ridge to look across the valley. Her horse came back without her. Then Mr. Johnson and some of the guys went out to look for them. They found Nathaniel's horse coming down the trail with Nathaniel kinda slumped over in the saddle"

"Alive?" Em looked in horror at Halloran.

"Oh geez, yeah. Found him up the road, trying to ride back at a walk. He has a dislocated shoulder and his wrist may be broken."

"Nathaniel put up a fight then. What happened?"

"He said two men came up the ridge in a pickup truck. They got out while he was helping Sandy mount up to head back. The men grabbed them."

Tears were in her voice. "Mom, they took Sandy. They didn't want Nathaniel. They said, 'Just leave the kid.'"

"Did they know who she was?" *Was it mistaken identity, was Deanna herself the intended target?* Em worried.

"Mom, I don't know." Deanna broke down in tears. "Aunt Marlene wants to talk to you."

"Emmie, now don't worry, dear. The sheriff and two deputies are on their way out to the Johnson place. I'll send our men out to search soon as it's light. Kidnapping is a federal crime, isn't it? I need to speak to that federal man of yours. Is he there?"

"Marlene, it's two thirty in the morning here. I'll have him call you."

"That's alright. I'm not the prude you think I am. Is he there? We need him now. The girls said they think you two are making it behind their backs, and that's why you didn't want to come to Texas with them."

Eyes rolling, Em hit the mute button on the conference phone so she could talk without being overheard by family in Texas. "Busted." Em looked at her intimate bedfellow.

"Give me the phone. I'm okay with this if you are." Halloran reached out covering her hand with his. She relinquished the phone to him.

"Might as well, at least it's not a Boy Scout troop." She hit the mute button again to enable Halloran to talk to Marlene.

"Mrs. Albrecht, did they know who they were taking? Was there any mention of why or a ransom?"

"Seems to me they had to know something. That jack-ass of a boy heard them say Sandy 'was supposed to be the easy one.' Can you imagine the boy went out there unarmed? When I get a hold of Sam Johnson I'm going to give him a piece of my mind, and he won't forget it soon!"

"It probably means they knew they had Sandy and not Deanna," Em remarked under her breath. "But why, did they say?"

"Not that the boy heard. Idiot!"

"Aunt Marlene, they pulled his arm out of its socket and broke his wrist. He was trying," Deanna piped up.

"It's Texas, honey. On vacation you take the gun and leave the cannoli, if they have any. There are animals and snakes out there," Em said. "Not to mention the occasional armed men." Now the initial shock had passed, she was able to think more clearly.

"Listen you two, you need to stay at the ranch. Marlene, get some men to stay in the house with you. I don't want them coming back after either one or both of you. Promise me."

"She's right. Please do as Em says, you're an announced candidate for public office. That puts a different light on the abduction of your house guest. Intimidation of political candidates is not acceptable. I'll make calls. Call immediately if there is any change." Halloran hauled himself up and out of bed and pulled on his shorts. He reached for his cell phone from under a piece of Em's casually tossed underwear and went out to the hall.

A sense of doom descending upon her, Em watched him go. Having Sandy who was as close as another daughter to her kidnapped, and her love life exposed in one short phone call, was a bit much for Em to handle. She repeated her injunction to Deanna to be watchful and to Marlene to stay in the house, to serve as a communications center and to keep out of the way of further harm. The point was also made, as a candidate Marlene should stay home and let the sheriff handle it. The good lady should not be seen as taking the law into her own hands, to which Marlene could be heard muttering in protest. The call ended with mutual expressions of support and not one word of "Mom, wish you were here." Deanna was clear what the repercussions of a visit from her mother might be, and hell to pay was the least of it.

Em barely had time to compose her wits before she was rejoined by Halloran.

"Need a bigger bed. Shove over."

"I should have gone with them, but we haven't found Kirbee yet. I hoped they would be safer with Marlene. Now I only hope they will do as I ask. Marlene's eighty if she's a day, but that won't stop her. She's perfectly capable of going into Bob's office, getting his gun, calling for her horse and riding out with her posse at dawn," Em said dramatically. "And I'm here in bed!"

"Yeah, and I'm glad of it or you'd be out riding with the posse yourself. I've made phone calls. I know people in the local office. They're good. They will be with Marlene and Deanna as soon as they can, should be well before dawn. And you will only complicate matters if you go rushing down there yourself. If it becomes necessary, I'll arrange for both of us to go."

"So what now? I won't be able to get to sleep." Em looked for sympathy.

"How about some strong tea? Do you have any whiskey?"

"I have some good brandy." Although this was not what Em had in mind.

"Brandy will have to do." Halloran was up and getting dressed.

An hour later, Em sat in the kitchen fully dressed, consoling herself with her second cup of tea and a buttered scone. Her overnight guest was frying eggs and Canadian bacon when the house phone rang. Em scrambled across the room, upsetting her chair in her haste to reach the phone on the wall.

"Mom, it's Josh. I'm getting an emergency signal from Sandy's key fob in Texas. Is everything alright down there?"

"Praise be! No, everything is not alright. Sandy's been kidnapped. Can you get a GPS fix from the signal?"

"Sure thing. Near as I can figure, it's about ten miles from the ranch, out in the middle of no- freakin'-where. It's moving around, too. Bobblin' up and down." Joshua, absorbed in his display, forgot to whom he was speaking.

"Give me the coordinates, please, then call Aunt Marlene. There will be officers at the house. Josh, you are a wonder!" Em wrote down the GPS coordinates on the wall pad.

"Why would anyone kidnap Sandy?" Josh was stunned.

"We're not sure. Call Texas. Deanna can tell you all about it. Hurry please."

A grin as wide as Em's cheeks met Halloran as he fried breakfast on the stove. "Sandy remembered the panic button this time."

14

KIDNAPPED!

SANDY WAS EXCITED, although she knew her friend Deanna might hate her forever and a day. Nathaniel was a good looking law student with those gentlemanly manners that she found hard to resist. *Lucas could use a dose of those manners,* she reflected. An invitation to supper at Nathaniel's grandfather's place, good chuck wagon style cooking and a ride out to watch the full moonrise, it seemed too good to be true. Sandy spent much of her time, energy and wits working to not be a burden to her host family. Vacation, and especially such enjoyment on vacation came rarely, and actually often only at Em's insistence.

In the family ranch house Deanna and Sandy occupied rooms close to Marlene's master bedroom. They were not large rooms, but each had a magnificent view across the countryside. Back home in the Spring House all they saw from their bedroom windows were the trees on the hill above the rock garden. In her room Sandy pulled on a shirt and jeans suitable for riding. She was not an avid rider, but you couldn't live with the Hubers and not know how to get on a horse and ride it. Em considered riding one of the valuable life skills for any child. After all, one might need to ride out with the Mujahedeen some-day, you never knew, and there was that old U.S. Cavalry saddle in Uncle Bob's office.

Sandy drew the line at spending her hard earned money on riding boots when Em was quite willing to lend her an old worn pair of stove pipe boots. They were nothing fancy, no embroidery, plain leather shank and good sturdy heels. The boots were half a size or more too large, wads of tissues in the toes usually handled it. In the afternoon as she pulled on the boots, Sandy stopped to think things through. They would be riding out into open country Sandy could only think of as the Wild West.

I'm probably being paranoid, she thought, but it was as if she could hear Em lecturing her right in the room. She went to her traveling bag and dug around in it. At the bottom of the bag she found what she was seeking. She wrapped one of the items in a small bandana to protect it. Jeans were tight fitting. The knit shirt had two chest pockets, no hope for concealment there. Carefully she placed the items down into the tall riding boots on the outside of her calves to avoid contact with horse and saddle while riding.

Disappointed, Deanna stomped up the stairs to Sandy's room, trying to maintain a cheerful demeanor. "Are you ready? Nathaniel is here. Have a good time. You'll have to tell me all about it."

"Yes, and you will have to tell me why you can't stop talking about Dave Anson," Sandy shot back, teasing her best friend. "He's probably got some girl back in Maine." She grinned at Deanna.

"I don't think so or he'd be up there now," replied Deanna who had given this question more than passing consideration. Deanna amused herself on the plane ride with speculations about her and Anson, and/or her and Nathaniel. It appeared the issue of Nathaniel had now been resolved in another direction.

Supper at the Johnson place was garden salad, tamale pie, sourdough biscuits and "Spotted Pup" for dessert. Spotted Pup was a delicious chuck wagon cook's version of rice pudding with the dark raisins providing the "Spots." Sam Johnson told cowboy stories and reminisced about the good old days when he, his deceased wife Bets, Bob and Marlene were young until Nathaniel could stand it no more.

Hoping to avoid any family war stories, assuming the tales owed a good deal to John Wayne's version of events, he rushed Sandy out to the stable. Much discussion at dinner, when he could steer the conversation, concerned the selection of a horse for Sandy to ride that evening. Nathaniel had his own chestnut Quarter Horse named appropriately Rusty. A half-Arabian Quarter Horse mare named Zuleika was decided upon for Sandy.

Nathaniel led Rusty out of the stable first followed by the stable manager who led Zuleika in a circle around the stable yard as Sandy looked on. Both horses were saddled, fresh and ready for a pleasant evening's ride. The stable manager handed Zuleika's reins to Nathaniel, said a few words, laughed and returned to the stable.

Zuleika was a pride of the barn. The buckskin mare was smaller than the standard Quarter Horse with a fine wedge shaped head and straight nose showing her Arabian ancestry and a solid compact body of a Texas bred Quarter Horse. Her coat was rich cream with a dark chocolate brown nose, mane, tail and high stockings, all of which made her quite handsome. Being half-Arab Zuleika was an intelligent horse that would take Sandy out and back with little for her rider to do but stay on.

"What was that about?" asked Sandy.

"Come and meet Zuleika and I'll tell you." He ran a fond hand down the mare's neck. "She's a smart girl and not happy with a tight girth around her. She has only one bad habit. To keep the girth loose she sucks in air and blows herself up while she's being saddled. You have to walk her around to get her to let it go. Then we tighten the girth. If we don't the saddle will slip and over you go!"

"Are you sure she's safe?" Sandy was ever cautious around large equines who didn't have to do anything they didn't want to do.

"She'll be fine with you, that's why we chose her. Horses are thinking animals. Because she's half-Arab, you have to reason with her, no heavy handed riding."

Sandy walked carefully around the mare's head to stand by her left side, prepared to mount up. Zuleika offered her velvety soft nose, which Sandy touched softly and then ran her hand down the smooth coated neck. Speaking quietly she told Zuleika what a beautiful horse she was, always a good approach with a mare. A soft voice, light hands, no sudden movements, no flapping clothing, and certainly no tissues to blow around to spook the horse, Sandy knew the ground rules. She was also a capable rider in the saddle.

With foresight, Em insisted her children learn to ride both English and Western styles of riding. Sandy remembered her arguing, *It's like learning to drive both standard and automatic cars. You need to be flexible, depending on the situations in which you find yourself when in need of emergency transportation.* Bareback was also a fun option Sandy had yet to try on anything but a pony.

Like a gentleman, Nathaniel helped Sandy to mount up, to find and adjust her stirrups to the right length. On Zuleika's back the Western saddle was as comfortable as a rocking chair on the Johnson's front porch. Its dark, almost black, leather smelled of saddle soap. Not quite as fond of the smells of horses, stables and saddle leather as Em, Celina and Deanna, Sandy guessed they might grow on her, under the right circumstances, in the right company.

They rode out of the stable yard in the gathering dusk. It was earlier than Nathaniel had planned, but perhaps more time on the ridge in the dark would be a plus. He carried a rolled blanket behind his saddle and had snacks in a pack. At first, the dirt road leading towards the ridge was wide enough to ride side by side, which they enjoyed. Sandy was easy company and laughed appreciatively at his jokes, so different from Deanna who constantly tried to one up his humor.

When they reached the base of the ridge the dirt road continued on below the ridge off to their right, and a narrower trail went up towards the brow of the long hill. A broad valley extended away to their left. As the moon rose, the landscape around them took on the sharp definition of a well-made black and white movie. Shadows were deep, moonlit rocks and leaves on the brush stood out in high contrast. It was truly beautiful. The air was crisp and clean.

Before they had gone too far along the ridgeline Nathaniel judged Sandy might find the narrowing of the trail a challenge. Zuleika, of course, would be fine, but a narrow trail and a hesitant rider were not a good combination. When they came to a hospitable part of the trail with flat areas on either side, he stopped. Zuleika stopped on her own behind him. He dismounted and tethered Rusty on the right side of the trail by looping the horse's reins lightly around a bush. He removed the blanket and packet of snacks from his saddle. Zuleika stood patiently while he assisted Sandy to dismount. This gave Nathaniel the opportunity to have Sandy land in his arms. She promptly kissed him.

Zuleika turned her head to watch them. A moonlight ride might only be a bit about the scenery. The mare became impatient to browse the grass with Rusty and shook her head.

Nathaniel and Sandy stepped apart. Sandy reached out

for the horse's soft nose.

"She's really a dear, isn't she?"

"A dear with a mind of her own. I'll tie her up. Why don't you spread out the blanket? Looks like a good spot over there." Nathaniel pulled a flashlight from his pocket and passed it to Sandy along with the blanket. By the time he returned to the valley side of the trail, Sandy was seated comfortably on the blanket, and he sat down close beside her. They tossed the pack aside and began the negotiation of who liked what where. Generously endowed and with an affectionate nature, Sandy easily attracted followers. What she chose to do with them after had always been an issue. Since they had agreed in advance they wouldn't be kicking off their cowboy boots that evening, she felt freer to get to know Nathaniel. Sandy found she liked his touch, and Nathaniel certainly appreciated it.

Truth be told, they did sit up at one point to admire the valley decked out in the clear moonlight before them. A rumbling pickup truck was making its way up the trail. The air was beginning to chill. Clouds had appeared unnoticed by Nathaniel and Sandy dimming the moon's light. The shadows in the landscape around them were now dimly muted. There was the temptation to wrap themselves up in the blanket and loosen a few more pieces of clothing, but the horses started to stir. A chill breeze rustled the bushes and swept through the wild grass. Rusty stamped his feet and tossed his head, and Zuleika gave a short whinny.

"Feels like the wind's changed. We'd better get back." Nathaniel kissed Sandy once more. "Let's do this again soon."

"I'd like that very much," Sandy said as she rose from the blanket. Nathaniel crossed the path and returned with both horses. Sandy had the blanket rolled and ready to go. The snacks were entirely untouched. Nathaniel had his hands full and was holding the reins of both horses as Sandy prepared to mount Zuleika, who startled and suddenly moved sideways.

Arms clothed in night camo reached out for Nathaniel and pulled him away from Sandy who screamed, "No!" The man was taller and heavier than her escort. A black ski mask covered his face. Fingers extended, she prepared to go for the man's eyes when another man grabbed both her arms from behind and lifted her off the ground kicking and screaming. Nathaniel fought back as best he could, striking out and landing a punch on the man's jaw. In the growing darkness, the assailant wrestled Nathaniel face down to the ground, grabbed his left arm and twisted it up straight behind his back.

"Stop screamin' girlie or we break the kid's arm!" the man clutching Sandy barked.

It took her a moment, but she did stop thrashing. Thinking hard to herself, *I am not letting this happen again.* With all the venom she could summon Sandy yelled, "Don't you touch him!" She stamped down on the foot of the man holding her, putting all her strength into the chunky heel of Em's riding boot.

"Yow! Son of a bitch! Are you sure we have the right one? She's supposed to be the easy one!" protested the husky voice. He attempted to tie Sandy's hands behind her back with a rope prepared with a cinch knot.

"Who cares? Take her and let's get out of here!" replied a younger voice.

"Leave her alone!" Nathaniel struggled and kicked out at the man holding his arm. There was the sound like a pop and Nathaniel howled in pain.

"Serves you right, kid!" He let Nathaniel's left arm go, hauled him up and punched him squarely in the face. Nathaniel sank to the ground.

As loud as ever she could Sandy screamed, her voice carrying across the valley. It took two men to get her tied up securely and duct tape over her mouth. The horses, startled by the violence, fled off to the right side of the ridge trail. The ongoing assault on their riders blocked the horses' escape down the trail. The hill dropped off too steeply to the right for them to go down that way in the darkness.

The man with the rasping voice started to force march Sandy back down the trail heading for their pickup truck. The younger man had an eye for a good horse and saw no reason not to appropriate two if he had a chance to do so. He attempted to approach Zuleika who was thoroughly alarmed and caught up her dangling reins, jerking the bit in her mouth. The mare flattened her ears back down against her head. She backed away hard and fast, like a cutting horse with a calf on the other end of the rope, and pulled him stumbling forward. Once she had him off balance, Zuleika struck out with one well-shod hoof and clipped the man on the arm. With a yell he fell back. The mare took off past him down the trail towards the ranch.

Rusty had other ideas, a powerful animal he reared up over the younger man who had the horse sense to run like hell after his partner and Sandy. Rusty came back down to the ground snorting. The horse let out one long challenging call and chased after the fleeing men. The horse stopped short as they sped away in the pickup truck. One man was driving, the other was in the back of the truck with the bound girl.

The stallion saw his quarry was fast departing and trotted back to where Nathaniel lay stunned on the ground. The Chinese have a saying, found in the *I Ching,* an ancient book of wisdom used for divining fortunes, to the effect of "if you lose your horse, or it runs away, don't chase it. If it is truly your horse, it will come back on its own." Rusty was Nathaniel's horse. Lowering his head he snuffled at Nathaniel's cheek and nudged him until

Nathaniel protested. "Rusty, enough!"

Grabbing a hold of Rusty's stirrup, Nathaniel pulled himself up and managed to stand beside the tall horse. Getting himself into the saddle would prove to be no easy feat. Without much hope Nathaniel said, "Down, Rusty, down." He had tried to teach Rusty to get down on the knees of his front legs and bow his head. Rusty refused to learn. Roy Rogers's palomino horse Trigger did this trick often.

This time the chestnut horse went down on his knees, immediately making it possible for Nathaniel to mount onto his back without having to use his arms to pull up into the saddle. Once his rider was in the saddle, the horse rose from his knees without being asked, and all Nathaniel had to say was "Home, Rusty." The horse started off at a brisk walk, but Nathaniel cried out involuntarily as the gait jostled his arm. Rusty took it slow and easy down the ridge trail after that.

Having liberated herself from the hateful men who hurt her gentle rider and Rusty's boy, Zuleika picked her way carefully down the ridge trail as quickly as she could safely do so. Horses are obsessively careful of their long thin legs. It was not too long before she reached the dirt road and could speed her pace. When she arrived in the stable yard, there was no one about. She stood in the center of the yard and whinnied her alarm into the air.

The stable manager was in the tack room repairing a harness. Hearing Zuleika's shrill whinny he dropped the harness on the floor as he ran for the stable door.

In the ranch house, Grandfather was engaged in rereading *Patton*. "Zuleika!" Johnson Senior exclaimed as the heavy biography of the famed World War II American general snapped closed.

A horse coming back riderless was a sure sign of trouble. Zuleika was shaking and stamping her feet with impatience. The stable manager tried to quiet the mare, but she would not let herself be led to the barn. She wheeled around and faced towards the dirt road in the direction of the ridge. After a quick meeting with Johnson Senior, while the mare fidgeted, the stable manager mounted Zuleika. He let her have her head intending she would lead them back to Sandy and Nathaniel. Johnson and one of the other men started up the vintage Jeep to follow.

The injured Nathaniel on Rusty were found as they left the ridge trail and were joining the dirt road. In hurried phrases Nathaniel told the men what had happened, that the assailants took off back up the dirt road away from the ranch house. It was quickly decided. Johnson would pursue the men in the pickup. Zuleika and her rider would escort Rusty and Nathaniel back to the ranch. There was no reliable cell phone service out this far. It was unavoidable, calls for assistance would have to wait until they reached the ranch.

15

CAPTURED

———◆———

SANDY WAS NOT blindfolded. There was nothing to see and it was too dark to make out any recognizable differences in the countryside around her. The man in the back of the pickup with her tried to hold her in one place by gripping her shoulders. But the two of them bounced around so badly both had a bruising ride. It seemed to last forever, although it was not a long time. The pickup sped down the rutted dirt road, then swung onto another one in a marginally better state of repair. Their destination did not seem to be a great distance from the ranch, and they never left the back roads.

The far from new pickup truck came to a halt in front of a wood frame house with no lights. The truck lights were quickly turned off, but Sandy did manage to see a barn with little paint and a door swinging on one hinge facing an old house across an overgrown yard. The masked men hustled Sandy out of the truck across the yard, up several creaking steps into the house. Sandy thought, *I am not going to pee my pants again, this time it's going to be different.* As they dragged her through the door, she saw the lock had been broken and the door forced. The house appeared unoccupied and consisted of two rooms side by side separated by a narrow staircase leading to the second floor.

Sandy did her best to make life difficult for her captors and went totally limp to create a hard to drag body. In the process of crossing the unfinished floors she picked up a few splinters in her fanny and in her calves. The masked men hauled her into what might have been a sitting room. The furniture was plain and some appeared to be handmade from planed wooden boards and straight tree branches. When they turned on the light, Sandy saw one bare bulb dangling from the middle of the ceiling. A table in the center of the room was flanked by the only factory made wooden chair. It was an armless side chair with tall spindles and a curved round top. It certainly looked less substantial than the Adirondack chairs in the backyard at home.

The men seemed to have misplaced the length of rope meant to secure her to the chair and the younger man went out to the pickup truck to get it. The older man held onto Sandy until the rope appeared. Having been mugged, bound and gagged once recently, Sandy had a unique perspective. She gauged her captors as less professional and certainly inexperienced. The use of rope gave her hope. They dropped Sandy onto the chair, only to discover her hands were tied behind her back and they could not get them tied behind the chair without untying her. An argument ensued with some pushing and shoving. With growing interest, the girl watched the interaction between the two men.

The younger man dressed in dark clothes had a long rip across the knee of his jeans and wore a ski mask which he scratched at every opportunity, perhaps hiding a beard. The older man had a gruff raspy voice and a smoker's cough. Both had work roughened hands and wore no gloves. The body language seemed to indicate a close relationship, perhaps even family.

To untie her hands, they loosened the cinch knot that tightened every time she struggled against it. When her arms were pinioned behind her chair and a knot retied, she did her best to keep the wrists apart. They wrapped the length of rope retrieved from the pickup around Sandy's ribs as she was seated in the chair. Stealing an idea from the clever Zuleika, Sandy sucked in a lung full of air and arched her back away from the chair as far as she dared.

The men then proceeded to try to tie Sandy's legs together with another section of rope. The legs of the chair were thin, and it creaked loudly as Sandy shifted her weight trying to give the impression she was resisting them. First, she got one leg free and stuck it out in an attempt to kick the younger man while the older man struggled to hang on to her other leg. She settled down as both legs were tied together and concentrated on keeping her boots apart and the items stashed there undiscovered.

The older man grunted and stood up. To her surprise he pulled a battered piece of paper out of his pocket and squinted at it. *I can't believe it*, she thought, *I've been kidnapped by a jerk who needs a cheat sheet.*

"Okay, we've got to ask her questions," he rasped.

"You gotta take the duct tape off so she can answer," itchy face replied. He stepped forward and grabbed a corner of the tape covering Sandy's mouth and yanked it free.

Sandy was prepared for this, and she roared, "Damn you! I hate duct tape! You ripped my mustache off!" She thought, *Or would have if I had one.*

"What did she say?" The younger man was appalled.

"How would you like it if I plastered duct tape all over your chest and ripped it off?" Sandy started spitting around her as if the duct tape had left a bad taste in her mouth. She wasn't as proficient as Deanna with this skill, but her captors were more easily put off.

"Are you sure we have the right girl? We were supposed to get the scared one," said the younger, taller man.

This settled it for Sandy, she determined to get herself the hell out of this. Although she knew she wasn't as capable of certain things as Deanna, she had a good head and was prepared to use it.

"What's your name girlie?"

"Matilda Louise. What's yours?"

"Yeah right, Matilda. It doesn't matter anyway. We ask the questions. You answer and we'll leave you here to maybe get found."

The older man stepped towards her and raised his hand making a threatening gesture. Sandy realized this man was not about to hit a girl first like her assailant in Connecticut and noticed killing her was not on his to do list.

Looking down at the folded note paper he said, "What did she find in the house?"

"Who do you mean and what do you mean?" she said with exaggerated patience, a bland look on her face.

The man checked his paper again. "Looks like Mrs. Hubert."

"Oh, not this again, it's Huber. She's not Mrs. Huber any more. She divorced Travis Huber."

"Shit, you're kidding?" the younger man said. "Fuck this."

"Listen you guys, it's like we told the guy who tried this back in Connecticut. She didn't find anything. She doesn't know what she's looking for. Alright? The answer hasn't changed."

"What do ya mean the other guy?" The older man grunted.

"This guy attacked us in the backyard in Connecticut. He tied us up like now. He asked us the same stupid questions. Only the feds came and rescued us. Of course, he's dead now. The people who hired him killed him. I got a text about it, actually more than one."

The younger man showed unhappiness with this by

tugging the chin of his mask hard as if pulling on a scraggly beard. "This is bullshit. What's she talking about?"

The older man shook his head.

"He got out of jail on bail, and they killed him before he could get out of town," Sandy repeated herself with good effect. *Idiots,* she thought.

"Are you telling the truth? We can leave you here forever," the older man growled.

"Why would I lie about that? You can check it on the Internet. It was written up in the papers." Sandy paused. *These men are not fast on the up take.* The men glared at each other. They moved off into a corner of the room as she watched them huddle in serious discussion. She waited patiently.

"You won't have any trouble finding it on the Internet. He turned up in a block of cement that got washed up by the storm." Sandy added helpfully, "I probably just saved your lives."

"Alright, we're going to get this over with." The older man advanced on Sandy. Her chest tightened. Her heart skipped beats and seemed to pound. "You gotta tell that Huber woman she has to leave it alone or she'll be next! Forget about it! Whatever the hell *it* is!"

Sandy sucked in a breath. "You mean you don't know what it is either? How come nobody knows what the freakin' thing is? I want a lawyer!" she yelled as loud as she could.

"This one's crazy. What the hell good would a lawyer be?" The younger man was pacing back and forth around Sandy, absentmindedly scratching the crotch of his jeans. He lowered his voice. "They're not paying us enough to end up in cement."

"Shut up!"

Both men stared at her. "Put the tape back on her mouth. I gotta make a call. See if we can't find out what the hell's going on." The older man let out a deep wet lung smoker's cough.

"If he spits that up, I'm going to be sick on your toes," Sandy remarked in a low voice to the younger man, who was not enjoying it either.

As the younger man plastered the same piece of duct tape over her mouth, Sandy let her jaw drop. Then the door slammed behind them. She was left sitting alone in the room with the light on. From what she could over-hear, it seemed they were checking for directions, and there might be only a few minutes to work with.

First, she forced every bit of air out of her lungs, then flattened her back against the chair and shimmied the rope down around her waist, which made life more com-fortable. Struggling with her boots, pulling the left foot out she wriggled the ankle past the rope. Along with her foot came the small object wrapped in her bandana. Right handed, she was also right footed. One foot free, the other came out easily. Two items tumbled to the floor. Using the left foot to hold the bandana down, she worked the small key fob out of the cloth and flipped it over. Stepping with the right big toe she depressed the small alarm button. A tiny red light began to blink.

Out in the other room an argument started. Sandy turned sharply towards the door and experienced a moment of panic. A flash of heat ran through her body. If the men returned to the room, she had a red checked bandana and several objects on the floor in front of her. Gently she nudged the key fob back into her boot with her toes.

Raised voices in the next room signaled trouble, the men were unable to reach their contact and cursed the unreliable cell service. "In the truck, you freakin' fool. Call on the CB." House lights went off. Frozen in place, toes curled around the fob in her boot, she listened as her abductors left the house, trudging down the sagging front steps.

Sandy couldn't believe her luck. The room was dark with only a trail of moonlight from the front and back windows. If they'd left the lights on the men would have been able to see her through the window if she managed to get out of the chair. Working as quickly as she could, she tried to haul around the knot that held her to the chair to her hands to untie it. That did not work.

She leaned back in the chair raising the front legs off the floor stressing the back of the chair, exactly the way Em told them not to at home. The chair creaked and the back began to give. *Eureka*, she thought. *Instead of getting me untied, I'll get the chair off of me.*

Using the surge of adrenalin, she grabbed two of the long spindles that formed the back of the chair and pulled upward. The chair only creaked under the strain. Frustrated, she slumped back down, took a deep breath, put both feet on the bottom rung of the chair and pushed with both feet and pulled with her arms as hard as she could. The rung cracked, and then she felt the back of the chair move, one side and then the other came loose from the solid wooden seat. Grabbing the back of the chair tightly, she rocked it back and forth and yanked it free. Suddenly the rope at her waist was loose. Careful to avoid dropping the back of the chair with a crash she lowered it to the floor and let it go.

Her maneuvers left her in her socks, sitting on the backless chair with her hands tied behind her back and the rope around her waist. She felt around on the floor in front of her until she found her Swiss Army knife. Standing up on one foot, she picked up the knife in her toes, turned around and raised the knife to place it on the seat of the now backless chair. Remarkable how handy feet could be. From there it was easy to bend down and grasp the knife in her hand. Using one of the short sharp blades she sawed at the rope. Care for the undersides of her wrists slowed her progress, but the blade was sharp and severed the rope.

Now free of constraint, Sandy was anxious to be away before the men returned. She ripped the tape off her mouth. It wasn't stuck nearly as tight the second time around. From the floor, she picked up the small cell phone and the key fob. She hesitated, then grabbed her boots and ran to the back window. The latch was rusted, but one of the knife blades came in handy to dig one side of the latch out of the window. The weathered wood gave way to her efforts. The window came up, and she climbed out into the night air.

Sitting, waiting before the men left the house, she'd been planning an escape route, only to discard the idea of running down the road, back the way they had come. It would be too obvious which way she might go to the men who brought her there. In stocking feet she circled the house moving away from it, up behind what might have been a garden and into a stand of bushes. She considered sneaking into the barn or around back but realized it might mean being caught crossing the beam of truck headlights. Instead, she retreated behind the house to a small rise. A position on the hill gave a view of the pickup truck and down the road. Hiding behind a scrub bush, she sat down to catch her breath. To camouflage her face she tied the bandana around her neck like a mask.

Less afraid of what might be on the ground beneath her stocking feet than she was of the men in the truck, she hunkered down. These were Texans from their voices, and she was not willing to see them angry. Someone wanted answers, and she had been unable to give the anticipated response. Most probably that person arranged to kill the man who assaulted her and Deanna in Connecticut. She wasn't about to be around when whoever that was came after these two men.

The key fob was in her hand, its tiny light blinking red. From the Spring House, the satellite was located in the sky to the southwest, but this was the southwest. In the palm of her hand she held the key fob straight up to the night sky. The night was so very still around her — no background noise from a highway or planes overhead. From the truck men's raised voices echoed against the silence.

When she lowered her hand the tiny light on the key fob blinked green, message sent and received. She heaved a sigh so loud she feared it must carry on the chill breeze. Voices from the pickup continued to carry up to her on the hill. If she kept low and moved around the bush she could see the pickup truck. More money was demanded and also a refusal to hurt her. Travis Fucking Huber's name was shouted aloud. *Well, at least he's good for something,* she thought. While the argument in the truck raged on, Sandy got the rope off her boots and was of two minds whether to put them back on. Her boots would leave a recognizable trail while her feet covered with socks left very little trace on the ground.

Time seemed to pass slowly. Her stomach rumbled. They had forgotten the snacks, she and Nathaniel had other things to do. In her mind she wandered back to the ridge, and she could hear Nathaniel scream in pain all over again. He was alive when they left him, she was sure, but imagined all sorts of complications. Em Huber sent them to Texas to keep out of the harm's way, she knew that now, and it brought disaster to her dream date. Typically female, she blamed herself with a barrage of would have, should have thoughts, followed by resolutions, including — be more flexible, go to gym classes, not just read on the treadmill, until she heard the truck doors slam. The men were returning to the house. Without hesitation she crawled on hands and knees into the bushes.

The lights went on in the house. Shouts of alarm and yells to find a flashlight split the night air. A man's head appeared out the back window and his body followed. But unable to find a trail even with a flashlight, he headed around the house in the opposite direction to the one Sandy had taken. He headed towards the dirt road and was met at the front of the house by the younger man. To Sandy's astonishment, they went to search the barn. In the distance she heard the noise, at first indistinct and then the recognizable sound of a rotor. With a grin, she pressed the small button labeled BCN on the key fob. A steady green light appeared above it. The key fob emitted a beacon, a steady tone, in addition to the emergency distress call.

In the helicopter above the Texas countryside and in Josh's apartment in Massachusetts the signal was received. Sandy was beaconing to her rescuers to enable them to find her location precisely.

Her abductors were searching the barn and that delayed the realization they were about to have unwelcome visitors. Two men raced out of the barn to see a chopper heading up the dirt road towards them. They ran for the pickup truck, but the helicopter was coming in for a landing directly in their path.

Four heavily armed Texas Rangers jumped from the helicopter as it landed in the middle of the dirt road. As Sandy watched from behind her bush on the hill, two of the Rangers ran towards the pickup to round up the now armed men. The older man in the driver's seat started the pickup with the intention of circling around the yard. Warning shots were fired overhead. One of the rangers stationed by the helicopter took aim at the truck tires and fired. Seeing escape was cutoff and their chances of survival were grim if they continued, the older man brought the pickup to a stop. It slewed around on flat tires.

Two Rangers yanked the truck doors open and pulled the masked men out into the yard. The older man went down on the ground. Two of the Rangers headed for the now lighted house where they found the broken chair, a strip of duct tape and the rope Sandy cut from her hands with traces of blood on it. One of the Rangers grabbed the younger man and slammed him back against the truck. He ripped the ski mask back over the younger man's head revealing a narrow face with a scraggly dark brown beard streaked with auburn. "Well, look who we have here. Anxious to go back inside?"

"Mother Fucker! I'll get a good lawyer this time," screamed the younger man, proving he wasn't as dim as Sandy assumed.

"The girl's not inside!" yelled a tall black Texas Ranger with a rifle cocked and ready, the short length of rope in his gloved hand. Up on the porch step he stood scanning the surrounding yard. "Back window's open but only large boot tracks leading out."

"Where is she?" The Ranger stuck his gun under the younger man's nose.

"She got away. We don't know where she is."

The Ranger tightened his grip on the man's neck.

"I swear!"

Sandy stayed under cover until she was sure the men were secured. Then, she stood up and came out from behind the bush, turned on her cell phone and held its lighted screen up towards them to show her position. The helicopter pilot spotted her light first.

"Hey, over there. Light on the hill."

And then Sandy, triumphant, marched down the hill still carrying her boots to meet her rescuers. She pulled down her bandana mask and grinned at the Rangers. Her first request was for Nathaniel.

16

ARMOR OF SILENCE

ONE EARLY MORNING call from Texas with Deanna, and briefly with Sandy, the reluctant celebrity, and Marlene settled matters for Em. Everyone was safely recovering from their ordeal. Sandy and Nathaniel would be meeting with the Rangers and the sheriff in the morning to make formal statements. Marlene and Em agreed to talk later in the afternoon about plans for the girls' return. The time difference of one hour gave Em a head start on her tasks for the morning.

The call had taken place as the sun began to lighten the deep blue of the night sky in the East. Deanna was relieved and ebullient. "Mom! Mom! Sandy's fine! Texas Rangers brought her back to the ranch. Aunt Marlene's making her take a shower. She's all covered with dust and dirt, and she's got slivers in her butt from being dragged across the floor of an old house. Aunt Marlene was going to pull them out herself, said she'd done enough buckshot in her day to know what she's doing."

"I'll bet she does, Dee."

"But Millie called the doctor, and she's coming out to do it and make a formal report. We can't wait to read it. Imagine, Mom, six slivers in left cheek and three in the right cheek…"

"Oh Deanna, so many? That must really hurt."

"Yeah, Sandy said she didn't notice it much until she sat down in the SUV on the ride home. Millie's going to write a press release for Aunt Marlene to give later this morning after they talk to the sheriff and everybody."

Deanna kept up a detailed narrative of Sandy's abduction, escape, rescue and current condition to which Em had little to do but add an occasional prompt, "and then what happened," whenever Deanna paused for breath. It seemed as soon as Sandy and her Ranger escort came within range of a cell phone tower she called Deanna and began a detailed narrative that did not stop until she reached the living room of the Albrecht ranch house. Sandy's one regret — she was not allowed to ride back in the helicopter with the Rangers.

"Nathaniel is going to be fine. Sandy can't wait to see him." Deanna sighed. "Maybe if we'd been able to make it a double date, this wouldn't have happened. It was so scary."

"I know. But it could have been worse, and someone could have been badly hurt. You couldn't know this was even a likely possibility. I didn't anticipate it either, and that may be the point. Find the weakest spot. Do the least likely thing."

"Mom, we need to talk about the case."

"Not yet Deanna, tomorrow, dear. We'll talk tomorrow. I have to think things out first. Let's talk again soon, when Sandy can come to the phone. One thing, no social networking on this. Not a word. Promise me. Postings are probably how Sandy and Nathaniel's plans were discovered."

"Oh, right, I didn't think of it. Oh, Mom."

"Don't 'Oh Mom' me. I'm serious. You know the drill. You both need to go silent. Wireline communications only, to home only. No texts. No emails. No social networking. No calling friends. And no credit cards. Silence is your best defense. Remember the old saying, 'Loose lips sink ships.' True then, true now."

"But Mom, everyone will want to know all about it…."

"They can wait. We have to consider everything we do as confidential from now on. You are off the Net, my dear, both of you. It's important to let the police make the statements and to let them control the details given out. Understand why?"

"Yes, Mom, gotta go. The sheriff needs to speak to me."

"Have Aunt Marlene call me, Deanna."

17

TARTAN FOR BREAKFAST

HALLORAN HAD BREAKFAST in clothes from the away bag he always kept handy in the trunk of his car, a white tee shirt and dark green tartan plaid boxers. He'd rejected "tighty whiteys" for the breakfast table.

"I'd offer to join you in the shower but I have work to do." Em smiled into her coffee cup. She was wrapped in a soft bathrobe over a tank top and flannel sleep shorts. Seeing the usually dignified Halloran come down to breakfast in his boxers amused her and suggested he might be a comfortable man to have hanging around the house. The thought of someone coming to the door and Halloran doing his best to sprint upstairs for cover made her glad it was only 6:30 in the morning. Huber never came to breakfast other than fully dressed, boots on, and expected her to do so as well.

Left alone after breakfast, she lingered over coffee. The Canadian bacon and eggs were long gone, and it was time for another scone and a serious sit down. Questions came to mind. The discipline of intelligence work reasserted itself — ask many questions, work to find answers, note the details, organize and analyze to recognize the patterns. Em was inordinately fond of spreadsheets, but once information was digitized in a computer, it was vulnerable to theft. Instead, she sought out a long yellow legal pad and set to work.

The first question was easily answered, how had abductors known exactly when Sandy and Nathaniel would be out alone under the stars down a long dirt road that night in Texas. Social media. Both posted their plans two days in advance and spread the news among their friends. This indicated access to a "friends" account, perhaps as a masquerade. Pulling down the friends list for both might find a screen name but not identify the guilty party. It would take precious time. With so many ways to be somebody else on the Net, Em preferred to keep on listing questions.

All clean and polished, Halloran came downstairs looking ready to take on a day at the office.

She expected denims and boat shoes but saw a crisp white shirt and pressed khaki pants. Em was still in soft flannel pants, tank top and bathrobe. *No fun and games this morning*, she thought.

"I'll need to go into the office to take reports from Texas."

"Before you go, come see what I've found. Internet savvy suspects, they must have a search program running on us, like a bot or a web spider. I have one I use. It picked up notice of George Waitely's promotion a few months ago."

"I'm familiar with the concept."

"I'll just bet you are. The government is always accused of patrolling the Net, and they would be silly if they didn't. Probably have whole rooms full of people doing it day and night in any written language." After a once over glance her gaze returned to the laptop screen. Her sensitive nose caught the scent of soap and aftershave.

Halloran chose not to comment. At the office a secure back room full of talented analysts trolled the Net.

"Which brings up a question. How do you search for a non-written language stored in an audio file? Like the

Code Talkers using the Navaho language in World War II?" Em teased him and truly didn't know how it could be accomplished.

"Not now, Em, keep on topic," Halloran stored the question in his memory, sound files, check on this.

"Okay." Em pulled her attention back to the task, away from the scent of his aftershave and his enticingly damp presence before her.

"The program they're using must be capable of pulling out the Texas newspaper coverage. It's perfectly simple. Here's the page from the local newspaper covering Marlene's announcement of her candidacy, full color picture of Sandy, Deanna and Nathaniel, who's looking quite interested in Sandy, to my eyes at least. The social section has an article on the girls' visit to the ranch. If we look at Sandy's personal page, we'll see she posted the plans for the moonlight ride in glowing detail."

Halloran leaned over her shoulder to stare at the screen.

"But, you have to tell me, Michael, does the typical perp use the Net like this?"

"A professional might," he replied.

"If this pattern holds, I think I know how we can find them. They are after technical specs and use technical tools to track us. Dirty jobs are hired out, sometimes to less than competent people like the two yahoos in Texas. Probably because they're not in the kidnapping and murder business and have few or no connections with people who are. I'll bet you when we do find them, we'll be looking at an executive type with higher level connections. Kirbee was right to hire me for this." Em reached out for his hand.

"I never doubted it," Halloran admitted.

"Did I remember to tell you I figured out why they marketed the three separate products based on SunSpryte Version 3?" These were the early non-classified plans stolen before the improvements and classified innovations were made for Version 5. *I know very well I haven't told him, but now's a good time, or not.*

"No, left something out, did you?"

"Well, not exactly. I was going to tell Frank Kirbee the afternoon he disappeared. And I didn't know what help it would be to the investigation when I first met you." She looked up at him sheepishly.

"Go on, Em," he said while admiring the line of her neck as it reached from her chin over her collar bones down into her bathrobe to a pretty cleavage.

Em was torn between wanting to be taken seriously as an investigator and reaching over to investigate the source of the scent drawing her attention to him.

"Here it is. I think they are field testing the product. On the websites of all three of the companies making the knockoff products there are the unusual guarantees. The warrantees are barely there, six months only. But the guarantees for replacement of defective units not only extend for eighteen months, if the defective unit is sent back with a completed questionnaire, in detail, the sender gets both a new unit and a fifty-dollar gift card. I've never seen anything like it."

"So what are you saying?"

"Like they're saying, here play with this, and when it breaks send us a full report. A group with extensive business knowledge and connections executed this. Somebody stole SunSprite Version 3, and they decided to bang it to the wall to get as many of the flaws out of it as possible. The group chose retail sales to do it, therefore we're looking for a scientist in the solar industry with retail experience.

"Grant money is tight," she continued. "Kirbee couldn't afford to do field testing this extensive in three geographical areas. The partners fixed the major flaws with Version 4. Professor Hussein went on to develop Version 5, which is the software or whatever they are searching for now."

"You mean to tell me they're wanting to steal a classified project for commercial gain?" Halloran's eyes darkened. This was not going to succeed on his watch.

"Well, it is industrial espionage, that's often what it's for. This is America, all for the all mighty, all powerful dollar." She laughed regretfully.

Halloran growled, suppressed anger coming from the tall man beside her. After a life in service to the country, he had little understanding and no patience for those who put money above all things.

"Michael, it all fits together. It's a consistent pattern of industrial espionage, successful and undiscovered. There is a profit, but it doesn't appear to be a large one. These are their tactics and what the thieves have done with their prize. Now, we need to anticipate their strategy."

"If they went to all this trouble to acquire and field test Version 3, they must have the capability to develop a corrected version. Probably in a research and development lab at the parent company, Transaxia. You might look for it there."

Raiding Transaxia had already occurred to Halloran's people who were working to build a case strong enough to get a warrant. Em's insight would give them specifics and a place to start looking. "So you think this is about developing a better product to market?" Halloran rubbed her shoulders.

"Possibly, but it wouldn't be a clean process. If they tried to patent it, Kirbee would find out. Since it is being developed under a government contract, they'd have a hell of a time defending a patent application. Suppose they use overseas marketing connections to shop the new product specs to a country where intellectual property rights are not respected?"

"One shot payment. No production expenses. No U.S. lawsuits. Greater return on investment is what you're saying." Halloran nodded.

"It's marketing. They want me off the case because I think the way they do. It takes one to catch one."

"Someone at Transaxia?"

"Looks most likely now." Em frowned. "Something's changed. Now there's overt violence. Maybe the buyer is pressuring them. Version 5 isn't finished yet, so they haven't been able to steal it. We've got to find Version 5 and Frank Kirbee before they do."

"Easier said than done, I'm afraid. He's gone dark. No trace. With his background it wouldn't be hard for him to disappear. None of his Army buddies have heard from him. One's dead. The rest swear he could call them any-time and they'd hide him. Vargas checked this."

"The threat of losing Version 5 scared Kirbee, though. Once the hardware is patented, it's public knowledge. It happens sometimes, a corporation won't patent a soft-ware innovation because they don't want anyone to know they have it. I expect the government does the same, right?" She raised her eyebrows, fully understand-ing there was no teasing this information from him.

"Em, you keep asking questions you know the answers to already. We call it classified information. I've got to get in to the office. Anything else you can think of you maybe didn't tell me?"

Em grinned and said sweetly, "No, dear, not right now." Halloran only half believed her, and she knew it.

All scrubbed and shaved, damp and smelling of after-shave, Halloran stood beside her, dressed and ready for work. Em rose, greeted him with appreciation, and couldn't resist taking a few little nibbles which led to some friendly gestures which managed to loosen her robe and almost had it off entirely. It took determination and some cooperation from Em for Halloran to get him-self out the door. Em thought, *I could keep that one.*

Anson had volunteered to meet him at the office so Halloran had time pressure to get there. He needed to follow up with Texas and coordinate electronic research. He planned to enlist several ingenuous minds in Analysis on the project.

WANTED — MOTHER HEN

As soon as Halloran was out the door, Em called Marlene on the wireline phone.

"Oh honey, I am so glad you called! You don't know what it's been like around here. I've had the sheriff and Texas Rangers in boots tracking dirt all through the house. And then we have the doctor in for Sandy. Such a brave girl. But she's not going to be able to sit down comfortably for a week. No riding for her."

"I heard about the slivers."

"Yes, and they were something, too," Marlene said with sympathy.

"How's Nathaniel?"

"Still in the hospital. Fixed his dislocated shoulder and put a cast on his wrist. They're keepin' him to watch for concussion 'cause he got hit pretty hard. His grandpa promised me to never let them go out again without a hand tagging along behind with a rifle." Marlene was indignant. "Don't know why he didn't think of it in the first place."

"There was no way Mr. Johnson could have known about the danger. That was the whole point, I think. To take us all by surprise."

"Still, your Uncle Bob would'ha had the sense to sneak a guard out after them."

This was not a point Em could win so she changed her approach. "You are so right, Aunt Marlene, that's *just* what I called to talk about. How can we get the girls home?"

"Well, they do have to stay here a while longer until the sheriff and those other fellows have finished investigating. Trampling all over my good carpets is what I call it."

"What would you think of changing their travel plans at the last minute, send them home by a different route for instance? Keep it all low key and quiet. No credit cards. All cash purchases from now on until they're home." Em paused. "And maybe provide them with a guard."

"I did think of sending Hank with them."

"I had something different in mind," suggested Em cautiously.

"I knew you'd have something to say about this, *dear,*" Aunt Marlene said into the phone.

"A bodyguard for the girls." Em waited for the response.

"You mean I should hire one of those private investigator fellows like you see on TV? It's not the money, I'll pay. All muscles and tattoos? Don't you think it would make them stand out too much?" Marlene did not sound enthusiastic.

"More like a mother hen with muscles. I can ask Deanna's boxing coach if she will go down and bring them back."

Marlene let out a laugh as big as Texas. "You do that, honey, and I'll pick up the tab."

18

HEADLINES

———◆———

A FTER A MOST pleasurable afternoon interlude on the couch with Halloran, Em made the mistake of stepping to her laptop. Her home office, comprised of a desk, padded rolling chair and printer on a two drawer file cabinet, was set off in the far corner of the living room.

Halloran was in the kitchen fetching his favorite Harpoon IPA, about to make Ben Franklin's ghost happy.

"Michael! Come here! You should see the newspaper coverage of Sandy's abduction. A reporter found out who Sandy's father is and wrote about his recent promotion. They think that's why she was taken. This is a disaster!"

Having spent the day in his office and receiving a thorough briefing from one of the analysts, Halloran knew exactly what the media reported. He was also apprised of the reports by the Texas Rangers and the local sheriff. Like most news media coverage, he'd seen nothing disastrous in it — an exaggeration for dramatic effect, some questionable grammar, a few spelling errors and more details than he would like to see released to the public. Clearly the local media had an inside source at the Albrecht ranch.

"What's so bad, Em?" Halloran came to stand by her side to read the screen over her shoulder.

"They found out Sandy is George Waitely's daughter. The article says he's recently been promoted to Vice President for Development at one of the largest software companies in the country. It's based on Long Island. Waitely commutes by boat from Stamford. They don't mention she hardly ever sees him. They wrote that she lives with the family of the ex-Mrs. Harley Travis Huber in a converted barn in the Connecticut woods. It's not a barn, it's never been a barn. I wish I'd changed my name to Magoo, anything but Huber."

Halloran smiled behind her back.

"Here's the thing, the article says she's the oldest child and only daughter of George Waitely, and that he has two step sons with his current wife."

Halloran said nothing. He waited.

"Sandy has a brother and a sister who went to live with her mother out of state. Maybe they got the details wrong and their source doesn't know about them. But, it says that Waitely's office confirmed this."

Em looked up at the quiet man standing by her side and continued. "I wonder if that means, if that's why Sandy couldn't go with her mother. She loves her brother and sister and wanted to move with them very much. When she first lived with us, after her mother and the children went home to Tennessee, I didn't know how I could take Sandy to a doctor or pay her medical bills. George Waitely arranged it. When she needed permission slips signed for school she mailed them to her father, who mailed them back. I never even spoke to him.

"Michael, suppose the article is right, suppose she is his only daughter, and that's why she couldn't leave the state," Em concluded.

"Court records of the divorce proceedings may be sealed, Em, concerning minor children and sensitive issues. Best leave it be," Halloran advised quietly.

"George Waitely is only obligated to pay in-state college tuition and college expenses. I've never seen a dime of child support and neither has she. I'm not concerned for myself, but she could have used money for music lessons and a good instrument."

"Let it go, Em. Don't open this up, for her sake." Halloran ran his hand across Em's shoulder.

"What do you know that I don't?"

"Trust me, leave this alone. It's a family matter. Let the Waitelys, father and daughter, work it out between them." Halloran looked very much like a father who'd been through a divorce with contested custody.

Searching for a way to change the topic, Halloran looked up at the pictures grouped on the wall over Em's desk. He spotted a vintage photograph of a handsome, hefty man in a turn of the twentieth century police uniform with its distinctive headgear. Broad shouldered with a deep chest, he looked almost too large for the uniform. The policeman stared out from the photograph with a direct and impatient gaze as if dressing up for a formal portrait was a sore trial.

"Who's the Keystone Cop?" Halloran asked Em referring to the comic disorganized policemen who were characters in the early silent movies made by Mack Sennett's Keystone Film Company in New York City.

"He's not a Keystone Cop, it's my Great Uncle Henry. He was a plain clothes detective in the Brooklyn Homicide Bureau."

"Maybe why he doesn't look comfortable in uniform."

"When I met him in his eighties, he was the biggest man I'd ever seen. Very tall. Broad. My mother told us when she was young he had to come up to Connecticut to visit them. They couldn't go into New York City to see him because he moved so often. They changed his phone number and the license plates on his car frequently because people were trying to kill him. One of his assignments was to chase Dutch Schultz, but of course,

Uncle Henry didn't get him. He was murdered instead.

"Remembering him, we used to laugh at James Bond's car, the one that changed license plates at the touch of a button on the dashboard. Uncle Henry probably had to get down and unscrew his license plates himself. I noticed the license plates on your car aren't always the same either." Em grinned up at Halloran who leaned on his cane next to her.

Halloran looked up at the portrait and back at Em, at the shape of her chin and the set of her eyes. "I can see a resemblance. If I were on the run, I wouldn't want either one of you chasing me. You know those two in Texas had a message to deliver to you, right?'

"Uh huh."

"Is it pointless to ask you to give up on this?"

"Yes, my dear man, it is."

He sighed in resignation. "Well then, let's put our wits together to catch him."

"I suggested that the first time we met at your office."

Halloran pulled a face. "'I told you so' is never a welcome comment."

"Let's think about who planned this, he... Or her. I asked myself, 'How would I do this?' The pattern, the strengths and weakness of the operation, it seems so familiar. As if…it's a woman." She paused, "This one's clever, has financial resources, tech savvy and organized. Also, significantly, can't seem to get good help when it comes to cheap thugs. We can be grateful she has no better connections. Meticulous planner, I swear it's got to be a woman."

"Women are not usually prominent in organized crime, Em."

"There are exceptional women in every field. Crime's no different, especially white-collar crime. Besides this is industrial espionage, and women make great spies. Think of Mata Hari."

Halloran frowned at her.

"I'm just saying, keep an open mind. In competitive intelligence you only need seventy percent certainty to call it, and I'm almost there. There's a missing connection."

19

WE NEED TO TALK

———◆———

SUNDAY WAS QUIET in the living room of the Spring House. Halloran was back from hours spent in his office and on the line with Texas.

"Michael, we need to talk."

"Now?" Halloran had a man's instinctive aversion to conversation opened by this womanly phrase. In his experience it was usually succeeded by a litany of his faults, errors, omissions, and assumed transgressions of an impossible to attain standard of male behavior. When married to Gillian, on the few times when he had made a true mistake, tantrums and tirades followed, punctuated by flying china.

"Yes, now before the girls get home." Em was seated facing Halloran on the Stickley couch. It was late afternoon. She took his hand in hers. Em's voice was soft and sounded worried. Based on previous experience, Halloran was concerned but not yet ready to run for cover.

"Since the phone call in the middle of last night, my family knows we were…" she paused.

"Sleeping together?" Halloran added helpfully.

"What Deanna figures out, she tells Sandy and Celina. Celina tells Josh. And now Aunt Marlene knows as well."

"You're embarrassed?" he surmised.

"I think we need to talk about where we're going with

this."

Halloran asked, "Is this the 'Do we have a relationship talk?'" *Could be worse.*

"I'm more worried I will embarrass you and compromise your career. If that's the case...."

"Wait a minute." He hadn't anticipated this.

Em didn't pause this time, she continued as if she just had to get it out. "What is this? Is it going to be an affair to remember? Once the case is over we're out of each other's lives? We've never talked about it. *We just did it.*"

Halloran put his hand over hers. "Yes, we did." He grinned.

"You get all wrapped up in the excitement of a new attraction, in the pleasure of the moment, and you can forget what you are doing has ramifications outside the bedroom."

"Or in our case the bed, the couch and the shower, and you had designs on the back lawn." Halloran teased, humor could deflect a lot.

"But don't you all have rules about this kind of thing?" she persisted. "If my kids know about us, your people are bound to find out. If it's going to get you fired or force you to resign, we should stop now. I can live with discretion, but I can't live with deception. People have told me I should never work in Marketing because I don't lie well."

"I won't ask you to," he paused, "unless absolutely necessary."

Em tried to pull her hand away from his.

"For national security I was going to say." Halloran knew he could lie like a fish (fishermen know this well), cheat and steal proficiently as his profession required, but he was basically a truthful man.

"How many times has national security been used as an excuse, I wonder?" she said, enjoying Halloran stroking the back of her hand, still grinning at her. "Be serious."

He thought a moment. "I could go for discretion. If certain people are aware of our relationship, there's no opportunity for blackmail. I'm just saying…"

"Michael!" The expression on her face changed to surprise.

"Are you married?" he queried, deciding to handle possible objections one at a time.

"You know I divorced Huber."

"Alright. I've been divorced for years, too. I'm not a general or an admiral, and I'm not up for Senate confirmation, or ever likely to be, Em. There's no one else who would be inconsolable if I never call again."

"But still…"

"And you? How about Stevenson of Geology?" he teased her with a motive, speculating on competition in the field for Em's affections.

"Cave man? No, thank you. I do like rocks, but I've had enough dinners with discussions of the substrata. He hasn't called back in any case." Em's expression hadn't brightened.

"You've been alone too long this afternoon and you've been worrying."

"If you tell me I worry too much, I'll shriek. I swear I will." Em squeezed his hand with a strength that surprised him, and his knuckles were feeling it. She obviously forgot lifting too many kettle bells gave Jill a strong grip, and she needed to go easy on her handshakes, too.

"What about your career? I don't want to derail it." Em would not be deterred before she had a satisfactory answer from him.

"Derail it? I'm perfectly capable of doing that myself. I have done it more than once." He hastily added, "without help from anyone else."

"I can walk away if I have to," she said quietly. Em held his hand and waited with a skeptical look on her face.

"Is that what you want, Em?"

Em looked down at their hands, fingers now twined together and replied softly, "No, but I can do it if it's for the best."

Halloran saw a fast change of tactics was needed. There was something on his mind as well, and he decided to go for it. "I've walked away from some myself, but you mean more to me. My running days are over."

She looked up at him expectantly.

"It's my leg. Field work is over for me. Eventually I may be able to walk without much of a hitch, but running is out. Even sitting in the office for a day is a real chore. I have to get up to walk around or it stiffens up."

"Can you take anything for the pain?" she asked with concern.

"Not on duty. Besides, I'd have to give up beer. You know what Ben Franklin said, 'Beer is proof that God loves us and wants us to be happy.'"

"So God and Ben Franklin want you to drink beer? Was Ben a friend of Sam Adams per chance?" Em quipped.

"Unindicted co-conspirators," he joked. "Listen, I retired from the Navy a few years back. That's another story. Went fishing for a couple months and was getting bored when a friend called about this job. My brief was to start up the agency, make sure it was strictly legal. It would only take a few years he said. I'd planned to hand the job over to Pete Leonard. It's not going to happen now."

"I'm sorry, Michael."

"My point is this. My career is behind me. This is my retirement job. If it needs to end, it can. It was supposed to be a limited term. I've had other offers to go into private consulting, even considered going into business for myself. There are extenuating circumstances here. Don't worry about it."

"I do worry. Harley blew up a promising academic career over an affair with an administrative assistant, and probably others, too."

"Em, our situation is different. Oh, by the way your security clearance has been updated."

"What? I didn't request that," Em responded in surprise.

"Frank Kirbee did it. He was always very thorough. Why are you surprised, Em? Did you read the non-disclosure contract and all the paperwork he asked you to sign?"

"Of course, I read everything. A habit really."

"Well, then you saw the clause that said security clearance might be necessary for some of the project."

She nodded in acknowledgement.

"You accepted payment, right? How did he pay you?"

"He paid me with a company check, which I cashed right away, just to be sure. I understood I wouldn't be allowed into the lab because I didn't have clearance."

"Right, well it's come through, and you were paid to be an investigator, on a subcontract. The original contract is with us, uh, the government." Halloran paused to observe her reaction.

"Does that mean I can go search the lab now?" Her eyes brightened as she anticipated another search and discovery mission. "It just struck me. Mrs. Howell Weiss warned me about government contractors on grants not knowing the source of their funding."

"It's been done already. The lab has been searched. Three times, and once by Andy Vargas who's good at it. He's thorough and he's ingenious." Halloran thought he had finally found a distraction that worked.

"When did the clearance come through, Michael? Before or after?" Em glared into his grey eyes.

For a moment Halloran considered playing innocent, but he chose the better part. "You asked me if I was a careful man."

"I meant…." she said ruefully.

"I know what you meant, and I am. And I was about this, too. The clearance came through before we slept together, if you must know." Halloran was rubbing her fingers slowly, deliberately, between his hands. It felt very good to her, especially the knuckles.

"Are you looking for a partner in your retirement?" she ventured.

"I think I've found the one I want. I probably should have said that right off, huh?" Halloran knew when he was licked and decided to enjoy it. He raised her fingers to his lips, looked deep into her warm brown eyes and watched to see her pupils dilate.

"It would have saved time. What am I going to do with you?" Exasperated, she'd had a few dubious moments in this conversation. As he looked into her eyes, she felt a rising sensation in her chest and a quiver inside. She could fight it. She knew she could back off. She knew she could throw him out and be done with it, but what she said was, "Oh, the hell with it."

"I can stay tonight so you won't be alone out here. I have to be at work early on Monday morning, my dear Em." This he said in a quiet voice as he eased a hand around her neck and gently drew her close.

20

HOME AGAIN

———◆———

LUCAS TURNED UP at the Spring House the day after Deanna and Sandy returned from Texas to take Sandy out for a long awaited supper and a movie. Sandy explained the presence of Halloran and Anson in the kitchen as visiting friends of Em's. Lucas readily accepted them. Around Em, he was on his best behavior, although he was reluctant to take off his shoes in the hall as Deanna suggested. Deanna was arch and she was teasing. Though Lucas knew he'd earned it, Deanna was a sore trial.

Lucas doubly tried when Mac, another of their high school friends, appeared unexpectedly at the house. Mac just happened by to see if Sandy was alright after her much publicized adventure in Texas. Sandy's time was spoken for by Lucas, which left Mac to lobby for an evening the following week.

A tall wide shouldered outspoken kid with long dark hair Mac had an unblemished face. Lucas always felt his few acne scars in comparison with Mac's determined good looks. Sandy preferred Lucas's not perfect, slightly rough cheeks, although he didn't know it. Lucas was now clear that acting like God's Gift to women had ended badly, in his case, with a trek through a swamp. Mac had yet to experience that kind of rejection and his tone towards Sandy said as much. He was confident of his appeal. Sandy had grown in his estimation to be worthy of him through her unexpected attachment to a highly successful, perhaps even wealthy, parent. Software development, stock options, corporate jets loomed up in Mac's fantasies.

Deanna looked at Mac with an interest she had not previously felt. The idea of a double date, supper and a movie taking her out for an evening away from the roost of her maternal parent was not unpleasant.

Sandy, conscious of her friend said, "Mac, why don't you come with us? Deanna can come, too. Right, Dee?"

Mac took a long look at Deanna in her tee shirt and jeans, and said, "Maybe next time. If we take the film critic here, we won't hear much of the movie. I remember the time we went to see the James Bond movie together, and all we heard was analysis of the stunts and the direction. Not to mention the acting. So at the end she says, 'I really liked the movie.' No thanks!"

Deanna became quite still, her face fell. Mac just laughed. This stunned Em who was about to step in when Deanna spoke up. "You'd better go find yourself someone nice and sweet who will say, 'Yes, Mac, No, Mac,' all night. I think I'm busy this evening." Deanna's voice was stony.

"Well, okay if that's the way you feel about it." Mac wasn't sure what to make of her reply.

Sandy whispered, "I'm so sorry, Dee." She took Lucas's arm and led them out through the hall, leaving Deanna standing on the living room rug, arms crossed, glaring at Mac's retreating back. Deanna flashed a look at her mother and headed wordlessly out the living room door to the garden.

Seated in the living room, Em, Halloran and Anson could not but hear the last exchange. Silence fell on the group until Anson excused himself to wash up. Once he was safely away, Em let out a long breath and turned troubled eyes on her companion.

"Oh dear, that's the second time in two weeks her self-esteem has taken a beating. She was so looking forward to seeing Nathaniel Johnson again, and it didn't work out, as we all know. And now this. I think Mac is only interested because Sandy is now known as Allesandra Waitely, daughter of George Waitely. He wasn't so interested when she was a girl left behind when her mother moved away with no money and limited prospects. He doesn't realize Sandy lives with us because she and her father barely speak to one another." Em was addressing Halloran.

Getting no reply Em said, "Maybe I should go out to Deanna." She sighed and started to rise from her seat on the couch next to Halloran.

"I'll go Ms. Huber." Anson was just returning from his errand. "If it's alright with you?" Em took a look at the expression on his face and nodded. The young agent was across the living room and out the door before she spoke.

"Oh! I wonder how much he overheard," Em remarked. Halloran reached over and held her arm to keep her seated by him.

"Dinner? Coffee? Desert? Something smells good, what is it?" he asked.

"Pot roast of beast. Since Deanna and Sandy were away for over a week, there was a little more money in the food budget this week. It's Black Angus pot roast. I bought it on sale at the butchers. Dessert will have to be blueberry pie and ice cream with those two in the house." She smiled knowingly. Em looked into Halloran's grey eyes and laughed softly. Halloran returned her laugh with a rusty chuckle of his own, which was a new sound for Em.

"I like any kind of pie. Especially yours, m'dear."

"What do you suppose he'll say out there?"

Intentionally casual Halloran remarked, "He'll be fine.

Anson's not exactly tongue tied. Don't worry about it, Em. He puts a foot out of line, and he knows he'll have to face me. Is there another Harpoon in the fridge? I think I'll go find out."

Sitting by herself in the living room, Em mused that she appreciated his protective instincts towards herself and her daughter. Protective instincts had not been high on Travis Huber's expressed qualifications for parenting. Em tried to sneak a look out one of the living room windows into the garden at Anson and Deanna without moving from her seat on the couch. All she could see was Anson's broad back as he stood in front of Deanna who was seated on one of the teak benches in the garden.

When Halloran returned with a bottle of Harpoon and a glass of flavored seltzer for Em, he found her leaning over almost flat on the couch, trying to improve her view of Anson and Deanna.

"Em, let it go for a while. Have something to drink with me." He gave her the bistro glass of sparkling pomegranate.

"You're right. It's time to plan the next move. I do believe it's time to find our friend Professor Kirbee." Raising her glass in a toast she said, "Here's to finding Kirbee alive, well and inventing."

———◆———

Deanna threw herself down on her favorite teakwood bench in the center of the hillside rock garden. The family meteorite poked its nearly black pockmarked top above the ground next to her. For Deanna sitting next to a hunk of old metal that had traveled so far to land in her backyard made her feel part of the universe above and around her. It usually made her realize her problems were small and fleeting. Deanna was looking up at the sky, tears starting in her eyes, trying to imagine the trajectory that brought the meteorite to her feet when Anson stepped out of the door onto the small stone porch.

Her attention was riveted back to earth as she watched Anson come carefully down the uneven stone steps from the house and walk towards her. He stopped a few feet directly in front of her and Deanna looked up at him mournfully.

"What's wrong with me? I say what I think. I can't take idiots seriously. I laugh too loud. Guys think I should be more feminine, does that mean I have to fake it? I can't fake dumb, and I can't pretend I don't understand what other people are thinking and feeling, when I do. I can't stand to see my friends bullied or insulted. And I don't forget and forgive quickly. Then there's my mother. I embarrassed her by spitting watermelon seeds all over the lawn. What's wrong with me?"

"Not much I can see," Anson replied in a low resonant voice.

"Yeah, you're just saying that to be nice." She sniffed.

"Deanna, you may be all the things you say, but you're also kind, intelligent and generous. Not many people would take in a friend the way you have. You're a feisty and sensitive person. That's not easy to be."

"Talented, you forgot talented."

"And you're funny. Sometimes very funny."

"No one wants to go out with me," Deanna protested with a moan and a sniff.

"I do," Anson replied.

Deanna looked up at the tall, broad shouldered man with a searching gaze. He was quite one of the largest men she'd ever known. "Thank you. You don't have to say that to make me feel better."

"I am trying to make you feel better. I'm also trying to tell you I like you the way you are."

To give herself time to process Deanna blinked rapidly. Seeing Anson as a friendly guy who used a wheelchair, then as an athlete capable of fielding a smoke grenade and subsequently as someone with a badge and a gun who rescued her, she was stunned. Her speculations about Anson during the plane ride to Dallas came to mind.

"Would you like to sit down?" This new view of Anson was worth investigating. Deanna moved over on the bench to provide room next to her. She hadn't quite moved to the end of the bench so Anson found he needed to sit close to her.

"What did you have in mind?" she asked, her sense of humor returning.

Ready for this one Anson replied, "There's a restaurant down on the west shore. It's right on the water. The seafood's supposed to be good. Live music. They import the lobsters from Maine. Not the same as the Five Islands shacks out on the water at home, but good enough. I've been wanting to try it. Would you like to go?" Left unsaid was the fact it was only a few blocks from his ground floor apartment. It was best to die another day on that one.

"When?" Deanna weighed the relative merits of pot roast or lobster, and the salve to her bruised feelings a dinner date with an attractive older man might provide. How could her mother object to an armed escort?

"When would you like to go?" Anson asked.

"How about now?" Deanna brightened.

"Now? Dinner smells awesome."

"It's pot roast. Treat me right and I'll invite you for leftovers." Deanna poked him in the arm playfully.

"Leftovers, Deanna, really?"

Realizing her strategic error in time, Deanna regrouped. "It's even better the second time, you can trust me on this."

Anson rested his arm on the back of the bench. She turned towards him and gave him a smile that could call him to her from across a crowded room. Since they were alone, he moved in to kiss her lightly on the lips. It was a pleasant friendly sort of a kiss. Deanna stayed close to admire the golden brown color of his eyes flecked with green and dark brown. Anson remembered to swallow first so he wouldn't slobber all over her like a happy St. Bernard and kissed her again. The kiss was still a little wet, but Deanna found the taste of it strangely intriguing and discovered she liked it. His arm drew around her closer and their tongues met briefly, tentatively and sweetly.

"I meant what I said." Anson was conscious that the old folks were at home.

"You mean dinner?" Deanna was dazed.

"Before that." Anson had both arms around her now.

"Ohhh…" She was not used to the warmth of his embrace, much less serious attentions. Flirting, exploring, teasing, playing around, and deciding whether she liked the guy or not, but courting with intent, not so much, never yet. The twenty something man with his arms around her might be older. For all his strength and experience, he was as vulnerable as she, for a whole set of reasons she did not yet understand.

Always her mother's daughter Deanna exclaimed, "I'm getting hungry. Let's go now."

Gazing towards the window, seeing them ready to get up from the garden bench, Em sat back.

"What's going on out there?" From his seat on the couch, Halloran's view was limited.

"A little pair bonding activity. You remember pair bonding?"

"Fondly. Intimately." He grinned at Em in a way that brought warmth to her cheeks and slowed her breath.

"They're not there yet." Em placed her hand on his chest.

By the time Anson and Deanna re-crossed the living room threshold, Em was in the kitchen and Halloran was seated at the kitchen table, right leg propped up as if he'd been there quite a long time altogether.

"Mom, guess what? Dave and I are going out to dinner," Deanna caroled happily. She had Anson by the hand.

"Tonight? What about my pot roast?" Em put up an obligatory protest, although it seemed her own prospects for the evening were suddenly looking up. "Where are you going?"

The restaurant Anson named was a good choice, both Halloran and Em agreed.

"Whose car are you taking?" asked her mother.

"Mom, can we borrow yours? I'll drive." Deanna smiled at a startled Anson. "I have to go up to change." Deanna took off upstairs to her room without waiting for an answer.

Left standing in a faceoff with Halloran, Anson held his ground.

"Take care of her. Keep it professional. Call in if you see anything suspicious," his boss ordered fully aware at least half of this warning was *pro forma* only.

Anson drew himself up straight to say, "Yessir, always," with warmth and determination.

"Good. Don't keep her out too late. Her mother will worry and she's had enough of that recently."

Anson heard tone of command in Halloran's voice. It took him a moment to digest this. He'd been expecting the possibility of a reprimand for unprofessional conduct not merely a warning.

In what for her was a short prep time, Deanna reappeared. Her makeup was perfectly understated. For the cool summer evening on the water, she appeared in black jeans and a charcoal grey finely knit top with three quarter sleeves. She hugged her mother impulsively and invited Anson to follow her out to the barn, which caused Em to raise her eyebrows and roll her eyes at the object of her own affections.

"I'm surprised you let them go. Don't you have rules about this sort of thing?"

"I told him to keep it professional. That's my respon-sibility. I'll see to it. As for telling them no, it wouldn't work anyway. Too young. She'll be going back to college soon, right? Let's not worry about a house on fire before we see more smoke than this."

"Very funny." She glowered at him. "At least this way we know where they're going for dinner. And we have the pot roast, blueberry pie and the house to ourselves."

"Let's eat before anything else happens." Halloran was savoring the mingled aromas of fresh baked pie and sim-mering pot roast that filled the kitchen and wished to do some pair bonding of their own.

Privately Halloran was not so sanguine about Deanna and Anson. He'd seen the look on Anson's face and heard the emotion underlying his voice. *If they become serious about each other, Anson hasn't had the job long enough to be thoroughly bitten by it. If it becomes a choice between the young woman in possession of his affections and the job, Anson is capable of chucking the job, taking the girl and heading back up the Interstate to Maine. If he did so*, Halloran reflected, *he wouldn't be the first man to have the direction of his life changed by the charms of a woman.* It was his pleasure to watch Em set their meal on the table before him.

———◆———

Dinner was a quiet companionable affair. The Black Angus made truly a grand pot roast, served resting in state on a stoneware platter among carrot chunks, peeled potato quarters, sweet potatoes and whole onions in a sauce of gravy. The gravy was redolent of bay leaves and fresh rosemary from the plants in the rock garden.

"Plenty of leftovers for next week," Em finished the last of her wine and pushed her chair back from the table.

"When would that be?" asked Halloran, hoping he might be asked for the encore.

"Two or three days. Would you like to meet this beast

again, sir?" Em asked with a smile. It felt satisfying to cook for someone who appreciated a good feed. "How about dessert in the living room?"

Without much thought, Em started to clear the table. Halloran had other things on his mind, but he put them aside temporarily to carry the heavy stoneware platter with the remaining pot roast into the kitchen. The sight of Em bending over the dishwasher to load the silverware and plates brought Halloran his opportunity. As if choreographed in an age old dance, Em rose and turned to face him as he moved in. He cornered her handily up against the kitchen counter. Pleased, she ran her arms around him and pressed her chest to his.

"Thank you for an excellent dinner," he murmured in her ear as he ran his lips down her cheek.

"If you liked dinner, you'll love dessert," she promised him.

"I'm counting on it. How long to do you think they'll be out?" Halloran nuzzled his way into the front of her blouse.

"No telling. That tickles you scratchy fellow!"

"Then we should have dessert soon, would you think?" He kissed her warmly enough and long enough to leave her in no doubt of his affection or his intentions.

"Shall I put water on for tea?" asked Em as she held him around the waist to rub his back above the kidneys. She could see him relax and feel his interest grow.

Halloran released her gradually. Regrettably he left his overnight kit in the car parked across the road in the barn. Bringing the bag in before dinner, with Em's family and guests all over the house, seemed less than discrete. Halloran wasn't a man to carry little foil packets in his wallet that might show themselves at inopportune moments. Having three boys in a household who were apt to raid their father's wallet while he was in the shower cured him. The best course seemed to retire to the living room and see how matters might develop.

He chose the long couch noting the pillows from all the other chairs in the room were now piled conveniently at either end. Clearly his fondness for the Stickley couch was growing.

Em busied herself in the kitchen thinking pleasant thoughts while she cut and served the pie and heaped on the home churned vanilla ice cream. They traded spring water for the ice cream with the dairyman's wife, and a good deal it was. She took down a large painted metal tray and loaded it with the pie plates, a teapot in which leaves of Assam were steeping, a small pitcher of milk, a bowl of crystalline brown sugar, spoons, forks and two Bennington Pottery mugs.

Picking up the heavy tray rattled the mugs against the teapot and clanked the silverware together. She made it into the living room barely missing a trip over Halloran's outstretched legs, landing the tray with a clatter on the coffee table and sat down next to him. His presence in her life was still so new even this closeness gave her a feeling of anticipation and excitement. As he watched her, heat spread upwards, her cheeks reddened as she poured the rich dark brew through the tea strainer. Em handed him his mug of tea and caught his gaze with a smile in her eyes.

Halloran was halfway through his piece of blueberry pie before he spoke. "Em, I've been thinking…" he started.

Oh, here it comes, she thought. *Business before play again. I'll have to sit on my hands if he keeps this up too long.*

"And?"

"When the girls go back to college you'll be alone out here in the woods. No close neighbors to see or hear you if there's trouble." He looked down at his pie. "This ice cream is very good."

"Homemade by the neighbor with the dairy. She's won prizes for her vanilla." Her eyes brightened, and she wondered, *Where can he be going with this line of inquiry? Would he offer to move in?*

"You heard what Sandy said about the assailant trying to warn you off the case."

Em nodded.

"You could be their next target. You may need twenty-four hour protection if that's the case." He paused. "I can only be around off duty, and it's unpredictable."

This was not going the way I anticipated. Em said quietly, "I'm not going anywhere, I'm staying right here. There's Josh's security system. My son's working on enhancements. Something novel he said."

"I'll bet, but that's not what I had in mind. We have a wounded warrior who could use some easy duty and a place to recuperate. We're not sure the sergeant will ever be able to return to full time duty. He's a good fellow. I think you will like him."

"Thank you for the thought, but I don't have a spare bedroom. Celina and Sandy share one already." Em tried to be gently discouraging.

"Jake won't need a room of his own, he can sleep in the hall if you don't want him in your bedroom," Halloran said cheerfully.

"My bedroom!" exclaimed Em.

"If you don't want the dog in the bedroom, he can sleep right outside in the hallway."

"Dog? You said wounded warrior."

"He was shot twice in a raid, the same raid where we lost Pete Leonard. They tried to kill the dog, too. He's a decorated veteran. Brave. What did you think I meant?" Halloran was puzzled, it was all clear to him.

"Someone like Anson. But, really, thank you for the offer. The medical expenses for a dog, I don't know…" Deanna and Sandy had been trying to persuade Em to get a dog for years but with the increase in the ability of veterinarians to treat canine patients had come increasingly expensive vet bills. "I can best afford only cats."

"The sergeant has medical benefits for as long as he lives. If he can't return to duty, he can be retired with a service pension for his upkeep. There will be a stipend for his expenses." This objection was anticipated and handled. The blueberry pie was finished with relish. He contemplated asking for seconds.

"But the cats, he'd scare the living daylights out of them," was Em's last ditch effort.

As Halloran raised his mug of hot tea to his mouth, he stopped in the midst. "Those two?" he said with emphasis.

Two pairs of cats' eyes stared back at him. Cleome had taken up a perch on the arm of Em's favorite chair, and Ash made himself at home on the hearth rug.

"Scare those two, not likely. Jake is trained to behave around other animals."

The descendants of the great cats of the Pharaohs looked well able to take care of the sergeant should he overstep his role in the household. Their philosophy — "Cats rule, dogs drool."

"I'd like you to meet the sergeant tomorrow. We can have his handler bring him over in the morning," Halloran said evenly, judging it best not to react to Em's surprise.

"Tomorrow morning? Why so soon?"

"It would be best to have him get used to the house, to your routines and to meet Deanna and Sandy before they go back to college."

"What if we don't like each other?"

"Miranda."

"Oh alright, but I'm just meeting him, no guarantees."

Through half closed eyes Halloran looked at Em sideways, smiled and thought, *She's a softy and Jake's a very good dog.*

Em considered the business meeting was now over.

Dessert was finished and she was ready for relaxation. She kicked off her flats, leaned back on the pillows at her end of the couch. Reclining gave her a full view of her friend at the other end. This pose was not working to her benefit. He was still drinking his tea. Unknown to Em, he'd decided he'd rushed her, and it was perhaps her turn. Em was thoughtful. She'd seen the sideward glance of the grey eyes, checking on her.

With only one glance and the faintest of smiles on his lips, it was enough for her sense of him, the pursuer wanted a little pursuit of his own. Em stared at him and gave him a winning grin, her eyes narrowed as she sat up with a graceful movement.

"More tea?" The good hostess moved down the couch towards him as if to pour herself another cup and came up beside him, shoulder to shoulder. "You want me to have the dog?"

"Yes, I can't be with you all the time. I think you will like him, and I know he will like you."

Her fingers ran down along his arm. Halloran put the mug down, leaned back on those strategically placed throw pillows and she followed him down. She owned a healthy female curiosity about human body parts she did not herself possess. And she was a nibbler. Given the chance, she would nibble on places where he hadn't often been nibbled before, which was remarkable for a man of his age and experience.

This evening with the limited privacy of the couch she started with his ear, nibbling and gently tugging at it. She progressed downward along his square jaw line to his Adam's apple, which seemed to hold a particular fascination for her as it was quite defined. She was earnestly nibbling on it when a beep sounded from the security panel on the living room wall.

"What's that?" Halloran asked as his hand made a pleasurable circle around her breast.

"It's nine o'clock. The security system is in night mode. Now I have to key in a code to let anyone in or they will set off the alarm. It lights up the doorbell so we can tell it is active from outside. We're locked in."

"Clever boy, your son."

21

THE SERGEANT SALUTES

———————

THE NEXT MORNING with Em's determined encouragement, Deanna and Sandy took the van out of the barn and pointed it to the nearest discount mall. It was time to complete the August ritual of back to school/college/fall weather shopping. Em cleaned the kitchen as she was nervously awaiting the arrival of her potential star boarder and his handler. When the doorbell rang she literally jumped as if she was expecting a ferocious beast. She dried her hands on the dishtowel and went to the front door, which she opened cautiously.

On her front step stood an admirably fit man in his thirties with what appeared to be a rather thin German Shepherd standing behind him.

"Haskins. Good morning, ma'am. Nice place you have here. Plenty of room for a dog."

"Should I come out or would you like to come in?" Em asked warily.

Haskins stepped aside. "This is Sergeant Jaeger of Saybrook. He's had a rough time and isn't as active as he could be." An exceptionally tall coal black dog with a baleful look in his brown eyes stared at Em. He was a distinguished looking dog with an intelligent face and tall straight black ears and a seemingly very long nose. The dog sat down.

"Come on Jake, show some spunk." The dog looked from Haskins to Em, without moving.

Em looked at the large sad eyes. "Is he in any pain?"

"He could be uncomfortable. He's had his meds for the day this morning."

"Is he friendly at all?" Em said softly. The dog's ears flicked.

"Oh yeah, probably too much so. At least he was before the shooting. He's off duty and I think he misses it," Haskins replied.

"Is he an attack dog?"

"Jake here is a finder. A real character, weird sense of humor. He finds things we want him to find, that other people don't want found. Sort of a jack of all scents." Haskins laughed at his own joke. "Jake's done bombs, dope and tracking people. Sometimes it seems as if he likes his work too much. He found us a field of marijuana once, we caught him sitting downwind when we burned it."

"He liked the smoke?"

"What I said, a real character."

Em couldn't hear much warmth in Haskins voice, and there seemed to be a strained relationship between dog and handler. Now she was concerned the sad looking creature was not going to be much of a companion, much less a guard.

"Should I try to pet him?" Em started her approach. She closed her right hand to present the back of it to the dog. In a soft voice she said, "You're handsome fellow. They tell me you need a place to rest up and get better."

Jake stepped forward to sniff the back of her closed hand that smelled of dish detergent and chicken fat, which meant home cooking. The dog gave the knuckles in front of him a tentative lick. He'd caught this female person's scent before and let her lay a gentle hand on his forehead.

"Do you think we could be friends? Why don't you both come in? Will he be alright with the cats?"

"Jake here grew up in a house full of other dogs and cats, and a ferret. He should be fine." Haskins gave Jake's leash a tug.

Em thought, *the operative term "should be" seems more like could be, might be or maybe.* She led her guests down the hall to the living room. Jake's toenails clicked against the slate tiles of the hall like ricocheting BBs as the dog took in the scents of the house. Smelling nothing of professional interest, Jake seemed to relax. As he reached the living room, there was a fearful howl and a hiss loud enough to be heard down the road.

Cleome leaped from her seat on Em's favorite chair and dived beneath it. *Need to watch out for that one,* thought the dog. Another one of those cranky scratchy creatures held his position on the hearth rug like a lord of the manor. A rumbling came from Ash's throat. The dog looked at the charcoal black cat and thought, *he and I can ignore each other safely.*

The dog turned his head towards the couch, keeping one eye on the fur ball on the floor in front of him, and sniffed. Jake didn't need to get any closer to the couch to know what went on there. His mouth opened in what Em would later describe as a wolfish grin and turned to look at Em, wagging his tail at her.

Oh Lord, thought Em, *it's a good thing this mutt can't talk.*

The dog's eyes lit up. He knew where he was now. This was the den of his best friend's mate. That's why he knew her scent. People collected all sorts of good smells on them, and then they tried to wash them off with water. Of course, there were times when they smelled so strongly he couldn't blame them for washing it off. People seemed to need stronger smells to scent anything, probably why they didn't know, or couldn't tell what was going on around them as well as he could. It was why they needed him.

Now all the nonsense of new training had a reason for Jake, guard the den, guard the females and guard the pesky young ones. Many generations of dogs and their wolf kin had lived with the families of men. It came as intuitive to them to chase with the hunters and to guard the human pack. From the smells of it, this was a den full of females, who in his experience as a pupster, could be gentle and generous with food. The house also smelled of mice, which was probably why they kept the assortment of sassy felines. Mice were beneath the notice of a guard dog. Limping with one back leg, Jake turned back to Em, panting in what sounded like laughter. He looked up at her with a *you can pet me now* look in his eyes.

Familiar with large dogs, Em reached down to run her hands over his forehead, around his ears and down onto his back. She was thinking, *You fresh fellow, don't you dare let on what you smelled on that couch.* What she said aloud was, "Good dog. Friends now?"

"Well, that's better, Jake." Haskins was relieved, he wasn't sure what changed their minds about each other, but things were looking more hopeful concerning Jake and Em.

Jake accepted Em's attentions gratefully, she smelled like cooking chicken. Jake's tall ears told him a familiar car approached the house. His raised head pointed towards the road to alert his handler and Em. Em watched the dog who remained quiet. Car doors slammed. The sound of two men's voices reached them. Sudden energetic tail wagging raised a breeze. *Here they come,* the dog antici-pated. *My friend and his hunting partner, the man whose feet leave little scent.* When Em went to the door to greet the new arrivals, Haskins let the dog follow her.

Jake wedged his way in front of Em. When she opened the door, he stood between her and the newcomers, tail batting her legs.

"Hi Sarge, how goes it?" Halloran reached down for the dog. "Sorry we're late Em." Noticeably tired, he leaned on his cane as he walked. Anson came in behind him also giving the dog a friendly greeting. Jake led the group back to the living room. Halloran looked around and set his course for the couch. The dog followed after him.

An elegant paw, claws extended, reached out from under a chair aimed at the dog. Jake gave a short sharp bark, to let Cleome know that cheap shots would not be tolerated.

Silently, Em watched as Jake planted himself in front of Halloran, who sat down in the middle of the couch. Halloran tousled the dog's ears for him. *A boy and his dog* passed through her mind.

"The boss was going to keep him, but he works long hours and there are too many stairs at his place," Haskins explained, nodding to acknowledge Halloran on the couch.

To Haskins Em said quietly, "Jake can stay here." She walked up behind the couch and placed her hand on Halloran's shoulder, and he reached up and placed his hand over hers. "I've told Haskins he can stay with me."

Haskins thought, *So, that's what Jake smelled on the couch, the boss has been here before. He can't keep the dog so he's doing the next best thing.*

"I'll go get his things. Where would you like his crate? And his jacket." Haskins was now anxious to be on his way.

"He has a crate?" Em sounded dubious.

"Yeah, he sleeps in it."

"How is he supposed to do guard duty if he's locked up in a cage all night? It can't be comfortable for his leg. He's going to need a nice soft dog bed." This last Em addressed to Halloran.

"Okay, whatever you say, Em."

Jake put his head on Halloran's lap.

"Need any help?" Anson offered to Haskins.

Haskins looked at Anson and replied, "You can hold the door."

"That's not what I had in mind. I can help you carry in the crate. She's not going to want it dragged across the floor." Jake heard the growl in Anson's voice, Em heard it too.

Haskins and Anson carried in the crate they had filled with dog food, bowls, an old blanket, a large mesh sack and a paper bag of meds with instructions.

"Thanks, Haskins. I can run through the commands with Ms. Huber and Jake. I know you will want to go pick up your new dog."

"You'll need to teach him the perimeter by walking him around the yard the same way every day for a week." Haskins remembered his duty. "Call me any time if you have questions, Ms. Huber."

"Will do. Thanks again and good luck with your new partner." Em wished him well out of her house.

Without even speaking a good-bye to Jake, Haskins left as expeditiously as he could. Truth be told, Jake did not seem sorry to see Haskins go either.

Carefully avoiding both cats, Anson found a seat in the chair next to the hearth. He was trying hard not to ask where Deanna and Sandy might be.

"What's up with that? How long were they working together? Weren't those two getting along?" Em could plainly see the dog was happier now with Halloran than he had been when she'd first set eyes on him.

"Anson, have you heard the story?" Halloran rested his hand on the dog.

"Andy Vargas told me some."

"Alright this doesn't go beyond this room. Jake here was the pick of a fine litter of pups. He was taller than the others and had different markings, none actually. As a young pup he was smart and outgoing, curious and friendly. We picked him out young and had him home-raised. Jake is a rare thing, an American German Shepherd certified with no hip dysplasia, a malformation of the hip joints that can result in painful arthritis in later life. So he got to keep his parts and his pups are fine, too."

"He does have that kind of knowing look about him," Em remarked.

"Maybe, but Jake needs a handler who respects his instincts. Haskins is an excellent handler who expects complete obedience. We're getting him another dog. Jake here is on leave."

"You said the dog was a hero, Michael."

"He is, to the embarrassment of his handler. He's a life saver. The night of their last assignment together, Haskins wanted to go one way along the shore, Jake wanted to go down an alley. The dog must have heard or smelled something. Jake couldn't convince Haskins to go with him so he cut up rough. Barked and jumped around until he attracted the attention of the other agents."

"Let me guess. No points for good behavior." Em looked at her canine guest with new eyes.

"All outright rebellion was what Vargas said," Anson agreed with a broad grin. "It's a legend."

"Damnedest thing. He got loose and barked at the other agents until they would follow him and then took off down the alley. Pete Leonard was one of the agents."

"Oh dear, what happened then?" Em was considering where to sit and was not willing to risk Cleome's claws any more than were the others. Halloran moved over on the couch to give her room to sit next to him and Jake.

"Dog runs down the alley. It was long. He was way ahead of the agents. Leaps at a man closing the back of a truck full of illegal Asian immigrants and pulls him down. The young women crying must be what he heard."

"Human trafficking?"

Halloran nodded soberly. "Nail salons and other occupations. Two other men ran for the cab of the truck, trying to get away with it. The agents were closing in on the truck. Jake went after the two heading for the cab. He delayed them long enough for them to come under fire."

"Is that how he was hit?"

"You mean friendly fire? No, it wasn't one of us. They were careful of the dog." Halloran was decisive.

"Wait a minute, I think I read about this in the paper. Wasn't one of the dogs in critical condition and not expected to live?"

Halloran smiled and Anson laughed. "Ma'am, there was no other dog. Jake was hit twice, serious enough but he had his vest on."

"Like the old saying, rumors of his death were exaggerated. Jake is a key witness. His testimony might not hold up in court, but he can tell us things we may not already know about who was there that night." Halloran was examining a bare patch on the right side of Jake's neck close to his shoulder.

"He'll need to wear a breakaway collar. Let's get this one off you, buddy. Jake responds well to voice commands, it shouldn't be a problem."

"So how was he shot?" Em had taken up a seat on the couch with Jake between her and Halloran.

"They must have had a lookout posted in a building above the alley. The dog made it past the first time. When Jake ran back towards the agents, he was heading for Pete Leonard when the lookout took aim and shot Pete. They singled him out." His voice dropped, Halloran paused. Em and Anson kept silent.

"When Jake pointed towards the source of the gunfire and ran towards it, the shooter tried to kill him too. Fortunately for Jake, seen straight on, he was a narrow moving target."

"My God, poor dog. And Pete Leonard, too."

"Bad night. What can I say? Jake took two glancing shots. This guy and his handler haven't gotten along since. If he can return to duty it will be with someone else."

"So, you would like me to care for him until he can return to duty?"

"You can say that's your part of the bargain. His part is to keep you safe. Jake, this is Em. Guard Em. Shake."

Jake raised his head, shifted his position carefully and raised his paw for Em to shake. For the first time, solemnly, Em took his large paw in her hand.

"Pleasure to meet you, Sergeant Jaeger."

Jake gave a bark that sounded like *yes*.

"If he's a key witness and everyone is supposed to think he's dead, is he undercover here?"

"Sort of the idea," Halloran acknowledged.

"Then he needs a cover story, doesn't he? I mean what am I supposed to tell people? I have a live-in bodyguard who is a decorated police sergeant?"

"Makes sense, sir," Anson agreed.

"We could change his name to something else. Maybe Che. No? We could call him Hunter, that's what Jaeger means in German. Could you be Hunter?" The dog did not look enthusiastic. "Was his name ever released to the media? I can check on the Internet," Em volunteered.

"Humph, not to my knowledge. What do you think would work for a cover?" Halloran was reluctant to dictate this one.

"Well, he doesn't look like a stray from the pound. I could say I'm caring for him for a friend who's sailing to the South Seas, going to the Galapagos Islands, moving to Timbuktu or who got laid off and is moving to an apartment and can't afford to keep the dog."

"Your choice, just let me know. The last option sounds like the best. What do you think, Anson?"

"I agree if you went with a lost dog story you'd have to make some sort of attempt to find the owner. Do you have an imaginary friend?" Anson asked.

"I have family in the Berkshires who can cover for me if we need it," replied Em. "What we will need are the breakaway collar and the dog bed. Deanna and Sandy are out mall crawling this morning. I wonder if there's any place they can stop on their way back."

"I know where we can get him a good one made in Maine. There's an outlet store upstate." Anson thought ahead. Em would need to stay with her new doggie. He could perhaps persuade the young women to go with him shopping for the dog.

"Good. Get it this afternoon. Use your card. I'll reimburse you." Halloran looked down at his good dog who was shedding all over his pants legs.

The dog's ears twitched, and he pointed his head towards the road. Laughter of two young females reached his ears from across the road. In a second or two, Em said, "I hear Deanna and Sandy too, Jake." Anson and Halloran looked at each other, the lady of the house certainly had sharp ears. Em patted the dog. "It's okay. It's family."

Sandy used her key and the two friends were laughing as they came down the hall. Deanna spotted Anson first, and then she saw the dog.

"Isn't he adorable?" Deanna was down on the floor petting the dog before anyone could caution her. There aren't too many adorable police dogs, but Jake was willing to give it a try and gave Deanna a friendly welcome. A long pink tongue came out and licked her face. She'd eaten a soft pretzel at the mall and still had salt on her cheeks. "Can we keep him, Mom? He doesn't have to go back, does he?"

"Now, see what you've done?" Em demanded of Halloran who smiled at her. He knew perfectly well what he was doing.

22

BUTTON, BUTTON

E M WAS TROUBLED the next afternoon, the storm and its aftermath, the kidnapping in Texas, so much had happened to her peaceful, dull and seemingly safe retirement. Life without Harley Travis Huber had settled into a pattern of housekeeping, garden keeping, young adult coaching and stretching to pay the bills. Time to sit and think was rare and precious. That's what she was doing, that afternoon sitting in her favorite chair by the fireplace, arms outstretched, feet at rest and staring into the corner of the room. Deanna took one look at her mother and recognized the perfect stillness. Only Em's eyes moved. Her daughter crept away towards the stairs to the second floor. She knew her mother was best not disturbed and found it an opportunity for some private time, too.

The subject of Em's concentrated thought was Francis Xavier Kirbee. But not in the way the gentleman might have preferred. Surely, he must have taken Version 5 with him. No one had succeeded in finding anything pertaining to it. Halloran's agents searched the house, the garage, the garden, his office, his lab and still nothing. Ditto for Professor Hussein's condominium apartment in an elegant brick pre-War building. *Did it make sense?* she wondered. *Why wouldn't Kirbee leave at least one backup copy where Halloran could find it? He wanted him to have it. Kirbee had been clear, I am to take care of the Siamese.*

Cleome was not wearing it in a collar around her neck like the cat in "Men in Black." The cat reviled collars and shed them quickly. In fact, while at the Spring House, Cleome developed a preference for the outdoor facilities offered to a cat by the bushes. The cat seemed determined not to use her special dustless litter and had taken up Ash's habit of pestering to be let out. Em had not changed her litter since Cleome arrived for her guest stay at the Spring House.

Em went from complete stillness, breathing slowed, to concentrated action. She hustled to the kitchen for garbage bags and disposable gloves and hurried down the front hall to the closet next to the stairs where Cleome's things were kept. The door was ajar to allow the cat access. Em pulled it open and went down on her hands and knees on the tile floor before the litter house. It was a plastic enclosure high enough so the cat could walk in, turn around and use the litter. It even had a curtain hung in the doorway. *This is the limit*, thought Em. *No wonder the poor thing prefers the woods. That curtain is a terribly gaudy print.* Em pulled out the pan of litter from its housing and surveyed it. It looked unused, but she carefully sifted through it with the poop scooper.

"If anyone sees me doing this they will think I'm crazy," she muttered. "Exactly."

Finding nothing in the litter, she dumped it unceremoniously into a plastic garbage bag. She carefully examined the pan and the inside of the litter house, although she believed it to be empty when they brought it home. Next she turned her attention to the reusable plastic container of fresh litter. As a young cat, Cleome proved to be allergic to litter dust. Kirbee purchased special dustless litter at a pet store by weight and brought it home in a specially designed sturdy plastic container with a spout and a hollow handle.

Em prepared to empty the contents of the container into the second garbage bag, thankful it was indeed dustless litter. The container was almost full so Em had a task getting it all sifted as it poured into the bag. Again, there was nothing in the litter. She turned her attention to the container itself.

The design of the item, with its half arch of a spout, precluded seeing anything more than a part of the inside of the spout. Em found a large square flashlight in the closet and directed the beam into the neck of the spout. She could see a little more of the back of the container. The molded plastic was thick enough the light did not show through to create any revealing shadows. She put the container down to think. *If I wanted to hide something in there, how would I do it? My hand is too large to go down the spout, and certainly Kirbee's hand is even larger.*

Briefly considering sawing the thing in half, she realized it might damage any concealed media. Cracking the plastic like a lobster's shell, likewise using a magnet were both out for obvious reasons. There was the questions of tools. Kirbee, the inventor, might have a collection of tools, including some flexible enough to enable him to place a small object down the neck of the container. Em had none. She did have tin snips in the cellar workshop, though.

For her piece of mind, with her inherently curious offspring to consider, Em placed the two bags of litter and the container back in the closet and closed the door firmly but quietly. Once down in the cellar at the work bench, Em searched through the extensive collection of tools. She found the long handled, short bladed pair of cutters designed to go through thin sheets of metal.

Brandishing the tin snips, Em made her way quickly back to the closet in the front hall. She listened intently. Faint music came from Deanna's room. Sandy was at work. Coast clear to proceed, she pulled the plastic container out of the closet into the hall for better light. Sitting on the cool tile floor, Em first cut straight down the spout as far as she could see. And then, she made a circular cut around the neck of the spout. By angling the cut, she could see down into the container, with no result. *That would be too easy and too gritty*, she thought.

The handle of the container was obviously hollow judging by the weight of the container. The top opening of the wide handle looked seam-sealed down the middle as if the container was made of only two molded halves. Em shook the container in frustration and heard the smallest of sounds. In careful haste, she cut around the handle in a wide oval to free it from the body of the container. Sure enough, there at the bottom of the handle was a circular seal. Judging the tin snips potential for damaging any media that might be hidden in the handle, she switched tools. On the shelf in the closet was a tool box with art supplies, oils, acrylics and best for her purposes, a variety of mat knives. Using a mat knife with a strong blade, she cut through the seal on the end of the handle. The light of the flash revealed a small square plastic case with a memory chip inside, carefully set in a glob of rubbery glue.

"McGuffin, McGuffin! So, I've found it, now how do I get rid of the thing?" She realized no one in the house was safe while the chip was in her possession. With hasty hands she removed all traces of her work, including accidentally spilled cat litter. The tools were stowed back in the closet along with the remains of the plastic container, minus the handle. Em quickly stuffed the handle into one of her own riding boots and hid it in the back of the closet. A Louisville Slugger came to hand. The door was again closed without a squeak.

Working on the floor in the front hall had the benefit of privacy. Em's project could not have been observed from any of the house windows. Staying low, Em edged along the wall, close to the security panel. In a low voice she said, "Electronic Umbrella up. Lock down three. Miranda Elice." The security system responded to her in a matched low volume. Em turned towards the kitchen, reached around the corner and snaked down the kitchen wireline phone from the wall.

"Mother!" Deanna howled from her room.

"In a minute," Em replied, her tone of voice brooking no argument. Taking in a few deep breaths, she punched in a number on the handset.

"Hullo," a casual woman's voice responded, familiar and reassuring.

"Gladys?"

"Yes, Em, how are you?" Gladys, at the Control Desk, waved to Garvey to get his attention. Stubbornly focused on his monitors Garvey had his head down, shoulders back in concentration. She snapped her fingers and brought him around and put Em's call on speaker.

"Fine, fine. Listen, I'm calling to invite that nice young woman who carries things and her friend to come out here." By this Em meant an evidence courier, Agent Esparza, nicknamed "Sparks," whose on the job ingenuity was a young legend.

"Oh? When would you like her to come? We're busy today." Gladys tried to figure out what was going on from Em's strained tone.

At this point Em lost her exaggerated caution. She was sitting on the tile floor of the hallway with the phone in one hand and the vintage baseball bat in the other.

"Now! I need her right now. Tell what's his name, Miranda called. He needs to come now." Em paused.

"Who's Miranda? He's on one of those over the moon calls, we can't go in there." Gladys had a puzzled look on her face. Scuttlebutt had it their boss was getting reamed out by the brass over the Kirbee and Version 5 affair. It was seriously not a good time to interrupt.

"It's me! I only let people call me that *in an emergency.* You have to tell him Miranda called. Gladys, please!"

"Are you under threat?" Gladys asked with growing concern.

"Not immediately, potentially very much. Gladys, please hurry. Button, button…"

Gladys turned towards Garvey, who bent over her shoulder to listen, and said, "Whose got the button?"

"Right, on their way. ASAP. Stay on the line, please." Gladys put her line on mute. To Garvey she remarked, "I need an agent foolhardy enough and heedless of their own career." Raising her voice she called out, "Anson! Get over here!"

David Anson, seated at his desk nearby, gave a guilty start. Gladys's shout interrupted him while cruising through an Army surplus equipment database searching for another potential acquisition for the group.

Guiltily he said, "Yes, ma'am?" and logged out of the database.

"Trainees call me sir." Seeing the look on Anson's face Gladys said, "I need you to take a message in to the boss."

"'Scuse me, meaning no disrespect, sir." Privately, Anson thought that anyone who called Gladys "sir" must be blind. She looked about ready to pop out a young one. Anson sighed, he could say ma'am with as much respect as he could say sir to a superior officer.

"Okay then, you need to go into the Executive Conference Room and get the boss out." Garvey gave a low whistle. Gladys ignored it. "Tell him Ms. Huber called. She said to tell him 'Miranda.' I think that's their emergency code for her. She needs an evidence courier with another agent. You know where the conference room is, go!" It seemed reasonable to Gladys that a war vet with Anson's record was not likely to be intimidated by a camera, or who was on the other end of it.

Stepping with long, stiff, determined strides in the direction, Anson turned away from her desk towards a narrow corridor with only one door at the end. Another agent stood outside the door, seemingly lounging against the wall.

Always hyper-organized, Gladys made a quick prioritized series of calls to field the expedition to the Spring House. Within minutes the first car left their parking lot. In the basement motor pool, Leroy pulled the command car out next, had it running, doors open, waiting.

Even at the Control Desk Gladys and Garvey could hear the argument down the corridor. Rapidly she said, "Did you tell DeCarlo to let Anson in? You better do it before Anson picks him up and slams him against the wall. Give Anson temp access to the door. I want everybody in one piece with no holes at the end of the shift, Garvey."

Doing as he was bid, Garvey spoke a few words into his mic and executed a few keystrokes. Suddenly there was silence in the corridor. Anson looked up at the camera in the requisite direction, planted his large hand on the reader and barged through the Executive Conference Room door.

Like an arresting officer, Anson strode into the room, stood stock still behind Michael Halloran. The newcomer took one look at the uniform shown on the video monitor, snapped to attention, saluted and said, "Your pardon, sir." He leaned down to Halloran and said in a low voice, "It's Ms. Huber. She called, said to say 'Miranda.' Gladys thinks that means emergency. She wants an evidence courier and said, 'Button....'"

"Damn! Joel, it sounds as if she may have found something. I've got to go. Apologies, General."

The cane eluded him temporarily. Since he'd been seated for nearly two hours taking a licking from the general, his right leg was cramped, reluctant to move. As

Halloran attempted to rise, Anson instinctively reached out, grasped his boss's arm and hauled him to his feet, and then escorted him out the door.

"That the new recruit, Lieutenant Anson?" the uniform on the screen asked.

"Yes, General," replied Joel Schwartz.

"He can pick them, can't he? Loyalty is a good thing, I can see that in Anson. Damn bad luck about Halloran's leg. Where were we? Contingency planning. Continue."

After he reshuffled the papers on the table in front of him, gathered his thoughts, Joel Schwartz took over the briefing, in fervent hope that Version 5 had been found.

"Evidence courier and guard are clearing the office driveway now, sir," Gladys reported in a voice that carried down the hall.

Halloran slowed his race walk as he approached the Control Desk with Anson a pace behind.

"Is she alright?" Halloran asked when he got within speaking distance of the desk.

Gladys spoke into her mic, "She's fine, won't talk straight though."

"Good." Halloran kept on going past the desk towards the elevator. Leroy had all the doors of the car open. Anson took the driver's side, to his surprise Halloran chose the front passenger seat. The car doors snapped closed using the driver's controls.

"Go, Anson. Fly low," Halloran directed.

Anson took him at his word, caught and passed the small black fleet car with the evidence courier out on the Interstate.

At the Control Desk, Gladys resumed a more comfortable position in her chair, feet elevated. She said into her mic, "Company's coming, on their way now. What are you serving your guests, lady?"

"I think I'll serve five cups of tea and a good strong brandy for me."

Gladys relayed the message, "Sir, she thinks she has Version 5."

"Call for additional backup," was his response.

The electronic jamming device, the "electronic umbrella," her brother Joshua installed at the Spring House cut off Deanna's Skype session with a friend. Deanna was growing restless, her mother had been on the wireline phone for ages. Always inquisitive, she decided to investigate and found her mother seated on the chilly slate hall floor, baseball bat and telephone in hand.

"Mom, what are you doing, are we under attack? What's with the bat, Minnie Mantle?"

At that moment, they heard two cars pull up onto the paving in front of the house.

"Help me up, Dee?" Em asked as she scrambled to her feet. "Let's see who's at the door, but don't open it."

Deanna looked out the peephole in the front door. "It's Dave and that tall boss of his. And a whole bunch of people. What's going on?"

"Company's here," Em told Gladys and hung up the phone. Again, she checked the peephole and found herself staring into two unmistakable light grey eyes.

"Unlock the door, Dee. Please."

Deanna stepped into the living room and entered her security code on the key pad.

Four people crowded into Em's narrow front hall. Deanna found Anson guiding her back towards the living room out of the action, to which she made a show of objecting.

To those assembled in her hallway Em announced quietly, "I've found a chip, it has to be Kirbee's. He hid it in Cleome's reusable litter container thing."

"What thing?" Halloran asked, but Em was already opening the closet door and bending over close in front of him, a sight which always inspired his pleasure.

Leaning forward, she reached into the closet to dislodge her riding boots, pulled the left boot out first and tossed it out of the closet. It landed on the hall floor at Halloran's feet. Chastened, he stepped back, all the better to admire the view of her bottom from his vantage point. Em kept rummaging in the closet until she found the hidden right boot. When she finally stood up with the boot in her hand she held it up to his chest. They were quite close, the boot held between them, and with a concerted effort, she pulled the truncated plastic handle from the toe of the boot.

"See? I had to cut the container to get to it. The chip is glued inside. He took real care to seal it in." Em was feeling very pleased and relieved, and it showed on her glowing cheeks.

"Well, I'll be damned." Halloran took the handle and stuck his long finger into it, wiggled it around and worked the chip loose from its glob of glue. A high capacity chip in its case dropped into his hand. Without looking up he returned the empty handle to Em and carefully opened the small plastic case. After one look, he snapped the case shut.

With a satisfied smile on her face and a light in her eyes, Em told them, "I got to thinking, the only things not in Kirbee's house when it was searched were Cleome's traveling kit. Because we had already taken them away."

Halloran nodded first, then laughed, a sound that surprised his staff. His clever lady friend may just have pulled their organizational feet out of the fire and gotten a general off his back. The situation might have been worse, it could have been an admiral.

He turned to the couriers. "Fully armed? Vests?"

"Yessir," they said in unison.

"Agent Moynihan, you are riding shot gun. Agent Esparza, do you have a secure case?" Halloran addressed the young blonde woman who was considerably shorter than the others. All he could see was a special carrier like a tough money belt made of Kevlar. To look unlike armed federal agents, both couriers were dressed in thrift store casual clothes and kept their lockers filled with many choice finds from the local budget stores.

"Sparks, are you kidding, sir? She's got a case for every occasion," Moynihan joked, his blue shirt was intentionally torn at the elbow.

"Several," Sparks replied with exaggerated patience for her partner. "We weren't sure what to bring into the house."

"Get one that's ... Get the biggest, oddest looking one you have." Halloran held the diminutive case in the outstretched palm of his hand.

"Oh yes, Mr. Halloran, got it." Sparks disappeared out the front door and reappeared with a battered road-weary trombone case. Em admitted her with her security code, laughing as she did so.

"I have a friend who plays the trombone. When he got a new case, I cadged this one. It's been specially retrofitted. We can blow it up if we have to," Sparks explained.

"Isn't that dangerous?" It crossed Em's mind to wonder how the young woman got the nickname Sparks but thought she better not ask.

"It's only the inside that blows up. We tested it, it works really well. Sort of goes THUMP! And hisses at you." Proud of her work, Sparks grinned.

Halloran realized early in his long career that when you give people the opportunity, they can do some pretty unpredictable things very well.

"Okay, let's do the transfer paperwork while we wait for your escort. Rankel and Vargas should be pulling in shortly." Back to business, Halloran was anxious to get their prize to a secure location to be analyzed and verified.

Sparks and her partner showed their surprise. They were too well disciplined to ask, *What the hell is on that thing?* Sparks was already considering the devious ways she could drive back to the office, with Rankel chasing her as escort. Her partner Moynihan was doing a mental inventory of the long guns and ammo in the car and considered borrowing something from Anson.

Meanwhile, Anson was not having luck trying to keep Deanna in the living room. Laying hands on her was a temptation best avoided for the present. Without trying to physically restrain her, which had definite downside potential, there was little he could do but stand in front of her to block her view. Well aware that he could not grab her, teasing him, she bobbed and weaved, and succeeded in getting past him, laughing as she did it. As it happened, she did manage to witness the transfer of the chip and the signoff.

"You found it, Mom?" she asked breathlessly on arriving in the hallway.

Em turned towards her youngest daughter and nodded, a smile playing across her face, and then she burst into a wide grin.

"High five!" Deanna raised her hand, Em reached up and slapped her daughter's open hand with her own. "So what was it anyway?" Deanna looked around.

Sparks laughed. She was wondering the same thing.

23

THE MIKE AND FRANK SHOW

———————

AFTER A NIGHT of simple pleasures, Halloran was sleeping on the outside of Em's single bed. It was growing light, the grey of dawn showed the mist in the backyard of the Spring House. A soft thud awakened him. A wet nose brushed his arm repeatedly until he turned over to face a long black nose and intent brown eyes. Jake was trained to alert his handler, or in this case his protectee, but not to bark out loud to give warning unless the situation was critical. Halloran was not moving fast enough for the dog, who grabbed the light blanket in his teeth and tugged at it.

Halloran looked the dog in the eye, willing him not to bark as that would wake Em who was asleep next to him. *Best to let the sleeping woman lie.* Halloran reached under the pillow, rolled over carefully and took time to get his legs under him. He reached into his overnight bag for his weapon. Looking down and seeing not a stitch of clothing, he decided pants and yesterday's polo shirt might be a good idea. Mornings were tough for him, his right leg was stiff. He managed to pull on plaid boxers, khakis, a shirt and an ankle holster. Socks were not going to happen yet.

The dog now stood calmly looking out the bedroom window towards the back lawn, indicating interest but no apparent threat.

From the other side of the bed, Em regarded him through half-closed eyes. Sensing slight movement, the dog pointed his nose at her. Halloran saw this and said quietly, without turning around, "Stay in bed. The dog has to go out."

"Huh, a two gun dog walk? It's not the wild turkeys again?"

"I mean it, Em."

"Of course you do." Em waited until he and Jake were far enough down the hall, and then quietly got out of bed. Her camisole was on the floor under the bed. She took a dive back over it to retrieve sleep shorts which were pulled on hastily. As she wrapped her bathrobe around her, there was a noise, an exclamation really, from the backyard. Keeping low, she approached the open window. What she saw astonished her.

Michael Halloran was standing in the backyard with his arms crossed. Jake was watering a nearby bush. Cleome sat upright like a sentinel on the porch of the Fred, their composition outhouse. From where he stood, Halloran listened to the rumbling coming from the outhouse.

"Come on out, Frank."

"I'm not done, dammit, Mike."

"I'll wait," Halloran said loud enough for Em to hear him clearly.

"Come in for breakfast," Em called out the window. *At least Frank won't be able to avoid Michael the way he has me,* she thought. Em washed and dressed hurriedly, she was in the kitchen making thin slices of onions and leftover baked potatoes for a Spanish omelet when she heard the two men arguing outside the living room door. The men might be trying to keep their voices down and tempers under control, but she could catch an occasional phrase. Of course, we have sharper ears when our own names are mentioned.

Halloran was giving Kirbee the benefit of his professional opinion and Kirbee was defending himself. "What the holy hell do you think you're doing, Frank?" Halloran tried not to yell at the top of his considerable lungs. Kirbee was not about to be intimidated by his poker buddy.

"They killed Al, I was afraid they would come after me, too." Kirbee was simmering mad.

"You should be in a safe place. You and that damned Version 5. How could you risk it? You know what's at stake better than any of us." Halloran's patience was rapidly fraying.

"There was someone in my backyard. It looked like he came from the garage. I guess I thought fast action was called for. I needed a place to finish Version 5. Now I am almost finished with the specs, and instructions for use and maintenance."

"If you panicked, why didn't you call me?"

"I didn't panic. Ending up in a safe house, people find those things, Mike." Kirbee was growing red in the face.

"I said safe place, not safe house," Halloran replied curtly.

"What? Go live in that damned bunker of yours? Nobody's found me." Kirbee took a risk with this statement. He was well aware Em Huber could have chased him down.

"The food's good. You would be safer there than in a cabin in the woods, with no john. Does it even have running water?" Halloran's frustration with Kirbee was beginning to ebb. "Frank, you are a threat to National Security if I ever met one walking around on two legs. Did you think if anything happened to you, we wouldn't know about it? Were you alone?"

"The friend who lent me the cabin and I have a check-in system. I wasn't dumb enough to take all of Version 5 with me, just the part of the User Manual I needed to finish." Kirbee's eyes glinted impishly. "Do you know where I put the backup?"

"We know. We have Version 5. Em Huber found your memory chip in the damned cat litter. Did she know you where you were?"

Kirbee could see the storm clouds gathering on Halloran's face. The implied ending to the question was, "and not tell me."

Kirbee could see he was on dangerous ground here. He tried a diversion.

"Speaking of Em, what the hell are you doing here at this time of the morning?"

Em was slicing the onions very thin at the time she overheard Kirbee ask the question. Although usually quite proficient with sharp objects, when she heard it, the knife slipped and took a nick out of her finger. The men moved farther back towards the rock garden on the hill and continued a heated discussion out of her hearing.

Kirbee could see the stubble of an early morning beard growing on his friend's unshaven chin. His glance aimed down to Halloran's bare feet. Halloran's shoes were inconveniently shoved too far under Em's bed for him to quickly find them with his morning-stiff right leg. "What are you doing with my intelligence consultant? Isn't that some sort of violation. Did you try to get to her to find me, did you?"

"Watch what you say, Frank." Halloran worked to keep his voice even. In no uncertain terms he let his friend Kirbee know he had a serious interest and believed it was returned. Kirbee better get used to the idea. Em would have been pleased, if she'd heard it. Kirbee learned the "I saw her first" argument wouldn't hold up. Halloran was an apparently serious contender and he, Kirbee, hadn't made it to first base. A just peace was negotiated.

As they walked into the house together, Halloran reflected gladly he'd chosen to make early advances to Em, and not to delay as had been his recent pattern.

Although unconvinced Kirbee would easily cede the competition for Em's affections, he was not about to see Em become the third Mrs. Frank Kirbee. But then Halloran was never a man to be without an action plan.

By the time Kirbee, followed by Halloran, came in the living room door, Em had the table set for breakfast, ketchup, tea and coffee on the table. Fresh bread was in the toaster, and she plated the omelet. Jake, Ash and Cleome came in with the two men and headed straight for their respective bowls. Em had observed the house rules, the pets get breakfast first.

"Good morning, gentlemen." Em decided to open on a cheerful note. Kirbee smiled at her, came forward and gave her a kiss on the cheek. He looked back at Halloran, who was slowly simmering.

Halloran remarked with asperity, "Look what I found in that outhouse of yours. You don't seem surprised, Em."

Em sighed. "No, but I am pleased you had better luck getting him to come in than I did. Where have you been, Frank?"

Kirbee grinned outright, mustache bristling.

"He's been staying in an old cabin out in the woods down the trail back there," Halloran informed her.

"You're kidding, the cabin's a wreck. I noticed Cleome kept sneaking off in that direction and coming back for meals. She stayed out through the storm and came back basically dry. Was the cat with you, Frank?"

Kirbee cut her off before she could mention she knew he was using the Fred. "You have her favorite cat food," he joked as he moved to sit down at the breakfast table.

"Would you like mango pineapple juice with this? It's become sort of a household specialty. Deanna is working on fifteen different ways to use mangos in a glass. Have a seat, Frank. I need to talk to you." Em's voice was firm.

"I've already..." Halloran began.

"Read him the Riot Act. I have a different issue. Working with a friend who is an FBI agent," Em looked at Halloran, "she and I developed a profile of the woman we believe was present when Professor Hussein was killed. Coffee?

"I need you to tell me if the description of the woman fits anyone you know. We even have a picture of someone who resembles her. A woman, not young, about 5'2", size 6 dress, so she would be thin and short, with a light complexion and dark hair. No grey showing, that doesn't mean it's not there underneath. She likes New York designer original dresses and has the resources to own them. Wears expensive gold jewelry, probably designer, too. She seems to be an executive type." Em noticed Kirbee had grown quiet, his smile faded, he seemed frozen in place. With a puzzled expression on his face Halloran watched him, too.

Em continued. "There is a possibility that she has a blue/green color blindness, that is rare in women, or…"

"Filomena," Kirbee said sadly, and he seemed to breathe again.

"Who's Filomena?" Em asked.

Kirbee hesitated.

"Tell her, Frank." Halloran was exasperated. *Could it be that simple?*

"My second ex-wife, Filomena Morena. I was afraid of that when you first asked me if I had any enemies," he admitted.

"Why is it always the ex?" Em huffed at the two men.

Halloran shrugged his shoulders, and Kirbee looked guilty.

"What makes you think it's your ex-wife, outside of the obvious reasons?" Em inquired, she was not yet convinced.

"It's the color blindness you mentioned. And she hates me. Filomena knew what I did for a living, and she married me anyway," Kirbee said apologetically. "She said I spent too much time in the lab and would never make real money from my damned inventions if I sold them to the government."

"You will be fairly compensated," Halloran said.

"But that isn't what she expected when we met at a professional convention. She represented a high-powered technology marketing company. We had drinks, and then dinner, and it seemed to, uh, move on from there. Filomena seemed genuinely interested in my work."

"I'll bet she was, with good reason, Frank." Em shook her head.

"When I met her she was in the process of divorcing Gerald Levitt. Jerry was into commercial real estate and collected modern art. Real estate tanked and so did their marriage. As part of her divorce settlement Filomena received paintings because Jerry was out of cash."

Em grew still more skeptical of his ex-wife's motives.

"I found out about the difficulty Filomena had seeing certain colors when she moved into my house here in New Haven. It was the paintings, especially one by Mark Rothko with bands of bright orange and red. All the paintings she chose were these vivid things with not much detail, and they went with her when she left."

"You let her take them with her? The Rothko alone is a high value item." Em was stunned, as one who had lost more than fair to an aggressive man and a very aggressive lawyer. After the fight to retain her own property during divorce, it seemed impossible a man could be that generous.

"The paintings were hers. My house doesn't have the proper temperature and humidity controls for them. They belong in a controlled environment. I told her that when she moved in," Kirbee replied with little care about their monetary value.

"So what happened, Frank? Lots of people work long hours and don't end up hating each other," puzzled, Em asked.

The expression on Halloran's face registered that this was old news, except the part concerning Filomena's vision. Kirbee never mentioned that interesting fact.

"We weren't together long before she wanted to get SunSprite developed into a marketable product." At this point, Em's eyebrows shot up. Kirbee continued without noticing the change in her expression, but Halloran caught it.

"We argued often. I tried to explain to her it needed further development and field testing. There was potential for a significant breakthrough and with it the possibility for a government contract that would make best use of the new technology. A government contract would put it beyond commercial marketing. She didn't want to hear it. Oh, could she be demanding," Kirbee continued. "And on that subject exceedingly difficult."

"Primary motive, I suppose," Em offered, a wry smile struggling across her face. "Everyone's heard of marrying for money, but marrying for technology? Perhaps Filomena Morena saw it as the same."

"In the middle of an argument about it, I asked her to leave. That's when she took the Rothko. And, she had taken down all my old maps, 19th century architectural and engineering drawings to hang her own paintings. Now I can't find them," Kirbee complained.

"This explains the blank walls in your house." Still in disbelief Em replied with the inquiry, "Why on earth did you marry her in the first place?"

"There were compensations," Frank Kirbee admitted with an ill-concealed smile. To a man, the answer to that question was obvious.

Em was thoughtful. "Old maps and drawings can be valuable, can't they Frank?"

"Filomena didn't like them, she said they were boring. Some of them were truly special. This obsession, always cleaning out, it drove me crazy," Kirbee said with gritted teeth.

"Give me a list, I may have a lead. Is there a finder's fee?" Em said half-joking. Return of personal property was not in their contract. The items could be highly collectible and easy to sell. Em had a good idea where they might be found and breathed a hope students from the Art & Architecture School had not yet discovered them.

Seeing his partner lost in what appeared to be abstract thought, Halloran had his own questions for Kirbee. Not all of these questions he proposed to have answered at breakfast in front of Em. "You can tell me how you found the cabin behind Em's house, and who recommended that you hire Em as a consultant later, Frank.

"Describe the man you saw in your backyard, the one who prompted you to pack up and head for the woods." Halloran frowned at Kirbee with the look federal agents dreaded, the one that said, you totally screwed up this time.

Kirbee, however, took it in stride. As far as he was concerned, this was a conversation between equals and his ruse worked well. "Young and not much more than a kid. Scrawny. Very light blond hair, almost white. Grey shirt and pants, like a workman, and he carried one of those large gate mouth bags like a plumber. But," Kirbee paused for effect, "I knew I didn't need a plumber, particularly not for the garage."

Em nodded at Halloran, who said, "Matter of fact, we got him. He planted a bomb in your Mercedes and several in your basement. Andy Vargas found a grounds keeper who saw him, too. He's lawyered up but just may know more than he's telling about some ill-cured cement."

Shocked, Kirbee replied in a ragged tone, his voice catching, "I read about the body in the harbor. Did he kill Al Hussein?"

"Not sure yet, Frank. I'm sorry," Halloran said quietly.

"We will need Filomena's current address."

"Good Lord, Mike. I don't keep track of the woman. All our correspondence goes through lawyers."

"Lawyer's name and address, then."

Deliberately stalling, Em poured herself a second cup of tea, hoping to come up with a way to explain to Halloran why she hadn't told him about the suspicious use of The Fred. Afraid she would have to make it a damned good explanation, she appeared absorbed by the leaves at the bottom of her cup and decided on a diversion.

"Frank, I thought you would run to one of your service buddies, but he," Em said gesturing towards Halloran, "said you didn't. You were in communications, weren't you? Would that mean Intelligence? Would it? Was it one of your covert service buddies?"

Halloran looked from Em to Kirbee and appeared to surmise she hadn't known who Kirbee touched for assistance.

"Excellent breakfast, my dear Em." Kirbee looked out over his coffee mug. "I must learn to make good coffee. I miss Al very much. This isn't only about Version 5. Please find the person, or the people, who killed the best friend and business partner a man could ever have. I know you can do it, I've always known that."

"We will, Frank, we will." Halloran looked across the table at Em who smiled as she rubbed her knee against his leg, trying to make sure he found his shoes.

Although it was still quite early, a black fleet car sped up the road to the Spring House. It pulled in almost to the front door. The doorbell rang.

"Are we expecting company?" Em asked Halloran. She nudged him under the table with her foot.

"Vargas and Rankel. Don't open for anyone else," was his reply.

Em was sorely tempted to say, *What if it's the milk man?* but thought better of it. The delivery from the nearby dairy farm wasn't due for several hours. Resigned, she rose from the table to answer the door and returned with Vargas and Rankel who eyed the remains of breakfast on the table with envy. An early morning call out left them both peckish.

"You are going with them into protective custody. No argument. Do it, Frank. I'm not losing another poker player."

The two men stared straight at each other, and Kirbee said, "I'm sorry about Pete. He came with you to my lab once, didn't he? Great loss. Alright, I'll go, I'm nearly done anyway. But my things are in the cabin," Kirbee protested as an afterthought.

With a quick gesture to the agents, Halloran spoke. "We'll give you an escort to go get them. A hike in the woods will be good field experience for them."

Kirbee smiled a mischievous smile.

"Stick to the trail, Frank, and keep them out of the swamp." To Em, his intentions were all over Frank's face. "I'll be watching!"

"Em, you are no fun." Kirbee laughed.

Halloran, the great investigator, slipped his feet into his shoes. With prompting, he finally found them under the breakfast table. He appreciated the considerate partner who fished them out from under her bed.

Kirbee studied Em and Halloran across the table for a long moment. "And I think you two deserve each other." Kirbee had found the shoes under the table first. Standing up a bit stiffly, Kirbee looked to Vargas and Rankel. "Follow me, 'gents, watch out for the poison ivy."

"Did you know where Frank was?" Once alone, Halloran accused Em, he couldn't resist.

"Deanna discovered a man had used the Fred and left a solar magazine. I left messages there, but there was no response. Cleome would disappear, as I said. I tried to watch, but I could never catch anyone. We are out often enough, he'd just have to wait. After we got the dog, it was probably more difficult." She neglected to mention she wrote the messages on the toilet paper and then rolled it back up for the next user to find. Some details were just not necessary.

"Why didn't you say something? We could have searched for him." He was exasperated.

"Because I wasn't sure. If I said anything and it turned out to be a neighbor, I'd be embarrassed. It wouldn't be the first time I've reported something, and it turned out to be nothing. Makes me feel dumb," she said ruefully. Years ago Em had learned her lesson the hard way not reporting an odd occurrence. The lesson still gave her nightmares, for reasons of her own, she failed to mention it.

"Besides, if we started searching, if it was Kirbee, he'd be gone. If Frank's managed to elude both of us, he's good at this," she reasoned. "The woods around here are full of rocky ledges, even caves, plenty of places to conceal a shelter or pitch a tent. That's where I thought he might be."

"You never considered the handy cabin down the trail?" he pressed his point.

"No, not really and it's still a puzzle. The girls and I found the cabin soon after we bought the house. But it looked to be uninhabitable. It looked like the roof leaked and there were animals living in it. There was a sturdy padlock on the door, probably to keep the neighborhood kids out. The windows were so dirty we couldn't see inside. No sign of wires. The outhouse was tumbled down, and it was too close to the stream anyway."

"Which is probably why he preferred yours," Halloran stopped, listening. "Make sure you go in with him, don't take no for an answer, Andy," he said into his collar.

Silently he listened to Agent Vargas's running description of the inside of the cabin.

"Sounds like someone converted the cabin into a hide. The outside still looks the way you describe it, but the inside is spotless. Frank tried to avoid having them see the interior. All the bare bones comforts powered by solar cells and hydro from the stream."

"I'll be damned, I mean there is one. Right below the cabin there is an old dam that creates a small pond. It's more like stepping stones placed across the stream. Leave it to Frank to use it for water power. I wonder how he managed it."

"Whoever did it, it wasn't done overnight," Halloran replied.

"Yes, whoever." Em certainly had ideas on the subject and quick research might verify it. "Truly, the neighbors around here are an interesting lot."

24

CAVE ART

———◆———

IT WAS A small nagging annoyance that started over breakfast coffee. Professor James Stevenson had not returned Em's phone calls. She missed his first call that was an attempt to follow up on his offer of project work during a very pleasant dinner first date. It seemed a dubious offer, perhaps from a government agency that might be related to Kirbee's disappearance. At first, it seemed they were playing the proverbial telephone tag, and she was not yet "it." But then Em grew worried. Jim Stevenson was reliable, conscientious, even on the dull and predictable side. Some might say dreadfully predictable in his daily routines. He answered his emails within twenty-four hours, the gold standard, and listened to his voice messages three times a day if he was within the country. He kept his appointments. In short, he was the preternatural opposite of Harley Travis Huber, her ex-husband, so Em felt she had grounds to worry. Once competitors for a prized appointment in the university geology department, although Em always found him likeable, Huber and the younger Stevenson were never friends. Receiving no answer at the professor's apartment, she then called his office number. The voice mail box was full and would not accept another message.

Deanna watched her mother from her seat in Em's

favorite chair in the living room. Sandy was upstairs engaged in packing and repacking her bags more efficiently for their imminent return to college for the fall term. Deanna, who simply threw most of what she owned into suitcases and hauled them along with her, never packed so much as two days in advance. Watching Em over the laptop screen her daughter guessed from the play of expressions across her mother's face, the fleeting frowns and the squinting eyes that something was up, and her mother was about to make a move.

Initially, after the divorce, Deanna had been unsure whether she would like living alone with her mother. After a short while she began to enjoy it. Em was hardly ever still unless it was late at night and she was reading a mystery. Without Huber Senior in the house, Em did as she pleased, when she pleased. Things did not have to be planned days in advance for his convenience. Deanna quickly learned the signs. Her mother was almost ready to make a break for it, and if she, Deanna, didn't stay alert, she'd be left home alone with the packing. Sandy was going out to lunch and an afternoon of shopping with two other girlfriends, leaving Deanna free to tail her mother.

The geology department office should be staffed by 8:30 a.m. or so. Em picked up her cell phone yet again. The administrative assistant, Charlene, answered on the first ring. She recognized the name on the caller ID as especially interesting to her because she replaced the younger woman who had been so attractive to Professor Huber.

"It's Em Huber, Charlene. I've left messages for Jim Stevenson, but he hasn't returned my calls. His voice mail is full. Have you seen him?" A quick explanation might help her cause. "We were discussing research."

Charlene managed the online department staff calendar, so she was aware Em and Stevenson had a dinner engagement. She thought it rather nice, Professor Stevenson needed someone steadier than that French ex-wife.

"You know, it's not like him, Mrs. Huber." Em winced at sound of "Mrs." "Oh, I'm sorry. *Ms. Huber.* But I've been so concerned. We haven't seen him. This is the second morning he hasn't come in or called. For some reason we have to keep track of Professor Stevenson. He checks in regularly even when he is in the field. Do you think I should call the chairman at home? We do have an emergency number to call if anything happens to Professor Stevenson. It's in Washington."

"I agree. It isn't like him. Has anyone looked in the lab? Perhaps he came in early and hasn't stopped by the office yet," Em suggested.

"There was no one there when I came in, and no one's gone by the office." Charlene was quite definite, and Em knew her well enough not to doubt her.

"Did he have any special plans for these two days? Any meetings?"

"I'm not seeing any on his calendar. For some reason, he always has to be accessible. It says 'cave,' day before yesterday. That would be the new little cave he and his students found in mid-state. He planned to measure it before turning it over to the archeology people. There were signs of use by native people, and others."

"Ah, where is the cave exactly, do you have the coordinates?" Em shared Stevenson's fondness for caves but hoped Stevenson wasn't lying somewhere injured in a heap of rock. Even with GPS coordinates a cave with a small opening might be a challenge to find.

"I can look it up, it may take me some time to find it. Do you think we should send someone out to his house? There should be someone else who can go." An urban dweller, her tone indicated Charlene was no fan of field work.

"I'm free this morning, I can go. You might call the

chairman, tell him I'm going to call on a professional friend of mine to go with me. I'll call you from Stevenson's place. Thanks." Em completed the call, which left Charlene understanding although Em might need the coordinates for the new cave, she didn't require the address of Jim Stevenson's apartment.

From her over large bag Em pulled out her wallet and searched it for a scrap of paper with a cell phone number. Her "professional friend," Nancy, answered on the third ring.

"Nancy, I'm so glad I caught you. Professor Stevenson's missing. He's been gone for at least a day and a half. Jim's the one who was so interested in Frank Kirbee's whereabouts. His office is about to call the Department Chair who will probably call the DOD if we can't find him. Can you meet me at his place? It's only a few blocks away from Frank Kirbee's house." Em gave her the address off Orange Street, in an area of large Victorian homes, many now converted to apartments inhabited by University faculty, staff and graduate students. As luck would have it, Nancy was at her desk inputting arrest data and more than happy to get away from it.

"Are we going caving?" Em looked up to find Deanna at her shoulder, boots on, prepared to march right out of the house.

"You can stay here, I'm just going to…" began Em.

"Look for a missing Professor, explore a cave and try not to get lost in the woods. I know. I'm coming, too. I'll tell Sandy where we're going." Deanna was not about to let her mother out of her sight, so she sent a text to Sandy, who was only upstairs.

Em could tell a lost cause when she saw one. "We can leave Jake with Anson. He's picking him up to take him to the vet at 10:00. Sandy can wait for them. He should enjoy that."

"Who, Dave or Jake?" Deanna was quickly typing a

text to Sandy about the dog. It was a measure of her loyalty to Em and of her sense of adventure that she was willing, at the moment, to forego seeing Dave Anson, if only briefly. Anson was not actively advancing his cause with her, and she had been cautioned by her mother as well.

"Both. Get the flashlights and the geology field kit. Don't forget the small pickaxes. The First Aid pack is in the car. I have to make a pit stop." Em took the stairs to her bedroom and changed into jeans and sturdy hiking boots as quickly as possible. Sandy poked her head out of her bedroom door as Em flew by on her way downstairs again.

"Don't forget to set the alarm and lock the house when you leave, Sandy."

Em and Deanna rolled up in front of a tall grey house with fancy white and rust trim. A wrap-around porch boasted original decorative turned wooden spindles under the railing and shorter spindles all around the top. Nancy's fleet car was waiting at the curb in front of the house. Em parked the aging van behind it. Deanna and Em met Nancy at the sidewalk.

"I've made a call so the folks Stevenson works for will know we're investigating. Should save time and aggravation. So what's the story? One professor dead, two missing, what's with the faculty all of a sudden?" Nancy asked.

Em looked at Deanna. "You're not hearing this, understand?"

"I never hear anything," her daughter replied dryly.

"Industrial espionage, more serious than I've seen before. Usually it's the opposition dumpster diving, messing with a website, phone phishing, getting someone hired into the competitor's business or pumping a drunken sales rep at a trade conference. This doesn't seem like the domestic article to me. I'm worried about him. Jim's geothermal, really top in his field, and spent three years in Washington into who only knows what. Huber's fossil fuel, and Kirbee's solar. I wonder, Nancy…"

"Then let's get going. I've got a ton of reports waiting for me back at the office." Nancy had done a fast database dive. "The landlady lives on the first floor. Her name is Schliemann, a widow with grown children who live out of state. She rents the second floor to our friend and the attic rooms to young married grad students named Margolis. They have a pair of toddlers."

"Schliemann? Really? A guy by that name dug up the ruins of ancient Troy." Em was intrigued. Archeologists in the nineteenth century often had the opportunity to hang on to some of their findings.

"Yes, really, I looked them up while you were on your way. What took you so long?" She was always impatient to be on the move, even short stakeouts were a sore challenge for Nancy.

"We were detained. Anson came early to pick up the dog." Em looked at Deanna who shrugged and bounded up the porch steps to ring the doorbell.

Mrs. Schliemann must have been watching for them at a window. The carved oak door with its thick glass panel neatly curtained opened immediately. A diminutive woman appeared with a curling head of white hair, immaculately clean, but a trifle disordered.

Anxious to welcome them the little lady said, "Oh, I do apologize, I've been cleaning. You must be Ms. Huber and her friends. The geology department called to tell me you were on your way. So nice, and so concerned. They are right, we haven't seen the professor. I checked with Mrs. Margolis. He's always so good with her children, too. And they are such a handful! Twin boys! Come in, come in. We'll go right up to the professor's apartment."

The landlady walked briskly towards the staircase. A gracefully curved banister hugged the left side of the entry hall. Mrs. Schliemann proceeded without waiting for further introductions. Em looked around curiously, looking for archeological relicts, but to her disappointment saw none. An old Turkish carpet lay on the floor of the hallway that stretched the full length of the house. The walls were papered with a faded light green William Morris floral pattern.

Nancy and Deanna got ahead of the landlady on the stairs, and Em only caught up with them at the door to Stevenson's rooms. Mrs. Schliemann unlocked the door, and stood aside so Nancy could enter first. "She's FBI, isn't she? The Department warned me," she said in a stage whisper to Em and Deanna.

"My, news travels fast in this town. Has anyone else been inquiring for the professor?" Nancy asked aloud.

"Oh, no, dear. You are the first," Mrs. Schliemann assured them.

The apartment was sunny. The windows would be considered oversized now. It had a rather funky smell Deanna quickly traced. "Oh, look at the ferret. Isn't it cute?" Beady sharp eyes on an active little animal greeted them from a wire cage. An odd assemblage of cardboard boxes taped together with small doors and windows stood next to the cage. "He's even got a playscape for the ferret. Looks like there's no food or water left. Can we feed it?"

"She," Mrs. Schliemann replied. "Her name is Monika. Let's find her some food."

Nancy, followed closely by Em, checked the three generously sized rooms and the kitchen and found it neat, but not overly so. Clean dishes were in the dish drainer, and rinsed breakfast dishes were waiting in the sink. Clothes were thrown on a chair in the bedroom, but the bed was made. Books, magazines and papers were spread all over the desk in the front room Stevenson used as an office. There was no sign of a laptop or other computer. On a wide wooden table a pile of U.S. Geological Survey maps were stacked neatly, held down at the corners by smooth stones, one of which looked for all the world like a dinosaur egg.

Pensive, Em stood over the stack of maps. With her finger she traced a thin black pen line to a tiny X on a hillside, its height indicated by elevation lines on the map. "I wonder if this is the cave." A call to the geology department was answered immediately.

"Charlene, we are at Jim Stevenson's apartment. Yes, we've met Mrs. Schliemann, thank you for calling ahead. He's not here. The ferret hasn't been fed so he's been away a while. Listen, I've found a map. Can you give me the coordinates for the new cave?" Em found a scrap of paper to write them down. Charlene told her what she remembered about the location of the cave.

"Thank you, yes, the FBI agent is with us. The cave will be our next stop, right, Nancy?"

Nancy had her gloves on and was making a systematic examination of the top dressing of Stevenson's desk. She shook her head, her auburn hair bounced around neatly, all in order. "Someone's been through this. No computer."

Overhead the Margolis twins were screeching with glee and being told to, "Get down out of there!" by a harried female voice.

Still maintaining cell phone contact Em said, "Stevenson must have a computer. Do you know what he used, Charlene?"

"A good bit of his work was done on the mainframe, his teaching assistant would know." Charlene pondered this for a moment. "There was a special hardened laptop he took into the field. He said it could 'take a lickin' and keep on tickin'."

"Good to know, we'll keep you posted. Tell the chairman hello for me." Em signed off.

"Are you all ready? Let's take the map. The GPS coordinates Charlene gave me match the little black mark here." Em pointed to the tiny mark so Deanna and Nancy could spot it easily. "The access is a dirt road through the woods. There's an old cabin at the end of it. I think she said it wasn't very far up the hill in the rock fall area." Em rolled up the map.

"You should use gloves," Nancy said without looking up as she finished examining the single desk drawer. "I can't tell if anything is missing, but it's been disturbed, that's certain. There's no sign of forced entry, but if they have him, they may have his keys, too."

"Mrs. Schliemann, did he take his car? Is it the same old Rover?" Em was on her way towards the apartment door. Deanna stopped teasing the ferret and rose quickly. Receiving an affirmative answer, they thanked the landlady who promised to be vigilant and to call Nancy if anyone came to look for Stevenson.

They were back out on the street trying to decide which car to take, Em arguing for the van, and Nancy for the fleet car. Deanna sized up the situation, went to the van to grab the backpack, First Aid kit, the pack with the geology field kit, flashlights and her own bag with snacks and water. She piled it all into the back seat of the fleet car.

"Mom, let's go. The last time you took a van down a dirt road you blew out the springs."

Nancy laughed. "Good that someone can make a decision. I'll drive, you navigate."

The trip up the highway and onto the secondary road took them only twenty minutes. Em was surprised by the power of the compact black fleet car. Nancy explained it was designed to look insignificant but had a capable engine and enhanced suspension. The secondary road led through houses widely spaced apart and set back from the road on acres of wooded land. The stone walls on either side looked as if they had spent two hundred years sinking back into the ground. Using the map, Em plotted a course to a winding two-lane road past farmland and then into deeper woods. At first, the road appeared to dead end for no apparent reason. But on reaching the end, they spotted a dirt road taking a right angle off towards the north.

"This must be it." Em wrangled the large map. "There's a dotted line on the survey map that indicates an unimproved road. Looking at the scale, there's a building about half a mile down here. Can we stop? Let's get out and check for tracks in the dirt." Em had no sooner spoken than Deanna was out of the car and walking down the right side of the dirt road, head down surveying the ground. Nancy joined her working the left side of the road.

"Em, it's two cars. Very distinctive treads. A second car went in and out over tracks of the first car, judging by the direction of the tread pattern. Any idea what tires are on the Range Rover?" Nancy knelt by a muddy patch, thoughtless of the pants legs of her working wardrobe.

"No, sorry. Whatever they are, they were expensive. The Rover has a checkered history. It was confiscated by police in a drug bust, and Jim Stevenson bought it. It has lots of hidden compartments. Hopefully, they're all empty now. He told me all about it at dinner."

"Let's get going." Nancy wasn't liking what she'd seen on the ground. "Don't slam the doors." To her, it appeared the Range Rover turned into the dirt road and had not come out. All three got themselves back in the car quietly. Nancy drove slowly down the dirt road. The low growing bushes closed around them, reaching in to scrape the car.

"Stop! This is not good." Em spoke as Nancy brought

the car to a halt. They could see the outline of a wooden porch through the trees ahead, but to their right they could see the Rover had been driven into the Autumn Olive bushes and left there. Scrapes on the branches of the bushes showed the Rover had been driven through them with some force. The bushes had then been pulled back up to hide the Rover.

"Mom, if you were expecting good, we wouldn't be here with Nancy," Deanna replied with attitude.

It was on the tip of Em's tongue to tell Deanna to stay in the car, instead she said, "You're right," and began loading her pockets with the essentials. "Take the First Aid kit. Leave the rest, Dee."

"I'm going to get the car off the road." Nancy backed the fleet car up until she found an opening along the side of the road and backed it in far enough to screen the vehicle from view.

After a brief conference, it was decided they would approach the Rover first, and then move on to the cabin, keeping out of sight as far as possible. The Rover was close so it was easy to keep to the side of the road and get into the bushes by the abandoned car. It was locked. To Em's relief, no one appeared to be in the vehicle, and there was no blood they could see. Working her way around the front of the Rover on the driver's side towards the cabin, Em spotted an earth-toned suede leather bound book and stooped to pick it up. Its natural color blended in with the dead leaves. There was no name on it, just page after page of outline sketches of prehistoric animals. Em recognized the carefully shaded images, among them a cave bear, two aurochs, the ancestors of modern cattle with their horns curling forward, a horse with a long nose, short legs and a roly poly body, and a mammoth. "These have to be Stevenson's drawings. He'd never have left this behind," Em concluded sadly.

Deanna came around the Rover so quickly she almost

fell over her mother who was still crouched close to the ground. Em stood up to show Nancy and Deanna the contents of the sketch book.

"Those are strange looking horses," Nancy said as she looked over Em's shoulder.

Three horse heads were drawn on the open page, one right over the other. "They were different then, 20,000 or 30,000 years ago. It's a copy of a famous wall painting from the Chauvet cave in France. It's his hobby." There was a catch in Em's voice.

Seeing Em's distress, Nancy said, "We'll find him. There's no sign anyone went into the woods from here. Whoever left the car walked out by the road. Probably towards the cabin. You two should stay here with the Rover."

"Like that's really going to happen." Deanna was emphatic.

"Yeah, like Deanna says." Em shook the sketch book at her friend.

"Alright then, stay behind me." Nancy called in the location of the Range Rover, giving its license plate and the circumstances of its discovery.

Ever so quietly they began their approach to the cabin, keeping under cover. There was no sound from the cabin until they approached quite close. Then, a male voice began singing in slurred French. It sounded as if the singer had been drinking, but the song had blurred semi-conscious quality to it.

"Could be Stevenson," Em told them.

"Sounds plastered and I don't even understand the language," Deanna whispered. "What if he's holed up in the cabin to be alone with a bottle?"

"Not likely," her mother replied as Nancy slipped off to get a look in one of the windows at the side. Em put her hand on Deanna's shoulder. "Wait for it."

Nancy, her gun drawn, disappeared around the side of

the building. In a few moments she emerged from the bushes growing next to the opposite side of the cabin. She motioned for them to join her by the porch. "There's a man inside tied up to a bedstead. It looks as if he's alone. You'll have to tell me if it's Stevenson."

"Take it easy, I'll go first just in case he isn't alone. Deanna, watch the road."

The peeling wooden door was locked. Em drew out her pocket knife and proceeded to carve out a nick by the lock. A blunt blade jammed into the gap popped the door open. Nancy entered first. The simple one room wood frame, hunting cabin had no place for anyone to hide. The few remaining pieces of furniture looked hand built and well worn, a table, several chairs and the bed.

"Who'sa that?" the half-clad man on the bed asked.

"It's Em Huber, Jim!" Em knelt by the side of the wooden bed frame where Stevenson lay on a disreputable looking mattress.

"Emmie, Emmie, so glad ... gotta go! Coming back. Soon. Nasty, *nasty* woman…." Speech was difficult, his mouth was dry. Eyes closed, he seemed about to lose consciousness. Stevenson's hands and feet were bound to the wooden bed frame with clothes line, new and still stiff. His arms and legs were bare and showed bruises, some fresh, some of which were older and had turned a sickly shade of green. Cuts and scratches, several deep, begged to be cleaned and dressed.

"We'd better get him out of here." Em looked around for Nancy who was examining items on a shelf on the other side of the room.

"He's not drunk. There's a collection of drugs, enough to do considerable damage. Some to keep him immobilized and some to get him to talk. Your friend's been interrogated here." Nancy pulled out her phone and made a call to a number on speed dial.

"Deanna, do we have any water? Good, get sugar and

salt out of the First Aid kit, put it in the water and shake it up. Then go watch the road," her mother instructed.

"She did it. Stuck me full of needles. Take me away, take me away…big noise coming in. In a day or two. Don't know for sure when. See if I'm for real. 'Course I'm real." Jim Stevenson's garbled speech caught his audience as if frozen in the frame.

With obvious effort, Stevenson struggled against the ropes that tied his hands and feet to the four bed posts. He gave a dry cough. His face was unshaven, and showed sweat, dust and the strain of his captivity. His shorts were intact, but his tee shirt was stained with sweat and traces of blood.

Em wiped his face with several days of bristles gently with a towelette from the First Aid kit while Deanna shook the water bottle.

"Drink this, Jim." Em held the plastic water bottle to his lips.

Stevenson gulped down the water. "Better, *mucch* better. Monique! Monique!"

"Girlfriend?" Nancy asked. "I'm calling for an ambulance."

"First wife." Em paused to think. "We fed your ferret, *Monika*, Jim. Hold still. I'll cut the ropes off." Using her pocket knife Em freed his right hand and placed the bottle of water in it. "Drink it slowly."

"Good." Stevenson finished the water off in three gulps. Deanna snickered.

"He named the ferret after his first wife?" Nancy exclaimed.

"Who's she?" Stevenson appeared to revive and made a determined effort to stay coherent.

"This is Nancy, she's an FBI agent who came along to rescue you. Damn, do you think they could have put any more rope around him? He's lucky they didn't cut off the circulation." The ropes were proving stubborn, and Em's knife was no longer sharp.

"Pretty. I like tall women! Neanderthals had red hair, too. Tall women. I'm part Neanderthal. We're all part Neanderthal." Stevenson was not wholly rational, but he was in there trying.

"I can easily believe that. You may have gotten more than your fair share, Professor." Em looked down at Stevenson's feet. "He even has hairy toes."

Stevenson closed his eyes, "Questions. So many questions. They teach you to lie. Promised me a villa, what do I want with villas?"

From her post at the window Deanna spoke in a low voice. "We've got company, Mom. Big black car. Fancy. I, uh, don't think it's the FBI. It's a man and punky little woman. The chick's staying in the car."

"Them! Get me loose!" Stevenson roared. He managed to snap the ropes on his left hand nearly sending Em sprawling. His legs were still firmly tied. She tumbled to the floor next to the bed.

"Get down, Deanna. Stay down!" Nancy stood behind the door, gun ready. Deanna ducked for cover into the corner by the front window.

The man came through the door with force, slamming it against Nancy. He saw Stevenson sit bolt upright on the bed, and then he whirled on Nancy. She gave him a solid punch to the torso with her left hand, grabbed his head and brought it crashing down on her knee. Stunned, he grappled with her. When they came within reach, although still tied to the bed, Stevenson flung himself forward and grabbed the intruder around the neck, pulling him away from Nancy. On the floor Em rolled out of the way. Stevenson got the man's neck in the crook of his arm, grabbed his own bicep with his other hand and choked him.

"Tap out *orr* pass out," Stevenson said loudly in his captive's ear.

The man chose to struggle. The professor tightened his choke hold and in seven seconds the accomplice dropped like a stone, nearly carrying Stevenson with him. Nancy recovered quickly, pulled out hand cuffs and swung the man's hands behind his back.

Stevenson landed back on the bed with a hard thump, panting.

"Any more water?" he intoned, eyes closing.

Deanna picked herself up from the floor in the corner to hand him their last bottle of spring water.

"Nice going Prof! Wow! Wait 'til I tell Sandy!" Deanna began rapidly texting.

"Stop that this instant, Dee! Haven't you learned yet? Go silent," her mother hissed.

Deanna looked up, chastened. "Oopsies! I'm putting it down."

"Em, can you get the rope off his feet in one piece. I want use it on this guy." Nancy hauled her captive straight out on the floor to tie his feet.

"Pierce, she called him Pierce," Stevenson added in a blurry voice.

"Where did she go, she's not in the car." Fidgeting with impatience, Deanna returned to the window. "Should we go find her?"

"In a minute, let me get the rope off Jim's legs. Deanna and I will go look for her. I think I know who it is. We can't let her get away again." Em was not about to give up the chase because they found Stevenson, although she could tell Nancy would object to this plan.

Stevenson finished off the water, rubbed his wrists briefly, then attempted to stand up next to the bed. Getting his balance he seemed to teeter in Nancy's direction. In a surprisingly agile move, he grabbed her around the waist, pulled her towards him and planted a lusty kiss on her mouth. Nancy still had her gun in her hand and instinctively raised it.

"Nancy don't shoot him! He's harmless, it's the drugs," Em exclaimed.

"Thanks for *ressscuing* me," Stevenson said to the tall red headed Nancy, a lopsided grin on his face.

Nancy pushed him away towards the bed. "Sit back down there. I ought to arrest you for assaulting an officer."

"Good one." James Stevenson, PhD, distinguished Professor of Geology, descendant of Neanderthals, grinned, squeezed his eyes shut and sank back down on the worn-out mattress. "Dizzy. Too many needles."

25

OVER THE EDGE

———◆———

COMING OUT OF the cabin in a rush, Em was determined to investigate the noise she heard at the back of the structure, towards the open hay field. Finding Stevenson alone and unguarded suggested a shortage of manpower to her. Otherwise, it seemed unlikely the man called Pierce would come by himself with only one woman to check on Stevenson's confinement. The car, possibly a rental, appeared to be a new luxury size model with New York plates. Certainly, it was a more expensive car than Em herself owned. The front passenger door was ajar. A small woman's Burberry raincoat lay draped haphazardly across the front seat as if it had been pulled towards the passenger side door, and then left behind. Deanna ran up to stand by her mother.

"She's here," Em exclaimed. "He drove, of course. She just had to have the Lincoln. The keys are probably still in his pocket. They're certainly not in the car, or she would have taken off with it."

"If she's from New York City, maybe she doesn't drive," her daughter suggested.

"Dee, she's in the wind. If we don't find her fast, she'll be gone, even out of the country. I think that's what they were planning for Stevenson, and Hussein, too." Em began searching the ground on the passenger side and stooped down to look under the car as well.

"You mean the game's on foot?" Deanna quipped.

"It's not funny, smarty. Start looking for footprints. Quick. We need to know what they look like."

"Mom, you're practically standing on them. Behind you."

"Oh shit! You're right." Em looked over her shoulder and stepped carefully away from the impression in the damp ground. "Look, it's small. About a size 6 narrow. It's hard to get a shoe this small. Flat heel, probably boots, looks like a hand stitched sole. You don't see that much anymore." Em walked briskly around the car, and then off back towards the cabin porch. No footprints led away from the cabin back down the dirt road.

"I pressed the panic button, Mom. I've got it on Beacon." The security fob dangled from her hand, a tiny light blinking.

"Good, we should have help coming. Let's hope I can catch up to her fast enough to delay her for them. Nancy will have people coming, too." Em started off towards the yard in back of the cabin with Deanna trailing behind her.

"You stay here, Dee. I'll bet she's armed."

"Sure, I let Mom go off by herself. And how am I supposed to explain it to the rest of the family?" Deanna remarked.

"So make yourself useful, tell Nancy what we're doing," Em replied, reminded of the consequences of righteous wrath from her older children towards Deanna.

Deanna took the porch steps two at a time. She darted into the cabin to alert Nancy, who had her hands full with the amorous Stevenson and the bruised and angry Pierce. The agent had Pierce in handcuffs, and she was trying to decide how best to deflect Stevenson's friendly advances without resorting to drastic measures. Slugging the rescued professor was not a high option. Deanna announced their intentions to follow the woman who had accompanied Pierce and turned to run back out of the cabin before Nancy could frame a reply demanding she and her mother stay put.

"Good luck, Professor!" Deanna yelled over her shoulder as she bolted out the front door, which left Nancy fuming.

Em followed the diminutive footprints around to the back of the cabin to a spot under the window where her quarry apparently stood listening. The direction of the footprints was confused and seemed to indicate she might have headed back to the car.

Deanna found her mother standing, listening and watching the woods to her left. Em turned to survey a field of tall grass in front of her. It was a hayfield that had not yet been mowed.

"Where would I go," Em asked aloud. "Alone and on foot." The breeze shifted, coming out of the northwest carrying with it the sound of truck and car traffic. "She'll head towards the nearest main road. There were no tracks on the dirt road I could see."

Deanna joined her mother actively scanning the ground in an arc along the edge of the field. Off towards the right side, in line with a hasty retreat from the car, Em found the trail of mashed down long grass leading across the field from the cabin.

"She's heading straight for the main road up there. I don't know why we didn't see her. You stay on the left side of her trail, I'll stay on the right. She's running scared. Let's go." Em took off at a fast jog with Deanna several paces ahead of her running easily. Not even halfway across the field Deanna stopped short to look over a larger area of matted grass.

"Mom, come look. I think she fell and sort of flailed around in the grass."

Breathing more rapidly Em ran up beside Deanna to

examine the ground. "I think you're right. It looks as if she went down hard. There's the rut that tripped her up. See her handprints here, too."

Deanna's sharp eyes caught a glint of light from deep in the grass. She got down on her knees and began pulling at the tuffs of grass until she reached the rust brown soil of the field.

"See something?"

"Yup, it looks like... an earring." Deanna held her prize up for her mother who carefully took it from her hand and held it out in the sunlight.

"Oh look what you found, pearls and diamonds." The two women looked with astonishment at a beautifully crafted gold earring. Its shape was a graceful S curve, two matched pearls in the center with two smaller round diamonds set on either end accented with tiny gold leaves.

"Finders keepers," Deanna breathed.

"It's evidence, honey." Em wrapped the earring in a tissue and carefully stowed it in her pocket. "Let's get going." The two women rose from the ground, looking to pick up the trail through the grass. It was not difficult to follow. They hadn't traced her tracks much farther across the field when her path took a sharp left turn and angled directly into the woods.

"Her strides are shorter now, she's going slower. I think she's walking, Mom." Deanna was ahead of her mother through the tall grass.

"Maybe she sprained an ankle, so she headed for the nearest cover. That's probably why we didn't see her in the open field."

"She's definitely walking, but not limping much."

"We need to be careful and quiet now. If she's hurt she may hide in the bushes. Remember, she could be armed." Em held it in her mind, someone had killed Professor Hussein.

Tangled vines and Autumn Olive bushes surrounded

the field at the edge of the tree line. Em and Deanna, keeping low, stepped cautiously into the underbrush. Wild rambling rose canes formed dense snarled barriers on either side of them. Paths created by small animals laced through the blackberry brambles at ground level. The rose briars above caught clothing and scratched the arms and legs of all three women who passed through the thicket. Halfway through the briars, Em was forced to stop and yank a branch of rose thorns out of her jeans. She emerged from the brambles to find Deanna kneeling over a fresh trail in the soft dark earth of the forest floor. A thin line of blood trickled down her cheek from a small scratch.

"Deer tracks under the boot tracks. Looks like a buck. She went that'a way," Deanna pointed out the direction of the tracks leading deeper into the woods. She straightened up and the two women started off at a good pace.

Once through the undergrowth, they found the forest on the hillside was densely wooded, a high canopy of leaves with deeply shaded open ground below. Their progress was quicker now. Tall maple, beech and several species of oak trees formed a dense canopy above them. Deep leaf mold covered the ground silencing their footsteps. It was not an old growth forest. The standing trees were not of great age, only a few with trunks too twisted to be logged had attained substantial size. To Em, who spotted the truly old low rotting stumps among the younger trees, it meant the hillside had not been cut for lumber since before the WW II. Here and there, sprouting from an ancient stump, she saw the distinctive leaves of the American Chestnut, now all but extinct.

They picked up her footprints easily as she headed along the wide straight path at the base of the hillside parallel to a free flowing stream. Em suspected the wide path they were following was an abandoned lumbering road and would lead through the woods, possibly up the hill, but might not lead to another road. The footprints continued along the stream for a short distance, and then led to the water's edge, appearing as sharply defined imprints in the wet sand on the stream's bank, and then plunged into the water. Like most streams, brooks and rivers in Connecticut, the stream's general direction of flow was north to south, towards Long Island Sound. Em and Deanna stood on the bank and looked up and down the stream.

"She's trying to hide her trail. Which way do we go, Mom?" Deanna was anxious to keep moving. "Probably thinks they'll use dogs to track her."

Em looked carefully into the stream and at the opposite bank, and began to chuckle. The stream flowed through a channel strewn with chunks of basalt of varying sizes, all rounded by tumbling in the flow of the stream.

"Could be, but someone forgot to tell her not to splash the rocks. She went north," Em observed.

Deanna started to put one foot into the water to follow the fleeing woman, but Em put out a hand to stop her. "Along the path. It will be quicker and quieter. Watch the banks." The two women started off immediately at a running walk, watching the bank as they went.

The path curved sharply around a mound of earth at the base of the hill forcing Em and Deanna to climb up a steep slope on hands and knees. At the top of the mound, Em signaled Deanna to stay low so they could look around the bend before continuing. Their quarry was still out of sight ahead of them. The sound of fast moving water rushing hard against the rocks reached them. They found themselves looking at a small pond formed by an old rock and earth dam.

The water still held behind the dam was too deep for the slight woman they were following to continue walking in the water. Even from the top of the mound, they could easily see where she clambered up the bank leaving a trail of muddy prints on the hillside. The glen was quiet as they crossed the mound to stand on the dam. The low murmur of traffic on the road beyond the hill reached them. The stream had breached the dam, finding its way around through a weak point at the hillside end.

"She's climbing up the hill right through dead leaves. She's going to be covered with ticks." Em shook her head.

"Yeah, might even be deer ticks. If we catch her we'll have to have her scrubbed before they settle in or she'll get Lyme Disease." Deanna was knowledgeable. She spent her childhood avoiding tick bites.

Em paused to reconnoiter. The land around the pond was gently sloping. On the other side she spotted a narrow path that appeared to lead to a wider trail up the hillside. At her feet, brook trout swam in the deepest water next to the dam. Always easily distracted, Deanna was hopping up and down on the dam at the edge of the pond scaring the frogs on the bank. They jumped off into the water with satisfying plops. Seeing healthy amphibians, Em reached down, cupped her hand, filled it with water and raised it to her lips.

"Mom, you're not supposed to do that," Deanna mocked.

"Hasn't killed me yet. Let's go."

The stream below the dam ran through a narrow channel and coursed over the rocks eroding the bank. Em chose to try their luck crossing the old dam. "Be careful. Don't fall in. If you fall in, don't scream."

"Yeah, right, Mom. Famous last words." Deanna knew her mother had a very distinctive shriek when provoked by the unforeseen.

Fortunately, Em made her way without incident across the first section of the dam. The sluice in the middle of the dam was dry, the water level now too low to flow over it. Water streamed around the end of the dam. Em walked up to the broken edge, backed up and took a few running steps and flung herself across the gap at the opposite bank. She landed in the soggy earth on the other side and stood up smiling with muddy knees and dirty hands. Em moved aside just in time as Deanna leaped more gracefully across the rushing water to land standing up on the bank. Moving quickly, Em dipped her hands in the pond and wiped them on a tuft of green grass. She pulled the smudged white sweatshirt off over her head revealing the sage green tee beneath. The grimy sweatshirt was then tied around her waist.

"Mom, we're on a path here."

"Jeez, she had to go up the steepest part of the hill. If we follow, she'll hear us or see us easily. Let's take the trail over there. It leads uphill and it's not as steep." Em headed off along the pond, picking up the pace, and turned onto the wider blazed trail. Blue squares were painted at shoulder height on the trees along one side spaced at irregular intervals.

"I hope you know what we're doing," Deanna muttered loud enough for her mother to hear her.

"We'll have to keep her tracks in sight, Dee."

Deanna was talking to herself about how they could be expected to do that but found it wasn't hard. The person they were following either had no sense of how to hide her tracks or indeed had stopped making any effort to do so. Em slowed as the wider path turned more directly uphill. Deanna kept up the faster pace longer, but soon she stopped and dropped down to hide behind the base of a fallen tree. Deanna made hand signals to her mother and pointed uphill to her left. Em crouched down as she approached Deanna's position at the side of the path behind the shield of upturned tree roots. Deanna pointed silently. Em crawled around the mass of roots. She could see the top of the hill was treeless and rocky.

Sitting down on the ground, her head between her knees, audibly panting was a small woman with short gleaming jet black hair. Her leather boots and pants legs were sopping and covered with dirt and wet leaves. A black bag rested on the exposed rock next to her. Off to the right, the sound of cars and the occasional truck could be heard.

Now with their fugitive in sight, truly only a good long stone's throw away, Em was unsure how to proceed. They were unarmed. The woman appeared an easy target, but the black bag worried Em. They would need to be closer if they wanted to stall her long enough for help to arrive. Em rubbed her hand over the knotted cord bracelet on her wrist. Reasoning a tired adversary would be easier to manage, Em motioned for Deanna to follow her farther up the path towards the top of the hill. They were working their way up the path around and above her. Tree cover became sparse.

Em could almost feel the moment the figure seated on the hill spotted them. Her body tensed, her hand went to the strap of the black leather bag. She clutched it tightly. It was too late for Em and Deanna to retreat. Em scanned the ground, for once there seemed to be no palm sized stones handy. The rock of the hilltop was bare, scoured by glaciers. Long narrow gouges ran parallel across the face of the basalt. Jagged boulders on the height had been carried along on the ice and dropped as it melted. The surface of the hill disappeared abruptly on the west in a sheer cliff. The cliff stopped the fleeing woman when she reached the top. Noise from the road below followed the updraft of the breeze to their ears.

With unexpected agility, she sprang to her feet. Em, with Deanna behind her, was almost clear of the tree line. There was little distance between them and the woman who had fled from the cabin.

"Who are you? Why are you following me?" she yelled.

Em put a disarming smile on her face but did not reply. She and Deanna continued to walk slowly up the rock slope towards her. Way off in the distance down the hill they heard a familiar bark. Once close to the top of the hill it was a surprise to see the cliff and the forty-foot drop between them and the road below. Trap rock, basalt, a dense old volcanic rock fractured in flat planes, forming sharp edges. The cliff was a straight drop with piles of talus, cobblestone sized rubble, at the base. The basalt ridge and the sheer cliff extended a good distance in either direction. For Em, at that moment, it was not a happy geological development.

Em stopped her advance when she was close enough to block retreat towards the road but near enough to run the woman down if she chose to take off to the south.

As she drew closer, the woman's eyes narrowed and she snarled at Em. "I know who you are. You bitch, I told you to stay out of it."

"Do I have the pleasure of addressing Filomena Morena Levitt Kirbee?" An impeccably groomed small woman with small features and an expensive high maintenance do faced her. The salon cut appeared longer on top, gave her more height and tapered to the neck. *Stall, stall, stall,* Em thought rapidly. The dog's bark was growing closer.

"Morena! Filomena Morena! You interfering bitch. Why couldn't you leave it alone?" She reached into a side pocket of the black bag and pulled out a small elegant pistol, which she pointed straight at Em.

"Nice purse," Deanna exclaimed enthusiastically.

Her mother frowned. *A concealed carry bag — she is very prepared this one.*

"Frank Kirbee hired me. I needed the money. What's he like in bed anyway?" Em worked to keep her voice steady.

"Mother!"

"Was there anything I should know? Why did you divorce him? A little dysfunction was it?" Em forced a casual tone and motioned Deanna to be quiet. "The young are so easily shocked, don't you think?"

"Nothing like that. He spent his life in the lab, with his brilliant buddy Al. When things were going well there, he hardly had time for me. When things went wrong, he was all over me."

"Oh, not promising," Em remarked.

"You, what do you know with that bed hopping husband of yours? Couldn't you keep him at home?" Filomena retorted.

"Is that why you stole SunSprite? To get even?" Em asked.

Deanna was rolling her eyes and fidgeting behind Em. She had never seen a verbal cat fight between two grown women.

"Yes. Frank had no time for me, so I stole his damned invention. Serves him right. And Al Hussein, too."

"What happened to Professor Hussein?" Em played for time, all the while thinking, *This kind of thing only happens in books.*

"All a big mistake, it was an accident. We offered him money, a great deal of money. But he wouldn't leave. He said *this* was home now. Al struggled, he shouldn't have done that."

"So he got shot? Okay, but how did you end up in the river?" Em was truly puzzled.

"Oh, you figured that out, did you? Someone was coming towards us from the street. I made a wrong turn and slipped off the bank. But it worked out, now they're looking for a dead woman in the river. They're not looking for me."

Filomena Morena waved the small elegant weapon in a way a seasoned shooter would never do.

Em locked her knees to keep them from shaking. *That's what you think, lady. I was looking for you. At least it's not a big gun, certainly not a Glock,* which was the extent of Em's knowledge of contemporary firearms.

"Why the field testing? Seems like serious development effort to go through," Em advanced her own pet theory.

"The people I'm selling it to don't take faulty goods lightly." Filomena was quite definite.

"Release no piece before it's fine. I wish all software developers felt that way. You have to have it perfect or risk your life?"

Her adversary nodded vigorously. "Yes, you have it right."

"Filomena, do you realize you're risking your life anyway? Sell it out of the country and it's espionage. What is it? The Russians? The Iranians? The Chinese? The North Koreans?" Em tried to read Filomena's expression for a clue to the identity of the purchasers.

The other woman laughed slyly.

"More than one?"

"It'll serve Frank right. All that talk about making it here in America. They will pay better." Filomena made a slow grin.

"You're crazy. There will be no place you can hide if anything goes wrong." Em had no hope she could talk Filomena out of her plans.

"Brazil is a very big country. Enough of this. Get over here. You're going to jump off the cliff or I'll shoot your daughter." Filomena Morena lowered her eyes and took aim at Deanna who stood next to her mother on the left.

"You're kidding, right?" Em heard a sharp intake of breath beside her. "This is like the old joke about if your friend asked you to jump off a bridge, would you do it?"

Em determined to stay in control, but she was growing alarmed. Help had not advanced quickly enough. One or two well-placed shots were all it would take. Then, Em noticed Filomena's hand shaking.

"I mean it, get moving! Jump, or I'll shoot your daughter." Filomena screwed up her face to look fierce.

"I jump and you'll shoot her anyway. Get behind me, Deanna." Em stood her ground, holding Filomena's eyes with her own. Beside her, Deanna, who did not follow her mother's direction, started to jump up and down lightly on her toes. Her fists came up to her waist.

"Stop that, Deanna," her mother ordered. "See what you've done now? She gets nervous and then she starts hopping around. Personality disorder, really." Em slipped her sweatshirt off her waist. "Calm down, Deanna." Quietly under her breath she said to her daughter, "Aek doe teen," which in Hindi or Urdu meant one two three. "Aek." Deanna continued to hop, moving around Em.

"What's wrong with her? Stay still!" Filomena demanded.

"Slightly demented, we try to cover it up. Doe."

Em whirled her muddy sweatshirt high and wide towards Filomena's head. She pushed Deanna out of the way and dived to the right out of the line of fire. "Teen," she exclaimed as she lunged to grab Filomena's right arm. Caught off guard Filomena let out a cry as Em wrestled with her for the gun. Although smaller, Filomena Morena was wiry and fought Em with the strength of an adrenalin rush. Em had a solid hold on her arm and forced it down, but she couldn't wrench the gun from her hand. The gun went off. Em felt a fiery pain sear across her left thigh.

At the base of the hill a dog barked excitedly.

"Dammit all, drop the gun!" Em tugged harder on Filomena and elbowed her in the ribs as hard as she could.

This was too much for Deanna. Em saw a fist fly past her to land on the side of Filomena's nose, snapping her head back. Filomena recovered, and a look of pure anger and hate filled her face. Em turned her body, attempting to block her blows. Filomena squeezed the trigger with a will this time, hitting Em low and outside, stunning Em who momentarily loosened her grasp.

Appalled, Deanna put all her weight and strength into her fist and landed a punch squarely on the women's jar. It knocked Filomena to the ground. The gun fell out of her hand as she fell, striking her head on the rock face.

"Yow, that hurts!" Em gasped as she gripped her hip.

"Did I kill her? I think she hit her head." Deanna was wringing a sore fist as she moved towards her mother.

"I doubt it. If someone holds a gun on you and *threatens* to shoot you, whatever damage you manage to do to them is self-defense, without killing them. Get her gun. I think you know how to use it." Em grimaced and swallowed hard.

"Yeah, Uncle Bob." Deanna stooped to pick up the small gun. "I like the purse."

"Don't even think about it." Em pulled the cord bracelet off her wrist. As she did so she saw the blood smear from her hip. She tossed the bracelet to Deanna. "Here, use this to tie her up. I've got a knife…" Em staggered as she stepped downhill to prop herself against a glacial boulder.

"I've got one." Placing the gun down on the rock carefully, well out of the unconscious woman's reach, Deanna stooped down. "She's breathing!" She pulled a Swiss Army knife from her pants pocket, unwound the bracelet and cut the cord in two. First she tied Filomena's feet together, which seemed illogical to Em. "She's got some sort of red rash on her arms. There's some on her face, too."

"I saw that." Em started to sing softly the old Blues tune, "'Poison Ivy, Poison Ivy.' She probably picked it up when they pulled Hussein's body off the path and dumped him in the weeds by the river."

"I'm not touching it." Deanna tied their captive's arms together above the wrist. "Those nice boots are ruined from all the mud."

"Yes, I'll say, and she ruined my Gloria's, too." Em

looked down ruefully at the dark stain growing on her thigh. "I think I hear Jake."

"Really? We could scream." Deanna sucked in a deep breath and reached to retrieve the gun.

"Why? We're done here. We got our woman, Dee." In pain, Em shifted against the rock.

"Let's sing. We need a fight song." Deanna began to yell at the top of her lungs an old football fight song, *Bulldog! Bulldog! Bow Wow Wow!* On the second chorus, her mother joined in, both ended with a burst of relieved laughter and the sound carried down the hillside.

A happy barking erupted from the path up the hill, and a large black dog broke cover and made his way up the rocks. Jake was followed by David Anson who trudged behind him. Anson stopped abruptly to take in the sight of Em propped against a rock, blood trickling down behind her, and Deanna standing next to her gun in hand.

"Hey, don't shoot! We're friendly." Into his collar Anson said, "They're okay. They disarmed the fugitive and tied her up. She's alive, right?" He hastened to check the woman and found normal respiration and pulse.

Deanna shrugged and stepped towards Anson "She shot my mother twice, Dave." As she spoke she turned to look at her mother. "There's blood on the rock. Where'd she get you, Mom?"

Em looked down, and then reluctantly at Anson and her daughter. "I know, it's embarrassing."

"Damn. Really? Watch the woman, Deanna. I'll take care of your mother. Guard the prisoner, Jake. Sit."

Jake looked up at Anson as if to say, "I knew that," and the police dog dutifully took up a position overlooking them.

Anson pulled the field First Aid kit off his shoulder. Em looked at him with resignation.

"Does she know how to use a gun?" he said, gesturing

towards Deanna.

"I'm afraid so. Not my idea," Em replied.

"Turn around please, ma'am."

A look of chagrin and resignation crossed Em's face.

He said, "Out in the field, it doesn't matter where they shoot you. Keep watching her, Deanna."

Anson tugged on disposable gloves, obviously a tight fit on his sizable hands. He removed a pair of blunt pointed scissors from his kit and began to enlarge the tear on the thigh of Em's favorite pair of jeans to reveal a long narrow flesh wound. The patient winced as he cleaned around the wound, applied antibiotic to gauze pads and taped them to her thigh. "Turn around again, please."

Em looked over her shoulder sheepishly as Anson with rapt concentration cut her jeans on the left rear to reveal an entrance and an exit wound. As Anson cleaned the wounds and bandaged them, she was forced to grit her teeth. Hands still for a moment, he watched as blood stained through the gauze pads. Working more quickly, he pulled the wrapping off still larger gauze pads and applied them directly over the first batch, taped them down securely and put pressure on the wound.

Into his collar Anson reported, "Clean shots. One graze and one through and through. Small caliber. We'll need evac. We're right up on top of a cliff. I can't walk them out. Not serious, but no walking. No, she'll be fine. They're in the, uh, leg area. Right, we'll wait here. Need two stretchers. The perp is still out cold, too. I'm not sure how exactly that happened, sir." He addressed his remarks as much to Em as to his collar.

"I punched her as hard as I could, that's how it happened!" Deanna piped up.

"Looks like the boxing lessons at the gym paid off. Your coach will be proud, Dee," her mother acknowledged.

"Can you sit down, ma'am?" Anson asked.

"Only on one side," Em said regretfully.

"Here's a better rock for you, ma'am." Anson helped Em over to a lower, smoother rock. As he did so, Deanna gave him a step by step, blow by blow, account of their pursuit and capture of Filomena Levitt Kirbee née Morena. She had just reached her description of the final scuffle when Jake stood up, looked over the edge of the cliff and barked a welcome.

26

DOWN THE CLIFF

———◆———

A NSON STOOD BESIDE Jake at the edge the cliff and looked down. It was a good forty foot drop to the top of the rubble below. He waved to the approaching cars and turned to Em and Deanna.

"Our ride's here."

Down on the road below, Leroy pulled the Humvee up towards the face of the cliff. The silver command car pulled off to the side of the road. Halloran got out. Rankel and Vargas jumped out of the back of the Humvee. They hauled out two long metal mesh baskets one inside the other containing coils of rope and a pack. Together they carried the baskets up the slope of the talus, the jumble of sharp edged rocks at the base of the cliff. As they did so, Leroy took the Humvee around in a tight turn to point it back towards the office, getting ready for a speedy departure.

Vargas looked dubiously up at the steep side of the cliff. He turned to Rankel. "So what do you think? Should we take the long way around and walk up?"

"Hell no, man, this is going to be good," his partner replied.

"Seriously?"

Rankel threw a coil of rope over his shoulder and walked several paces down the pile of sharp edged cobblestones.

An experienced climber, he picked the spot without hesitation and with a grin on his face started climbing. There was some very good climbing in Connecticut although not widely recognized, and he appreciated it. When he'd climbed ten feet, his grin turned to a look of concentration, and then to a frown.

"Andy, get out from under," Rankel shouted as his footing gave way sending a cascade of paving stone sized rocks down beneath him.

Vargas moved aside quickly. "You missed me! I'm okay, can you keep going?"

"I have to go slower. The ice splits the rock every winter. There's stuff that hasn't fallen yet." The face of a cliff had not so much as a bush with roots to grab for a handhold. Making his way more cautiously, Rankel carefully sited each hand and foot hold. He amazed the watchers on the ground with the skill and strength it took to make the climb.

Once, only ten feet from the top, high enough to be badly injured if he fell, Rankel had a hard time finding a handhold to advance. Sensing trouble, Anson went down on his knees at the edge of the cliff and ordered Deanna back away from the edge, just in case. Anson made ready to grab Rankle and pull him up. Another shower of rock let go from the cliff face, and Rankel swung to the side to avoid most of the falling rocks. One gave him a sound thump on the arm as it passed to hit the top of the talus and clattered down to the feet of the three men who stood watching tensely below.

The last ten feet were truly the worst. Clinging to the rock face, Rankel managed to unwind a length of the rope he carried over his shoulder. He'd prepared one end of the rope with a round throwing knot the size of a baseball called a "Monkey Paw." He grasped the knotted ball on the end of the rope and threw it. Anson reached down and snatched it from the air with a fielder's precision. A much larger man than Rankel, Anson braced himself against the rocks, leveraged his weight and pulled Rankel swiftly up the remaining distance. To the watchers on the ground, Rankel appeared to fly up the rock wall and over the edge in an instant.

"Glad to see you. Did you bring extra bandages?" Anson asked this before Rankel had a chance to rise to his feet.

"They're in the baskets.

"'Ullo Ms. H. How's it going this afternoon? Ready for a ride down?" Rankel waved to Em who leaned against a boulder with a red stain growing behind her and an armed Deanna who stood poised close to Filomena Morena's motionless body.

Rankel and Anson set to work — Rankel securing one end of the rope around a glacial boulder. Anson tossed the other end of the rope down to Andy Vargas on the talus heap who clipped the baskets' harness onto it. Braced against a rock, Anson hauled the baskets up quickly hand over hand. He took the pack from the basket, searched through it for the largest gauze bandages and dragged them out. Without thinking about his movements, Anson got up and motioned for Em to turn around. He quickly applied the fresh bandages to the through and through wound on Em's left buttocks. The bleeding from the flesh wound on the side of her thigh showed signs of slowing.

"We're going to take you down first. The boss called Smitty. He'll be waiting for you. He's called an ambulance for the other one here." Anson hurried, the boss wanted them safe and out of sight fast. The last thing Halloran wanted was media coverage of their activities.

"Smitty says he enjoys flesh wounds, doesn't he, Dave?" Deanna teased. Now with the agents she reacted with relief and high spirits.

Rankel looked up from his work rigging the first basket for transport down the cliff. "Ready." He picked up

Em's sweatshirt, turned it inside out and used it to pad the bottom of the basket. "Hop in, or rather climb in face down, please."

"Face down? Do I have to?" Em moaned, she began to feel light headed.

"Yes, ma'am," replied Anson, "or you'll ruin my beautiful bandaging job." He motioned to Deanna to help her mother.

"More likely drip blood all over," Em said, loud enough for Deanna to hear as she helped her mother into the basket. Then Rankel strapped her in. Together with Anson they began lowering her down to Vargas who was joined by Leroy and his assistant.

Em was not happy, she could see through the wire mesh of the basket. Although not terribly afraid of heights, for this trip she made an exception. Vertigo overtook her. She had not realized how high the cliff was, and with every bump on the rocks her thigh banged against the basket. At one point the basket banged so forcefully against the face of the cliff she squeezed her eyes shut, gritted her teeth and prayed they wouldn't drop her.

The three men at the base of the cliff received Em's basket carefully and sent the rope back up to the top at once. Leroy and his assistant carried Em, who was still in the basket, down the rest of the way to the ground where Halloran stood waiting for them. He directed them to place Em in the Humvee and to prepare her for transport back to the city. Em was feeling dizzy and weaker. She said only this to him, "Make Deanna give Anson the gun."

Inside the Humvee a petite woman in scrubs with close cropped blonde hair met Em. She introduced herself as Trixie, physician assistant to Dr. Smithers Williamson. Trixie was not sent out into the field often. She needed to put on her track shoes to sprint over to catch a ride in the Humvee. The PA assessed Em's vitals and took a quick medical history. Consulting with the doctor via cell, it was determined she should start an IV line.

"Have you had anything to drink this afternoon, ma'am. You seem dehydrated, I mean besides the obvious," Trixie asked.

Em confessed to feeling tired and thirsty after the pursuit up the hillside and the wrestling match with Filomena. Halloran was close, she could hear his voice as he gave directions and received reports right outside the Humvee. Nancy Dombroski was taking Pierce directly into FBI custody, and they would transport Professor Stevenson to the university hospital. Despite aching, she felt herself drifting in and out of a light sleep, perhaps helped along by medication administered in the IV.

Assured Em was stable, in no immediate danger, Halloran turned back to watch the progress of the suspect down the cliff. Into his collar, he asked Anson what on earth Em meant about a gun. He'd heard only two shots, and those from a distance. Her mother had two wounds so it followed Deanna had now appropriated the weapon.

Up on the rocks above the cliff, disarming Deanna was the least of Anson's worries. She and the dog were watching with rapt attention as he and Rankel attempted to transfer the slight form of Filomena onto a backboard. They were trying to do it gently without adding any further to her injuries, but Filomena showed signs of regaining consciousness.

"Watch out! She's nasty when she's mad," warned Deanna.

The words were no sooner out of Deanna's mouth when Filomena's eyes shot open and she began to struggle. It was an unfocussed effort and she relapsed into silence. But she had given her rescuers a shock. They worked more quickly still to secure her on the backboard and into the basket. Rankel and Anson had her over the side of the cliff and were starting to lower her down.

An updraft of wind from the valley floor below swept up rocking the basket and jarring her into consciousness again. She looked straight up at the faces of Anson and Rankel and started to scream at them in language disjointed and increasingly graphic. She struggled against the straps holding her in the basket until it swayed in the wind.

"Stay still, dammit! You're forty feet up in the air. Do you want to end up on the rocks?" Rankel yelled back at her.

Filomena gasped. "No! Don't drop me!"

Deanna joined Anson and Rankel to peer down over the cliff at the woman descending in the basket.

"Get the little bitch out of my sight!" she screamed, hysteria tingeing her cry. Filomena's voice echoed off the cliff. The sound was so loud Em even heard her in the Humvee, and she laughed softly.

"Company's coming," Em said aloud to Trixie, who was seated by her patient.

Anson looked at Deanna who had her hand on his back for support and could see the gleam coming into her eyes. She was forming a snarky reply. "Come on Deanna, back off quietly." She looked at him and eased back out of view, leaving her hand where it rested. This did not displease him.

"She's the second person to call me a little bitch, and I don't like it, Dave," Deanna sputtered.

"Understandably so, Dee," he replied.

Filomena made a safe and smoother journey down the cliff. The rope handlers had learned a few lessons from Em's rather bumpy ride. The basket was promptly carried off down the slope to a waiting ambulance.

As soon as the rope was free, Rankel prepared to rappel down to the ground. Deanna yelled, "Can I try that?"

Both men yelled back, "No!"

Anson qualified it by adding, "Not without training.

You and I and the dog are walking out of here as soon as Rankel hits the ground."

On cue, Rankel disappeared over the edge of the cliff, laughing to himself. Laughter was of short duration. Concentration was needed for a safe descent. It was not exactly the same route he used on the way up. Loose rock sloughed off from the rock face threatening to take his footing out from under him and to slam him against the sharp angles of the basalt. After more than one misstep, he reached the top of the talus and signaled Anson to drop the rope.

Up on cliff top, Anson undid the rope from around the boulder, dropped it and waved. Deanna and Jake stood waiting for him by the access path. He picked up his kit and gave the area a preliminary search for the bullets, which were not visible. After a thorough scan, he took a quick picture of bullet strike marks on the rock face.

"We need to get moving, Dee. The boss wants this all wrapped up before the FBI takes custody of the suspect. He says if we follow the blazed trail north, we'll find an easier way down." He paused. "Time to give me the gun."

Deanna pulled a face. "Can't I keep it until we get down to the cars?"

"No, you can't keep it until we get down to the cars. It's evidence. Hand it over." Anson yanked an evidence bag out of the kit as Deanna extracted the small ladies' gun from her jacket.

"You can't walk around with a loaded weapon like that. We don't need any more bullet wounds today," he commented dryly.

"I put the safety on before I put it in my pocket. I'm not that dumb, *Dave*."

Deanna appreciated the confidence Anson showed in his walk. Lunch hours spent hiking on the treadmill in the gym at the office were paying off for him. She stood in front of him and reached out for his hand.

"Thank you for coming for us. Thank you for bandaging up my mother's fanny. She may never get over that." Deanna's voice cracked. Tears started in her eyes. "She would have killed us if she could have."

Anson took her in his arms in a bear hug, hoping they could not be seen, but well aware they could be overheard. Jake looked on. But, when their hug was about to turn into an embrace, it had lasted longer than the dog's patience, and he gave a short sharp bark.

Deanna stepped away, tugging at Anson's hand. "I'll race you guys down!"

"That's no fair, Deanna. The dog will win." He laughed.

The three companions started off together on the trail following the ridge line, and then quite suddenly it turned straight down through the wooded hillside. The angle of descent at the top was quite steep. Fortunately, the blazed trail down the hill was a dirt track. Small trees grew on both sides, and one or two were in the middle of the trail itself. Rocks embedded in the soil served as natural foot holds. Half way down there was a boulder to one side of the trail providing an often used stopping place.

Jake bounded to the head of the trail, and on a signal from Anson, the dog started down, digging his claws in for traction. Deanna hesitated, waiting for Anson to lead.

"You go down next." Seeing her reluctance he said, "Can you do this by yourself? If I fall, I'll take you with me. Go ahead, if I can't stand I'll slide down."

By holding onto trees and scrambling along they started down the steep slope with Jake in the lead as predicted. Deanna headed down next, crabwise with her feet sideways against the slant of the hill. Without ripping it off Anson had no way to turn off his mic, so the open channel was punctuated at irregular intervals with the sounds of their travails down the slope, including occasional descriptive phrases picked up during service in 'Stan.

Deanna reached the boulder rest stop first. She turned uphill quickly towards him when Anson issued curses in a language she didn't need to understand as he tripped on a root, then followed with a shout of "Saleh!"

"Tarzan! The grapevine!" she yelled as Anson struggled to regain his balance. Having noticed Anson's upper body strength while up on the rocks, she quickly realized the stout wild grape vine next to the trail had distinct possibilities. "On the right," she sprang up from her seat on the rock, ready to charge up the hill.

Anson reached out with one long arm to grasp the vine. The grape vine was firmly anchored in the ground and again in the upper story of the trees by many years of unhindered growth. It held his weight, enabled him to catch his balance and advance towards Deanna down the steepest part of the trail. Jake shifted quickly to make way for Anson who came to rest with a final stride next to Deanna on the boulder.

U.S. Army vocabulary is functional, highly descriptive, and not always ready for prime time. Deanna was familiar with the WWII version of the lingo from time spent with Bob Albrecht, who tried not to curse and swear in front of the women folks. But there were times when he couldn't help himself. So Deanna could swear like a trooper, too, but she learned a few new ones from Anson that afternoon.

"Well done, Ape Man." Deanna greeted him with relief and awe in her voice.

"Thanks for the hint, Jane. I nearly bought it up there. Sorry about the language."

"All you said I could understand was 'brother-in-law.'"

They were seated close together on the rock, facing up hill. Jake stationed himself facing downhill and listened to activity down along the road that lay at the base. Long black ears were pointing off towards the left. Deanna slid her arm around the arm next to her, and he let her do it.

Anson pulled the mic off his shirt and removed the ear-bud, and held them in his tightly closed hand, and then negotiations began.

"Halloran says I have to wait until after the case is closed to ask you out again," he said quietly.

"I got the lecture, too."

"You'll be going back to college real soon."

"I'll be home for fall break and Thanksgiving vacation. Would you like to come for Thanksgiving dinner? Mom said I could ask you. There's always too much food, and she does a great turkey and apple stuffing."

"Does she shoot the bird in your own backyard?"

Appalled Deanna replied, "Oh no, we wouldn't let her. She buys it from a local turkey farm. Mom's threatened to throttle the Tom turkey that wakes her up so early in the morning, but she'll never catch him. They can fly, you know, drum sticks and all."

"Only if the case is over, Dee." He rubbed the arm that rested around his. Anson turned towards her sweating with exertion.

The scent acted on Deanna like the most expensive aftershave. She licked her lips, reached over and planted a rather damp kiss on his cheek and stayed in close. "I passed calculus, it took work. And statistics, too. But I'm not good at that kind of math." She tugged gently on his arm, smiled at him, and he kissed her, which was exactly what she wanted him to do. It was a warm kiss that lingered enough to be memorable.

Anson knew they needed to keep it short before he gave into the temptation to really play Tarzan with Jane.

"We need to get going before they come looking for us." He hauled her up off the rock and gave her a playful push. "You first. I'd like to come to dinner. In November. Do you think you can stay out of trouble until then?" With a conspirator's grin, he replaced the earbud and tiny mic.

"We'll see about that. I make no promises." Recent fear for her life momentarily forgotten, Deanna grinned back at him. Other possibilities had successfully overtaken her.

Happily, negotiations concluded to their mutual satisfaction, they started down the remaining distance to the valley floor. The descent was only half as steep, and Anson was able to better control downhill momentum by walking sideways. Deanna and Jake just ran down. Anson halted for a moment. When Deanna's back was towards him, he ran the palm of his hand across the damp spot on his cheek, not realizing his hand left a telltale streak.

At the base of the grade they made a sharp right turn along the trail parallel to the road, heading due south. They could hear and see that operations at the base of the cliff were winding down. Anson, Deanna and Jake hiked towards the vehicle in tandem, Jake at heel beside Anson.

By the time Anson, Deanna and Jake reached the field below the cliff, black SUVs were arriving in strength. Following directions from Halloran, Deanna and Jake were hustled into the silver car. Rankel and Vargas stood by the ambulance. On a signal from Halloran his agents swapped places with three FBI agents, one of whom climbed into the back of the ambulance for the ride.

Rankel walked over to intercept Anson on his way to check in with Halloran.

"I wanted to say thanks and nice catch up there. We have a team and we could use a good short stop. We play the locals sometimes and stuff. It's time they stopped winning. You interested?"

"Sounds good. We had a team on deployment, but I haven't played since…."

"Yeah, well that's okay. But listen, I saw you two. You might want to wipe your face off before the old man sees it." Rankel gave the much larger man a punch on the arm and walked off.

"Oh, damn," Anson muttered under his breath.

Halloran spotted Anson dutifully scrubbing his cheek and turned away shaking his head. The director had his own problems to deal with, one of them had gotten herself shot twice helping to break the case. The best course of action, he decided, was to get the hell out of there before local officers arrived to ask more questions than he was prepared to answer. Their work was not done yet, of that he was sure.

The Humvee packed with Em, Trixie and the agents pulled out smartly before any questions could be raised. In the command car Anson and Halloran took off after them passing incoming state police cruisers. Deanna rode in state in the backseat of the silver car, her arms around Jake who sat beside her like a sentry on guard, both enjoying every minute of it. She aimed a smile at Dave Anson in the rearview mirror.

27

A COUPLE OF CRAZYASS PATIENTS

THE RIDE FROM the base of the cliff downtown held few memories for Em except a sense of speed in motion. To say Leroy flew low in the Humvee would capture the experience. Em had cross questioned Deanna and Sandy together and separately in detail about their visit to the doctor after the backyard attack, so she was sure where they were going.

"Leroy, for God's sake, slow down. You're jostling my patient. We all need to get there alive. Period." Trixie was clinging to her bench seat.

"Relax, we have to keep up with Anson. He just passed me. Marvin, don't touch that." Leroy barked at his assistant who sat next him in the front seat. "It's the satellite uplink. Anson's got so much communications stuff in here we can disrupt radio communications for a mile and a half if we want to." Marvin opened his mouth to speak. "Don't ask which satellites, or whose. He wants ground penetrating radar, but the boss won't sign for it yet, says navigational radar should be enough."

"Navigational radar? Like for boats? Does this thing float?" A competitive small boat sailor, Marvin was intrigued. Marine engines were his specialty.

"Naw, Anson wants a duck boat."

"Hey look, we're almost there." Marvin grabbed the

door handle and hung on as Leroy made the final turn before their destination. The bag of saline solution dripping into Em's arm swung around in a wide arc over her head.

"Dammit all Leroy, don't stop short," Trixie yelled from the rear seat, and he didn't. The Humvee coasted to a stop and backed into the loading dock neatly.

Trixie crisply directed the agents to carry Em into the facility. They woke Em up completely transferring her out of the Humvee onto a gurney and into a special airlock entrance in the building harboring Smitty's treatment suite. Anson, the dog and Deanna were assigned to stay with Em. Halloran hitched a ride back to the office with Leroy and Marvin to make his report and to dispatch V.J. Agarwal to take down Deanna's statement.

Deanna, Anson and Jake headed down the hall to the break room, a mini self-service cafeteria. Deanna was still in high gear, her steps active and her mind alert. Anson threw his pack down on one of the tables and pulled out an evidence gathering kit while Deanna roamed around the room looking at everything, sizing up the possibilities for an extended snack. The dog took up a guard's position on the carpet near the door.

"Dee, either sit down or stand still. I need to test your hands for residue from the gun," he asked with some exasperation. "Jake, do you need some water, buddy?"

"Why? Why do you have to do that? I didn't fire the gun?" She looked at him quizzically.

"So you said, but we need to do it anyway. V.J. will be here to take down your statement, and we need to get this done so you can go wash up," he said, seeing her hands were still showing mud from their downhill trek. "Before you eat anything, right?"

"Wash up, right. Okay, here I am." Deanna submitted her hands, the knuckles on her right were swelling.

"You'll need some ice on that hand." He held it gently

in his palm.

Deanna felt her fingers tingle.

"Why can't you take my statement?" she asked, her hand still resting lightly in Anson's strong hand. Being alone in a room with Anson held its own attractions, which was precisely why Halloran dispatched V.J. promptly to do the interview.

"The boss requires that someone not present at the incident take the witness's statement, if it's possible. You and I were there. We know what the land looks like and what happened while we were present. By telling a third person, you will have to give him details you and I might take for granted. V.J. will also ask questions an investigator hearing about the incident for the first time would ask. Agents write their own reports, boss reads everything and puts it all together.

"Let's hope there's no second time," he remarked with a grimace.

"I'm going to go wash up and look for ticks. Would you do a tick check for me?" She smiled invitingly.

"That depends on where you want me to check. You need to keep your clothes on in here." Anson was not about to let her take liberties in a secure, watch what you say, watch what you do or else facility.

With a burst of nervous laughter Deanna said, "I'm just going to hold my hair up off my neck, and you look for the deer ticks, little black pin heads or the big ugly wood ticks. Take it off if you find one. Look along the hair line and behind my ears. Then I'm going to go wash up. Do you think Lyme Disease really escaped from Plum Island? That's the rumor." She stood in front of Anson, held up her hair, turned her back on him and said, "See anything, Tarzan?"

Anson had no knowledge of this and he wasn't sure if people were supposed to know where Plum Island was, or what it was, so he let it pass unanswered.

The sight of Deanna's bare neck, the graceful tilt of her head and the soft curve of her cheek provoked a reaction in Anson he was trying to mask with a professional demeanor. As he was seriously looking behind Deanna's ears, a gauze bandage in hand, V.J. Agarwal arrived, armed with a note pad and small recorder. Later, Anson reflected that V.J.'s timely arrival was most probably a good thing.

"Good day, Ms. Huber. Anson. And what is this? Some sort on new evidence gathering investigation?" V.J. always seemed in pleasant humor. Certainly his skill with people made gathering evidence and information from interviews less painful and more productive. "Getting blood" from an uncooperative stone was his specialty. Never in a rush, he never seemed to lose focus.

"Hey, V.J. Deanna, this is V.J. Agarwal. Just checking for ticks. You're fine." Anson took a step back away from his charge and suppressed a sigh of relief and regret.

"So funny, here the dangerous wild life is so small. In West Bengal, there are tigers in the jungles, even white ones with blue eyes, elephants and water buffaloes. And gharials, those are the Ganges crocodilians, in the river," V.J. reminisced.

This piqued Deanna's interest. "Sounds like fun. We're starting to have bears in Connecticut again. My brother screamed like a girl when a mother bear chased him. He said it was just to be funny. I'm going to go wash up now. If I put popcorn in the microwave, will you pull it out?" Deanna was starting to itch, and she was anxious to get up close and personal with soap and water.

"How about a hot shower and shampoo, Ms. Huber?" Trixie stuck her head into the break room. "Can I offer you some clean scrubs? We're going to do the same for your mom, perhaps you could help."

"Sounds great!" Deanna exclaimed.

V.J. and Anson looked at one another. Anson sighed. "Looks like you'll have to wait V.J."

"I am in no rush. What are we dealing with? You can fill me in. Is there any decent tea in this place?" V.J. headed for the counter with the coffee maker and the hot water carafe. "I don't think that I will ever get used to tea in these little bags. Tea dust, that's what it is. Leaves are required for a good cup of tea."

———◆———

Em arrived in the treatment suite and was transferred quickly to a waiting exam table. She looked up to see a man even larger than Anson with straight black hair, olive skin and the build of a weight lifter dressed in scrubs.

Seeing the look of surprise on Em's face, Trixie piped up, "Ms. Huber, meet our scrub nurse, Salvatore. We call him Sal, *but never Sallie.*" She grinned and proceeded to give an update on Em's condition and asked him if the doctor had arrived yet.

"On his way, ma'am. The wife had him out to a dog show, and he's relieved to be out of there. Said there were Corgis all over the place, and they had enough of them at home."

The scrub nurse, Sal, began by redoing Em's vital signs and was peeling the bandage off her thigh when Dr. Roland Smithers Williams, III literally trotted into the room dressed in scrubs.

"Well, who do we have here? The mother of the clan. Pleased to meet you. I'm Smitty, but I'm guessing you already know that. Let's see what new injury we have." Smitty peered around Salvatore. "Good. Nice clean shot."

"I wish I could say it's my pleasure, Doctor," Em replied.

"There, there, you'll be fine. That's a good graze. It will clean up nicely. Keep peeling away the bandages on the derriere, Sal. Someone's been to the gym. You'd be surprised what you can tell about the health of a patient from their bottom. No need for all that middle aged sagging when exercise will firm it up. Men lose theirs entirely if they don't exercise, of course. Very nice." Smitty paused. "Ah, the bandage job I mean. Who did it?"

"That would be Agent Anson initially, Doctor," Trixie put in as she worked to prepare an instrument tray.

"We'll have to check his level of training and get him Advanced First Aid. Could be a useful skill to have in the field, especially with this crew. They have a way of falling over things or into things, or getting shot by someone unsavory. This looks like an amateur attempt, quite close range. Lucky for you, Ms. Huber." Smitty chuckled.

Lying face down on the exam table Em did not find this humorous. "I was struggling to get the gun away from her. My daughter knocked her out cold."

"Well, well, well, the charming Miss Deanna, such a nice girl. The last time she was here she had pounded a man's ribs to bits, all for a good cause of course. Trixie can have a look at her later."

"We're going to need to take a closer view of this wound. It's through and through but you never know what came along for the ride," the doctor concluded. "Trixie, where are you? Trixie, now where has that woman gone?" Smitty looked around the room conspicuously at his own eye level, over Trixie's head, in what appeared to be a standing joke.

"Right next to you, Doctor." Smitty was a man of average height, by no means tall, but Trixie barely reached his shoulder.

"Oh, yes there you are. Let's clean and re-bandage these wounds. Cover them with waterproof tape, and give our lovely guest the spa treatment. I like my patients sparkling. Are you comfortable, Ms. Huber? Good," he said cheerfully.

Sal and Trixie regarded their patient's wounds critically. Hands were still in need of thorough cleaning, jeans muddy at the calves, dry leaves and dirt clinging to her pants.

"Yes, indeed, Doctor. I'll see to it. Salvatore can finish the preparations," Trixie was in charge.

"While you're doing that, I'll phone over to check on my other two patients. Fortunately, neither of them is bleeding." Smitty shook his head. "But apparently that is the least of our worries with them. The nursing staff is complaining vociferously. Carry on, regardless," Smitty said with an accent and a twinkle in his eye. The doctor stalked off to make phone calls from the office across the hall.

"If you ask me, he's been watching old British movies again," Trixie remarked under her breath.

"Wasn't there one called *Carry On, Nurse?* Slapstick humor, like Charlie Chaplin," Em asked with an attempt at conversation.

"Please don't encourage him, we have a hard enough time working for the old tyrant," Trixie joked.

"And keeping a straight face. Patients don't understand it when the whole team in the operating room bursts into laughter. Plus his choice of music, who operates to the '1812 Overture?' All those cannons!"

Trixie gave Salvatore a severe look.

"I'm just saying."

"Sal, help me get these jeans off first, then finish the prep. Hand me scissors, these *have got* to come off." Trixie was determined to get Em into the shower as expeditiously as possible.

"Not my Gloria's," Em protested uselessly.

"Ma'am, you are never going to want to wear these again and they are evidence," Sal consoled her.

In short order Sal and Trixie cut off Em's jeans. Sal was sent back to his prep task, and Trixie re-bandaged Em's wounds with waterproof dressings and wrapped her up in a hospital gown. Under Trixie's watchful eyes, Sal pushed the exam table towards an airlock door at the end of the hall. They rousted out Deanna along the way, and all headed into "The Spa."

After the patient received a thorough scrubbing, Sal retrieved Em who was gently placed on clean table to wheel her back to the treatment suite.

"Why didn't you tell me it was a decontamination chamber? I'm so freakin' clean my eye lashes are squeaking." Em was back lying on her stomach, hands under her chin alternately squeezing her eyes shut and batting her eye lashes from the effects of the soap spray.

"That's what we do here, ma'am," Sal replied.

"Fun wasn't it, Mom? Like going through an automated car wash, except you're out of the car. I remember something sorta like it in *Dr. No*. My hair is never going to be the same. It feels like a fright wig!" Deanna was refreshed. "Wait 'til Anson sees this. I hope he remembered to take the popcorn out of the microwave." Deanna race walked along next to Sal to keep pace with him down the hall back to the treatment suite.

"Calm down, Deanna, just give them your statement," her mother warned quietly.

Em was sore, weary in mind and body. The images of a nice long nap with a certain man for an amiable companion played in her thoughts. Assuming the case was over, she wondered, *Will I ever even see him again?* and tried to put the sense of loss that would cause her out of her mind. After all, there were still unanswered questions. They parted company with Deanna, who had an appointment to keep with V.J. Agarwal for her interview.

———————◆———————

"Are we all gowned, masked, gloved and ready? I do think it helps to look the part. As a patient, I would never have confidence in medical staff that didn't come *en mufti.*" Smitty paused to look at his attendants. "That's all dressed up in Arabic." A fourth figure in surgical scrubs joined them.

"Are we all ready? Good. Lights, camera, action!" The fourth figure stepped to a console, and bright overhead lights flooded the table and surrounding area. A whirring sounded overhead, a camera traveled along a rail to a position directly above Em's fanny.

"Do I dare ask what that is?" Em attempted to turn over onto her side.

"You must be quite still, my dear, although you are the star of the show. Ready now? Good." Smitty reached for his first instrument.

"Don't tell me you're recording this? You didn't do this for Deanna and Sandy. Why me?" Em blurted out.

"No, I believe it's wholly digital. The young ladies required only basic care, filming that would be boring indeed. Still photos were fine for them. For the record…." The doctor went on to give the patient's name, time, date and the names of the medical attendants of the procedure to be documented.

"Now let's proceed. Graze on the upper outside left thigh, we'll clean and bandage this apparent gunshot wound." As the doctor worked, he kept up a running commentary punctuated by requests to his staff for one implement after another.

"We certainly do need to talk to you, Ms. Huber. We could use your insight with our other two patients. Hospital staff placed them in separate wards. I'll come to why in a minute. Sponge. I can tell you there is one red faced FBI agent over there. Magnifier. I think we have some detritus to remove. Good. Much better. Professor Stevenson won't let her out of his sight. He laughs and repeats he's been arrested for assaulting a federal officer. Then he says, 'Sweet Nan, let's do it again. You can lock me up for life!' High as a kite still on whatever they gave him. One can only wonder. Any truth to that, Ms. Huber?"

The doctor took a breath and continued. "Salvatore, I'll let you bandage. Fortunately for us Agent Dombroski had the presence of mind to bring all the vials she found at the scene in to us rather than sending them to Evidence first. Good job. That should heal up nicely. You'll have bragging rights on that scar." Smitty inspected the tray of instruments and flexed his fingers in preparation for the next phase of the treatment. Em moaned softly.

"Too many drugs in his system for us to give him anything to speed the recovery process. Quite a mix actually. Professor claims a short 'nasty woman' punched him, kicked him and shot him up with drugs. He'll have to come down in his own good time. But he has taken quite a fancy to the lady." Smitty seemed to have no trouble narrating as he worked.

"Let's change her position, Sal. Good. What can you tell us, my dear, while we're preparing?"

Em responded as much to keep her mind off the procedure as to oblige the doctor. "Jim Stevenson was barely coherent when we found him. The nasty woman was probably Filomena Morena, your other patient. He expressed his gratitude to Nancy for rescuing him. What ever happened was well meant. No harm done that I could see." Em remained silent on the details on camera. "Ouch!"

"Just some anesthetic here and there. In a few minutes, you'll be nice and numb for the rest of the afternoon. So, Professor Stevenson is not quite off his head, yes? Good to know.

"Ready? Feel that? No? Good. You may feel some pressure. Try to keep very still. If it hurts raise your hand and I'll stop." Smitty took up his surgical instrument in earnest. The entry wound absorbed his attention. "Powder burns around the wound. Looks close to point blank range, eh, my dear? Small caliber. Handgun?"

"Yes, that was her second shot," Em confirmed.

Trixie spoke up. "Doctor, we have cloth missing from the jeans and the under garment."

"Then we'll go fishing for them. Ready? Hold still now."

Em winced and gritted her teeth.

"Good. I've got the jeans material." Smitty placed the blood soaked fragment of denim on the tray. "Let's find the other piece now. What am I looking for? Grandma's cotton under drawers?"

"No, doctor, thin blue nylon with polka dots," Trixie replied.

Em heard a snicker behind her. She was glad that she made a practice of throwing out the potentially embarrassing holey underwear that mothers always warned about. Something about the snicker hit a familiar note.

"Shame I'm not artistic. We could cover the scar with a tattoo, how about a rosette right there? What do you think, Mike?" Smitty inquired.

Em turned her head to try to look up. A pair of grey eyes crinkled at the corners met her gaze and held it. Halloran was dressed in scrubs and standing at the video controls.

I might have known he wouldn't miss this. It relieved her feelings to know he was by her side, grinning from beneath a surgical mask.

"You two know each other, I presume. Mike, you might give her something to hold on to. I'm going to need to do some deep sea fishing here."

Halloran reached out to grasp Em's hand and squeezed it gently. Em hung on to it, increasing the strength of her grip as Smitty probed for the missing shred of nylon. Pressure increased in the wound as Smitty probed deeper. After what seemed like a long fishing expedition, she felt the probe being withdrawn, and it felt as if it was tugging a good bit with it.

"Ah, look what we have. Pink polka dots, were they? We're going to need to open this up a wee bit more. Scalpel. There's something else in there."

Em moaned. "You're not done yet?"

"Very good so far. I'll stitch up whatever work I do," he assured her lightly.

"Auwh."

"Eureka! A twig. How nice. Sal, let's clean this out. There you go. Good. While I'm stitching we can talk, can't we? My second patient over there is turning into a more serious issue. Perhaps you can help me understand her situation."

"What's that I feel?" Em was not Smitty's worst patient, at least not in the number of complaints. Smitty preferred his patients awake and sassy. It speeded recovery.

"Hem stitch. A little stitch here, a little stitch there. Not that you need any work done." Smitty finished his last stitch and asked Sal to snip the thread. "On to the exit wound."

"Are you finished?" Em asked, she was growing weary of holding still.

"Quit complaining, my dear. You'll have more than this before you're twice married. That's what my grand-mother used to say. Of course, she was only married once for a very long time. This wound is much cleaner," the doctor commented as he probed around gently.

"About Filomena Morena, Doctor, you were saying?" Em's curiosity was aroused in spite of the circumstances.

"Staff thinks she's had some sort of psychotic break. They're about to send her off to a Psych ward," Smitty said, demonstrating his handy ability to stitch away while talking.

"Maybe, she was pretty crazy up there on the ridge," Em agreed. "She wanted me to jump off the cliff. Perhaps that's why she clawed her way straight up the hill to the top through the trees. I mean, to jump herself. It would have been much easier to go up the trail the way we did. Doc, do you have to do that again? What is she saying?" Em gripped Halloran's hand so firmly that his knuckles were beginning to ache.

"Here it is then, she screams that it is all Frank's fault, whoever he is. Do we know him? Then she becomes hysterical, claiming they have to let her go so she can get to Bolivia because people will be trying to kill her once they find out. She won't say what about. First it's the Chinese who will kill her, then the North Koreans, and that's if the Russians don't send the Bulgarian after her. Any of this make any sense?" Smitty looked up from his handiwork at both Halloran and his patient.

"All of it makes sense, Smitty. Frank's her ex-husband. She needs to name names for us." Into his collar, Halloran said, "Who's with the woman? Andy get in there. Get her to tell us who she's afraid of, we need to know everything you can find out. Tell her we will protect her if she talks. Find out what she planned for Professor Stevenson. Tell the FBI and local police we need guards 24/7 on her room. Not just yourself. Right."

To Smitty, Halloran said, "She may be psychotic, which seems likely, but she's still our best link to the agencies behind this."

"Are we done yet? Can I roll over?"

"No my dear, not quite yet. Sal, do your magic with the bandages. Trixie, where is that woman when we need her?" Smitty stepped back away from the table.

"Right here, Doctor, at your elbow, as usual." Trixie's voice was so close that it startled Smitty, which made her grin.

"Give our charming patient a tetanus booster. I read she can't remember the date of her last shot. Can't have been recent. Start an antibiotic drip and something to give her some rest this afternoon. She can have something to eat later. Monitor her here for at least three hours."

Mask off, still holding Em's hand Halloran said, "I'll have the café send over soup. Mrs. Maresca came in this morning. She terrorized the staff about their tomato sauce and made Italian Wedding soup and lasagna for dinner. The customers will be lucky to get any of it. We have most of it reserved already." This was said with relish.

"Can we get on the list? Good job everyone. Procedure completed." The doctor gave the time and a brief summary. The recording equipment and the lights were switched off. "Let's send our lovely guest home with walker and a jelly donut."

Em looked puzzled, Smitty laughed.

Trixie explained, "Jelly donut is what the doctor calls a ring pillow of silicone, kind of like a bicycle seat pad. Some of our patients really get to like them." She smiled at Sal in a private joke.

"Some of them too much," was Sal's response.

"If all's well, she can go home later this afternoon. Will there be someone there to care for her? She's not going to be hopping around for a few days yet. Anyone?" Smitty asked into the air.

"Deanna and Sandy will be there," Em said.

"Hmm. Let's think about that, we may need to make some arrangements. I'm off to the hospital. Mike, your man will need my permission to interview that ranting woman, you know. Good. So much more fun than a kennel full of yapping corgis." Smitty nodded to Halloran who followed the doctor out of the treatment suite into the hall.

Trixie settled Em into a quiet corner of the room surrounded by curtains, propped her patient up on one side with a full body pillow against her back, covered her with a sheet and an open weave white cotton blanket. She adjusted the medication drip and withdrew to a desk near the doorway.

Back in plain clothes, Halloran returned from his consultation with the doctor. Stopping at Trixie's desk, he asked to see Em.

"Of course you can talk to her. You have five to ten

minutes until lights out," Trixie replied cheerfully.

"What? I need to interview her, I should have told you." Halloran was stricken. In need of Em's help, he was prepared to deliver a good, well supported lecture on not taking things into her own hands.

"Doctor prescribed a mild sedative. I've given her something so she will get some rest and to help keep her still for a while after the procedure. She'll be more comfortable that way," the physician's assistant assured him.

Halloran thanked Trixie, pulled a small notebook from his pocket, frowned and walked thoughtfully towards the curtained corner of the room. Ten minutes was not nearly enough time to talk through the liberation of Stevenson, and the pursuit and capture of Filomena Morena, especially with the anticipated effects of the sedative coming on. It would have to be quick and focused, and he would have to forego the lecture.

After Sal finished cleaning and disinfecting the treatment area, he came to rest in a chair next to Trixie at the table they used for a desk. Paperwork was the order of their afternoon and monitoring a single sleeping patient.

"He's back. Did you see the way they looked at each other?" Trixie said in a hushed voice. "We don't usually see the boss here."

"Not unless he needs patching up again. Last time was a close call. I've seen a few injuries, but I have to admit I didn't expect to see him back to work walking around on that leg." Even Sal's quiet voice sounded like the ground rumbling.

"Good surgeons and good care, we can take some of the credit. We can't have undercover personnel checking into the hospital under whatever cover name they are using at the time. Medical records would be inconsistent, and the billing would be all screwed up. I meant, first we had the girls, then the mom. He doesn't order chicken soup for all our patients." She kept her voice low.

"It's your imagination. She's some sort of special consultant." Sal was not about to admit that he'd missed something. "I could go for some of that lasagna."

"Spare me, you big gallute, the last thing you need is a plateful of lasagna." Trixie grinned at her scrub nurse. It was satisfying to have such competent and sizable staff.

Across the room Halloran found a chair and dragged it up next to Em's bed, sat down and stretched out his right leg.

"How are you?" he asked as if seeing her for the first time that day. Em looked up at her guest, who looked down at his collar. He then cast his eyes up towards the corner of the room letting her know the concealed microphone was still live, and there was a surveillance camera above her.

"Tired and sore and fading fast," she replied with a weak smile and a sigh. "Not the way I hoped to end a day in the country."

"No, I expect not. Since only the girls will be at home with you, we're sending a nurse for added security. We haven't located everyone involved in this yet." Halloran voiced his concern.

"A nurse for security? Trixie's a wonderful care giver, but protection...."

"You would be surprised about Trixie, but the nurse I have in mind is Salvatore. He'll take good care of you and guard your family as well."

———◆———

Back in the office at the Control Center desk, Bertha and Garvey were monitoring the ongoing activities of Halloran and the agents in the field, listening to conversations and logging in reports.

"Lucky lady. She gets to take Sal home with her. I wouldn't mind some attention from that fine man. It might almost be worth getting shot in the ass for it."

Bertha gave a rich earthy laugh. Their microphones were on mute, of course.

"Don't tell me that. I can't wait until Gladys gets back so you can tell her all that girlie stuff," Garvey scoffed.

"I'm just too damned healthy." Bertha feigned regret. "Sounds like I'd best get back to the Armory to make up a travel kit for Sal, *Salvatore*. The desk is all yours Garvey."

Garvey gave her an exasperated look, he had a server to defrag. Bertha took herself off to the Armory with a spring in her step, Garvey noticed. Doing Control Desk duty was okay with Bertha, if there was nothing more interesting to do.

———◆———

Em suppressed a yawn. "Oh, I see. Deanna will be calling Celina, but she may not be able to get away, Josh either." Sore, she tried to move cautiously, stretching down against the pillows.

"I need to ask you questions. I listened to Deanna's story in the car on the way back. She's short on details, long on drama." Halloran watched her carefully out of thoughtful, half closed eyes.

"She would be," Em yawned. This was not a good sign to Halloran.

"What did Filomena say exactly about her plans?"

Em yawned again.

"Stay with me!"

"They shot Hussein, it was an accident. They offered him money to defect somewhere. Don't know where. He refused. She planned to sell Version 5 to multiple buyers not specified. The ones she's afraid of make sense, countries with northern latitudes, not friendly…." Her eyes slowly closed.

"Em, anything else?" There was urgency in his voice.

"She did it for revenge on Frank. Jealous of his work, of his friendship with Professor Ali Hussein. Crazyass woman was not rational about that."

"I understand that. Why did they take Professor Stevenson?"

"This may be her lucky day, we've saved her life. No way they'd let her live after this, if she knows who they are..." Em's thoughts were drifting away.

"Names, places, anything at all?" Fading fast, he was losing her attention.

"I ... I think they were planning to export Jim Stevenson without his consent. I would tell you if I knew." She struggled to stay awake and was losing the battle.

"Em!"

"Ask Stevenson, he knows more." Em slipped into well-deserved sleep.

Her breathing was slow and regular, in medication induced sleep. Halloran kept watch beside Em's bed, an active man with a sharply analytical mind, not often given to contemplation, and then only in short bursts. It was not that he couldn't turn his mind to consider the meanings of things, when he did, often the results didn't please. Thinking how close she and her daughter had come to harm, Halloran felt what that meant to him. This strengthened his resolve to find those behind the murder, this attempt at espionage and kidnapping. Fervently he wished discussion with Smitty had been minutes shorter, and he could have asked for Em's help planning their next moves.

Sitting there, looking at Em asleep, freshly washed hair, uncombed and curling on the pillow, brought images to mind that banished the blue mood. He knew he'd rushed Em, but spent a few moments contemplating the more than satisfactory results — sleeping curled up around her body, and waking to find her sleeping sprawled across his chest, snoring with that soft purr of hers. Imagining a strategically placed rose tattoo cheered him, although she probably wouldn't do it. Retirement, long an anathema suggesting long hours of painful inactivity, even fishing hadn't helped, began to have its attractions. With Em's wits for company, it certainly wouldn't be dull, and there was good cooking, too.

When Trixie came to check on her now quiet patient she found him scribbling earnestly in his note book. Stevenson was his next target. He spoke into his collar to give Rankel a list of questions to attempt with the professor. The leg had begun to ache in a spot on top of his shin, and he wanted to give it a rest at home.

Late that afternoon, after Halloran returned to the office, Em was released. Anson loaded the staff car, Deanna in the back seat, the dog riding shotgun and happy to do it. Sal wheeled Em out of the building and lifted her gently into the back seat of the car and settled his patient onto the donut for the ride home. The small companion wheelchair was folded up and stowed in the trunk along with a walker adjusted to Em's height.

A heavy coat of sprayed on road dust camouflaged the compact black fleet car Sal drove. He was to meet them at the house and stopped briefly at the office to pick up a boxed dinner and a satchel resembling a doctor's bag full of small arms. It held several of Bertha's gadgets to be deployed in the house and around the grounds as he saw fit. His own custom XXL vest was kept in the car because he never knew with this job. It wasn't Special Forces, although there had been times in the ER when he wished he had the protective Kevlar vest on, but that was his day job.

Deanna spent the short trip back to the Spring House on her cell phone first to an amazed Sandy, and with dread to her older sister Celina who she caught between graduate school classes and lab time. It was decided between them, after Celina was enjoined not to be so bossy, that Em could best be accommodated on the sleep sofa in the ground floor sunroom. They decided to relegate the nurse to the living room couch with the hope it would be long enough.

When the car pulled up at the house Sandy was at the door waiting for them, sheets, towels and blankets all ready. Em was lifted into the wheelchair and pushed inside. Sal placed a few of the items from Bertha's bag around the house while Sandy and Deanna were busy making the bed for Em and assisting her out of the wheelchair into it. The inhabitants of the Spring House passed a peaceful evening, replete with Mrs. Maresca's lasagna, garlic bread, garden salad, and an assortment of Italian pastries including cannolis for Em.

28

DAY SPRING

———◆———

IT BEGAN ABOUT dawn, and long about nine-thirty in the morning, Em was desperate. Sandy and Deanna made themselves scarce upstairs after breakfast. The dog lay on the rug next to the pullout sofa, alert but unhelpful. Em had spent a restful, but not entirely comfortable night in the now very bright sunroom on the ground floor. Determined, she reached her cell phone on the end table by the sofa bed, wincing as she twisted around.

"Halloran."

"You have to rescue me," she begged.

"What's wrong, Em?"

"Can you hear that? Listen to them. They've been arguing like that since she arrived at six o'clock this morning." Em held the phone out towards the doorway into the living room. Two raised voices could be distinctly heard.

Celina, Em's oldest daughter, had arrived close to dawn. She tripped the tiny alarm Sal had placed in the grass by the front door, waking him. He greeted her at the door in fresh scrubs and shorts and announced that he was Ms. Huber's private duty nurse. Shock registered on Celina's face. She proceeded to bully her way by him, although Sal could easily recognize her by her strong resemblance to her mother.

"You're not giving her that stuff," a deep male voice boomed.

"She's my mother!" A foot stamp resounded across the living room.

"She's my patient."

"Hear that? All I want is a cup of tea and a scone, and I can't make myself heard. And a pee. Sal is not a fan of herbal medicine, to put it mildly. He's more than twice her size, and I think she can take him," Em sounded exasperated.

"Have you had any breakfast?" Halloran tried hard to keep the amusement out of his voice.

"Yes, Celina fixed it. It was very good." French toast had arrived quite early made from her own bread, cinnamon and fresh eggs with a tiny warmed pitcher of their own maple syrup, accompanied by a pot of English Breakfast tea, leaves and all. And then the fun had begun in earnest.

"They have discussed the relative merits of traditional remedies and Western medicine *ad nauseam*. I may never get to take another aspirin, she believes in the original willow bark tea." Em paused for breath.

"Then, they moved on to the difficulties of maintaining consistent potency in plant-based medicines and the value of their complex chemistry. Celina is arguing that plant-based medicines can be compounded specifically for patients on doctor's orders. Sal is having none of it. You'd think she was defending her dissertation to listen to her. Please rescue me!" she wailed.

"Good morning to you, too. I'm glad to hear you're feeling more like yourself. What are we drinking this morning?" He was relieved to hear her complaining, surely a sign of recovery.

"I think some Ceylon tea might be nice. I can't think Sal would object," Em answered.

"Hold the line, I'll call him." Halloran switched to his

outside line.

In the living room, Sal's cell gave a loud angry buzz. He jumped. Celina reacted with surprise. She hadn't imagined a simple call could affect the substantial man who faced off against her. She put the tray with the Ceylon tea and the plate of scones down on the dining table.

"Sal, quit arguing with Ms. Huber's daughter. I can hear you both from here. She wants tea, make it Ceylon and send in the scones. After a personal break. Do it now. And apologize."

"Yessir," Sal replied, cowed for the moment.

"We'll send Trixie to relieve you at one o'clock. Keep the peace until then. Think you can do it?"

"Yessir," Sal said quietly into his cell phone, glad they were not on the comm channel.

"Good. Keep it up. Think of it as hazardous duty. I need to talk to Ms. Huber about the abduction of Stevenson," he ended the call after indicating to Sal he knew what the nurse might be going through with Celina. Halloran sat at his desk scratching his head, this was not an outcome he anticipated when he assigned Sal guard duty. His sore leg had not improved measurably since the previous afternoon, and he stretched it out under his desk.

To Em, who was waiting on the other line he said, "Everything okay now?"

"All of a sudden it's quiet, and I think I hear tea cups clinking. What did you say to him?"

"A reminder. Can you talk? Need a few minutes?" Receiving no negative response, Halloran forged ahead. "No joy with Stevenson. The more rational he becomes, the less he remembers. The last thing you said to me yesterday was Stevenson knew more. What did you mean?"

"Let me think a minute. Give me a hint, what were we talking about?" Em's memory of their last conversation was hazy at best.

"Filomena's plans for Stevenson. Anything you can tell

me," Halloran hoped for patience although he realized her situation. His plan to question her again in person that morning was delayed by other developments that might or might not be related to the case.

"He wasn't coherent when we found him, but he was trying to tell us what happened to him. He seemed anxious, frightened almost, they would be coming back for him to take him away. In a day or two someone was coming in to check that he was the real deal. They needed to keep him quiet until then. Villas. They promised a villa of his own."

"Did he say who? Where and when? Try to remember, Em. Agent Dombroski wasn't wearing a wire. We have no record." He regretted this and never let his agents go anywhere without comm of some kind or other.

"Can't she remember anything else?" Em assumed Nancy would relay everything to Halloran.

"Apparently she was too busy subduing Pierce to hear everything Stevenson said to you."

"Let me think it through. Leave the tea please, I'm fine, really. Thank you very much, Celina. Stevenson said someone important was coming in, in a day or two. They couldn't tell exactly when he would arrive. Then he started on about checking the bona fides and repeating of course he was who he said he was. But I don't think that's what *they* meant." Em was remembering her struggle with the ropes that tied Stevenson to the bed.

"Yes, and?" Halloran prompted.

"I think they were expecting someone who could tell if Stevenson was truly an expert in his field. Someone worth buying. I think Filomena couldn't produce Version 5 or Hussein, and Stevenson was her fall back. Terrible, isn't it?"

"'*Coming in*,' were those his exact words?" Halloran pressed his query.

"Yes, I'm sure, I can hear them that way." Em's memory

for sound was excellent.

"Em, as soon as you can, write down everything you can remember, everything said, any detail you think we need to know, even the ones that don't seem relevant to you. Call V.J. Agarwal on a landline when you're done and read it to him." He hesitated to tell her to call immediately if she had a sudden revelation. He hoped she'd have the good sense to do it. Anyone who would think to call him for a cup of tea and scones could surely follow through.

"Can it wait a few minutes? I have to take a walk down the hall, or ride," Em reminded him.

"Of course, glad you're better." Halloran ended the call. There was another piece of rather disturbing intelligence to deal with that morning.

Em thought, a little hurt, *Not that you asked me how I am or anything like that*, and she let go of the hope for a personal visit from Halloran.

29

HARBOR CHASE

——◆——

"SIR, THE ANALYSTS are not happy."
Michael Halloran looked up from the paperwork on his desk. It was puzzling. What the hell was David Anson trying to order now? Day duty officer Gladys Rodriquez stood in front of him with her arms crossed high up above her pregnant belly.

"Tell me something I don't know."

"It's worse than I've ever seen them. They can't seem to sit still. They are threatening to break out of their offices and head for the roof."

"Need fresh air and sunlight? How's the air quality in there?" Halloran conjectured as he put his pen down.

Gladys needed to make her point quickly. "No, I checked first. It's the information you brought back from the evening in the bar. They think they are onto something. Chatter is increasing, sir, on low frequency channels."

Halloran sat up. It was unusual for Gladys to leave her post at the Control Desk to report directly to him. "Why the roof?"

"They think we need to watch the harbor, especially the oil tanks and the tanker on the east shore. They may be under threat, sir."

"Do it, get observers on the roof. Not the analysts.

Alert the Coast Guard. I want a summary report ASAP, no longer than one page, in no longer than ten minutes."

"Thank you, sir. They'll like that." The analysts lived to have their work taken seriously, and Halloran understood.

"Gladys, how are you doing?"

"We're fine, fine." She grinned. "Will there be anything else?"

"Your recommendation, Agent Rodriquez."

"How reliable was your source, sir?"

"Two confirming sources, one highly credible. What are the analysts saying?" Halloran was rubbing his chin. It was a thinking tell.

"They called me, and at their request, which you gotta know never happens, I went in to see them. They're up out of their chairs, streaming marine radio traffic from Portland to New York, and coastline police frequencies, ears on the roof scanning the Sound where they're picking up the low level chatter. Maps projected all over the walls. Something set them off early this morning. Like a piece of information fell into place. Night shift is staying through. They are at fifty percent certainty, sir. Only need seventy percent certainty to call it...."

"Your recommendation?" Halloran repeated.

"I think we need to recall field staff."

"Do it."

"Done."

"Good. As I said, alert the Coast Guard, Canadian border to Washington. Raise the alert status here, have staff ready to roll out if necessary. Fully armed. Tell Bertha, heavy field equipment. Find Joel. Is he back from lunch? Tell him to put his boots on and bring his special. V.J. too. Tell Leroy to ready command, Humvee and a 'penny black.'"

"Anson wants to go, sir, up on the roof." Gladys watched her boss weigh his options. "Relevant battle field experience."

"No, we'll take him with us if we go. Send José. I want three spotters on the roof."

"That all, sir?" Gladys was anxious to get a move on.

"Do it, Agent Rodriquez, you're in charge. I'm going to call the 'ant hill' down the hall." Halloran picked up the telephone headset he'd tossed to the corner of his desk post-Washington conference call. To call the Chief of the Analysis section he began pounding buttons on his desk set.

Down the hall in Analysis, a short, pudgy man with flyaway white hair and the rotund build of Shakespeare's Falstaff, and similar drinking habits, grabbed the phone off his desk. The habitually genial man was red and puffing.

"What?" a grouched out voice answered.

"Do I need to come down there?"

"Here's your damned report, Halloran. We're picking up increasing traffic, gone low tech, using walkie-talkies until out of range, for cripe's sake. Most of the perps use cell phones now because they think they are harder to tap. Now they appear to be using lights to signal from ship to shore. A boater out fishing reported a light signaling Morse Code in a language he didn't understand. Who the hell does that anymore? It's coming from the shore, aimed at a medium sized motorboat stopped midway in the Sound east of here."

"Did he relay the message? Get it translated? Do we have tracking?" Halloran issued his questions in rapid fire.

"Yes. We called European Languages at the University. Not good. Plain language code. The guy in the boat has been fishing to keep watch for us."

Silence on the end of the phone.

"Could be they are reluctant to use our cell network technology. Not sure of NSA's intercept capabilities. Meyerson?" Halloran barked.

"Dammit all to hell. Got another signal, the boat's moving, heading west towards NH. Two guys. It just passed the fisherman who says the motorboat is riding heavy, moderate speed. Sound is choppy. Looked like four oil drums in the back of the boat. Balls! The boat is heading closer towards the north shore of the Sound."

"Objective?" Halloran prompted sharply as he hauled open a locked desk drawer to retrieve his preferred service piece and holster.

"Potential attack, low tech and soon. I can't think they're going to blow up Cosey Beach. We're the closest high value target. Traffic indicates timing essential, keywords oil and pumping, implies tanker in the harbor. Secondary, middle pier, that's got to be one of the harbor bridges."

"Good job. We'll roll out," Halloran yelled in Meyerson's ear. "Rodriquez! Field team to the garage, now! Tell Bertha I need my new cane."

In the Analysis office, a red light flashed above the duty roster board. Meyerson gave a thumbs up to his staff. Halloran could hear a jumble of voices in the background of the call before he disconnected and threw his expensive telephone headset down on the desk. He hoisted himself out of the deep ergonomic chair and strapped on his gun. On the way out the door, he grabbed his vest off the coat rack in the corner.

In the Control Center, Garvey announced a facility lockdown and raised the security levels on the Internet ports and the physical access points.

Anson finished lacing up his field boots when Halloran stalked by his desk.

"You're driving. Get your damned vest on." Anson was well armed already.

The new recruit shot a look at Gladys Rodriquez and scrambled up to chase Halloran down the hall.

"Sir, where are we going?" Anson was trying to keep

up with Halloran who gripped his cane like a club.

"Across the harbor bridge, in front of the oil tanks. Move it, Lieutenant."

Halloran stalked down the hall to the Armory. Several now mobilized analysts passed the two men, intent on taking up their relief positions as back up in the Control Center for Anson and in the café for José.

One of the women murmured to her colleague, "Their guns are bigger than ours."

Her friend replied, "Yeah, Bertha says ours are for personal protection, easy to conceal, accurate at short range. They can probably hit what they shoot at, too. Did you see the big guy? He's new."

Halloran banged on the door of the Armory with his serpent-headed cane and glared into the retina scanner. Bertha threw open the door. Wordlessly, she handed Anson extra ammunition for both men.

"Here you go, sir. Can I come? I so want to…" She snatched the wooden cane out of Halloran's extended hand, replacing it with a gleaming coal black one with a pistol grip handle.

"Bertha, I need you here. Back up Rodriquez and Garvey. Keep the analysts off the roof."

"How am I supposed to do that? Some of them outrank me," she balked.

"You are a field agent. You have the authority. Don't let them sneak up the back stairs," Halloran warned her.

"I guess we can't have the 'ants' running around the antenna farm on the roof. They'll just trip and break stuff, like the last time," Bertha replied.

But Halloran, with Anson at his heels, was already at the elevator door being held open for him by Agent DeCarlo, dressed in tactical gear. DeCarlo looked askance at the hefty new recruit holding the ammo. Anson struggled to get into his vest in the elevator car without knocking into Halloran or a fully armed Agent Amy Cardozo standing next to him. She was barely recognizable in her tactical gear. DeCarlo hit the button for the garage and wisely said nothing.

Down in the lower level garage, Leroy and his assistant, Marvin, had the Humvee, the command car, and the third intentionally dusty small black fleet car lined up with the doors open and motors running. Flexible tubing attached to their tail pipes drew off the exhaust. Halloran and Anson were the last of the field team to arrive.

Halloran's agents gathered around him. "We are going to take up a defensive position in front of the oil tanks on the east side of the harbor. Leroy, you lead. Joel, V.J. and Leroy, command car. Humvee, DeCarlo, Cardozo, Halloran, Anson drives. Vargas, Rankel rear guard." To the surprise of the staff he said, "Joel, weapons loaded?" and received an affirmative nod.

Into the mic in his collar Halloran said, "Garvey, ready when you are. Okay? Traffic lights are on stop. Let's go!"

Halloran called out "Shotgun!" and climbed into the passenger seat of the Humvee. He said to Anson, who was climbing into the driver's seat, "Fly low. Don't hit the civilians."

Leroy's assistant hit the button on the wall that raised the garage doors. The vehicle engines revved. The silver command car pulled out of the garage, followed by the Humvee with Anson pressing close behind and the black compact at the rear.

In the café, two middle aged business men were enjoying a late lunch. They picked up their heads when a young woman diner pointed towards the front of the café and exclaimed aloud, "Did you see that? Does the Mob have a Hummer?" The silver command car passed by the front windows followed by the Humvee now decked out in Anson's custom urban camouflage design. The cooks and their new counter person, a woman from Analysis, looked around as if it was another quiet afternoon.

"Do we?" asked one of the business men of the other.

"Do we what?" The well dressed man opposite him blotted his lips on a napkin.

"Do we have a Humvee?"

Still holding his napkin to his mouth, he replied, "No, but it's an idea. We can tell the boss when we take him his cannolis." With a secretive expression on his face the businessman resumed eating an overstuffed sausage and peppers sub.

The three vehicle convoy took the short cut to the nearest entrance to the Interstate highway. It motored past an astonished Sergeant Gianelli whose patrol car was stopped at a traffic light that seemed to last forever.

"The feds are on the move, three vehicles moving fast heading to the intersection of I-91 and I-95. There's trouble if I ever saw it. I'm following them," he said. Not one to miss the action, he pulled the patrol car around a VW with a carful of teenagers. The dispatcher knew better than to tell Giannelli to hold his position. Rodriquez had already called it in, but Gianelli bolted the light and was already providing a fast-paced escort over the harbor bridge. Leroy set pace across the bridge that scared the bejeezus out of the local commuters and traffic hardened New Yorkers alike.

"Keep it tight," Halloran directed as if his drivers needed it said.

Gianelli was sharply told to block the road to the oil docks and under no circumstances to allow access. The convoy took the first exit after the bridge. The black and white with Gianelli driving swerved at the entrance to the tank farm and came to a stop blocking the road.

"We've lost our tail, boss," Vargas reported to Halloran as Gianelli pulled to a stop.

"He has his standing orders. Good to have access restricted. Locals need to stay there." Halloran realized this could was an unexpectedly prompt asset. Gianelli would slow any incursion on their operation.

On the comm channel they could hear Meyerson sounding like a sports announcer. "Subjects stopped in front of the harbor. They're coming about to trajectory of primary target, as plotted. They appear to be waiting for something. The Sound is choppy. It's making it difficult to see their approach straight on."

There was a light haze on the water. The north shore of Long Island across the Sound appeared like a continuous smudge about half an inch high stretching along the southern horizon.

"Control, Coast Guard status?" Halloran requested.

"They're out towards BPT, had a distress call past Bridgeport towards Stamford. They can't find anything. They think it's a crank call."

"Call them back! Tell them we need them here. Now," ordered Halloran.

"Yessir."

Next to him Anson heard a constant sub-verbal rumbling from Halloran. Leroy threaded his way through the massive oil tanks, past the company offices, and out to the edge of the harbor. An oil tanker tied up to the dock, surrounded by oil slick booms, had begun to unload its cargo, its most vulnerable time. The Coast Guard would already have advised it to cease operations.

Meyerson's voice crackled across the comm channel. "Subject starting to move towards target, speed increasing."

"Anson, pull up in front, between those two tanks." Halloran rode the Humvee up over the rutted gravel track with his hand on the door ready to jump out as soon as it came to a halt, or close enough. The command car and the fleet car stopped short and stayed on the gravel road behind the tanks.

The agents were out of the cars and taking up positions

in front of the tanks, facing the mouth of the harbor. V.J. climbed out of the command car with a sniper rifle. Anson caught sight of two rocket launchers carried forward by DeCarlo and Cardozo. The launchers looked older, certainly not like the ones he'd seen on deployment. When he turned back to grab the high powered binoculars, he missed seeing Joel Schwartz take up a shoulder fired weapon and hoist it into position. Schwartz, head of Finance, took his stance in the front of the agents on the high berm above the water. The shore was lined with a metal bulkhead that held it well above the high tide mark. Schwartz narrowed his eyes as he attempted to gauge the wind drift and distance.

Reporting from the office roof, José's voice started as restrained, but he ended up forgetting it. "Subject is attempting to increase speed but fighting tide flow and waves. They've passed the breakwater. Now passing Lighthouse Point. Running heavy, low in the water. Roof confirming two men and oil drums. Sir, we can see wires leading to the drums. They're coming straight at you. Incoming, I repeat, incoming," he exclaimed.

"Where's the Coast Guard?" Halloran yelled into his mic.

"Puddle Pirates are on the way, sir. Got a ways to go yet," Gladys replied.

The voice of an older man, familiar to Halloran, was heard on the comm channel. The voice began giving the bearings and estimated speed of the oncoming boat as well as reading out the wind speed and direction. Frank Kirbee had almost finished his work on Halloran's moving target practice system. Left to his own devices in his basement living quarters during the facility lockdown, Kirbee had found a way up the back stairs to the roof.

"Sounds like someone has experience," Anson remarked.

"Yeah, some experience is never lost," Halloran replied,

mentally chiding himself for forgetting to tell Bertha to watch out for his unpredictable friend and reluctant guest Frank Kirbee.

On the raised berm next to Halloran, Anson stood scanning the oncoming motor boat. "Did Al Qaeda issue parachutes on 9/11, sir? These guys have life jackets on under their clothes."

"What the bloody hell? Give me the glasses!" Halloran grabbed the glasses away, he could see jackets were concealing bulky vests thick as life jackets. Those around him heard a string of nautical curses whose origins probably went back to the flood.

"Is there an order in there, sir? I don't speak Navy very well," asked Anson dubiously.

"Decoys. V.J., I want those men in the water. I want them alive, we have questions I need answered. Put two over their heads. Close. Don't hit them. Try not to hit anything on Long Island either."

"Yessir." V.J. popped off two shots so close over the heads of the men so quickly they had little time to respond, proving he deserved the high score on the range.

Halloran flipped up the black cane, sited it on his outstretched left arm and squeezed the black pistol shaped handle. A red laser dot target finder projected from Halloran's cane onto the windscreen of the approaching boat, it bounced up and down with the boat's rise in the waves. The driver needed no more incentive but tied off the wheel securely. He yelled to the other man, who took the opportunity to jump off the opposite side and plunged into the murky green, oil slicked water of the harbor. Now pilotless, the boat headed in directly at the tanker and the oil tanks on the shore.

"Control, call the local police. The fire boat must be standing by. There is going to be a fire in the harbor." Halloran stood with the binoculars pressed to his eyes, legs apart as standing on the deck of a ship.

"Mr. Schwartz, fire when ready."

Joel Schwartz lined up his shot, waiting long enough so the blow back would miss the power station on the east shore and the men in the water. The missile fired true, and the boat's explosion was a deep deafening wave of sound and a fish killing, building shaking, window shattering blast impact. The waves of sound and impact rushed passed the agents who managed to stay on their feet. On shore side, car alarms wailed and building security alarms lit up the consoles in monitoring centers sending their stunned minders a series of programmed reports. Police phone lines maxed out immediately. Folks on Long Island witnessed the blast and swore to their local media New Haven was under attack.

On the roof of the IIA office building, the observers braced for the impact before the missile shot. But Frank Kirbee stumbled backwards and was saved from falling by a quick grab from José and a steadying arm from another agent. It took the two of them to keep Frank, an able forward observer, on his feet.

Inside the Analysis office two shifts of analysts were silently watching moving images from the rooftop cameras. Garvey directed two cameras forward, one trained on the party of agents in front of the oil tanks, the second camera aimed at the boat. Although they could not see his face, the analysts recognized Joel Schwartz. Even in their secure bunker in the center of the building they could feel the blast. Cheers of relief and high fives followed. Meyerson held up his hand and said, "I'm buying the first round."

"It was a bomb," Anson remarked with serious understatement. A tall plume of smoke drifted towards the shore in the prevailing wind.

"Yes, but if I'm right, it was a diversion. Control, fireboat?" Halloran asked briskly.

"The *Nathan Hale* is launched. She's on her way." Uhu–

ra–like, Gladys's reply was clipped.

"Have her stop at the dock here to pick up an evidence team."

"Feds are on their way," Gladys relayed. "I'm just saying, you'll have company coming. They could see it, hear it and feel it from their building. Half the city is rocking from that one."

Over the harbor to the north, cars and trucks were slowed to a staggered crawl as the rubber necking began in earnest. Not a few fenders were dented over this one. High above the harbor on the Interstate Bridge, traffic had a bird's eye view. Cars and trucks on the lower local drawbridge shared a view closer to water level. Several standard issue black SUVs were making a winding progress across the now overcrowded local drawbridge. Later, the two tiers of witnesses swore they saw a missile trail from the east shore towards the boat right before it blew up. This, of course, was denied to the media. If anyone had a video to post, it was quickly confiscated on the grounds of national security, which it certainly was.

"Sir, isn't Mr. Schwartz in Finance?" Anson was truly puzzled.

"Yes. Our friend is a man of many talents and useful skills. Joel's made some determined enemies in the course of his career. Until the situation is resolved, he's here with us so he and family can keep a low profile. The fewer people who see him here the better."

"I want to do that, too," Anson said loud enough for those around him to hear.

"Do what?" Halloran looked at his newest agent, standing straight and tall next to him.

"I mean the shoulder fired weapon, sir. If needed, it can be fired from a kneeling position, too."

To hide the smile struggling to cross his face, Halloran looked at the wreckage in the harbor. Just to keep Anson in suspense, he considered the request for a moment.

From a wheelchair to shoulder fired rockets, surely this is progress. His gaze rested briefly on the expectant face of his new agent. "Alright, I'll speak to Joel to see if he can get you practice time at the National Guard range. If you do well, you can be his backup. We don't often do this, but we never know."

Anson grinned at his boss. "This is turning out to be one hell of a good desk job, sir."

"Cardozo, DeCarlo. Go out with the fireboat. Swap out your gear for life jackets. Make sure you take the bullet proof ones with the black linings from the Humvee. Take the evidence kits. Don't let the firemen blast the evidence to hell. Tell them to snuff the thing, we need all the pieces for the FBI lab." Business on shore needed to wrap up, Halloran was on to other matters.

Amy Cardozo took off her helmet and shook out her hair. She understood what Halloran was about. Piece by piece she and DeCarlo began shedding tactical gear on the way back to the Humvee.

"Vargas, Rankel, take the car, go get our swimmers." Halloran was watching the progress of the SUVs across the bridge, calculating how long they had to accomplish what needed to be done before the other agency put feet on the ground.

"V.J., police your brass. Stash the gun." V.J. raised a hand showing two shells casings, and he, too, headed for the Humvee.

"Anson, Leroy get those launchers into the Humvee." Leroy took the spent launcher from Joel Schwartz and unceremoniously jammed it at Anson, reached down, grabbed the spare and slung the launcher over his shoulder. Weapons were hustled into the Humvee. They left Schwartz, using the binoculars to check his work and Halloran alone on the bank of the shore.

"Nice shooting, Tex. This could have been one hell of a mess. You better head for the bus, too. Make sure they lock it behind you." Halloran clapped Joel on the shoulder as Joel handed back the binoculars.

"It's good to get out of the office once in a while. Thanks," Joel Schwartz replied.

DeCarlo and Cardozo came to stand in front of Halloran where they remained until the fire boat arrived. They were soon joined by Anson and V.J. who formed a protective ring around the man with the very effective black cane. Curious, Anson looked tempted to ask Halloran what the cane could do but decided to save it for another day.

Into his collar Halloran said, "Patch me into the Coast Guard." He greeted the officer, who was his first floor tenant, as an old friend, certainly not sounding as if a boat had blown up in mid harbor, not all that far from the Coast Guard station. "We have a situation. You heard what happened in the harbor."

"My ears are still ringing."

"What do you have coming in? A freighter? What's its registry? What's the cargo?" With each question, his agents around him could tell Halloran liked the answers less and less. "Has it been inspected?"

"The armed crew are about to go out to board it now. They're late starting," the Coast Guard officer replied. "Civilian inspectors are holding 'til the ship is cleared."

Since 9/11 all ships entering U.S. waters are boarded and inspected by the U.S. Coast Guard and cleared either before they make port, or in port before anyone is allowed to leave or unload. Cargo is checked against manifests. It can be a harbor pilot who comes aboard, takes command and guides the ship into port. Foreign flag ships' masters are wary, even afraid of the U.S. Coast Guard. Safety violations are an especially sore part of inspection results.

In a measured tone that carried more weight than an outburst of temper from another man, Halloran spoke. "Call back the inspectors. You need to hold up until we get there. Double the detachment of guards and inspectors. We have reason to search that ship more thoroughly, even take it apart if we have to. We will need a bomb squad. And dogs."

"They are not going to be happy, Mr. Halloran. The captain is already complaining about having to be boarded." The officer sounded disgusted with the captain of the freighter.

"I don't give a damn if you're a month late. This is our water, and they can damned well wait on us. With that registry, there's no telling what's on the ship. Or who. Can you get the commander for me? Thanks.

"Bud? It's Halloran. I need that freighter surrounded. No one gets on. No one gets off. No boarding party until we get there with additional resources and personnel. You heard right, bomb squad and dogs. I'll borrow two dogs, that's right, two. One to start at each end and work towards mid-ships.

"Right. Where's the cutter? Can you get it there? Have the captain take up a firing position between the freighter and New Haven. Everything waits for us. We'll have a team to go onboard. I want photo recognition on every member of the crew and the passengers, if any. The captain should have all IDs and passports in the ships' safe. If they don't match with those on board, we've got them."

The commander offered the benefit of caution and wasn't ready to blast the freighter out of the water yet and provoke an international incident. At this point the harbor pilot would be on board and could hold the ship for the extended search. The Captain of the Port issued an order for the ship to stay at anchorage outside the harbor to hold it for the extended search.

"I don't give a .... No, I'm not concerned with that. You think *that* ship's owners are going to protest? State will show them the door. Someone tried to blow up New Haven Harbor, I'd call that probable cause."

"Did you call Washington, Mike? I'll have to check on this." The commander needed to cover his bases.

"You know who to call, and you know that I have the authority to do this in case of a threat to National Security." Now, this was something that the agents surrounding Halloran did not previously know. IIA staff were never sure what exactly their leader could and could not do and suspected he would do the necessary thing, regardless.

"Of course, we will file a full report as soon as possible." Halloran cut off the call as a phalanx of black SUVs pulled down the gravel road behind them. By this time, Joel Schwartz had taken himself off to climb into the Humvee, and Cardozo and DeCarlo had boarded the *Nathan Hale.*

The agents continued to watch the fireboat now carefully pumping foam on the burning wreckage of the boat. The agents on the fireboat were using long handled nets to scoop up the fragments before the debris sank or dispersed too far from the site. Dead fish floated to the surface and had to be shaken from the nets.

"Hell of a way to go fishing," Halloran remarked causally and handed the binoculars to V.J.

Anson looked out at the harbor and said aloud to no none in particular, "We need a boat."

Leroy, who stood next to him chuckled, and told him, "Ignore our guests," and walked away towards the knot of men and a woman in suits wearing bullet proof vests. "Nice of you to turn out. The boss is down there." Leroy kept on walking by towards the road.

"Whatcha got in there?" one of the FBI agents demanded and grasping the handle on the back of the Humvee tugged at it.

"Wouldn't you like to know? Beach blankets and picnic baskets. Get your hands off," Leroy growled.

The IIA agents and Halloran were on the shoreline,

looking at the burning wreckage as if they had not a thing to do with it. The lead FBI agent approached the group with his partner close behind, not knowing whom to address as Halloran had not turned around to meet him.

"Who's in charge here?" he barked in the distinctive tone of command voice that so irritated. "We got reports of a rocket hitting a boat. What's that about?"

Halloran slowly turned around to face the oncoming agent. His own agents fell back around him. The newcomer stopped in his tracks at the sight of the tall man with the cane. The lead agent had never seen Halloran up this close before and certainly not out in the field. Although, he had heard stories.

"It blew up. Better out there than right here in the middle of the oil tanks, or into that tanker, wouldn't you say? I would." Halloran gave the FBI agents the once over and let them see him do it.

"They were headed here?" The lead agent was suddenly apprehensive.

"We had credible intelligence to infer that, yes. You are standing next to their primary target. The bridge was the secondary target."

"Crrrap!" said the agent in the suit.

"We're leaving now. We have further business to do. You can take over the scene. There are two agents collecting evidence for your lab out there." Halloran gestured towards the fire boat. "Two men went overboard before the boat exploded. When they make it to shore, we will have two wet suspects to deliver to you. We will want to interrogate them. Don't answer any media questions, but you know that."

"What if they saw the rocket thing?" asked the FBI agent reluctantly. Balding and getting heavy around the middle, he didn't relish facing the press without a podium in front of him.

"The usual bull, neither confirm nor deny, ongoing investigation, sun in their eyes, glare off the water, maybe. Don't get too creative." Halloran spoke into his collar. "Good, they have them both. Have them brought back here to turn over to the FBI." To the agents in the suits he said, "Your suspects are coming special delivery, on their way now."

Halloran motioned to his agents who fell into formation around him as he walked towards their transportation. Ahead of him, Leroy argued with two other federal agents insisting they move their SUVs so his team could leave. The dispute could be heard across the intervening distance.

"Back up!" Halloran seldom found it necessary to raise his voice. When he did, it was obvious he was well used to making himself heard on deck. The more formally dressed agents headed promptly for their cars. In a quieter voice to the men who surrounded him, he said, "Leroy take the Humvee, Schwartz and V.J. back to the office. Start reports. Vargas and Rankel can pick up Cardozo and DeCarlo. Anson and I will take the car. We're going to pick up the dog. I think we will need Sergeant Jaeger."

Vargas and Rankel, with two suspects wetting down the back seat of the black fleet car, drove past the Humvee and the silver command car on the way to meet the FBI. Their orders were to wait for Cardozo and DeCarlo to return. The fire was out, the bits and pieces left of the boat were not extensive.

On the bank in front of the oil tanks, the FBI agents had little to do but wait and watch. His partner turned to the lead agent. "Was that really who I think it was?"

"Pretty sure."

"How come they have a Humvee and we don't?"

"How the blazes should I know? I don't even know what the hell they're supposed to do," replied the lead agent.

"Do you think they actually did it? I don't see any evidence of a missile strike from shore, do you?"

"By the time we got around that cop car, they had plenty of time to conceal it. Martins checked the back of the Humvee, it was already locked tight. It will be in some report classified way over us. We get to pick up the blast fragments, and if we're lucky we can get the story out of the two guys they fished out of the water for us. If we get to keep them long enough, and Homeland doesn't get them. Here they come now." The lead agent sucked in his gut, ready to take charge and take credit for apprehending suspected bombers.

30

JAKE'S LAST COLLAR

———◆———

A NSON PULLED THE silver command car past the
black SUVs, skirted around a row of oil tanks, huge
light grey drums wider than they were tall with gravel
access roads between them. Sailors from the tanker tried
to flag them down. Anson slowed to avoid hitting them,
grinned, made a thumbs up sign and drove on. In the
passenger seat next to him, Halloran was on his satellite
phone.

"Em, we need the dog. Can you have him ready in five,
maybe ten minutes at the most? Give him something to
eat, not too much. Put on his working collar and leash,
he'll understand. And take him for a quick walk."

"Good Lord, Michael! What happened? We heard an
explosion south of here. The TV news said a small boat
exploded in the harbor. There are unconfirmed reports
of a surface to surface missile. Someone out walking on
the west shore said they saw a missile trail from the opposite shore as it hit the boat. It's all over the Internet, but
the pictures aren't clear."

Since Halloran offered no comment, Em continued. "Is
that why you need the dog?"

"Huh." Halloran thought they'd need to capture those
images not already confiscated and maybe shop them. A
good project for Gladys Rodriquez, who was proficient

at sanitizing documents and images.

"Is that a 'huh, yes' or a 'huh, no,' or a 'huh, don't ask me?'" Em persisted.

"Hmm."

"Are you alright? You're not hurt, are you?"

"Fine, Em. Can you have one of the girls bring the dog to the front door? We're on our way *now*."

"Okay. Jake, where are you buddy?" Em called. There was an answering bark. Jake was in the living room lying on the best oriental carpet, positioned where he could watch both girls in the kitchen and be close to Em propped up on the Stickley couch. "Get your leash, you're going out. Deanna, I need you to take the dog out. No, now, right now!"

Before Em could ply him with another barrage of questions, Halloran hung up, an amused smile struggling across his face.

Jake, pulling Deanna, made a quick circle around the house, out the side door, down the back lawn, past the gardens and along the brook side. They reached the cobblestone paving in front of the house when the silver car executed a tight U turn and came to a halt next to them. The back door of the car closest to them popped open. Halloran gave a low, on-key whistle. Jake looked up at Deanna who dropped the leash, and the black dog bounded into the back seat. The door snapped shut, and the car was in motion without so much as a wave.

Deanna turned on her heel and took the short distance to the house at a run. In the living room the TV news was blaring an update, interrupting a favorite cooking show. Em and Sandy were transfixed. Deanna dropped down to sit on the floor next to the couch. Over their heads Celina watched from the kitchen, dish towel in hand.

"Dee, tell me who it was. Which way did they go?" Em placed her hand on her daughter's shoulder.

"It was Dave and his boss in their car. Barely even stopped. They came over the hill and went back the same way."

"So they came from the highway, and they're going back to the harbor. If they came up from there, they made fast time." Em glanced at her watch. "They must have other dogs, I wonder why they need Jake."

"Boy, was he happy to go. He ran right into the car."

"Oh, no." Em stared at the flat screen. "Look at that, who does it look like?" A grainy and much enlarged camera phone image appeared, men on the shore in front of the massive oil tanks. The camera wobbled and the image changed to show the burning wreckage of a small boat.

"You would never recognize them if you didn't suspect who they are to begin with," said Em dryly. They could make out the shape of a large blond man in a black vest, a sidearm strapped to his leg. Next to him, away from the camera's direct view, barely visible, was another tall man with binoculars held to his eyes. In front of them stood several others, two in tactical gear. They were surrounding a shorter man, almost obscuring him from view.

Celina looked puzzled, "Who are they?" She hadn't met any of the agents yet, much less Halloran and Anson.

"Can we see that again?" Deanna asked excitedly when the short video clip ended.

"I'm recording it now. I doubt if you will ever see it again on the evening news. I wonder where they're off to now with the dog." Em sighed, shifted her weight from her sore cheek, and wondered would they ever see Halloran and the dog again. She bit her lip and looked away.

Deanna looked up in time to see the expression on her mother's face. "They'll be fine, Mom. They're together." She reached over to lay her hand on her mother's shoulder, who smiled in return. They watched the "continuing coverage" from the local station's mobile news van of the fire boat dowsing the flaming pieces. Men and a woman in dark suits with vests labeled FBI now lined up in front of the oil tanks. They replaced the team shown in the cell phone video and were receiving on screen credit for their prompt arrival.

———————

Halloran directed Anson to return to the Interstate that followed the shore route to Boston, paralleling the old US Route 1, locally called the Boston Post Road. However, their drive towards the Rhode Island border required avoiding the Interchange with the north/south highway at the head of New Haven Harbor. Traffic there slowed to an agonizing crawl. The Interstate was backed up solid in either direction with drivers gawking and picture taking in turn as they crossed the bridge. Mysteriously, all cell phone service failed in that locale around this time. It was blamed on cell switch overload, an unlikely occurrence since it affected all carriers at once. Guided by Halloran and onboard satellite GPS, Anson wound his way through back roads, around the traffic jam until they could rejoin the highway farther along to the east.

On the way to their destination, Halloran arranged for the Coast Guard to form a blockade around the incoming cargo ship, which now waited at anchor to be boarded for inspection. Jake, an experienced passenger, could anticipate action from the tone of Halloran's voice. Retirement at the Spring House was all well and good, but he was still a young dog who enjoyed the hunt. The journey took them down to the shoreline, through warehouses that never could retain paint in the salt spray of a southern exposure, in a climate prone to hurricanes one half the year and Nor'easters the other half.

The task group was assembling close to the dock when the silver car pulled down the road made of sand and crushed shells. "Pull the car between the buildings, keep it out of sight," Halloran instructed. He got out of the car slowly, no sense in hurrying as his team was not yet complete. A dusty black fleet car rolled in and hid itself behind one of the warehouses. Carrying gym bags Rankel and Vargas wandered in the back door of an office building close by the dock. Halloran and Anson followed them inside.

Already waiting for them was a Coast Guard boarding party with an officer in charge. The dusty office was full of battered metal desks of indeterminate age on a worn wooden floor. It was crowded with armed Coast Guard men and women and their civilian inspectors in vests and coveralls who would wait until the ship was cleared. Vargas and Rankel dropped their casual act, put on their vests, labeled in white simply USA, and pulled out their automatic weapons. They brought a full body vest for Jake, who stood patiently as they strapped it on him.

"Sir, we have the ship surrounded with smaller craft per your orders. No one on or off into the water. What are we waiting for?" A Coast Guard Academy ring wearing Lieutenant named Carey walked over to Vargas, who pointed him to Halloran. Lieutenant Carey repeated the question.

"We are waiting for two teams with dogs. You are going to search this ship for drugs, contraband and especially people." Halloran spoke so that the room could hear him.

"Isn't one dog enough, sir?" The junior officer was looking straight in the eye of a very serious, and large, jet black Shepherd.

"This is Sergeant Jaeger. He's staying on shore." Halloran continued to address the room without obviously taking command away from the officer. The room grew quiet to better hear him.

"Specifically, sir, what are we to look for?" The Lieutenant wanted orders so there would be no errors or omissions.

"Everything we can find. Bring the crew and any passengers up on deck first. Two dogs, each starting from the opposite ends of the ship and working to mid-ships. Dig into the cooking stores. Measure the bulkheads for any hidden spaces. Ask Agent Vargas for search strategy if you have questions. We will be doing facial recognition on everyone on board." Halloran continued in a voice that could easily be heard.

The tall black American Shepherd stood up and pointed his head towards the office door.

"Looks like the canine units are here, we're almost ready. We are waiting for two more agents to get into position to cover access to the docks from the main road. They were busy," Halloran explained.

"At the harbor, sir?" queried Lieutenant Carey. "The commander sends his regards. He has the Captain of the Port order already written, and says you better be right about this one, too. Are you coming with us?"

"We're the welcoming party on shore." Halloran's eyes darkened. "Huh?" He was listening to a report from Bertha in the Control Center. She told him that the Coast Guard cutter was still ten minutes out, and that they should see it approach soon. "Make sure they get the message to take up a firing position between the cargo ship and New Haven Harbor."

"Sir?" said the lieutenant in surprise. It suddenly occurred to him that the news reports concerning a shore based missile fired at the small boat might be correct. The junior officer looked at Anson, who shook his head and shrugged his shoulders. The new agent was learning to keep their activities under cover.

"Okay to go, Lieutenant Carey. The agents are in place. Agents Vargas and Rankel, over there, will coordinate the search and identity verification onboard with you. They have brought evidence gathering kits. Consider anyone on board armed and dangerous. Remember the cook in *Hunt for the Red October*." Halloran looked down. "No casualties. I want everyone back alive, any prisoners, too."

Rankel called out, "Cruiser's on station."

One of the Coast Guardsmen muttered, "It isn't a cruiser, idiot."

"Go now. Split up your boarding party. You have more than two launches waiting, I understand." Halloran found the habit of issuing orders to younger officers impossible to drop.

Lieutenant Carey stepped up to the assembled boarding party and split them into three teams then ordered them out of the office to join the waiting canine units. Before leaving, the Coast Guard officer turned, gave a salute to Halloran and addressed him as captain.

"He looks young for this, sir." Anson gave his opinion of Carey freely.

The corners of Halloran's mouth tugged upward. Lieutenant Carey was Anson's contemporary, or near enough. "He's hand-picked for this assignment. The whole party is. The commander saw to that. You and I and Jake are going to wait out there on the boardwalk, behind the cover of the buildings." Halloran led them out the back door and around towards the front of the building. The older man's limp was more pronounced, and he leaned more heavily on the black cane.

From their position on the boardwalk they had a partial view of the launches as they approached and prepared to board the ship. Shouts of consternation came from the ship's crew as the dogs were hauled aboard. Several minutes later, the crew and passengers were paraded up onto the deck and lined up for inspection to be individually searched and photographed. Through his technically advanced binoculars Anson watched the process attentively.

To relieve the weight on his sore right shin, Halloran leaned against the building, rubbing weathering white paint onto the shoulder of his jacket. Progress reports from Rankel and Vargas came in as they worked with Coast Guard personnel to search the ship. Civilian inspectors waited on shore. They do not go on armed boardings. Halloran kept eyes and ears out towards the main shore road in anticipation. Anson called his attention to the ship as two Coast Guardsmen dragged a struggling man up on deck. The line of crew and passengers, who had been standing sullen and resentful, began animated movements to see the new arrival. Suddenly several of them moved to attack an Asian and had to be hauled off him and handcuffed to control them.

Agent Vargas's voice came across the comm channel. "Sir, we have a South Korean with papers, not one of the crew, a stowaway, asking to be taken to the head of this operation. Says he won't speak to anyone else. The crew seem to want to kill him before we question him."

"Get him off the ship right now, under guard. Transfer to the cutter. I'll speak with him as soon as I can. Say you are my deputy. There's a second cutter on the way."

Rankel came on the comm channel. "Lieutenant Carey has found maybe ten or twelve women and some kids. He took your advice, he said, and measured the internal walls. They were hidden in a narrow space. The Coast Guard commander gave orders to arrest the crew and passengers. Something about putting them in irons, he was that incensed. I told him we don't have any leg irons handy, but I made sure we had plenty of cuffs this time."

"Make sure they're on a different ship than the South Korean. No slip ups. Take him with you if you have to. If they start to take the crew off, make sure they do it on the off shore side. We're still waiting here for their contacts." Halloran was calculating the potential intelligence value of new material witnesses.

"Oh shit, one of them wants off the boat real bad. It's the captain. He's trying to go overboard. That is so not happening. Get him back before he hits the water. Good going!" Rankel yelled into his mic.

"One of the canine units is calling for a demolitions team. This thing's rigged to blow," Andy Vargas reported. "Hey, do you have any more evidence bags? I'm running out."

"Strip search the prisoners down to their skivvies. Get their shoes off. Jackets, too. Make sure they have no way to set off the explosives. Keep them in the center of the deck. The captain wanted off the boat for some pressing reason, didn't he? Make sure they have no way to kill themselves if captured." Halloran paused. "Above all, keep them away from the South Korean. Get him off the ship, and get him some place where he can talk."

"You were right, sir. Unbelievable. Can we go now?" Anson was anxious to get moving, the rest of the team was seeing action, he wasn't.

"We're not done yet, Anson. Stay where you are." Very active staff members were nothing new to Halloran. By way of explanation he spoke to Anson in a low voice. "The wind has picked up. The tide has turned. They were planning to miss the high tide. So, they would be forced to stay until dawn tomorrow, giving them time to unload their cargo here along the shore, not in the harbor. Smuggler's Moon tonight. We're going to wait for their onshore contacts to arrive."

The dog waited quietly. Anson could do waiting if he knew action would follow. Jake had settled down to lie at their feet, but only minutes later he was back up and pointing his nose towards the main road.

"Pickup truck approaching," Agent Cardozo's voice came across the comm channel.

Nose up, sniffing the breeze, Jake stepped forward. The battered pickup, its paint worn down to an indeterminate color pulled slowly down the sandy road towards the dock. It stopped well short of their position and fortunately, out of view of the ship. The pickup pulled into what appeared to be an unused warehouse. Men's voices, muted and furtive, could barely be heard. Jake's fangs appeared, his lips pulled back, and a deep subdued rumbling came from his throat.

"Stay, Jake," Halloran told him. The dog was not convinced, but stood impatiently, shifting his weight from one side to the other as if preparing to race forward.

Three men could be heard walking down the road towards them, their footsteps crunching on the broken shells of the lane that turned and led down to the dock. A change in the direction of the breeze brought their scents to Jake. Halloran knew he could not restrain the dog much longer, pulled his gun and made sure Anson had his ready.

When he judged the men close enough, Halloran spoke, "Anson. Don't shoot unless you have to. Drop the leash. Ready, go."

"Federal officers," Halloran's voice boomed.

Jake gave a snarl like a wolf. Anson had never heard one like it. Hackles raised across his back, the black dog seemed to fly off the boardwalk towards the approaching men with great leaps. Three men, not one very tall or fast, yelled at the sight of the dog and turned to run back to the warehouse in a strung out line. To Anson's surprise, Jake ran past the nearest runner, to bring down the second man by grabbing his jacket is his jaws. Anson followed the dog at a steady jog in his heavy field boots, service weapon raised.

Michael Halloran stepped straight off the boardwalk. And in his haste, he turned twisting his right shin so badly he stumbled and nearly went down. Using the stout black cane, he recovered his footing, propped himself up and transferred his gun to his less accurate left hand.

Down the road, the dog seemed possessed. Jake barked loudly and snapped his teeth in an unmistakable threat at the man on the ground who rolled over and attempted to pull a gun out of his pocket. Jake grabbed his wrist and shook it hard. Anson pulled up right by them just in time, once running, it was hard for him to check his speed to stop short.

The other two men kept on running and reached the warehouse. They made no attempt to free the fallen man. No shots were fired. Their only imperative was to flee the trap set for them. The pickup backed up preparing to escape, leaving the third man behind. Once turned, they sped up towards the main road, gravel flying out from under their wheels. There, at the head of the gravel road, was a dusty black fleet car pulled across to block their escape. Agents DeCarlo and Cardozo in full tactical gear were poised ready to greet them.

"Okay, Jake." Anson was unsure how to get the angry dog to let go of his quarry. Instead, he yelled at the downed man, "Drop your gun. Now. Throw it over there."

"Get him away! He's ripping my arm off!" The man tried to throw the gun as instructed but could only drop it at Jake's feet.

"Jake. Let him go, I've got him."

Jake dropped the arm and continued growling with determination and gave a series of short sharp barks.

"Like the dog says, federal officer, you are under arrest. Move and he'll bite your ass off."

Jake turned and yapped at Anson.

"Alright, it wasn't your ass he had in mind," Anson corrected his translation.

The dog moved in again, barking in the man's face and giving Anson no time to retrieve the gun.

Halloran walked up to stand on the other side of their quarry who struggled to get away from Jake's jaws and teeth. Jake was so close that the man could see the scar on the dog's neck.

"I shot this dog. He should be dead," he yelled.

Anson looked at Halloran who said in a flat voice, "You

shot this dog? Are you sure?"

"Yeah. It can't be just a dog, is it a wolf? Get him away from me!" he cried in fear as Jake lunged at him as he tried to roll away. The dog grabbed his sleeve and tore it off.

"You are under arrest for the murder of federal officer Pierre Leonard and the assault and attempted murder of this federal officer, Sergeant Jaeger of Saybrook. Also for resisting arrest. Stand down, Jake. Now. Heel." Jake reluctantly let go of the ragged piece of cloth from the jacket, spit it out, and came about to stand by Halloran's side. Growls still rumbled in his throat. Halloran rested his hand on the dog's head to quiet him.

"The other two got away, should we pursue, sir?" Anson was ready for more.

"No need, I guess you had trouble hearing, Cardozo and DeCarlo have them in custody. Agent Anson, his gun, your cuffs." Into his collar Halloran said, "We need a bus."

"Feds are on their way," Bertha replied to his request on the comm channel. "We have custody of a man who claims he is a South Korean government agent. Coast Guard has the crew and listed passengers being held for Homeland. The unlisted passengers will be receiving medical attention. We have interpreters on the way to see what's the story with the women and children held against their wills. Several speak English well enough to tell us who they are and where they were taken from. I hate this, I truly do," Bertha fumed.

"Understood. Good job everyone." The black dog with the eyes of a wolf and an incredibly long nose and a too long tail sat down next to Michael Halloran, who leaned heavily on his cane. Whenever the suspect, who was now standing, held securely by Anson, moved an inch, Jake showed his impressive fangs.

In the Control Center with her microphone on mute, Bertha turned around towards Garvey who was hanging over her shoulder watching the video feeds from the cargo ship and Halloran's vest camera. She looked towards Gladys who was sitting in her chair counting and taking deep breaths. "The boss got his man."

Garvey said, "You mean Jake got his man, right?"

31

HOME SWEET SPRING HOUSE

"MOVE OVER, JAKE!" Halloran let go of Anson's arm, eased himself down onto the backseat of his command car and gingerly swung his legs around into the car. He tried to stretch out his painful right leg and gave up that idea.

"Maybe he should ride up front with me, sir," Anson offered.

"He barks orders when he rides shotgun. I'll keep him back here with me."

"If you are sure, sir." Anson mused, *Great, now I have two backseat drivers.*

Jake put his chin on Halloran's lap, and his hand came to rest on the dog's head. "Good day's work, Sergeant."

"Vargas says we should clear out now, before the media shows up." Anson was listening to Vargas's report on the comm channel.

"We're done here. Back to the office. Have Gladys set up a video conference with Washington. Story and pictures. Get the results of facial recognition mounted with photos, names, countries of origin, and any criminal or missing persons' records. Note any still in process. She knows the drill. Get the team back to report as soon as they can manage it. Anson, evasive action, take us back the long way."

The car pulled out of the alley where they had concealed it. Vargas stood out on the opposite side of the gravel road, spoke into his collar and the drive ahead of the car miraculously cleared. Two canine units moved off the road to let the car pass. Coasties and officers from several local and federal agencies stood by. Anson drove out to the main road. At the corner, Agents Cardozo and DeCarlo waved them on when the road ahead was clear. Anson drove off in the opposite direction from the office, down the shore road away from New Haven Harbor.

Halloran closed his eyes. The ache in his leg increased sharply with each bump in the road, and then receded. Time was needed to process in quiet without the chatter in his earbud. Surely they had made a significant catch. But Halloran was a relentless hunter, and he focused on what he did not know and who they had not yet caught. He asked himself questions. Where was the young Korean girl for whom a foreign agent risked his life and his country's diplomatic relations with the U.S. to find? If they found her, what else might they find? Who bankrolled this operation? Who were the buyers the Morena woman dealt with for SunSprite Version 5? Where were they planning to take Stevenson? And most pressing, what where they planning to do with the high grade weapons they were attempting to smuggle into an area halfway between Boston and New York City? Their colleagues, the Gucci police, would surely want to impound the counterfeit goods, handbags, scarves, sneakers and ski jackets.

By the time they passed through the rural town of Killingworth, Halloran had his plans in order. "We've seen enough of the state. We should try New Haven next." In response, Anson turned back and found his way to the first traffic circle in Madison to change direction to drive south and east.

"Sir, Gladys has most of the information you wanted

put together, but she's not feeling so good. She's over with Trixie who says she's fine but's holding her for bed rest. Bertha and Garvey tried to reach the husband, but he's not picking up his cell phone. He's out West on business." Anson looked in the rearview mirror, saw the scowl on Halloran's face and realized he would never want to merit that look on his boss's face.

"Have them recall Agent Vargas. Assign him to escort Agent Rodriquez as needed, for as long as needed. Tell her it's an order," Halloran said in a measured tone.

In the Control Center Bertha turned to Garvey. "I heard that. Does that man know everything? Gladys's husband better be glad he's far away, 'cause I bet the boss would send the troops after him."

"He may do it yet," Garvey replied. Into his mic he said to José, "Incoming. Here's the pizza order. I don't care if you're out of the fresh ones. Don't put any damned canned clams on mine!"

———◆———

The video conference call with Washington was over for the evening. The duty officers there were fully apprised of the situation and were earnestly engaged in analyzing and reanalyzing the information given to create reports for the morning intelligence briefing. Their addition to the effort was national and international data. Their tasks included preparation of excerpts of data for approval to share with allied intelligence agencies, and heaven forbid, for the State Department to pass to several embassies. Risky business.

Almost free to go, Halloran retreated to his office taking several slices of specially ordered red pizza covered in sausage, peppers, mushrooms, onions, pepperoni and mozzarella cheese. This was the house specialty known covertly as "Halloran's Bomb." He was doing his email, eating his pizza and washing it down with Foxon Park

Kola. Jake lay on the floor by his desk chomping down on still another pizza crust. The Shepherd was a big fan of the "Bomb," too.

———◆———

Anson made a phone call. In the University Hospital the hulking trauma nurse, Salvatore, felt the special cell phone hidden carefully in his scrubs buzz urgently. Sal finished deftly running the IV line into the little old lady who came in severely dehydrated. He was good at this and could get an IV started even if the veins rolled or were barely visible. The nurse went to find a quiet corner to answer the summons on the phone. He took his dinner break from the Hospital Emergency Room at an unusual time and headed out the front of the ER to meet Anson in the staff car.

Two men cornered Halloran in his office. The office was a small one for two such large men as David Anson and the former Army medic turned scrub nurse. The black Shepherd dog took a good section of the office floor space as well. Jake looked up at the two interlopers speculatively. One word from Halloran and he would run them off. There were times when his friend behind the desk refused company.

"Sir, I'm here to look at your leg," Sal announced in his best professional voice as he placed a small unobtrusive medical bag of supplies on Michael Halloran's desk.

"No, you're not. I'm not done here." Halloran knew where this was going and frowned at Anson over his last slice of pizza.

The dog looked from his friend to the two men, waiting for the command that didn't come.

"Sir, respectfully, we need to evaluate an injury I understand you sustained in the field." Sal was positive from the odd angle of Halloran's right leg his trip to the office was justified and wondered if he could even put weight on it.

"No, you don't," Halloran replied, chewing thought-fully.

A strong clear woman's voice came from the Control Desk. "I heard that. Sir, not the right answer. As duty officer it is my responsibility to see that all personnel get appropriate medical attention." Bertha paused for a split second. "If you don't do it, how am I going to get the rest of them to do it? They get shot up and mangled every which way. And do they want to see the doctor? No way. You're only the first one. I heard you could barely walk back to the car, now you're limping around here. And there's Rankel. He dived into the water after some damned people-smuggling foreigner, and he's got a lump upside the head and he's holding his side. He probably cracked those ribs again. If you don't do it, how am I going to get Rankel to let Sal look at him?"

Halloran frowned and reluctantly put down the remaining end of his pizza slice. "Alright, Bertha. Tell Rankel he's next, and that's an order." Misery truly did love company. "Move over Jake, let Sal through."

"Let's roll up your pants leg, sir. Make way, Jake old man." Sal moved agilely around the dog who was getting up slowly.

"I'll take him out for a walk, sir." Anson judged it best to leave Sal alone with his patient. As one who understood reluctance to have others see your injuries, he suspected the boss might feel the same.

In what seemed a short time, Sal emerged from Hallo-ran's office to find Bertha standing waiting for him, her arms crossed. "Well?"

"He needs to be off his feet. He's eaten so we can't do anything tonight. I'll report to Smitty and arrange it for first thing tomorrow morning. It's a pin in his shinbone working loose would be my guess. It may be ready to come out, and he will feel a whole hell of a lot better after. He won't take anything for the pain."

"Off duty?" she asked.

"Yes, a couple days. I'd give him half an hour to clear his desk, then have someone drive him home. Where's my next patient? The one with the ribs who's going to need an X-ray and won't be happy about it. Again." Sal chuckled and Bertha shook her head.

———◆———

"Sir, Anson's assigned to take you home. He's taken the dog out for a stroll. Half an hour. Sal says it's best, that it must be painful. I'm to tell you, Joel says to go, he'll take over for you." Bertha could stand it no longer.

"Hmm." Halloran looked up from his report. "How's Gladys?"

"Trixie has her resting over in the medical building. The contractions stopped again. She's going to keep her there overnight to monitor the baby because there's nobody at home for her. It's almost time, they'll make a decision tomorrow."

"Oh?" Halloran had been through this three times with his ex-wife and knew enough to be concerned.

Seeing the look on his face Bertha replied to reassure him. "It seems the baby's just lining herself up right. Nothing to worry about. Everything's good so far." She fervently hoped this was true.

"Vargas?" he asked.

"He's there, too."

"As long as it takes, he can stay with her. Any luck contacting the husband?"

"No sir, none. I told Vargas if that rat of a husband does ever show up, he should tell him he's Gladys's bodyguard. I didn't have to tell him to look like he meant it."

Halloran's eyes narrowed dangerously. "Have Vargas call if he needs backup. If he does, send Cardozo. Let me know if the husband shows."

"Between me, yourself and Vargas, I would not want

to be that man when he does come around her," Bertha said quietly. "Anything else I can do for you, *before you go home?*"

"Call the Spring House. Tell Ms. Huber we're bringing the dog back this evening."

"What else can I tell her?" Bertha was angling for tacit permission to spill it to her new friend.

"Just the facts. Keep it simple. Only what she might read in the newspaper or hear on the evening news. I've got a call to make, to Peter's widow."

"Yes, sir, will do." Bertha respectfully withdrew from Halloran's office. His guidance on what to tell Em Huber was nowhere near as strict as he intended. It left Bertha to her own best judgment on what a media correspondent might say, and we all know what liberties might be taken in the service of the public's right to know.

Time passed. Halloran still made no move to leave his office. Bertha and David Anson stood together by the Control Desk. The Control was quiet. Evening staff were beginning to arrive.

Bertha sighed. "It's been over two hours since Sal left off inspecting and taping up those cracked ribs. We've got Rankel on the road home to that cubbyhole he calls his apartment. I can't see how he lives there. He's got no space for anything but those guitars and the amps to go with them."

"I'm not surprised. He bought another electric blue one at the Spring House shindig, said it was the perfect cover." Anson laughed at the memory that seemed long ago now, although it was only in June.

"Oh, I heard all of that you know. And I'll tell you we got a good recording of his Jimi Hendrix riff. Garvey over here thinks we should use it like our theme song, complete with the gunshot sound effects."

Garvey laughed. "You know I could program the phone system so when we put a call on hold, the person on the other end has to listen to the national anthem.''

"That must be against some government regulation somewhere, Garvey. But keep thinking." She wagged her head happily and hummed a few bars.

"I could use it on some cyber pirates I'm tracking, maybe they would enjoy it." Garvey turned back to his desk and began typing furiously on his keyboard, grinning.

"But this all begs the question. How are we going to get the boss out of his office and get him to go home? He's got that dog in there with him, too. Can he walk, Anson? Do you think that's the problem?"

Anson looked down at his own feet. He ran his hand through his thoroughly unruly ash blond hair. "I've been thinking about that. Did he ever use a chair after his accident?"

"Come to think of it, yes he did. I can call over to Trixie to see if we still have his spare. It's time for me to check on Gladys anyway. You think you can actually get him to use it? I cannot see us wheeling him down the hall in that ergonomic beast of a chair he's sitting in now."

"Give me a few minutes, I've got something in my car." Anson stalked off down the hall to the elevator. Bertha watched him go, amazed that Anson who started work a short time ago using only a wheelchair, reluctant to use his feet, was now bounding off, somewhat stiff legged, but determined.

Shortly, Anson returned pushing a gun metal grey low-seated wheeled chair unlike any Bertha and Garvey had ever seen. The seat was down between two wheels that were angled, and it had two smaller wheels in front. The larger wheels were wider and had deeper treads, resembling dirt bike tires.

"It's my all terrain chair," Anson explained. "I keep it in my car in case I feel like taking it out for exercise." He pushed the chair to the door of Halloran's office and announced, "Sir, your ride is here. Time to go."

"What is that?" Halloran looked down at the chair.

"It's my hiking chair. You might like to try it out on the way to the car. We should get the dog back to the Spring House before they close up for the night. Come on, Jake, let's go."

The Shepherd got up readily. He was bored and craving something more to eat than pizza crusts, as much as he appreciated them. Halloran looked at the expectant face of the canine hero of the day, logged out and turned off his computer.

With assistance from Anson, Michael Halloran lowered himself down onto the chair. In truth, he'd been hoping the ache in his leg would moderate so he could try to walk to the elevator, and from there to the car.

"Watch it, sir. It's fast and it turns on a dime."

Halloran wheeled himself out of the office, past Anson and the dog, and did a 360 degree turn in the open floor space between his office and the Control Desk where Bertha stood.

"Tell Joel he's up. I'll call in. Keep me posted on any developments from Interpol. I'm hoping they can give us a readout on the ownership of the freighter. And especially Gladys." With that, Halloran made a sharp turn, pointed the chair towards the elevator and took off, with his detail in tow. The dog did a fast trot next to him. His driver and bodyguard David Anson followed behind carrying his cane as if it were a spear.

When the elevator door closed safely behind the three figures, Bertha turned to Garvey. "Boys and their toys. I swear men invented the wheel. They do love them so much. We invented other things." Her voice insinuated interesting conceptions.

Garvey let go with a big deep baritone laugh. "I do believe you, sister. Now some of the rest of us can go home, too."

———

Anson pulled the command car smoothly out the driveway past the lighted café, which was doing a healthy evening business.

Leaning back against the smooth leather seat, Halloran tried to extend his sore leg past the large dog who had his head right up against him and closed his eyes. He was weary, tired in body and mind, but also relieved of a great weight. He'd found his close friend's killer and would see the man delivered to justice. There would be favorable reviews for the field agents and recriminations at the upper levels of the organization. A ring of smugglers had been caught, but what else could they be missing? It could mean increasing security, and ultimately more work, and the need for more staff. Increased staff, the thought made him even more tired. Halloran realized all he wanted right now was to crawl into Em's warm bed and to stay there with her until morning.

On arrival at the Spring House, a trip made in close to record time, Anson backed the car on the cobblestones as close as he could get to the front door. The dog was out of the car first. Jake high tailed it to his favorite clump of bushes. Halloran pulled his legs slowly around to the open car door and reached out for the cane in Anson's hand.

"Grab my bag out of the trunk, will you?" Halloran asked as he began to extricate himself from the car. He looked up at Anson, nodded towards the house and said, "I'm keeping that one. Just so you know."

Now this was not unanticipated, Anson could see how the wind was blowing in Em's direction. However, the idea of sitting down to Thanksgiving dinner at the Spring House with the Huber family, and his boss Halloran, gave him pause.

Anson retrieved the bag from the trunk and turned in time to catch Halloran as he tried to take the first step on the injured right leg. The disabled soldier hauled the older man up and half carried him to the house. Jake planted himself in front of the door to use his own voice key, barked twice and waited. With foresight, Joshua Huber programmed the key for Jake, and Deanna taught the dog how to use it.

"Jake. Front door. Voice print positive," the small security system panel inside the house announced in Joshua Huber's digitized voice.

"Jeez, Josh, I can hear the dog bark." Deanna often spoke to the security system as if her brother was in the room with them. She skidded on the hall rug in her effort to race to the front door. When she opened the stout wooden door, she froze at the sight. The dog sat attentively waiting. David Anson, black bag in one hand, was supporting Michael Halloran. The strain was apparent on the older man's face. She opened the screen door as wide as she could to allow the men to enter the narrow hallway. Jake bounded in. Deanna reached out to take the bag from Anson's hand and followed the new arrivals down the hall, dropping the black bag in the hall by the closet door.

"Sit him down in the kitchen, Dave." Deanna pulled a Windsor chair out from under the table and positioned it facing outward towards the men. "Celina!" she called to her older sister in a quiet but insistent voice.

"What happened to him?" Celina asked Anson as she and Sandy came from the living room to stand close to the blond man.

"He stepped down off a curb the wrong way. They think that something is working loose in his leg," was the reply. Halloran frowned as Anson settled him onto the chair.

Three concerned young women's faces looked at Halloran. "It's nothing. Don't fuss over me," he remonstrated as they closed in on him. Deanna grinned at Celina, her expression saying, "Oh that is so not going to happen." He'd run an all-male household for years but had vivid memories of his mother and sister hovering over him, bandaging scraped knees and worse. It still gave him the willies to think about it.

"Let's see how we can make you more comfortable, Mr. Halloran. Sandy, heat some of spring water from the tank for us, please. Has he seen a doctor?" Celina began rummaging in a low cabinet to retrieve the First Aid supplies.

"What did Smitty say?" Deanna tugged on Anson's sleeve, who shrugged his shoulders.

"It was Sal who looked at it."

"I'll call Smitty. He gave us his cell phone number, remember? Celina can talk to him," Deanna said under her breath to Anson.

Anxious to be of help Sandy asked, "Are you both hungry? Would you like something to eat? Jake's gone right to his bowl." The dog stood begging discretely by his food and water bowls. The kettle of water went on the stove. Sandy picked up the dog's bowl to fill it with his usual mixture of special diet dried food, olive oil and evening meds. "House rules. The pets get theirs first," she explained.

"No wonder the dog likes it here," Anson remarked. "What do you have to eat?"

Like a server in a bistro Sandy listed, "Barbecue chicken, rice and beans. I'll warm them up for you. We finished the zucchini."

"Sounds good to me. I can eat it cold," volunteered Anson. The zucchini squash was no loss to him. "Sir?"

"Fine with me either way." Halloran tried to stretch his injured leg out but was only partially successful.

Celina approached her patient with a basin for the

water and a pack stuffed with First Aid supplies and set both on the table next to him. Deanna handed Celina the cell phone and mouthed, "Doctor."

To cover the phone call Sandy distracted Halloran and Anson with cold grilled chicken smothered in Em's famous barbecue sauce. A pan of leftover rice and red beans was warming for them on the stove.

Thanks to Salvatore and Trixie, Celina's reputation had preceded her. Smitty knew to whom he was speaking and gave instructions accordingly. To which she replied, "Uh huh," several times and concluded with, "We can do that, thank you, Doctor."

"Would you gentlemen like a beer? My brother keeps a stock here, but I see that something new has been added. Harpoon or Sam Adams?" Celina looked Halloran straight in the eye, a little smile on her lips. Anson was about to ask for a Sam when the young woman said, "Harpoon for you, Mr. Halloran?"

Deanna suppressed a snicker behind Anson's back and handed him a bottle of brother Joshua's Sam Adams without waiting for his reply.

Wisely Halloran choose not to reply but accepted the bottle of Harpoon with good grace. The chicken was excellent, and the rice and beans would go nicely with it.

"Now let's see what we have here. I understand that you have an appointment first thing in the morning to possibly have a pin removed. The doctor asked that I take a look at the wound and change the bandage. I have an antibiotic dressing to apply for the night." Celina was prepared to go to work.

"It's okay. No need." Halloran was wary.

"Oh, yes, there is. The doctor told me I need to remove the brace." This was said with her best soothe the patient grin. "He's concerned that it shouldn't stay on overnight, you know."

Now, this was serious. Halloran had no wish to have

this happen.

Reading the expression on his face, Deanna quickly added, "My mother's asleep in the sunroom. Should we wake her up? I bet she could get it off for him." She grinned at their patient.

Resistance was futile, and he tugged at the knee of his trousers to pull up the leg of his pants. This revealed a padded black brace that covered the shin bone and wrapped completely around the lower leg. Celina slipped on exam gloves. Deanna spotted the Velcro closings on the outside of his leg brace and tugged at them gently, removing the brace.

"Hey, what is this? There's a knife in it," Deanna remarked. "Cool."

"Give it to Anson," Halloran directed. Deanna continued to marvel at the several vertical pockets in the brace and was about to open another one when the owner objected. "Get it away from her, Anson."

"Hand it over, Deanna." Anson gave her the benefit of his best tone of command voice, to which she responded with a wry look and handed the brace to him. Anson, for his part, made a determined effort not to explore the contents of the leg brace any further but wondered if he might somehow come across another one if he asked Bertha about it.

Negotiations complete, Celina soaked off the gauze bandage that covered a spot of abraded skin about the size of a quarter. The hot Wintergreen Spring water seemed to soothe the injury, and she let a hot compress rest there for a few moments while she cut the medicated yellow dressing to size and shape. This she placed directly on the raised wound and covered it again with gauze. Using a cling bandage, she wrapped the long strip around the shin several times extending above and below the white gauze and finally taped the ends with adhesive paper tape.

Halloran had to admit that his leg felt much better, and he said so and thanked Celina for her care. She smiled back at him quietly.

"The rice and beans are ready. I wonder how your mother is doing?" Sandy brought bowls of steaming rice to the kitchen table. "Would you like some tea or coffee and dessert? It's orange custard."

"Let me make the tea," Celina offered with something special in mind.

"Having finished his dinner now, Jake looked around and realized someone was missing. Leaving his friends in the kitchen, he headed off into the living room following his nose towards the sunroom.

Stirring sleepily, Em heard the approaching click clack of the dog's claws on the hardwood floor. She rolled over to meet a pair of intelligent brown eyes and a long wet black nose close to her face.

"Jake, you're home." She threw her arms around the dog's neck and hugged him. "I heard what you did, you are such a good dog." Em held him in her arms. Sergeant Jaeger of Saybrook, canine federal officer, basked in her attention and the sound of her voice was sweet to his ears. It was better than sitting still and having a man with a stern and formal voice pin another shiny thing onto his dress collar. Hugging him seemed to please the lady. When she finally let go of his neck and drew back, he sent his impossibly long tongue out to lick her cheeks.

"No, Jake, not the lips," she exclaimed. He licked her nose instead. "Oh, Jake, now I'm all dog spit. Is your friend here? Is Michael here?" She wiped the bridge of her nose with her hand.

One bark and the dog trotted back to the kitchen to fetch him.

———◆———

HALLORAN'S PART

Michael Halloran hobbled down the length of the living room to the sunroom door, leaned heavily on his cane, barely touched down with his right foot. Anxiously waiting, Em heard him coming and leaned over the arm of the sofa bed towards him. When he reached the doorway he looked around for the nearest place to sit, only to find Ash gazing at him from the nearest chair. Tucked into the far corner of the room, Cleome was happily ensconced on the only other chair.

With relief and joy, Em greeted him. Halloran's clothes were rumpled, the legs of his trousers showed traces of sandy mud. From the weary look in his eyes and the strain on his face she could see he was very much in need of rest.

"Michael, I'm so glad you are all back safe. Come tell me about it. We heard the abbreviated version from Anson. And Bertha, too."

She shifted her body towards the middle of the sofa that folded out to a double bed. "Here, sit on the bed with me. I thought I could sleep down here to avoid having to trek up and down the stairs. I'm still pretty sore," she said ruefully and patted the spot next to her. "It's the only double bed in the house now. We can share the pillows."

For Halloran, it was cheering. He sat down next to her and looked around. "Need a bigger bed upstairs, Em. Too many windows here." He tried to straighten out his injured leg and settled down next to her.

"When we moved in, Josh said the same thing. The windows are alarmed, but he wanted to replace them. At the time, I told him I couldn't afford it."

His eyes closed, Halloran took in a deep breath as he

lay next to her, and made a mental note to have a conversation with Joshua Huber about windows and security.

"There's a nice old double brass bedstead upstairs in the attic. We can use that," she suggested quietly.

"I'll find a new mattress," he said, letting out a long deep breath.

A familiar floral scent filled the air around them. Em burst into a wide amused smile. The ever-helpful Celina had likely given him her double strength, double brewed Chamomile Knockout tea. This would be a short conversation.

The bed shook beneath them, Halloran opened his eyes a slit. "Get off the bed, Jake," he ordered in a drowsy voice.

"He's concerned about you, he won't budge." The dog looked at Em expectantly. "He can stay. And so can you." Jake settled his head on his paws to listen.

"I need a shower," he sighed.

"Uhm, yes, you do." There was a smile in her voice. Em liked squeaky clean straight from the shower, but she also enjoyed his presence a bit sweaty.

Halloran tried to stretch out. "Can you keep Cleo for a while longer? We're sending Frank to work in a secure lab until Version 5 is finished to everyone's satisfaction."

"Is he going to agree to that? He hid out in a cabin in the woods with no flush toilet instead of asking for protection." Em was doubtful.

"I called some friends. They'll feed him all the crab cakes and beer he can handle. They play a fair game of poker. Frank'll be fine. When he's done, he can come back and restart the business with a new partner. Al left his share of the business to his eldest son." Halloran's throat rumbled in a tired chuckle. "The son takes strongly after Al. He'll keep Frank in line and on track. It will be a step down for him to join the startup, but he'll respect his promise to his father."

Halloran stretched his back. "Need a bigger bed, Em."

"So you've said, and I agreed. We heard Jake caught the man who killed your friend Peter. Tell me what happened down on the shore this evening. With the freighter."

"Yes, Sergeant Jaeger made a good collar. Merits a promotion for that one. The Coast Guard boarded a freighter, rusty on the outside, not so much on the inside. New cabins. Walls didn't match the outside dimensions. A CG officer found ten young women and two children in a narrow hidden compartment. Some of them were abducted in their native countries. We'll be working with their embassies to send them home to their families. We also bagged an Asian officer who stowed away in an attempt to locate the missing daughter of an official of his government. He's convinced she's already here."

Halloran coughed to clear his throat, he was deciding how much to tell her. "You will appreciate this. The boarding party also found a man who didn't fit the smugglers' profile, a passenger masquerading as a crew member. He couldn't answer their basic questions about the ship or navigation. Not good preparation. When they started to collect pictures for facial recognition, he decided to take his chances in the water. Rankel chased him across the deck." He laughed silently. "They said when the man got up on the railing to dive in, Rankel jumped the railing and caught him in mid-air and went into the water with him. Even the smugglers were impressed. The boarding party had less trouble with them afterwards. Should make quite a report. I'll enjoy sending it to Washington."

"Who is he?" Em believed she might have a clue as to what he was.

"Interpol had a file on him that was suggestive." Here he paused to edit his thoughts. "If certain things check out, I'd say it is likely he was coming to verify Stevenson's creds. If so, he's a significant asset. That's all I can say, Em. And, it's more that I should tell you."

Oh, thank you for telling me. "When did you know both cases were coming together, Michael?"

"That night at the bar. Information we received made me suspect it," he replied, smiling to himself. *That was a good report as well. I enjoyed writing that one up.*

And you didn't share, she thought.

"Cargo was significant, too. Other contraband, counterfeit medicines, and a whole laundry list of consumer goods. And military grade weapons, did I mention that? Bertha's excited about them. She hasn't managed to collect some of those before. A very successful raid. Kudos and glory for the Coast Guard." Halloran's breathing slowed as he relaxed into sleep.

"You can tell me more tomorrow," Em said as she eased herself around.

"I have to go to work. Reports," he muttered sleepily.

"Sure you do. Tomorrow." She rubbed his arm gently, moving in still closer, to slip one arm gently across his chest. Without thought for any others in the house, an arm reached around her and drew her in to settle her head against his shoulder. His chin rubbed her forehead and stayed pressed gently there for several moments. Then on the crown of her head she felt his kiss. In appreciation she responded with a hug that lingered as Em settled in to enjoy his slightly sweaty, comforting, man scent.

CELINA'S PART

Approaching midnight, David Anson was sitting very close to Deanna on the Turkish carpet in the living room. Halloran's newest agent was reviewing, still one more time, the DVR version of the afternoon newscast of the explosion of the small boat in New Haven Harbor. Now termed accidental, the evening news coverage somehow managed to leave out the images of their team blowing up the boat. Fancy that. Anson was earnestly trying to convince Deanna to delete their copy of the earlier coverage, with no success. She was enjoying his attentions and teased him in return. Sandy watched her friend with pleasure from her seat in Em's favorite chair.

Celina had taken up the position on the couch vacated by her mother. More discretely, she watched the pair seated on the rug together alternately arguing and teasing. She and her brother Joshua frequently expressed despair at marrying Deanna off. Now Celina was not so sure. She resolved to consult with Joshua at the earliest opportunity. Time to check on Em and that man Halloran, their quiet talk out in the sunroom had stopped. Celina could hear a sound like a lion purring, and she launched herself carefully from the rather valuable antique Stickley couch. To make her way around Deanna and Anson, she rested her hand for balance on the couch's wooden frame.

As Celina came nearer to the sunroom door, the purring sound grew distinctly louder. In the sunroom, one of the small table lamps was still lit. Standing in the doorway she was quite close to the foldout sofa. The adults had fallen asleep together. Halloran was lying on his back fully dressed, his eyes closed in sleep, with Em curled up around him. Her head and hand rested on his chest, and her knee was placed over his good leg. Halloran's chin rested on her mother's forehead and Em had the smallest of smiles on her face. One of his arms encircled her shoulders, and his right hand had wandered around onto her mother's breast. The dog lay on the foot of the bed, his head down on his large front paws, snoring.

Celina stood for a moment lost in a sadness she could not have predicted. In all the long years of her parents' marriage, not once had she seen them in such peaceful intimacy. She stood silently. Deanna and Sandy came up behind her. Craning her neck to see around her older sister, Deanna began to snicker softly. The dog opened his eyes to stare at them.

"Aw look, Ma, Pa and the pooch." Deanna called quietly, "Come on, Jake. Time to go out, buddy."

The black dog lifted his head and with great delicacy took himself down off the bed and headed out towards the living room. The three young women backed up to let him pass and followed him to the door that led to the rock garden.

"What should we do?" Sandy asked as she let Jake out the door onto the side porch.

Deanna nodded sagely. "Best let sleeping mothers lie. You can go home now, Anson. I think we have another house guest for the night. They are both asleep."

"I can't just leave him, I'm his guard. I think he'd be safe at his place. He's due to see the doctor first thing in the morning," Anson objected.

Deanna gave a severe look at Anson, which made the watchful Sandy smile to herself. Sandy recognized reading each other's non-verbal cues as a sign of growing friendship between Anson and Deanna.

"It's my responsibility to get him there." Anson picked up a stray piece of popcorn from the rug and accurately landed it in the fireplace.

"If you insist, you can have the couch. I'm going to bed." Celina pronounced this like the order of the day.

JAKE'S PART

Jake stood on the stone porch in the rock garden and pointed his nose towards the backyard. Life was good for a dog at the Spring House. Jake understood his role, guard the den of his human pack's females, especially his best friend's mate. He would oblige by chasing pesky little ones, if there ever were any. The females in the house were gentle, affectionate and generous with food. They played with their animal companions. And he never had to sleep in the blasted crate. If he was canny and cautious, he could sleep on the couch and keep a sharp eye on the vermin-chasing felines from there. He only wore a leash when he had to take a person with him. His new hunting partner, the man whose feet left little scent, understood that.

Fortunately for Jake, the young alpha female Deanna's idea of a perimeter search was to let Jake out the back door and let him back in the front door after a while. He sniffed the midnight air, sensing nothing to raise his threat level. At the Spring House, there were turkeys and deer to chase and foxes and coyotes to scare off. But best of all, there was a desirable Golden Retriever down the road. When the wind was favorable, her enticing scent reached him. She was going into heat. Some morning soon, he'd do his perimeter search, then take R&R for himself. While he was recovering from his service-related injuries here in the country, someone had omitted to arrange his usual and regular matings with various Shepherd females. It was time to take initiative on his own, this could be good, too. With his hip feeling better, he could easily jump their backyard fence to pay a visit. The Golden was quite attractive with soft golden fur, and when they first met, she was not at all unfriendly. She seemed to welcome his company, always a good sign.

———◆———

SANDY'S PART

———◆———

Sandy had been sitting quietly in Em's favorite chair by the fireplace, watching her foster family take on a new shape as it added at least one new member. It was a good warm feeling for her. Em Huber had found herself a new companion after years of adjusting more and sometimes less well to a single life, even as she had been alone within a marriage. The way Dave Anson's eyes followed Deanna around the room when she wasn't looking made Sandy smile for her friend. All of this was in time for her own impending changes. She was universally known as her father's only daughter, it brought possibilities and a chance for a reckoning she would rather avoid. Her father acknowledged this and had written to her with an invitation to visit during her next vacation. She could not remember if he had ever done so before. It might give an unexpected opportunity to negotiate for assistance with graduate school, a possibility she had not dared to hope for until quite recently.

While Em launched her new business venture, and Deanna dragged Sandy into it, Sandy flourished on her own in her summer internship in epidemiology at the university hospital. It confirmed her aptitude for the work and increased her resolve to pursue the study of human epidemic disease as a career. Meticulous, and highly organized with a good grasp of the basics of the subject, she had an instinct for research. Em's instruction in research methods were not lost on her. Sandy had grown up hearing Em's stories about a family member who survived the Spanish Flu epidemic of the early 20th century. This oral history sparked her interest in the study of the patterns of epidemic disease. Now, if she could only convince her father of its value.

Sandy willingly followed Celina up the stairs to the second floor. Celina stopped at the head of the stairs.

"We're missing someone, where's Deanna?" Celina asked in a low tone.

The two young women turned back towards the stairway. Celina was about to call out to her sister when Sandy touched her arm and raised one finger to her lips for silence. Sandy walked back to the head of the stairs to listen. The stairwell carried Anson and Deanna's voices clearly to her. With a delighted grin, she beckoned Celina to join her to listen.

———————

ANSON'S PART

———————

"I've got to take him home, Deanna."

"Keep your voice down, *Dave*. Are you really going to go there? Wake him up to take him home?"

Anson and Deanna had taken their argument to the front hall to be as far away from the sunroom as they could manage. Deanna opened the front door to let the waiting dog back into the house after his nightly constitutional and perimeter search. Jake sniffed Deanna and Anson and trotted through the living room towards the sunroom.

"That's the idea," he said firmly, although with misgivings in his voice.

"You can do all that brave man stuff some other time. You have no idea what you could be in for. He's hurt. My mother cares for him. She is not going to let him go anywhere."

Seeing Anson preparing to object again, Deanna raised her hand. "You didn't see them. They are curled up asleep together. And she's got him pinned down, so he can't get up without waking her." This was an accurate assessment of what Deanna had seen in the sunroom. "And, you'll have to get by the dog to get to them."

Jake had taken up his position lying on the rug next to the pullout bed with his long nose on his paws, pointing towards Deanna and Anson. The guard dog watched and listened to them argue, perhaps he was even amused.

"What do you want me to do? I can't just leave," Anson

asked in frustration.

There were several ways she could go with this — she chose the better part. "If you take him back to his place, are you planning to camp out with him all night?"

"You mean stay with him? No, I wasn't planning to do that."

In the narrow hallway, they were standing rather close to each other. Anson was conscious his sport shirt was long past acceptable for mixed company. It was one thing to sweat it out with the guys. Hell, even the damned dog had sniffed and looked offended.

"But if he stays here, someone will be with him all night. I overheard Celina talking about watching for blood clots in his leg. Alone is not good for that, Dave." She crossed her arms.

"Oh." Anson's voice rumbled in his chest, he had not considered this.

An opening presented itself and Deanna took it. "If you really can't leave him, do what Celina suggested, sleep on the couch. That way, you'll be here first thing in the morning and can help him get ready to go see Smitty and his friends." Seeing no objection, she continued. "We'll get you bedding and towels. You can take a shower down here in the small bathroom. There is a plastic bench to use to sit down in the shower." Here Deanna caught herself. "For him to sit down in the shower." She had no idea whether Anson could wear his feet in the shower or not, but she knew a shower was definitely in order.

At the head of the stairs, Celina and Sandy, sneaking a listen, went to get a blanket, a sheet, a pillow and enough towels for two men to shower.

"I'm sorry, but I don't think we have any extra clothes that would fit you, you're… a lot taller than my brother," she said. But she was thinking, *Oh, so much bigger than my brother. Hmmm.*

"Alright, I'll stay, but how the hell am I supposed to

explain this?" Anson spoke up more forcefully than he meant to do.

Deanna's eyes began to tear up, which appalled Anson. Eyes burning, she tried desperately not to cry. It had been a long day, and she had been so worried about him. Now she felt he was yelling at her.

"Deanna, I'm not mad at you."

Without replying, Deanna looked at him sadly, showing wounded feelings.

Anson leaned forward to plant what he hoped would be a brotherly kiss on her cheek. Deanna anticipated him, and moved in. The movement diverted his aim enough to land his kiss closer to her lips. At first they nibbled each other's lips gently and once again found they liked it. Not so gradually, it became a good lip lock of a kiss. Arms slipped around his waist, almost too low. Anson put a gentle hand on her cheek, caught himself reaching to draw her in tighter. It had been a while since Anson tasted anything so sweet, fresh and shall we say invigorating. Rocking on his feet, Anson had his arm well around her before he pulled back.

"You need to go upstairs. I'm on duty. We can't be doing this…" he hesitated, caught.

"Every chance we get?" she asked with a mischievous smile.

"With my boss around. I'm on duty." This he stated with what he hoped would pass for authority.

As if to take the disappointment out of it, he rubbed her back. Her head rested on his broad chest, the same way she had seen Em sleeping on Halloran's chest and learned quickly by example. Anson let her stay there as long as he dared, and then carefully moved away so they could look at one another.

"Deanna, please. Go."

"I'll be back for fall break. And then you can come to Thanksgiving dinner. Will you?" Engrossed, she was admiring his eyes. In the muted light in the old hallway, they seemed to glow gold. A shadow of a beard, a deeper amber color than his blond hair grew across a strong jaw line. Her chest grew tight. The air between them seemed suddenly quite hot, her face flushed red, a new sensation for her. The flush spread downward and left her shaky, and it wasn't embarrassment.

"I will," he said in a moment, although sitting across the Thanksgiving dinner table from Halloran gave him pause. "You need to go up to bed now." He caught a glint in her eye. "Stay there until breakfast." The girl had been teasing him all evening, and he wasn't sure she knew what she was doing, but she was damned good at it. A cold shower was certainly in order, and maybe a chance to walk it off.

Presence of mind restored, laughing impishly, she turned on her heel and ran up the stairs without a word. As she came barreling around the corner into the hallway she bumped into Sandy, who carried a heap of towels and bedding with a pillow balanced on top.

"I hope you enjoyed yourselves listening. Gawd, I thought you were Mom," Deanna exclaimed at the sight of Celina standing in the center of the hall arms folded across her chest. Hoots of laughter followed.

"I'll take these down to *Dave,*" Sandy teased. On reaching the hall below, carrying the shifting load of soft goods, she caught sight of Anson's back as he beat a retreat into the living room.

In his haste, Anson tripped over a black satchel. It was the away bag he'd brought in from the car for Halloran when they first arrived. *Damn,* he thought, *we've been arguing about taking him to his place, and Halloran always meant to stay here.*

EM'S PART

As soon as her daughters and Sandy were back in the living room and Em could hear their restrained voices debating what to do next, she opened her eyes and stirred against Halloran's chest. He rubbed her breast in friendly response.

"Busted again," she murmured.

"No surprise there from the sound of it," a sleepy voice replied.

"I've been thinking." Em rested her chin on his chest to look at him. Half asleep, salt and pepper beard growing in, to her he looked delectably scruffy.

"They are adults now. There's no real reason I can't be more open about my personal life. The last few years of marriage with Harley made me so miserable, I didn't want to share it. They didn't want to hear it, either." She paused, then said in a soft and warm voice, "I'm not unhappy now," and waited to hear what he might say.

A reply was expected. Halloran roused himself, but it surprised her when he spoke. "My son wants to meet you and the girls and Joshua, of course. Jamie will be here in October. After my accident he took a leave of absence to come to stay with me. The stair glider was his idea. The two of them, he and Jake got me through it. He worries, says I shouldn't live alone. I think you'll like Jamie. I know he will like you." Eyes now at half mast closed again.

"I think I'd like that." Em smiled.

He could feel it rather than see it. "I have to get up. I have to go to work tomorrow."

"Before or after your doctor friend Smitty takes the hunk of metal out of your leg bone? Don't be silly, Michael." In a low husky voice she added, "Come back to me afterwards."

"My dear, that would be indiscrete," he said with a chuckle. It was, however, what Halloran had in mind. After all, windows on three sides, even with the shades down, he could hardly let her sleep alone in this ground floor room.

"I'm okay with that if you are." Em watched a slow smile creep across Halloran's face tug at the corners of his mouth and crinkle his eyes. "Seriously, Michael, you are welcome to stay with us." Chin on one hand, she rubbed the other across his chest. "We can convalesce together." Soft brown eyes looked into his. She raised her eyebrows at him, and he laughed, more aware now. They both had more than convalescing in mind.

"Thank you."

"I have dinner next week with some women friends. It's at a restaurant down on the shore. We get together every month or so, and they called to check on me. When we worked together at the company, we used to go out for break together every morning, and it became kind of a sisterhood. We saw each other through lots of changes, personal and professional – downsizing, right sizing, layoffs, outsourcing, retirements, divorce, illness and death of parents. One or two are still working there. The youngest one of us figured out that we were so close because either we are only children or have only brothers. They moved the dinner date up, I think they want to grill me on my new business venture or my summer adventures."

"Em, it may not be wise to go out yet. Which shore are we talking here?"

Hearing the name of the restaurant and where it was, Halloran groaned audibly. The location was not far from where they had intercepted the freighter.

"Michael, you worry too much. No one would be interested in me. It's only a women's night out. Besides, I'm already starting to go stir crazy." Em was determined to go.

"Precautions will need to be taken," he replied.

"Dee and Sandy will be going back to college soon," she continued. "I only hope that Deanna can stay clear of trouble for one whole academic year and graduate without a hitch. It's not that she does anything really wrong. Things get complicated and she manages to get into other peoples' business. She usually drags Sandy in with her. I can't think who she takes after."

"You can't, Em?" This time Halloran laughed outright.

"Very funny. I know Machiavelli wrote you should never go anywhere unarmed, but may I ask you to take off your gun? Put it under the pillow or something. It feels like a rock."

"Which one? Which gun?" he asked.

"Oh, Michael."

EPILOGUE

BREW PUB

———◆———

"SPEED LIMIT, ANSON!" Michael Halloran ordered from the shadowy back seat in a tone of habitually exasperated patience with his newest subordinate.

The driver, David Anson, obliged his boss by slowing a few miles an hour. Looking into his rearview mirror, he remarked, "Sir, what on earth's the use of having a truly capable pursuit car if I can't let it out on the Interstate?" And he mumbled quietly, "Connecticut's a small state, how far can we get anyway?"

Two passengers in the backseat, Em Huber and Michael Halloran, debated discreetly from the moment she wedged herself carefully into the repurposed general's staff car. Trying not to act like a couple who enjoyed more than simple verbal sparring, they stared intently at each other. Em broke down and snickered but was not a thoroughly happy woman — she was sore. A comfortable angle to sit was difficult to find as her gunshot wound was not completely healed. Scooching around on the leather seat only made it worse. And on top of that, her brains were too tightly constrained by the new bustier. The argument concerned her evening plans. But now she wasn't so sure the idea was wise, considering the events of this summer. The interior of the car was dark. The back windows were heavily tinted so they barely saw each other's expressions. A sure tell of agitation of mind, she ran her fingers through her curly dark grey hair, raking it back and out of any semblance of order.

"No arguments like this in a Humvee in 'Stan. Just the old folks at home," Anson said to himself more quietly, trying to ignore the dynamic in the backseat. A whisper of this reached Em's keen ears. She smiled.

"I wish you wouldn't do this, Em. We still have suspects at large out there."

"You worry too much. It's not like I'm special. They won't be interested in me. It's an evening out with the girls," she said, trying to convince herself it was true. Listening to the higher tone and inflection, she knew she must sound anxious.

"Don't forget the cane," his deep voice with a little gravel in it reminded her. "Only use it if you need to, and be careful. There is not another one like it."

"So you've said," Em stated. The sound of the low notes in his voice made her wish to haul him down onto the smooth, supple leather of the general's backseat. It had been a few days since they'd stolen time together. Considering the line of sight from the driver's mirror, sneaking under it, her hand found his sore knee, and her finger tips ran around it, barely touching in gentle circles. Stealthy fingers moved to the inside of his thigh above his sensitive knee and began to massage back and forth. The hand of the fabric, the texture to the touch, of good wool flannel suiting beguiled her, and Em imagined the leg beneath his trousers. All the while she was aware they might be overheard by more than Anson if the comm channel was active.

"I'm fond of that cane," Halloran attempted a grumble.

"Stop worrying. I'll be fine. It's dinner with a bunch of women friends from my former job. What can happen?" Trying to sound cheerful, inwardly she cursed. It hurt to walk. Bullet wounds took a long time to heal. Unsure she could sit through a leisurely dinner on a wooden bench seat without giving herself away, doubts overtook her. Almost absentmindedly, thumb up, her fingers started a slow progress moving lightly up his thigh.

"Heavens to *Betsey*, what am I going to do with you?" As he spoke, Halloran interlaced his fingers with hers, holding them down, giving a most pleasant sensation. Almost causing her to forget her wound's discomfort.

Soft laughter, a cocktail alto chuckle, was her response to hearing the *nom de guerre* she had used when undercover with him.

Distracted by her fond attention Halloran spoke *sotto voce*, "What indeed? With you there are so many options. There is no telling what might happen." Grasping her hand gently he said, "I can't very well go in with you. At least agree to take the cane. I know you refused the dog, which is understandable.

"They pay me to worry. An imagination for disaster is a valuable thing. A requirement really, in my work. I never hire anyone without it," he spoke, his tone low and serious while trying and failing to keep her hand still. "Your house is safer, why insist on going out now, outside of plain stubbornness? If we hadn't been willing to pick you up, I'm sure you'd have found a way around us." This was said as he gently encouraged her fingers away from their intended target.

"I do understand, but not this time. I've been cooped up in the house for *weeks*." Down close to the seat the little hand wrestling match continued. As the car took the corner at the end of the Interstate exit ramp at speed, Em pressed against the door.

"Ouch! We're not late, Anson. No need to rush," she expostulated as she worked to regain proximity to Halloran who now had a firm hold on her hand.

"One week, ten days, Em. That's all you've been laid up," he reminded her. A deep sigh expressed it was long for him, too. Concentrating on wrapping his fingers around hers, he fell prey to a sneak attack by a second hand. Because any rebuke would be overheard, he resigned to defend himself silently from his teasing lady.

Down along the shoreline, through a twisting road lined with small cottages, the fast car with no discernible markings made its way. The car pulled into a gravel parking lot with a line of boulders between it and an old smuggler's channel that led out to Long Island Sound. The wind off the North Atlantic picked up as the sun went down and was now blowing across the salt marsh grasses in waves. The wind carried with it the smell of salt water, the stink of mud flats at low tide, and when it turned and swooped over the long low shack by the parking lot, the delectable odor of fried seafood.

The long low building, originally a lobstermen's shack with a notorious past, kept its weather beaten red paint look, regardless of how often it was painted. Sea spray, sand and storms wore the paint so thin the boards showed through. Protected by marshes, it was far enough from the beach that only the most severe ocean-borne storms swamped it. The lights in the Brew Pub's small high windows were incandescent-warm, and the neon signs in the windows advertised favorite beers. Across the marsh down the channel, and across the water, tiny navigation and channel lights dotted the north shore of Long Island only seventeen miles away.

The car pulled up to the pub's doorway. The mood lightened considerably by a little playfulness, Em, a woman of a certain age, no longer young, quite a bit wiser, eased herself out of the car, gingerly poking the carved wooden cane out ahead. Straightening up, and pulling her skirt down to walk forward towards the pub door, she carefully steadied herself. Before closing the door, Em softly addressed the darkened interior of the car. "You can go now."

"Call us when you're ready to leave, *Betsey.* Someone will be close by." His growl, humor edged, gave her the shivers and provoked a wish that the fun and games could be extended later that evening.

Damn and blast it, she thought, her mind still absorbed by the man in the car. *He's going to have someone in the parking lot.* She turned to make a swift reply, the car slipped away, and she was standing alone. A ripple of doubt caused her to wonder, *Have I gone too far teasing him just now? In bed he can be a tease, even playful as a teenager, but oh so experienced. Truly enjoyable technique, warm with feeling. But on the job, he's detached, all focus and no fun. Is this how a mistress feels, only half his life shared? Is that all I want?* Sense memories distracted her thoughts, the taste of raspberries, the sound of his voice low and warm, the scratch of his morning beard, and images of their shared pleasure. *Dinner, I have to go in to dinner. I can't just stand here wanting him back. It really is the same as being a teenager or not so much.*

Though still early, she had made certain of that, Em hoped to be seated before the others arrived. The pub door was old and rather heavy, and she struggled to get it open. This was part of the original roadhouse converted from the 1920's smugglers' fishing shack. It was whispered bootleggers brought their Canadian cargo up the channel from the Sound to the shack during Prohibition. The doors were stout to delay raids by competitors or the police.

After Prohibition ended, things became tamer. The summer cottages were winterized gradually and became year round homes. A deck reaching out over the marsh was added to the restaurant and live music could be heard there on weekends. Em wondered absently if all the hiding places and bolt holes were still in the premises. Still and all, the food was surprisingly good. People came down to the marsh for boiled lobster, salted red potatoes and corn on the cob. No one asked questions about where the lobsters came from.

With effort, Em managed to get the door open. The interior of the pub was all bare wood and dark oak rafters. Tongue-in-groove bead boards covered the walls to half their height. Water stains on the boards six inches above the floor showed the recent highwater mark. Old prints and photographs of sailing ships and a few genuine marine artifacts provided the only attempt at decor. The bar was a long antique of a thing that stood along one wall. Booths with built-in benches and longer stand-alone tables in dark wood filled the interior. Initials carved into the tables declared wait times for meal service were productively used.

A tall youth, black hair slicked back, wearing a white barman's apron approached Em to show her to her seat. Although carrying a cane, she was not using it very well. At the Brew Pub she was known as one of a group of women that came every month or two. They reserved the large round table in the corner. Some wait staff believed women didn't tip well, but this group was a welcome one, paid cash, tipped liberally and said thank you, too.

Em chose a seat back to the wall, with a full view of the dining room, especially the door. And sat down cautiously, all the while keeping the cane out of sight but close at hand. The server missed the sharp glance that followed him back to the center of the room. From behind the menu she knew by heart, Em cruised the dining room with her eyes. Tucking the feel of Michael Halloran's trousers back into a special corner of her mind, to be enjoyed at leisure, was not easy.

There were few diners, more patrons at the bar than in the booths or at the tables. It was mid-week in early September and even the lobster special seemed not to draw heavy traffic. A young professional couple debated a point of law regarding search and seizure. Two outrageously active young boys and their family were having an early supper. The parents were pushing plates of fried onion rings at their reluctant offspring.

Rankel, acting as the waiter serving the family's table, arrived with a second round of soda. A small man, wiry, with alert and active eyes, he carried the tray with oversized glasses loaded full of ice with practiced assurance. Agent Rankel's appearance at the table provoked the boys, and he dexterously avoided a swipe by the hand of the six-year old that would have caused a shower of soda and ice to land in his mother's lap. The father was grateful. Someone deserved a good tip for quick action.

Amused, reassured, stifling a laugh, Em peered down into the menu to hide her smile. Easy to anticipate that Halloran couldn't leave well enough alone, so he sent in an agent to watch her. The mercy was he didn't come into the pub himself.

"Well, well, well, aren't we early? Where shall I sit? Can you move at all, honey?" A tall distinguished woman in a tailored black business suit sat down next to her friend. A bright orange print blouse highlighted her *café au lait* complexion.

"Yes, Tina, but let's keep it between us. I'm not talking about it in a restaurant. You know what they say, 'Telephone, telegraph, tell somebody at ....'"

"I know. With this group news would be on the wire fast. Did your son send the security stuff down for installation yet? We could use something like that for the data center. When I asked him, he said, 'It's not invented yet. So far it's only for fish.' Now I ask you, if it's good enough for his mother, why not me, too?" Tina Wallace laughed. "Where is the waiter? I could use a seltzer. And then something stronger.

"It's been a long thirsty day since they took out the water coolers. I came right from work. We had a meeting with a vendor about the next security software upgrade.

I told him exactly what I wanted to see in it and don't send me anything less. Too many cyber hacks lately. You'd think those Russians and Chinese didn't have anything else to play with. Hello, Susie, so good to see you!" Tina looked up at the new arrival.

Almost to a minute of the appointed time, a bevy of women arrived and seemed to take charge of the dining room in the way a large party of friends can do with familiarity and a vibrant female energy. They greeted each other warmly and with laughter. After all, they hadn't seen each other all summer since their vacation schedules wouldn't line up. Friends with history of shared joys and struggles, both personal and professional, some were still working, others retired, several laid off or outsourced to other companies. The group of middle management women could be as many as twelve or fourteen, but that night only eight gathered for gossip, seafood, and most importantly, dessert.

Although Em held her chosen seat at the table, she felt compelled to shift her weight frequently from one hip to the other and worked to hurry their order. The menu offered lobster rolls, southern Connecticut style hot dog buns filled with lobster meat drenched in melted butter with a touch of lemon, fried shrimp, clams or broiled fish. One or two planned to brave the pound and half boiled lobster special. Drinks were ordered. Wine and water glasses crowded the table. Appetizers drew greater attention. Fried calamari, fried mozzarella sticks and seafood stuffed mushroom caps came to their table in rapid succession.

The table with two boys was in the center of the room, a most fortunate placement as it turned out. The children were loud and rambunctious, which meant the group of women would in no way disturb them with laughter and the occasional hoot. The eight women who met for dinner were the sparkplugs of their friendship group.

On one side of the room, a table with four men in plaid short sleeved shirts with different shades of white hair all cut short sat in discussion. A slightly younger man lectured the other three who listened with reserved attention.

Tina's eyes landed at the men's table, and she said under her breath for the other women to hear, "Look over there, shop stewards and the union rep. Do we have a strike due? Working conditions lately for *all* of us, wouldn't surprise me one bit." Eight pairs of management women's eyes turned on the four men. It took a moment, but the backs of the men stiffened as if hit by darts. One of them saw the source and alerted the others. They hastily called for their check and left as soon as possible. Having cleared the room, the women went back to passing the appetizers.

Over at the family's table hot dog and hamburger platters arrived, piled high with golden French fries. The children dug into their fries with gusto. Ketchup, the boys' vegetable of choice, flew through the air propelled from a squeeze bottle and landed on the wide board wooden floor. Mustard and pickle relish joined the fray. The boys seemed to be having a contest to see who could finish their hot dog first. Their mother could be heard enjoining them to slow down and chew their food. Immune to the chaos at the table, the father was engrossed in savoring a huge double burger.

As the room grew warmer, Em felt constrained by her undergarment. She stretched and wriggled in her seat as subtly as possible but in ways not usually seen at a dinner table. When she started to scratch discretely under her arm pit, Tina, who was still seated next to her, noticed.

"What's wrong Emmie? Bed bugs biting? You can't seem to sit still," Tina whispered,

Reluctantly Em slid her hand back into her lap. Scratching had been so satisfying. "Nothing like that," she replied. "New long line bra. Must be a tag or a seam. It's not quite right yet. I have to sit up too straight to be comfortable. I can't seem to relax in it." Em dropped her voice. Her attention was drawn to a table across the room.

"You are looking kind of perky under that sweater. It's a nice look for you. For anybody special? Where is he this evening?" Tina stared at Em, whose eyes were fixed on the table with two small boys. The older child was growing flushed, his eyes were wide and his arms were flapping. The younger boy laughed gleefully at the expression on his older brother's face. Em watched him for a few more seconds, then bolted from her seat moving as fast as she could. Favoring one leg, she hopped over to the six-year old.

"I think your son is choking!" she said to the startled mother seated on the opposite side of the table. The father's mouth was too full for him to speak. Em and the child's mother urged him to speak or cough, but he could do neither.

"Jeremy, stop fooling around. Cough," his father ordered sharply.

The child's face grew alarmingly red. Other diners sensed something wrong, but no one else moved to help. The room became dead silent. With the parents' permission, Em stood behind Jeremy, wrapped her hands around his middle, and gave him a quick firm squeeze. Nothing happened. His little brother gave a fearful cry.

Silently praying, Em took a deep breath, adjusted her hands, and squeezed the child again. *More quickly*, popped into her mind, and she gave him a third firm squeeze upward in faster succession. With a deep gurgling gagging sound, a chunk of hot dog flew from Jeremy's mouth. The over large bite shot across the table, striking his mother on her breast bone, and dropped down into the front of her blouse. Jeremy gasped several times. His color quickly returned to normal, and his eyes began to tear.

"The next time, mind your mother and chew your hot dog." Placing her hands on his shoulders gently, she said this into his ear. Thanks from his parents were waved off. Jeremy's mother extricated the hot dog from her bra. Trying not to limp, Em made her way back to her seat.

At a table across the room, Agent DeCarlo defended a legal point in conversation and had his argument vigorously pursued by his companion. Watching the action at the children's table he remarked to her, "Fast acting. Amy, I can't believe Ms. Huber did that."

"Why on earth not? We've seen her jump in before. I got it. They're probably enjoying this video feed back in the office as we speak," under her breath Agent Amy Cardozo, his partner, replied.

Returning to the table Em met seven pairs of eyes focused on her. Were they watching her limp? *If only I can avoid detection*, she thought, *make it a quiet dinner and sneak out without having to answer the questions such as, "So how was your summer, Em? How's your new business venture?"* Questions flew at her as she eased herself onto the regrettably hard seat. Fortunately, the cane was well out of view, hidden down between her and Tina. The beautifully carved Irish burl cane with the head of a sea monster was a good lead-in to the story. It was a rather long yarn, and she was determined not to unravel it all at dinner.

Providing a welcome reprieve two waiters approached with their main courses. One of them was the short wiry man who had served the family. As Agent Rankel delivered her plate he leaned towards Em and said softly, "Nice going, ma'am. That's two saves."

Em gave him a swift warning look, and her face warmed with color.

New England scrod, baby cod, in a crust of seasoned

bread crumbs, surrounded by shrimp in a cream sauce, accompanied by steamed fresh vegetables and wild rice pilaf arrived for Em. As the friends settled down to their main course, Em relaxed enough to swallow down some of the house white wine. She hoped the house brewed beer was better. It had the best reputation around. The lingering presence of brewing, scents of yeast, hops and salt marsh air, with an undertone of deep fat frying, formed the comfortable pub ambiance that would follow her home in her clothes. The scrod was excellent that evening, very fresh.

A perennially cheerful woman for a database administrator, Elaine twisted the front arms off her carmine red boiled lobster with obvious enjoyment. Putting a nut cracker to good use she attacked the two large claws, extracted the sweet meat with a pick and dipped it in melted butter. Complaining about her on call status, she threatened any client who might interrupt their evening with the fate suffered by the delectable crustacean on the plate in front of her.

Em staunchly avoided ordering a whole lobster in a restaurant other than an outdoor seaside venue. Having grown up eating lobster, she was reluctant to show her skill at sucking the meat out of all those little legs bit by tiny bit. It was a family custom, best practiced at home, so as not to embarrass her children.

"It's not as sweet as a Maine lobster, must be from down here. Maybe it's from Massachusetts or even the Sound." Elaine stopped to savor the tender meat from the claw.

"Did you see the electric blue lobster in the tank up front? They are valuable. They don't catch too many of those. The sign says he's going to an aquarium. He doesn't look happy about it," Andrea from financial systems remarked. Sitting close to Elaine, she leaned back to avoid the salt water spattering from the boiled lobster. Andrea was a small person, who found it a challenge to buy adult women's clothes in size 4, but her mind and tongue were sharp. Auditors walked softly in her presence, an unusual phenomenon.

New Englanders can tell a Maine lobster from its freshwater cousin the crayfish a mile away. The presence of dead crustaceans *Homarus americanus* belly up on the table was a constant source of contentment. Em relaxed. The topic was to her liking until Andrea said, "So Em, tell us about your new career. I understand you've found the solution to senior unemployment. We're anxious to hear about it. That's why we moved the date for dinner up a week." Andrea smiled, cat-like and a bit sly.

The shrimp on Em's fork went back down onto her plate. In reflection she thought, *A coward dies a thousand deaths; a brave woman might be able to cut that in half. If anyone in this group is going to pin me down, it will be Andrea.*

"Okay, here's to new beginnings." Em raised her wine glass and waited for her friends to raise their assorted glasses in a toast. Thereby giving herself time to think, *Where to start? What to say? And most importantly, what to leave unsaid in a public restaurant. Especially with at least one of Halloran's agents hovering around me.*

"Get it over with, Em, it's the only way," Tina spoke behind her napkin. "And let the brain trust be with you."

Em took the opportunity to drain her wine glass, decided it was drinkable after all, and began. "It started with our discussion at dinner last spring when we closed that Italian restaurant on Wooster Street. We got so involved that we lost track of time."

Samantha, the birthday celebrant, reminisced. "I remember. We had the waitress and waiters lined up along the wall listening to us, and we bribed them with pieces of triple chocolate birthday cake so they'd let us stay."

"They'll probably never be tempted to work for a corporation," remarked Andrea.

"God forbid," interjected Sarah, the quiet one, whose job had been outsourced to Brazil.

"Maybe, you never know. We talked about layoffs at the magic age of fifty-seven and outsourcing jobs to countries where the workers require armed guards to come to work," Em remembered. "Fifty-seven must seem like a long way off to them yet. You can't exactly have someone off-shore serve dinner or tend bar."

Elaine worked the tail meat out of her lobster as she spoke. "We dissed executives whose stock options vested immediately while the rest of us are stuck with Jacques Cousteau options, that is to say underwater." This was greeted with rueful laughter all around. "Mine were supposed to help put my kids through college. No such luck for us."

"Em analyzed the relationship between Wall Street expectations for company earnings that were driving corporate management to make short term decisions costing US jobs and income. Sacrificing employees to boost earnings for Wall Street, and corporate bonuses, that is," Andrea rejoined.

After saluting the group with her wine glass, Andrea continued. "It doesn't take a financial genius to see if you outsource jobs to other countries there will be fewer jobs here. If there are fewer paying jobs here, there will be fewer customers for goods and services and that will affect the economy in an adverse way. If you lay off people to make numbers to impress Wall Street analysts, who know little to nothing about the actual running of their subject businesses, you waste human capital."

The women all stared at Andrea, their resident financial expert.

Sarah took a turn as the discussion rounded the table, "Continuous twenty-four hour coverage is one thing. Outsourcing to avoid paying foreign workers benefits, that's another. Seems so simple when you think it through. Unless you're an economist or a CEO, then it's an impenetrable mystery. I'm just saying… they have a lot to answer for." All eyes around the friends' table turned in astonishment on Sarah. Complacently finishing her house Caesar salad, the youngest in the group who rarely spoke up, said, "What?"

"Right, well, that still leaves many of us unemployed or minimally employable due to age discrimination. I did my stint in retail, and I can tell you that's not an easy gig," remarked Susan, formerly executive assistant to the head of Marketing. Her typing speed was legendary until the advent of computer keyboards, which were significantly slower than her IBM Selectric. Susan dyed her hair a jet black because people in Marketing can never be seen to age, whereas many people in Information Technology didn't bother with hair dye or Botox — customers never saw them.

Tina picked up, "You know I think they're under-estimating how mad people are about this. Not good. Labor tensions build up, negotiations go sour, threatening behavior used to turn to violence. Either side. Both sides. Labor History 401, Professor Melvin played an LP record in class over and over again. Can you believe it, an LP? Until we knew the old organizing songs by heart. We were convinced they'd be on that final." Imitating a limited range, slightly off key marching song voice Tina began, "The union is behind…." The laughter around the table certainly was a guilty pleasure for middle management.

"Are we starting this all over again or do you want to hear what I decided to do about it?" Em asked reluctantly. Encouraging words were said all around, and Em took up the flow of her narrative. "Like so many other people, a couple years ago I got the invitation to play musical jobs, your job has been eliminated, find another or leave."

"So, you left in a huff," Tina teased as she popped a whole bellied fried clam into her mouth.

"I thought I retired gracefully, and I am never going back there. Corporations can be dangerous places," Em countered to laughter. "Anyway, it didn't take long to figure out after the divorce from Harley and buying the Spring House last year I would have to find some way of earning money. There are no jobs for people with resumés as long my arm. I can't exactly pretend to be thirty years old again."

"That wouldn't do you any good, honey," Tina interjected.

"How is Harley Travis Huber, our favorite marital miscreant anyway?" Samantha asked between bites of shrimp scampi with a determined lack of tact on her open good humored strawberry freckled face. Well she understood the satisfaction of catharsis, the emotional relief achieved by complaining to a sympathetic group of women friends.

"Haven't seen him in months and don't want to either. Harley would rather see me go belly up than anything else in this world…." Em replied with asperity.

"You said you were done with that!" Tina spoke in mock surprise, hoots of laughter followed.

"Financially, Tina, belly up financially, as in broke. And I am not about to let that happen." It was going to be a struggle to proceed with the story without serious kidding from her friends.

"Well, apparently he's up to his old shenanigans and screwed up again in Texas." This was greeted by snickering laughter and comments very much not *sotto voce*. Comments ignored, Em forged through the easy update. "My children were beginning to accept Brigitte as his live-in when she suddenly moved out screaming and in tears. His Aunt Marlene Albrecht is livid. I heard it all from her. It seems he treated Brigitte the way he treated me. The kids were upset, especially Deanna, who was looking forward to spending vacation time back in Texas."

"She would be the most upset, Em. Deanna's the youngest. She will get over it. Honey, the children figure it out eventually. Give her time." Never fond of Harley Travis Huber, Tina offered some rather cool comfort.

"Yes, but you haven't heard the best part. Brigitte married someone else. A very old, very rich someone else."

"Gold digger on the rebound?" interposed Andrea.

"I don't know, but I hope she's done better than Harley." Em sighed and stared down at her plate.

"Enough about Harley, tell us about your new career," Andrea suggested firmly.

"You haven't lived until you've been laughed at by Unemployment," Em rallied. "I gave them my resumé, and they asked how much I'd been paid and burst out laughing when I told them. 'You did all that, and that's all you were paid?' they said. I was embarrassed, really. Apparently women *are* paid less than they are worth for the same job."

"Everyone here can agree on that." Elaine humorously pointed the empty shell of a lobster claw around at them for emphasis. This was met with nods of rueful agreement and regretful smiles around the table. The plastic lobster bib was doing duty as an oversized napkin on her lap for just such occasions.

"The federal government doesn't know how to help workers over fifty who have become unemployed. They really don't. I could retrain to do something I probably wouldn't be good at. All they could suggest for people my age was to start your own business. I'd already bought the Spring House, and I wasn't about to make the mortgage payments selling spring water. Now where are we supposed to get capital to start a business?" Em paused. "So, I started to think, what are my assets? Stop laughing, Tina. That's not helpful."

"I'm laughing because it's typical. You got yourself in

some serious stuff by thinking about it."

"A foreign competitor emailed me, fishing for that one sheeter, I am never going back inside one."

A hearty generous laugh splashed the wine in Tina's hand. "Never say never, it's a sure jinx, Em."

"Look at us, there's enough talent around this table to run a major corporation, which is what we were doing before the bottom fell out. It's a major waste, and I had no ideas for manufacturing the next great widget, so I decided to go another way. Why not do what I'm good at, like my old job?" Em concluded.

"What exactly was it you did? I never quite got that," asked Elaine as she dunked a piece of lobster meat from the tail in the melted butter.

"Generally speaking, *Here goes the canned speach*, it was business competitive intelligence. It's sort of like military intelligence but for business. Competitive intelligence, well, it's the secret weapon that corporations use to assess competitive threats and opportunities to best each other in the marketplace. It's supposed to be strictly legal, gathering information about the competition and analyzing it. But, there is room for some creativity." Smiling she said more to herself, "It's the creativity that I was good at."

"Yes, so then what?" encouraged Tina in an insinuating tone.

"I decided, go into business for myself. You'd laugh if I told you how serious I was. I did a business plan, a marketing plan and got business cards and stationery. I even looked into errors and omissions insurance before I decided the hell with it and took my first client."

Em saw her scrod was growing cold. The cream sauce over the remaining shrimp was congealing on the plate. She begged to be allowed to eat before continuing. Another round of drinks was ordered. One of her friends wisely made sure Em got another glass of a different wine, although she did not request it. The new wine tasted better to her than the first glass. A tiny smirk on his face, the short waiter hovered at the side of the dining room. The family with the two boys finished their meal in relative quiet and stopped on their way out for Jeremy to thank Em. In the corner, the couple were nursing their drinks and debated the relative merits of dessert over the need for additional exercise.

Dinner time passed more slowly with discussion of college-aged children and upcoming weddings. Desserts were ordered. After prolonged negotiations, only two women opted to share dessert. The rest indulged their individual pleasures with chocolate, fresh raspberries, tiramisu, New York cheesecake with strawberry glaze or other delicacies with high calorie counts. With relish Em finished her wine and was more than ready to begin again.

"So my first client, such a disappointment, she was a young woman who hadn't been married long and wanted me to trace her ex-husband. I am never doing divorce work again. My client was so mad at me when I told her what I found I ran right to the bank to deposit her check. The ex was back home, living with his sister's family. Well, that case did pay car insurance for a month. My second client wasn't much better, and this has to stay here at the table, I did a statewide survey of funeral costs, complete with charts, graphs, maps. Overkill really," Em spoke confidentially.

"No pun intended, of course!" Andrea was half way through her crème brulée.

"Of course, not, no! My third client paid for the new washer and dryer and dinner tonight. They say three's a charm...."

"Good thing you were charmed, honey, and got to walk away from that one. So what can you tell us? We only know what we saw on TV or read on the Internet." Elaine was happily sipping espresso with her carrot cake.

"Shootings, kidnapping, *murder*. Do you carry a gun now?" Despite requests to share it, Susan was getting through her chocolate lava cake all by herself.

"No guns," Em exclaimed. "I'm not a private investigator."

Moving into range, Rankel busied himself clearing the family's table, wiping away ketchup and mustard spills meticulously, several times, hiding a laugh.

Em sank her fork into a piece of autumn apple tart and swirled it around in the fresh whipped cream. Earl Grey was steeping in the diminutive white teapot next to her cup.

"It's strictly business intelligence gathering, so far anyway." Em proceeded to tell the bare bones version behind the media coverage assuming they had all seen it and that there had been a stream of shared emails about it. After all, there was client confidentiality to be maintained, a nice retainer to be earned and bills to be paid with it. Now there is a business problem with retainers, which Em did not anticipate. As she later realized your client expects you to be at their beck and call. Frank Kirbee was not likely to forget that. Em's resolution to stay away from corporate would be sorely tested in a remarkably short time.

The dining room was almost empty, and the bar was growing rowdy by the time Em finished her version of "what I did over the summer," for her longtime friends. The women rose from their seats at the table and went through the good-bye ritual of hugs and good wishes. Two went off to the ladies' room, four departed together for the parking lot, leaving Tina and Em as the last to leave. As she retrieved the cane Em looked around the dining room. The waiter had disappeared.

"Nice cane. Borrowed for the evening? His, I'm guessing," Tina mused.

With a nod and a smirky eye roll, using the serpent

headed cane for balance, Em carefully rose from the hard wooden seat.

Together Em and Tina walked out of the dining room, passed the bar of happily carousing patrons, and were walking towards the side door out into the parking lot. Feeling the pleasant effects of two glasses of wine, Em wavered in her walk. In front of her, Tina pushed the heavy door open. Seemingly on cue, a dirty white panel truck drove up in front of the entrance and abruptly stopped.

As Em came through the door she felt movement behind her. A man from the bar in a dark hoodie and ripped blue jeans, not quite sober, grabbed her around the neck. His breath smelled of a yeasty brew and spicy beer nuts. As hard as she could, Em jabbed her elbow backward, catching the man in his solar plexus and doubling him forward. She kicked his shin and scraped her boot heel down his leg and was about to bring her head up to bash him on the face. But suddenly he was pulled backward and away from her. The lightly built waiter, the loosely disguised Agent Rankel, tackled the larger assailant from behind and brought him to his knees.

Another barfly of a man in a black leather jacket caught Tina by surprise and had her arms pinioned behind her back. As she struggled to free herself Tina swore at him energetically. Em turned towards her, pressed the bump on the handle of the cane, and jabbed its tip onto his leg. The assailant froze, a stunned expression on his face, dropped to his knees, and then flat to the pavement.

Two agents from the dining room burst through the door in time to see Em drop the man who had been struggling with Tina. Cardozo, with the legal mind, pulled out a gun and aimed it at the man on the ground. Her partner, DeCarlo, produced a pair of handcuffs, shackled him with them and yelled, "On your feet!" Leather jacket moaned and took up cursing where Tina left off.

Agent Amy Cardozo, gun in her hand, pulled out a pair of handcuffs and handed them to Agent Rankel, the slender waiter who held Em's assailant. "Here you go, have a real pair. No need to use your usual twist ties on this guy."

In several long strides Anson covered the ground between their car and the driver's side of the van. He wrenched open the van door and pulled out the man in the driver's seat. The driver was a young slack jawed ferret of a man with stubble on his chin. Anson picked him up bodily, grabbed the gun from the man's belt and shook him. A box cutter dropped to the pavement. "You holding anything else?" He shook him again harder. The terrified driver, hardly out of his teens, gasped, his eyes wide in surprise.

Across the parking lot, the tall older man in a jacket and tie got out of the specially modified fleet car. Halloran leaned against it, his right leg extended. "Federal agent, you are under arrest," he prompted the younger man. Anson repeated that loudly into the face of the van driver.

"For…." was Halloran's next prompt.

"For attempted abduction and whatever else we can get you for," the new agent yelled.

"I think that's 'other charges to be determined.' We'll let the FBI figure that out. You can put him down now. Good first collar, Anson."

A man of mid height with the build of a boxer and a regulation short haircut emerged from his cover behind a bank of thorny beach roses. With his gun drawn he walked up next to Anson. "I'll take him now, buddy." Vargas proceeded to lead their suspect away to an FBI classic black SUV that pulled up promptly out on the road in front of the restaurant.

Anson walked around the van to gather up his charge. "Your ride is here, ma'am," he said to Em. She peered around the van to see the figure leaning against a car in the shadows, beyond the circle of light from the restaurant. A feeling of relief and anticipated pleasure rose to her breast, her heart beat still more quickly.

"So there he is," remarked Tina. "I did wonder. Never a dull moment with you. I'm heading home now. I've got work tomorrow. You might think on keeping that one."

"He's not supposed to be out of the car," Em exclaimed.

"You try telling him that, ma'am," replied Anson.

"Try telling the boss anything," said Rankel the waiter. "I have to go return my apron."

"Thank you all, by the way," Em told the agents over her shoulder, already on her way to the car. Smack in front of the tall man she stopped. "I'm not sure I like being the cheese." The car door popped open for them.

"I told you so. This should finish it." Michael Halloran's voice was deep and quiet. "I want my cane back."

"You were right, it came in handy." Sliding cautiously on the well cared for leather, Em eased herself along the seat. Wriggling her shoulders, she thumped Halloran with an elbow in an attempt to pull her new bulletproof long line bra down into some semblance of a comfortable position for the ride home. "This thing is still too damned tight around the middle. It's definitely still a work in progress. Maybe it's dinner."

With a rusty chuckle he said, "Don't take it off in the car," and placed his hand on her knee and began to lightly stroke it with his long capable fingers.

ACKNOWLEDGEMENTS

One novel grew and grew into two, *Harbor Chase* is the second book in the Spring House Mysteries series. Chapters migrated between the books. Several chapters were removed to be saved for another day, or perhaps to be part of book 3 tentatively titled *Once Lost. Harbor Chase* was completed before the pandemic in a time that now seems so much more secure. A hearty and much deserved thank you to my first readers of the two Spring House Mysteries, they read the works in pieces, some of them not in order, not even finally in the same book, and still they persevered. Each reader added their insights, caught my inconsistencies, and raised questions for me. I enjoyed the process, I hope they did, too; Rachelle Cooper, Frederick Walters, and our trainer Jenni Keenan-Shettleworth, owner of Fighting Fitness Performance Centers, Orange, CT, for martial arts consulting. Thanks to John McLeod for consulting on maritime terminology. Most especially I owe a debt of gratitude to Barbara Whitcomb Walters, now deceased, who at 80 years old caught the smallest typos that snuck by the rest of us. She let me know that I needed to finish both books so that she could, too. The last chapters were returned to me with her notes after she passed. For her patience with a first-time author, and her guidance, thanks to the woman who never met a comma she couldn't delete, my editor Judy Roth. Believe me when I say, the errors are all mine.

My three children Kate, Dan and Beth were endlessly patient and supportive of me and my work. Kate especially listened and listened until she could recite the plot details. Special thanks to my cover illustrator, my daughter in law, Beth Janelle Stone. The cover of *Mystery at the Spring House* was a Mother's Day gift. The tree in the center is a New England sugar maple. The dark cover for *Harbor Chase* reflects a challenging time. It is the Southwest Ledge Light, East Haven, CT, which is just outside New Haven Harbor.

For my corporate sisterhood, through downsizing, "right sizing," outsourcing, layoffs and retirement offers we hang together. Many thanks for the inspiration and comradery, Rachelle Cooper, Carole Vissicchio, Lisa Hess McLeod, Lorrie Young, Norma Simmons, Karen Kimble and from California Jackie Kirby. We lost one sister Giovanina "Johnnie" Mancini in February 2020.

Two books owe their existence to the contacts, mutual support, mentoring, and resources of the Connecticut Chapter, RWA, and Sisters in Crime Guppies. If you have any thoughts of writing novels, join up, come swim with the Guppies.

ABOUT THE AUTHOR

K.M. Umbricht right out of college apprenticed at the Yale Co-op, the largest independent academic bookstore between New York and Boston, where she learned from Manager Theodore Wilentz that booksellers could be publishers, too. After a twenty-year career in Information Technology research, she "took the offer" to leave the competitive intelligence group of the largest American telecommunications corporation. She founded Black Crow Press LLC with a nod to the memory of TW.

She lives on a glacial lake in woodsy Connecticut where red foxes casually patrol the shoreline looking for their favorite meal of Canada Goose, while coyotes slink off into the trees. Ospreys splash down from height fishing with talons first in the pond. Snapping turtles lay their eggs in the herb garden. Peepers, tiny little tree frogs, fill the spring evenings with their music. Bull frogs chorus at night under the windows. Night Herons wake to fish. At midnight you can sometimes hear a fisher cat scream. Sadly, she is cat-less after the passing of Shadow, the elegant, intelligent and highly vocal model for Ash in the stories and his younger fellow stray Patches. A daughter working for her PhD shares the place.